BLOOD
BENEATH
the SNOW

TITLES BY ALEXANDRA KENNINGTON

✦ ✦ ✦ ✦

Blood Beneath the Snow

BLOOD
BENEATH
the SNOW

ALEXANDRA KENNINGTON

ACE

NEW YORK

ACE
Published by Berkley
An imprint of Penguin Random House LLC
1745 Broadway, New York, NY 10019
penguinrandomhouse.com

Book design by Daniel Brount

Library of Congress Cataloging-in-Publication Data

Names: Kennington, Alexandra, author.
Title: Blood beneath the snow / Alexandra Kennington.
Description: New York : Ace, 2025.
Identifiers: LCCN 2024032713 (print) | LCCN 2024032714 (ebook) |
ISBN 9780593820117 (hardcover) | ISBN 9780593820124 (ebook)
Subjects: LCGFT: Fantasy fiction. | Romance fiction. | Novels.
Classification: LCC PS3611.E6683 B58 2025 (print) | LCC PS3611.E6683 (ebook) |
DDC 813/.6—dc23/eng/20240722
LC record available at https://lccn.loc.gov/2024032713
LC ebook record available at https://lccn.loc.gov/2024032714

Printed in the United States of America
1st Printing

The authorized representative in the EU for product safety and compliance is
Penguin Random House Ireland, Morrison Chambers, 32 Nassau Street,
Dublin D02 YH68, Ireland, https://eu-contact.penguin.ie.

For Owen.
Every moment of my life is better with you in it.

AUTHOR'S NOTE

This novel contains heavy themes and topics that might not be suitable for all readers. I hope the following list will be helpful in allowing you to decide whether reading this novel is in your best interest. Whether you choose to continue reading or not, I'm grateful you took the time to pick up this book. Take care of yourself, friend.

This book includes the following: alcoholism (side character); attempted murder of an infant; blood and mild gore; deaths of loved ones; discussion of suicidal ideation and mention of a suicide attempt (past, no graphic details); domestic abuse of an adult child by a parent (includes physical abuse); emotional abuse by religious leaders; explicit sex scenes, all consensual; homophobia by political leaders; kidnapping; murder; self-harm; strong language; war; and violence.

BLOOD
BENEATH
the SNOW

1

I STOOD SHIVERING BENEATH MY CLOAK IN THE TEMPLE PLAZA and wondered what would happen if I spat in the face of a god.

The press of bodies against me on every side still wasn't enough to keep the chill at bay in the frigid early-morning temperatures. I glared up at the statue in front of me, one of the seven adorning the steps of the temple. The god of fire, Hjalmar, stared off into the distance, with stone flames dancing over his outstretched palms. It was fitting I'd end up in front of him, considering he'd blessed the worst of my brothers.

If I spat in his face, would gasps echo across the crowd? Would priests descend from the temple steps, scythes in hand, to haul me away? Would Hjalmar himself cause me to burst into flames where I stood until I was nothing more than a pile of ash?

The gods of air, water, earth, sky, and body on either side of him were almost identical, the only differences lying in the depiction of their abilities carved in the stone. To the right of Hjalmar, directly in the center of the seven, was the only goddess: Aloisa, who gave gifts of the soul.

Seven deities. And every single one of them hated me.

My best friend nudged me, clearly sensing the emotions bubbling beneath my surface. "You good?" Freja muttered, quietly enough that only I could hear. Around us, the buzz of excited conversation hummed. The streets were packed to the brim, and we were surrounded on every side by the godtouched.

Freja and I blended in with those standing in the front of the crowd—today we looked like wealthy citizens and obedient worshipers. Our realities couldn't have been further from our disguises. The hoods of our cloaks were pulled tight around our faces, obscuring us from easy recognition in the dawn light. The last thing we wanted was anyone noticing two of the most infamous godforsaken hiding in plain sight at the front of the crowd on a ritual day.

As Freja waited for my answer, a single curl slipped across her forehead, unable to stay contained. I calmed the anger flaring in my chest and reached out to push the lock of hair behind her ear once more. Glancing down for what must have been the tenth time in five minutes to check that the bundle of decoy fabric was in Freja's arms, I nodded sharply. "Fine."

She shifted her weight from one foot to the other; whether from cold or nerves, I couldn't tell. This small act of rebellion felt heavier than the others we'd carried out before. Today was my last chance to make an impact before I was carted off to another country to become the wife of a man I'd never met.

When the godtouched whispered of our anarchy, they often used the word *barbarous*. But I doubted anything Freja, Halvar— our other partner in crime—and I concocted was as "barbarous" as using one's only daughter as a political pawn.

"You shouldn't have given me your breakfast," Freja said, crossing her arms. "You always get irritable when you haven't eaten."

I forced a smile. "I wanted to make sure you had a clear head for this. Don't begrudge me that."

With the war draining our supplies so quickly and this winter being so harsh, there was never enough food to go around. Of course, that meant Freja and the other godforsaken were rationing their food, while the godtouched still managed to eat three meals a day. I tried to offer a portion of my food to her or Arne—our other friend—every day, but they usually refused. If not for her trepidation about this morning's plan, I doubted she would have accepted my offering today.

The temple loomed in front of us. As was the case every time I observed it, I resisted the urge to roll my eyes. Once, in my grandparents' time, the building had been an homage to our country's roots—but after our neighboring country to the south, Kryllian, opened their borders to visitors, those same grandparents decided they appreciated the smoother lines and expensive stone of foreign architecture. The old temple was torn down and rebuilt into what it was today: a creation of white stone so pure, the falling flakes disappeared in its orbit. The roof pivoted into two sharp angles representing two hands reaching for the heavens, where the pantheon of gods we all worshiped remained.

I tapped my foot, growing impatient. The ritual and ceremony were supposed to start first thing in the morning, while the sun rose over the hills in the east. But here we all stood, blowing hot puffs of breath over our numbing hands, still waiting as the sun ascended in the sky.

The chatter of the crowd closed in around me and I fumed at how normal the godtouched sounded. They discussed what might still be available at the market despite the shortages, what parties they were attending later this week, whether their spouses and children were due back from the front lines in this round of military rotations. All the while, their expensive jewelry flashed in the dappled sunlight and they basked in the warmth of their fur-lined cloaks—as if they all weren't here to witness a murder.

I tried not to think about the godforsaken—my own people. The ones at the back of the crowd, dreading what the next hour would bring. Knowing they'd see blood of their own spilled on the altar of the gods and then be expected to go about their day as if nothing had happened. I wondered if any would lose toes or fingers from frostbite after enduring the frigid conditions of midwinter in their worn shoes and their thin cloaks, fraying at the edges. Whether their children's ribs were showing in the wake of a war they despised. Whether they'd go home and cry silently for a few moments, hugging their families tight as they wondered why it was worth living another day.

My thoughts were interrupted by the temple doors swinging open. The crowd fell silent immediately, every head bowing low. I stared at the priests for a moment too long before Freja elbowed me, and I directed my gaze to the ground as well.

The holy men still managed to make me shudder, even after having spent a lifetime in close contact with them. They dressed entirely in white, in robes stretching from their necks to their wrists and ankles. Veils covered their hair and faces so that they blended in perfectly with the snowy landscape—except for the eyes.

The fabric of their veils was pinned to the necklines of their robes, meaning not a single inch of skin was visible on any of the priests. Above each one's forehead was an eye embroidered with bloodred thread, eerie enough to make both the godtouched and the godforsaken feel the priest was peering directly into the depths of their soul.

I hated the priests almost as much as I hated the gods.

An endless stream of them flooded out the doors until they had filled the steps of the structure, the blades of their scythes winking in the sun. The last to exit brought with him a white cloth with another embroidered eye on it to drape over the altar. Fury ripped through me at the sight, but I forced myself to stay still. My fingernails bit half-moons into the flesh of my palms and I busied my mind with the reminder of what I was here to do.

"Every priest in the country must be here," Freja whispered as we surveyed them. "I've never seen this many in one place before. Do you think they traveled for the ritual?"

"Who knows," I murmured, feeling the telltale furrow of my brows appear. "I wasn't expecting them all to be here. This might be harder than we thought."

My friend nodded, readjusting the bundle of fabric in her arms. "Guess we'll see how fast we can run."

Another figure exited the temple. The queen. She'd once confided to me when I was a small child that the crown she wore today was her favorite: an arch that stretched from behind one ear to the other, hugging tightly to her hair, rays projecting out like a halo to frame her face. The gold of it glimmered in the morning sunlight, contrasting against her dark black hair. Her gown was a deep blood red, one of our national colors. It flowed like liquid, and I found myself wondering if she was freezing beneath the fabric. It certainly didn't look warm.

She stepped to the center of the dais and stood before the altar. My eyes found my feet and I clenched my jaw as if the tension would prevent her from seeing me, recognizing me. A priest came forward to stand next to her, facing the crowd. In one synchronized movement, the other priests pounded the wooden handles of their scythes on the temple's stone steps, sending a booming echo through the square. The ceremony had begun.

"Ready?" I asked Freja. My heart pounded with anticipation.

She nodded. "Let's hope this works."

The priest at the altar began speaking in a resounding voice. "Welcome to the Winter Ritual, beloved citizens of Bhorglid. Today marks the beginning of a new year, one filled with great hope for our country. Even now, we wage holy war against Kryllian, our armies drawing closer to taking over the southernmost country in the Fjordlands."

A cheer erupted around us, and I suppressed a sigh of irritation. The godtouched in the crowd, whose partners, parents, and children fought on the front lines, were ecstatic to hear it repeated: their loved ones weren't fighting in just any war. No, it was a *holy* war. Decreed by the gods.

The priest continued, "Generations ago, the Fjordlands were stolen from us. We, who communicate directly with the gods. Instead of harmony, discord was wrought and the Fjordlands were split into three. For thirteen generations, the gods have mourned with us as we have waited for their perfect timing. Now you are blessed to be part of the chosen few alive to see this miracle come to pass. Kryllian shall be rightfully ours. The gods have declared it."

I tried not to let my emotions show on my face. The speech had been the same every year since the war began, but it never failed to make me wince. Halvar had been the one to explain to me years ago how the priest's version of this story had been edited in Bhorglid's favor. Only those who passed on the original stories verbally still knew the truth. He'd been lucky enough to come from a family that didn't embrace the revisionist version of our history.

In actuality, the Fjordlands had been filled with wandering people, those with magical abilities and those without living in peace— until a pair with powers far beyond what was necessary for mortal man decided they could speak with the gods. And according to them, the gods said those with abilities had been blessed. *Godtouched*.

The rest of us were *godforsaken*. Forgotten by our holy pantheon, called unworthy from the moment we entered the world. While the godtouched enjoyed innate abilities that allowed them to manipulate elements of the world around them, the way the gods had once done as they walked the land millennia ago, the rest of us were normal. Shunted to the edge of a society where an invisible group of gods claimed we were lesser.

The speech grated against my nerves like the screech of a metal fork across a ceramic plate. Enduring the rest of this drivel was going to kill me. I was ready to move, ready to wreak havoc, ready to wrap my hands around the nearest priest's throat and rip their veil off. Only watching the light fade from their eyes would be enough to calm me.

Freja snatched my hand and squeezed. "No," she hissed. "We have to wait until they've brought out the child."

My hands shook with fury against hers. But she was right. The priests enabled the foul treatment of the godforsaken, but we weren't here to rid ourselves of them. Today was about saving a life, not taking it.

Even if I wished it were possible to do both.

The priest droned on, but I focused on Freja's words and nodded, forcing myself to breathe deeply. The godtouched around us were too intent on listening to the priests to notice me acting strangely.

The ritual speech continued despite my swirling thoughts. "As we perform the new year ritual, this unholy blood will be a tribute to the gods. In exchange for our sacrifice, they will grant us their power. We will gain a powerful advantage in this war; with the vanquishing of this life, we will be able to defeat the Hellbringer. The gods have declared it so."

Freja squeezed my hand again, barely in time to keep an indignant huff from escaping me. This part of the speech was new, the logic as incomprehensible as the rest. How would killing an infant grant us the power to stop the most powerful godtouched being to exist in any of our lifetimes and end the war? As Freja released my hand, the queen gestured to the side of the stage for several acolytes to bring someone forward. I glanced over but couldn't make out the woman's face; the figure was hunched at an odd angle and a low moan emanated from her mouth. There was a wriggling bundle clutched to her chest. My stomach sank, the way it did every year.

The priest took the infant out of the person's arms and began to move toward the altar.

The figure left in the shadows—undoubtedly the child's mother, a godforsaken woman—let out a haunting scream, her wail of anguish echoing through the square and silencing everyone, even the godtouched. I clenched my teeth. The screams were always the worst part. Worse than the blood. The mother collapsed to her knees and howling sobs cracked the silence.

Freja and I were the only ones who appeared affected. The priests' expressions were carefully hidden behind their face coverings and the godtouched on either side of us were reverently silent, waiting for spilled blood to spell their salvation. The queen curled her lip at the bundle in the priest's arms as he set it carefully on the altar.

As he laid it down, it wriggled, and a tiny hand emerged from the blankets.

Seeing the movement made my throat raw. The last child born to godforsaken parents each year was always culled—a horrifying euphemism—as a sacrifice to the gods. Only the youngest, freshest blood would do for this brutal tradition, repeated winter after winter.

"Now," I said to Freja as anger sparked in my stomach. "We go now."

She reached into her pocket and pressed something. The infant let out a wail. The godtouched were poised, on their toes, ready for action; behind me, I could feel the raw defeat of the godforsaken.

Without warning, a boom echoed through the courtyard and smoke began to pour from the top of the temple, obscuring the priests and the queen from view. The gray clouds billowed out into the square. Cries of panic rose from the blindness.

"Good work," I whispered to Freja. When Freja had first mentioned Halvar was training her to use explosives, I was wary—now I had no time for anything but gratitude. We dashed up the temple steps toward the chaotic scene.

The priests were coughing, having a more difficult time breathing through their veils. The queen fanned the air with a hand, snarling. But there was no time to think; the priest at the altar raised his scythe above his head, undeterred and ready to strike.

I pulled my sword from under my cloak and lunged forward until the sound of metal on metal grated against my ears.

The priest hadn't expected the collision. When the scythe connected with my sword, he stumbled, and I seized my opportunity. Sprinting forward, I grabbed the infant off the altar and dashed the other way.

The queen let out an angry scream.

"They're coming," I said, voice panicked as I handed the baby to Freja. The shadows of the alleyway where she waited obscured her features. "Run."

She traded me a bundle of fabric for the infant and took off, sprinting through the streets.

I sent up a silent prayer. *Gods, if you're real, please keep that baby from crying.*

The smoke was clearing. Footsteps pounded behind me. The priest from the altar was getting closer. People in the crowd coughed, crying out with fear and confusion.

Freja was close to getting around the first corner. I bounced on the balls of my feet, heart pounding. As soon as she was out of sight, as soon as I guaranteed they were following me and not her, I could run.

Right as I moved to take off, a white-gloved hand landed on my shoulder, tightening hard enough to bruise.

On instinct, I pulled a knife out of my belt with my free hand and whirled, slashing until it connected with something solid. Red sprayed over white fabric and the priest cried out in pain. Time was up. I leapt into action, running as fast as I could down the uneven streets.

"There's two of them!" someone shouted behind me.

A curse escaped me. They'd seen Freja. If I didn't act quickly, they'd send search parties after both of us.

Time to play our most valuable hand. I pulled my hood down, exposing my jet-black hair and well-known face. My mother rarely smiled, but when she did, we had the same feral grin. In one swift moment I became the most recognizable person at the ceremony. "Over here!" I called, drawing the priests' attention.

They looked my way, forgetting about Freja.

"The princess," one roared. "Get her!"

I grinned. Exactly as we planned.

Sprinting past run-down buildings, through puddles of melted snow and hidden alleyways, my mind took over. This part of the city was a maze ingrained in my memory.

I clutched the bundle of fabric to my chest, heading away from Freja as if my life depended on it. "Out of the way," I ordered a group of godforsaken standing in my path. The people moved without complaint, recognizing me and filling in behind, slowing my pursuers.

As I moved to turn another corner, the ground in front of me erupted, forming a wall where there had once been a clear path. I stumbled slightly and cursed. When we made our plan, we accounted for every possibility—but predicting the abilities of the priests who pursued me was impossible.

Clearly, at least one of them had been touched by Isak, god of earth. I growled in frustration and sprinted back the way I had come, down another clear path, ignoring the rumble of the ground beneath my feet. My only advantage was knowing the streets of the lower side of town better than they did.

I heaved air into my lungs. Keeping them away from Freja long enough for her to get back to Halvar's was crucial. *A little farther*, I told myself. *Come on.*

I stretched my hand out and clutched the edge of a building, using the leverage to propel me around the corner.

A few steps down the street, a block of ice shot out in front of my face, too fast to dodge. I slammed directly into it and fell flat on my back, stars blooming in my peripheral vision as I gasped for breath. Wetness on my lip spoke to the blood pouring from my nose as a result of the collision. My wits were scattered across the cobblestones, but I had enough left about me to curse the priests and their horrible gods once again.

A strong hand wrapped around my bicep and hauled me to my feet. The motion made my vision spin and nausea writhe in my stomach. Half of me was disappointed when I didn't vomit all over the white robes of the priest holding me. His fingers pressed so roughly against my skin that I knew I'd have a hand-shaped bruise there in the morning—he was likely godtouched with strength, a gift from Asger, god of the body. The same ability my oldest brother, Erik, possessed.

The bundle of fabric had fallen when I collided with the ice structure. Another priest was unrolling it while three other members of the Holy Order stood laughing among themselves at my predicament. I dredged up a mouthful of saliva and blood and spat it at the closest one.

He howled at the mess now covering his robes and I grinned at him. It must have been a horrid sight, considering my broken nose and the bruises I felt forming around at least one of my eyes. I could taste the blood staining my front teeth.

The one with inhuman strength twisted my arm behind me at an unnatural angle and a hiss escaped me. The other returned with the now unwound bundle of fabric, clearly not containing the infant they'd been looking for. I imagined he was scowling behind the veil covering his face.

"These were my favorite pants," I said, glancing down at the muddy stains now coating the fabric. "I hope you're prepared to replace them."

"Where's the sacrifice?" he demanded, holding up the empty stretch of fabric. I made a valiant effort to hide my smirk.

I shrugged. They may have caught me, but if they didn't find Freja, then it didn't matter. There was no replacing a baby born on the last day of the year. The ritual sacrifice could not be supplanted. "You probably should've kept better track of it."

The priest tilted his head and grabbed a fistful of my tunic, yanking me closer until he was right in my face. His voice trembled with anger. More priests appeared behind him, finally catching up to the chase. "Little bitch. Do you know the punishment for interfering with our rituals, Princess? Your hands are cut off at the wrists. It's quite painful. No healers are permitted to tend to the wounds. The perpetrator almost always dies of blood loss."

I shrugged. "If you want to explain to my parents how you cut off my hands, be my guest. But I certainly wouldn't recommend it."

"The king and queen don't care what happens to you," a priest behind him sneered.

Heat flushed my face. "They don't. But they do care about the treaty. I don't think the Fastian royal family would be too thrilled to marry off their son to a thief with no hands."

For a moment the hold on my arm tightened. The priests had arranged the treaty—and my impending marriage—in the first place. Even they weren't stupid enough to risk ruining it now.

If the war continued for another full season, people would begin dying of starvation. In exchange for regular deliveries of food, the Fastians would receive the support of our soldiers at their borders.

The seal between a war-mongering country and a distrustful agricultural nation? A loveless marriage between two royal children.

The priest in front of me growled, the fabric of his veil fluttering as he prepared to continue arguing.

"Enough."

The familiar voice came from behind me, and I snapped my head around to see my mother standing there, her displeasure as icy cold as the water she froze with her magic. My head throbbed with the sudden movement and I inhaled raggedly, blinking away stars from my vision. I didn't think I had a concussion, but now the injury seemed more than likely.

The priest's hold on my arm tightened once more as the queen stepped up to face me and placed two long fingers beneath my chin. Revulsion filled me at the touch, her digits as cold as the ice running through her veins. I jerked my face away and snapped my teeth threateningly close to her fingers.

The priest holding me hauled me backward and my mother slapped me across the face. My skull throbbed. "Insolent brat," she said. My face stung and I held back tears from the shock of the abrasion in the freezing air. "Tell me where your disgusting friend has taken the sacrifice."

"No." My voice was thick with blood, my nose swelling from my earlier collision. I felt like a fish, mouth hanging open in order to keep breathing. The taste of blood passed my lips.

Mother sighed and I looked up at her from where my head hung. Her cold eyes, the same green as mine, were filled with disgust. "You could have made your life as painless as possible, you know. Being godforsaken as a member of the royal family . . . you're already an embarrassment. We advised you to keep to the shadows, where you belong. Lower your head and accept your station. Do what's right for the benefit of your country. And yet you've never listened. Now here you are, toying with the idea of *rebellion*. Ruining your home one ritual at a time. Dreaming of things that don't belong to you. Like you have any clue what it takes to run a country."

"You could find out," I suggested, allowing the edge of malice in my voice to show its claws. "Throw me in the ring with the others during the Bloodshed Trials. You never know. Perhaps I'd manage to come out on top, at the end of things."

The once-in-a-generation competition for the throne was mere weeks away now—it wasn't an entirely preposterous suggestion that I join my brothers in the fight to the death that would decide who ascended to power, taking our father's place. I had enough training that, even without magic, I might be able to hold my own in the ritual sacrifice of heirs. But no; even allowing a godforsaken to fight was too far. Instead, I was good for one thing: to be married off to seal an alliance.

She laughed. "You're many horrible things already, daughter mine. Queen won't be one of them." To my surprise, Mother ordered, "Let her go."

"Your Majesty?" The priest holding me sounded as shocked as I must have looked.

"You heard me."

The hand released its bruising clutch on my bicep and I stumbled slightly before catching myself on the wall of the building in front of me. Everything ached. I wondered whether I'd be able to convince the royal healer to mend me up or if Halvar would have to reset my nose again.

"That's it?" My voice trembled when I spoke, knowing I was inviting Mother's wrath.

But she scoffed. "I'll let your father deal with you. He'll know what punishment suits you best."

Mother knew it as well as I did: Father had a knack for consequences that cut to the bone but left no visible scars.

I shuddered at the thought of what my future might hold when he next returned from the front lines, then swallowed the river of blood pooling in my throat. The queen walked away as if nothing had happened, as if the blood from my nose hadn't dripped onto her fingers.

The priest turned to face his two companions, murmuring something I couldn't make out as they moved away.

"Revna Thorunsdotter, consider yourself lucky to be royalty," he called over his shoulder as he retreated. "Otherwise, you would not be leaving here with your life."

I managed a smirk. "Oh, I know."

2

By the time I felt a new set of eyes on me, carefully tracking my every movement, the early signs of a storm were blowing in.

I'd been wandering the streets for the last hour, fully aware the priests had been following me since they set me free. They didn't blend in well in the lower side of the city, where the buildings were still constructed with dark wood from the trees growing in the forest to the west instead of the expensive gray stone the godtouched were able to build their homes from. The white robes made them look like haunting specters.

I could sense them itching to punish me, anxious to slice their scythes through my cloak and flesh until my blood pooled in the street. Swift revenge for undermining their power. If they did, I doubted anyone in my family would care, except maybe my brothers Frode and Jac. But the acolytes had a king to please, and since my mother had declared my punishment his choice, they wouldn't make a move.

The decoy fabric was now wrapped around my neck as a scarf to shield me from the descending snowflakes, leaving my hands unfettered and protecting my battered face from the cold. It allowed my broken nose to peek out, and the freezing wind eased the pain a bit. My sword and knife were sheathed under my cloak, and I fidgeted with the hilts, wondering whether Freja had made it back to the Sharpened Axe—the tavern Halvar ran on the godforsaken side of town—with the infant. If she'd been caught, I'd never forgive myself.

On either side of the street, I watched godtouched women walk in and out of shops, gossiping with their friends about the newest army recruits and advancements. The few soldiers who were home for a month in between war calls glared at me from where they stood guard. All wore bright cloaks and makeup. Some were adorned with copious amounts of jewelry.

The energy in the market plaza was different than usual. The godforsaken ran businesses here, homes often built above the bottom level of each shop. Instead of the depressing, soul-sucking sadness that usually permeated every aspect of the streets, today there was a lightness in the air. Godforsaken smiled at each other and dealt with the snide comments from their godtouched customers with an ease I'd never seen before.

But with the aura of relief came backlash. The godtouched were in a foul mood, especially knowing I'd stolen away their sacrifice of blood and life. The priests would now pivot to teaching how the pantheon would retaliate in anger because of my actions. And because the godtouched couldn't take their anger out on me, they would take it out on my people.

I allowed my thoughts to encompass me, wondering if there was any drastic measure I could take to turn the fury of the upper class to me while I was still here for another month before my fiancé arrived to whisk me away to another country. But my senses sharpened when the hair on the back of my neck stood up straight, my hand reaching automatically for the hilt of my sword.

I knew the feeling of unfriendly eyes chasing my movements as well as any godforsaken.

Turning in a slow circle, I observed the sights around me. Past the plaza and into the part of town where the other godforsaken lived, the cobblestone streets were fairly empty. Everyone was inside, preparing for the incoming storm. The inches of snow covering the road showed footprints treading back and forth with the occasional set from a stray cat or a horse alongside them. Priests stood watch every few houses, their scythes reflecting the lazy flakes making their way down from the sky. The shops and homes lining this stretch of road appeared the same as always. The priests who had been tailing me had finally seen fit to vanish back to their posts.

No one was paying me any attention.

But the nudge in my gut persisted, and I knew better than to ignore it. Warily, I continued forward, relaxing my stance and forcing myself to appear calm and unperturbed. Perhaps it was a godtouched trying to locate Freja by following me. Invisibility was a rare ability, but not unheard-of. Whoever this bastard was, I would find them.

Taking an unpredictable path was easy. I knew the godforsaken streets better than I knew the interior of the palace. Twisting and turning down abandoned back alleys filled with mud and refuse, I did my best to lure my follower out of the safety of their distant hiding spot. If they were truly intent on catching up with me, I would make them work for it.

When I knew they'd have to be sprinting to keep pace with me, I fell back into the doorframe of a shop. Dark clouds had descended as I wove my path, and the alleys were submerged in shadow. Now I had the advantage.

I waited, wondering who would dare pursue me so blatantly. Everyone knew I was the princess—the godforsaken royal, the shame of her family, the bargaining chip that would save us from starving before we could win the war. Who would dare seek me out and attempt to harm me before the alliance with Faste was finalized?

I ran through the options in my mind. The priests had already proven they couldn't touch me, and I knew they would never go against my father. The godtouched hated me, but not as much as they wanted to eat a full meal again or overtake Kryllian. Perhaps one of my brothers was playing another nasty trick on me—but they were all still at the war front for another three days. I quietly pulled my knife from its sheath, my heart pounding a bruising rhythm against my ribcage.

Another moment passed before a dark shadow descended over my hiding place. I didn't hesitate. I leapt out, brandishing my dagger, fully prepared to stab my pursuer . . .

But the alleyway was empty. My eyes caught the flash of a cloak disappearing around the corner of the shop.

Not just a pursuer, but a cowardly one. I growled and took off running after them, racing down the alley. I spared a half thought of gratitude for the winter wind in my face, keeping my broken nose from swelling too horribly. We raced past the back doors of shops and houses, and when we finally reached the end of the road, they stopped abruptly in the open, causing their hood to fall and expose the back of their head.

I froze at the sight. The person was wearing a dark mask that covered their entire head, obscuring their face. But I still knew exactly who it was. I would recognize that carved visage anywhere, as would anyone else in Bhorglid.

And him, being here? It was impossible.

Nonetheless, fear crept up my spine and I gasped, taking a swift step back—

"Revna!"

The call broke me from my reverie and I whirled to see Halvar leaning out the back door of the Sharpened Axe. "The hell are you doing? We've been waiting for you."

"I . . ." I turned back around, expecting to see the masked figure waiting in the street, but they were gone. My pulse thudded in my veins. Surely there was no way I'd imagined seeing *him*. But I shook my head. "Right. Coming."

Halvar held the door for me, but I still had to squeeze past his large frame to make my way into the back room of the tavern. Once I ensured no eyes lingered in the shadows of the room, I pulled open the trapdoor in the floor, revealing the ladder beneath it.

It took mere seconds to slide down the rungs and land gently with my feet on the floor. Freja sat in the closest corner, half immersed in darkness, rocking the rescued baby back and forth in her arms.

The child whimpered but didn't scream. Good. The last thing we needed was to be found now, after we'd gotten so far.

Halvar slid down the ladder behind me, tugging on a rope until the trapdoor above closed with a thud. He struck a match and used it to light the few lamps in the vast hidden space with its stashes of weapons, then sat down with his back against the wall. I moved to sit next to him, bumping my shoulder against his. "We did it," I said softly.

He offered me a small smile. "We did. You two did. The little one is safe for the time being."

"The plan was yours," I reminded him. "You take at least a third of the credit."

Halvar chuckled and ran a hand through his graying beard. When he'd first taken me—a godforsaken princess who knew nothing of the world she belonged to—under his wing eleven years ago, his hair had been dark, and his energy had been endless. Now there were crow's-feet around both his eyes and an air of exhaustion he couldn't seem to shake. Bitterness rose in me when I considered how time was stealing away the only father figure in my life.

Freja shushed us and we both lowered our voices. "Were you caught?" she mouthed at me.

I nodded and smirked, sending a throb through my nose. "What gave it away?"

She raised an eyebrow and scrunched up her own nose. I chuckled and placed a gentle finger to mine, wincing when it made an ache bloom beneath the swollen flesh. "I'll have to see if I can bribe the palace healer to work his magic on me." I sighed at the thought of trying to convince the crotchety old man to use his godtouched gift on one so lowly as I.

"Ingrid and Anders are anxious to see their little girl again," Halvar said, nodding to the infant. "How did the streets look? Still too many priests to sneak her to the edge of the city?"

I nodded. "Unfortunately, yes. I say we wait another few hours, as long as we can keep her fed until then. After things calm down, they should be able to leave the city without too much hassle." I frowned, thinking of the person who'd followed me through the alley and led me on a chase. If he was who I thought he was, then perhaps there was need for even more caution.

"What happened?" Freja asked.

I glanced up, hating how obvious my thoughts were most of the time. "I was on my way here, but I felt someone watching me. Following me. I waited to try and ambush them, but then they fled before I got the chance. I ran after them, their hood fell off, and . . ." I shook my head. "I could have sworn I was looking at the Hellbringer."

Freja and Halvar were both silent. Then the latter finally spoke. "The Hellbringer? The one fighting on the front lines of the war?"

I nodded, feeling slightly ridiculous. "Yes. He wore the mask all the soldiers talk about—the one carved to look like a wolf's skull."

They were quiet for a few heartbeats before my best friend spoke up again. "Anyone can wear a mask, Revna," she said softly. "And besides, if the Hellbringer were here, the war front would be, too. Maybe it was someone trying to scare you. He would have used his godtouch to kill you instantly if it were really him."

I mulled it over. It wouldn't be the first time someone had tried to take advantage of me with a scare tactic, but it was the first time anyone had bothered to disguise themselves as the culprit. The feeling of his hidden gaze following me as I walked the streets remained, and I pulled my shoulders back as if it would help.

"Maybe," I conceded. "But you're right. The whole city would be corpses in the streets if it really were him."

The Hellbringer was known for his terrifying godtouch—the ability to kill anyone in sight with no more than a flick of his finger. He'd single-handedly turned the tide of the war in Kryllian's favor. My father had been trying to capture him for almost seven years, to no avail. The general was a difficult man to find.

No one knew his true identity, despite his powerful magic. I thought again of the dark, blank eyes of the carved mask staring at me from the street. They'd bored into me, looking into the depths of my soul.

Halvar spoke up. "They're saying he's Aloisa-touched. That he might be Callum reincarnated." He used his knife to clean the dirt from underneath his nails, nonchalant as ever.

I raised an eyebrow. Callum, the original Silencer. Legend had it he could take a person's godtouch. Stop their ability to use magic with nothing more than a snap of his fingers. I didn't put much stock in the stories, but the godtouched spoke of him in hushed, fearful voices when his name came up in temple worship or speeches by the priests. They told their children stories of Callum when they misbehaved.

While all the pantheon blessed the godtouched with gifts and supernatural abilities, Aloisa, the goddess of the soul, had never given a human any gift. Callum was the exception. A godtouch was innate, part of a person's soul. Only her blessing could offer such a powerful ability.

Callum and his wife, Arraya, were also the first to claim they spoke to the gods. They had believed themselves superior to the godforsaken—to the extent that they'd coined the terms in the first place. They created the Holy Order of Priests and attempted to take over the Fjordlands. Only swift opposition from two rebel groups, now our neighboring countries, kept them from succeeding.

They'd been killed in the war soon after the Fjordlands were split into three. Only their demise had allowed an unsteady peace to reign.

"I haven't heard that," I said, unable to suppress a frown.

Halvar gave me a sympathetic look. "You haven't heard about it because you don't run in the lowest of the godforsaken circles. Not like we do." He gestured to himself and Freja.

I nodded, acquiescing with a frown. He was right. No matter how hard I tried, I couldn't escape my family's influence, which meant none of the godforsaken truly trusted me with any confidential information. "If he's Callum reincarnate, does that make Kryllian the rightful country to rule the Fjordlands?"

Freja looked thoughtful, the light flickering over her dark skin as she leaned back against the wall, still cradling the newborn. "Probably depends on who you ask. I'm sure there are others like us who believe the whole story is hogwash. Then there's the group who believe we're the ones who rightfully own the land—Callum's worthiest ancestors."

"Meaning all of the godtouched in Bhorglid," I said.

She nodded. "And then there have to be some godforsaken who wonder if this means the priests have it wrong. Who wonder if maybe Kryllian is supposed to rule it all."

I sighed and rubbed a hand over my forehead. The priests would undoubtedly twist the rumors to their advantage as soon as they could manage. My chest constricted at the thought of the godforsaken who believed everything the religious leaders taught. Many—like Freja,

Halvar, and me—kept up with the façade of corrupt religion only to prevent drawing undue attention. But plenty of others truly believed they were lesser than their godtouched peers.

Halvar hummed, his brow furrowed. "Regardless, the three of us know the truth: Callum was just a man in history who had an incredible ability that he used to persecute those with less power than him. And now, society looks like this." He gestured to the rest of the basement, where we hid with an infant born to godforsaken parents. If anything spoke to the cruelty of our world today, it was this. "The greedy godtouched bastards never feel like it's enough, so they keep warring and warring and warring until one day someone wins for a time. And then it starts all over again."

It was easy to hear the frustration in his voice. I placed a gentle hand on his knee and he sighed. "Sorry. I get fed up with it is all."

"I know." Not for the first time, my heart ached, wishing I could do more for Halvar and Freja. And if the rest of the godforsaken benefited, that wouldn't be the worst thing to happen.

He turned to meet my eyes with a half smile. "If we had a godforsaken queen, this wouldn't be an issue."

I moved my hand back to my lap and sighed. "It's not possible. They'd never let me compete; you know that. And if they did, I wouldn't win. Not against four men with incredibly powerful godtouches."

"And even if she did win, the nearest priest would shoot her dead before she made her first move as queen," Freja pointed out.

"Disrupting the rituals will have to be enough for our little rebellion." I stood and stretched. "Regardless, you're all right. There's no way the Hellbringer is in the city. Whoever it was must have been playing a nasty trick."

"Exactly," Freja said. I watched her shoulders relax slightly. Had she been afraid? "Headed back home?"

"Yes. I'm late to meet Arne. He'll kick my ass in training if I don't get there soon."

"And I'll see you back here tonight, you hear?" Halvar ordered.

I grinned as I began to ascend the ladder leading to the trapdoor in the ceiling. "I wouldn't miss it."

STANDING ALONG THE MOUNTAIN PATH OVERLOOKING THE city, I couldn't tell the roads on the godforsaken side of town were in desperate need of repair. From a distance it all looked almost beautiful. A thin layer of white snow covered everything, refusing to melt in the frigid air.

Surveying the city from a distance kept me grounded. It served as a reminder of all the good the godforsaken did and lit a fire within me at the same time, urging me to do what it took to ensure my people were finally treated equally.

For a moment I just looked while I caught my breath. As my lungs steadied, I stepped back from the edge and turned to the path again. If I continued along the familiar switchbacks to the cliffside, the castle would come into view. But my brothers and father remained at the war front for another three days, and I had no intention of going home now.

Snow-covered foliage obscured the trail, packed down enough to show that several travelers had come this way over the past few hours. Probably priests doing their rounds or godtouched coming to socialize with my mother, hoping to gain her favor. But the main path wasn't the one my eye snagged on. Through the towering pines and between the frosted greenery, half-smudged footprints traversed the untouched landscape, headed into the unmarked part of the mountainside. Anyone who wasn't looking for them wouldn't have spared a second glance.

Careful not to leave noticeable footprints of my own, I followed the path to the west side of the mountain. Soon enough, the main road was out of sight. My only company was the occasional squirrel skittering up a tree.

No one would be able to find me unless they knew where to look.

With each step through the film of ice on the ground, I relaxed a little more. Here, I bore no responsibility to the throne or the godforsaken. Here, I was Revna. Nothing more.

By the time I reached my destination, the sun had arced its way high into the sky. When I pushed through the last pair of bushes and into the clearing, a familiar voice called out: "You're late."

Arne sat on a tree stump, once the foundation for a magnificent oak. It made a nice resting place for anyone in the clearing who wasn't sparring. Then again, few people frequented the clearing besides the two of us and Freja.

I'd first met Halvar here. I smiled fondly at the memory—running away from another punishment at the hands of my father simply for asking to sit at the table with the rest of the family instead of on the floor, where the godforsaken were designated to eat. Losing the priests chasing after me had been easy at ten years old, my tiny form fast and small enough to crawl through spaces where my pursuers would never fit. When I stumbled through the bushes, unsure of my destination, I found Halvar sitting on the tree stump, staring at me with wide eyes. At the time it had been summer, and wildflowers dotted the grass. He'd been taking puffs of a cigar but hesitated at the sight of me.

It had taken every ounce of bravery in my fiery heart to stand tall in the face of him. Even then, it was clear he was strong, more than capable of holding me captive until my father found me and lashed fire across my back. "Are you godtouched?" I'd asked, hands curled into fists.

He shot me a bewildered look. "No, Princess."

With a deep breath, every muscle in my body had relaxed and I'd thrown my arms around him in a hug as relief flooded through me. Rough, hardened Halvar hardly knew what to do with himself, but eventually found his own arms wrapped around me, too.

Since then, Halvar had shared the clearing's location with Freja and Arne. But besides the four of us, no one was the wiser to its existence. It was nice, knowing this place belonged to us and no one else.

Arne balanced his sword on his knee, using a whetstone to sharpen it. His dark hair was pulled back, exposing the shaved sides of his head. Beaten armor covered his casual clothes.

He pushed to his feet and his tall, gangly frame moved toward me. When he got close enough, I had to tilt my head back to maintain eye contact.

Arne offered me a half smile—the most happiness he ever expressed—and leaned down to press his lips to mine.

I leaned into the kiss, the expression of affection calmingly familiar until our noses brushed. I hissed from the pain and he pulled back with a wince. "Sorry. Do I need to set your nose again?"

"I don't think so," I muttered, wishing the persistent throb would make its exit already. "I'm going to try and persuade Waddell to heal it for me before dinner."

Arne scowled. "I hate that you have to bargain with him for the same healing your brothers are *entitled* to."

I wrapped an arm around his waist and rested my cheek against his chest with a chuckle. Arne was fiercely protective of Freja and me. If he could stand guard at our sides all day, I had no doubt he would.

With a sigh, he intertwined our fingers. My stomach chose that moment to growl loudly. Arne frowned. "You gave your food to Freja today?"

"Yes." He knew better than to argue with me about it. "She needed her strength."

"Hopefully we'll be able to put our hungry days behind us soon," he murmured, pressing a gentle kiss to the top of my head.

I stiffened at his words—at the reminder of my arranged marriage, coming far too soon for my liking. In a month, I would marry the Fastian Prince in exchange for shipments of food to keep our people from dying out while most of our supplies were funneled to the wastelands, where the fighting took place.

Arne didn't notice my discomfort. "I missed you."

Saying it back should have been as easy as breathing, but the words weighed heavy on my tongue, remaining unspoken this time. Wishing I could say it wasn't enough to force the words through my lips for once. I pulled back slightly. "Can we spar?"

His smile disappeared. "Of course."

Our relationship—if it could be called that—was complicated at best. With my twenty-first birthday having passed two weeks ago, my engagement to the Fastian Prince approached quickly. Pursuing more than friendship with Arne was foolish and rash. I'd kissed him for the first time nine months ago after my father revealed he'd arranged a marriage for me. The panic of the moment broke me, made me ache for something that was mine and no one else's.

I didn't want to imagine a first kiss with a person I didn't love—didn't *know*. And in the chaos, it was simple to press my lips to Arne's and tangle my fingers in his hair.

I told myself we knew where it was going from the start. A relationship with a short fuse, unable to live past its beginning stages of passion. Arne didn't seem to mind, but lately I found myself wondering if our feelings were aligned. If he wanted something more than a safe place to practice his firsts with a friend.

Did it matter, though? In the coming weeks we would go our separate ways. Neither of us would be able to stop it.

Forcing the thoughts from my mind was easy. I didn't have time to dwell on the sick feeling burrowing deep in my stomach whenever Arne kissed me these days or the hunger gnawing at my insides. I needed to train, to learn how to fight, to take care of myself. Things that were impossible when my family was in the city instead of on the war front. I had to take advantage of my limited time. I would not place my fate so securely in the hands of a husband I didn't know.

Unsheathing my sword was the most natural motion in the world, the sound like music to my ears. Here, I could forget my run-in with the priests. I could forget the way the robed figure held the scythe over the infant's chest while she wailed.

I closed my eyes and tried to shake the image from my head. Remembering the gruesome scene would only make me angrier. Freja was getting the baby to safety—no one had died senselessly at the hands of the priests today. It was more than I could hope for.

One ritual of many, my thoughts whispered. *A life saved now, perhaps. But will it make a difference in the end?*

Arne didn't wait for me to get set before he swung his blade, the metal arcing toward me. I stepped back and leaned so the blade didn't swipe me.

"How did it go today?" Arne asked as he turned and swung again. "Is Freja all right?"

I braced my hands on my hilt and parried, wrists shaking from the impact. Arne might be skinny, but he was strong. Every clash of our swords rattled my bones, but today I was glad. It would distract me from the baby's cry ringing in my ears.

"Good, I think." I saw an opening and lunged, but Arne dodged easily. "The priests managed to grab me, but they didn't catch Freja and she had the baby, so . . ." I would have shrugged if I wasn't parrying his next blow.

Arne narrowed his eyes, though I felt some of the tension drain out of him when I mentioned Freja's safety. The two had grown up together long before I knew them. If I didn't know better, I might assume they were siblings. "They caught you? Your father is going to give you hell."

"I know. My mother already did."

We were falling into a rhythm. Parry, thrust, swing, block.

"And you don't care?"

I frowned and tried to surprise him with a twist he wasn't expecting, but I wasn't as sneaky as I'd hoped, and the blow was easy to block.

"I've never cared." My breathing was getting heavy. "Especially not now, right after my birthday. The Bloodshed Trials are in six weeks. The Fastians arrive in a month for an engagement ceremony and the wedding. I'll be gone soon enough—might as well get as many blows in as I can beforehand."

Arne's voice was strained. "And you don't mind?" he asked. "Being married off to the Prince of Faste?"

Then I saw it—a gaping hole in his defenses. I swung and he tried to parry but missed, and my sword cracked against his armor. Finally, a win.

We both relaxed, breathing hard. I pushed loose strands of hair out of my face and shivered at the cold breeze rustling the leaves on the trees. "It doesn't matter if I mind," I said. "It's not like I have a choice."

Arne shrugged.

I held back a sigh. He was so open with his feelings, and I . . . well, I wasn't, but it didn't stop him from reading me like a book. He was disappointed our time together was coming to an end.

Arne didn't appear interested in sparring anymore, his sword hanging at his side, so I practiced my stances. He watched me silently, offering no comments. The blade felt like home in my hands. I sliced it through the air, enjoying the feel of the momentum.

"Besides, what else would they do with their godforsaken disappointment of a daughter?" I asked, my voice razor sharp at the edges. Arne asked me these questions over and over; he knew the answers.

"My family always does what the priests say. 'Sacrifice infants.' 'Treat the godforsaken like trash.' 'Go to war against Kryllian.' When Faste offered to send food in exchange for my hand in marriage"—I relaxed my stance and shrugged—"the priests thought it was too good to be true."

Arne sheathed his sword. "You're not something to be traded," he muttered.

I sheathed my own sword and turned to him, quick as a whip. "What would you have me do?" I demanded. "I won't run. I won't show them I'm afraid. That's one thing they don't get to hold over me. Otherwise, I'm a slave to my own fate."

His face was red; whether from the cold or from the sting of my words, I wasn't sure. Either way, his eyes didn't meet mine.

"Halvar thinks I should compete for the throne," I continued, my words cold. I already knew exactly how Arne would feel about this. "Force my way into the Bloodshed Trials."

"And you're considering this?" Apparently I wasn't the only one who could put up a mask when threatened.

I shrugged. "Why not? If you want me to stay here so desperately, then competing is the only way."

"You know that's not what I meant."

I shook my head and sighed, the fight leaving me in a rush. We had so little time left. Did I really want to spend it arguing? "I'm sorry. We've had this same talk—"

"About a million times. I know." His fingers ran around the edges of the armor on his opposite arm.

"There's nothing we can do." My voice was quiet now. "I don't want to leave. But if I have to, to keep you and Freja safe, I will."

"You can't protect us forever."

"Doesn't stop me from trying."

We practiced for the next hour in silence. Another person might find it disconcerting to spend so much time without exchanging words. But Arne preferred it, and I didn't mind.

Today my mind was occupied trying to imagine my life in Faste: wife to a spoiled godtouched prince in a country that cared more about agriculture than the art of war. So far, "decent enough" was the most I dared to hope for.

In Bhorglid, it was unseemly for a godforsaken to know how to fight. In Faste, it was unseemly for *anyone* to know how to fight.

Regardless of where I ended up, I would be forced to hide this part of myself—the part of me craving to defend the godforsaken against their oppressors. Only Arne, Freja, and Halvar saw through the façade forced on me.

These thoughts followed me as Arne and I traveled back to the main path when we finished sparring. His gloomy expression told me he was tangled in his own inner turmoil. Steeling myself against the torrent in my mind, I clapped a hand on his arm. "Don't be so glum," I said. "You and Freja will have plenty of fun without me. And I'll send letters, so it's not like we'll never talk."

Arne stilled, his face contorted into an expression I didn't recognize. He opened his mouth, but before he could speak, quick movement from below caught in my peripheral vision.

I whirled, turning to look at the cobblestone streets. Sure enough, five riders were making their way toward the path leading up to the castle, their matching fire-red hair noticeable from my position high above them. I shut my eyes and groaned. My worst nightmare. "They're back. Three days early."

When I opened my eyes, Arne wore an expression of concern. I knew he cared about me, but this was the first time I noticed it was leaving permanent frown lines around his eyes.

We concealed ourselves in the trees so my father and four older brothers wouldn't notice us when they passed. My father's booming voice echoed from the horse at the front of the group. "Well done, Björn. We'll have you as our captain in no time."

I massaged my temples. What a headache of a day.

Arne put a hand on my shoulder and gently rubbed my tense muscles. "It's nothing you haven't dealt with before. They'll be too busy talking about the Trials and the Hellbringer to pay you any attention."

Good point. With the Trials being so close, it was unlikely either of my less-than-friendly brothers would antagonize me. And while stories of the Hellbringer were always morbid, I found them fascinating in a strange way.

"Dinner will be an hour at the longest," Arne reminded me. "Stay quiet and things will be fine."

Eat and stay quiet. Should be easy enough.

"You should get going," I said.

He stood but glanced back. "Are you coming to Halvar's tonight?"

"Of course."

The worry evaporated from his face and a bit of light returned to his eyes. "Good. I'll see you there." He left, and I was alone.

I swallowed the lump in my throat, trying to remember the morning's victory. Freja and I had successfully disrupted the new year ritual. We saved an innocent life.

A cold wind blew over me and I shivered. By the end of the month I'd be in Faste, too far to help anyone. The castle loomed into view as I ascended the rest of the path.

The white stone edifice comprised four towers and five levels. On the bottom floor, an odd section jutted out from the original foundation: the armory, expanded to its current size only fifty years ago. The landscaping included a huge courtyard for sparring and hosting parties, a rose garden that bloomed only for a few weeks each summer, and the stables. A few priests milled about, weapons in hand to guard against any imagined threat. Their embroidered eyes stared me down as I made my way to the doors.

My home served as another unwelcome reminder of why we'd truly gone to war. The priests and the godtouched might claim it was a holy crusade, but the castle's towers and smooth, sloping arches told another story. The original castle my ancestors had built long ago had been a mighty wooden structure with sharp angles and straight lines. The new home my grandparents had commissioned was an imitation of the palace in Kryllian—a fact I only knew because my father often bragged about taking everything from our enemies. Their land, their culture, their lives—all of it was ours in his eyes.

My father and his father before him had a bad habit of wanting anything they didn't have. What had once been an admiration of Kryllian's ways had quickly festered into an obsession. And obsession always led to war.

At least signs of the approaching storm had disappeared. The winter sun danced idly on the grass, and I took my time walking across the courtyard. The crisp air had a particular taste and I inhaled deeply, clearing my lungs. The tip of my swollen nose was numb, but the sensation steadied me.

In the spring, the sight of the white castle against the green grass was stunning. Now it was nearly invisible before the snowcapped mountain. Its spot high above the valley was meant to give us a unique perspective in case of an invasion. From the top tower's vantage point, a person could see out to the southern sea on a clear day.

As of yet, the predicted invasion hadn't happened. If it ever did, I pitied the army who attempted it.

I reached the ornate front doors and took a deep breath. Now to prepare to deal with my family.

They went off to the front lines frequently enough that I knew their routine: they would head straight to their rooms to rinse off the month's grime before they came to dinner. My father would briefly consult with the Holy Order of Priests regarding updates on the war front as well. If I gave them enough time, I wouldn't run into anyone before dinner. And hopefully I'd be able to convince the palace healer to mend my face.

The front doors of the castle were huge and, of course, squeaky on their hinges. I closed them quickly and relaxed when the noise finally stopped.

All the bedrooms were on the third level. After ascending the stairs, I peered into the hallway to make sure my brothers' doors were closed before walking to my own door, which was cracked open slightly.

There were no guards or priests in the castle to give me trouble. If we were attacked, my brothers were expected to protect themselves. During the war, we couldn't waste soldiers. A single unit of fifty—the ones home on rotation—remained in the city while the rest fought on the front lines. The priests claimed law enforcement duties, but they all knew better than to intervene if I was in danger—no one cared if I lived or died.

Thanks to Halvar and Arne's training, I'd stand my ground if an attacker made their way into the castle. Otherwise, only two of my brothers cared enough to help me.

In the familiar, comforting space of my room, I threw on a maroon dress with sleeves long enough to hide the purpling bruise the priest gave me this morning. Then I brushed through my long sheet of dark hair, wavy after being in braids all day. I stared at my reflection, eyes hollow from long nights spent planning the morning's disruption with Freja and from bruises spreading away from my nose.

Where I saw strength glittering in my green eyes, my father saw defiance. Now I only hoped he saw little enough of it for me to make it through dinner unscathed.

First things first, though: I needed my nose to stop hurting so I could hold my own at the dinner table. I dashed down the stairs to the floor below, where my father's personal healer resided, and knocked on the door.

The wizened old man opened it, his back hunched forward, and glared at me. I offered him what I hoped was a winning smile, though I knew there was likely still blood on my teeth.

"Waddell," I greeted him. "As you can undoubtedly see, my nose is broken. I was hoping you'd be kind enough to heal it for me before I attend dinner with my family."

He didn't answer, simply scowled deeper. I wondered how it was possible.

I sighed. "I'll trade you for it." My brothers and my parents were treated well by Waddell, but whenever I needed healing, I was forced to barter. Even if the injury was dire, I knew he'd stand above me, tapping his foot while he waited for me to offer up my firstborn child in exchange for his services.

"I want a piece of jewelry," he said, voice cracking around the edges like a withered piece of paper.

I nodded. "Done."

He knew me well enough to know I'd follow through. So he reached forward and pressed two fingers hard to the broken bone and let his magic flow through them.

With a loud snap, the displaced pieces of my nose flew back together. It didn't hurt, but the feeling of bone writhing beneath my skin made me gag. Soon I felt the swelling recede and knew the dark bruises were vanishing. When he was done, I made the short trip upstairs to fetch him a necklace from my slowly dwindling jewelry box.

"Giving this to a fine friend?" I said, attempting a teasing tone.

His expression was serious. "No. I simply enjoy being able to take everything from you."

Waddell slammed the door behind him, leaving me fuming in the corridor.

◆ ◆ ◆ ◆ ◆

I DESPISED FAMILY DINNERS, WHICH WAS UNFORTUNATE, BECAUSE Mother insisted on having one every time Father and my brothers were back from the front lines. Attendance was mandatory; no exceptions.

I fidgeted in my seat, trying not to pull my legs up underneath me. Imagining the look Mother would give me kept me from doing it. On a normal day, I'd relish her glare, enjoying every minute she spent scolding me for petty rebellion, but I was too exhausted to fight back tonight.

My four redheaded older brothers sat on the sides of the table, my mother next to them, and my father sat at the head of the table, across from me. The foot of the table was my assigned place. Still better than the floor.

Directly on my left, my youngest brother, Björn, rambled on about some battle they'd been part of in the north. "The last one who tried to kill me had the godtouch of air. Probably thought he had the advantage over my fire, but I had the advantage in swordplay." He smirked. "It didn't take long to get rid of him."

I wondered whether the soldier had quenched Björn's fire by pulling the oxygen out of the air. Godtouched gifts were different in subtle ways—while many people could control the basic elements, they each had different limits and specific abilities. As a child, I spent years wondering what part of the gods' magic I possessed, which valuable talent would be my godtouched gift. When no magic ever manifested itself, I spent years languishing in disappointment.

When Björn finished rambling, I rolled my eyes and glanced to my right, where Frode, my second-oldest brother, sat across from Björn. Frode's hair was distinctly curly, unlike the rest of ours. He kept it cropped short against his head. He'd changed out of his military uniform and was dressed in a casual shirt and pair of pants. I wondered if Erik scolded him on the way to dinner for his outfit choice.

I channeled my thoughts in Frode's direction. *Is Björn this prissy when the temperatures are far below zero at night?*

Frode didn't say anything but smirked as he brought another bite of food to his mouth. I grinned. His godtouch was my favorite out of all my brothers: he could hear thoughts. It made for interesting fights and fun dinnertime conversations. The conversations were one-way, but I was glad someone appreciated my snippy comments, even if I didn't say them out loud.

Frode and I both despised Björn, and Frode once told me our other brothers, Erik and Jac, would sympathize if they were able to voice their thoughts without being lashed for it. "Erik only cares because he thinks Björn is neglecting the gods' demand to be more like them," Frode had told me with an eye roll. "Self-righteous of him." I took him at his word; Frode was terrible at lying and he didn't have any reason to.

Father watched Erik, the oldest, and Jac, a year and a half younger than Frode, more closely than he did the two of us. Perhaps because he had written Frode off as a potential candidate for the throne long ago. And it was no secret the king wished I never existed in the first place.

Björn continued to drone on about the war. I didn't pay much attention—the war was old news to me. Everything in Bhorglid was always about fighting, conquering, finding victory over someone else. Over time, the concept became boring. Not to mention Björn had a way of getting under people's skin enough to make them snap. If he didn't shoot fire from his fingers, I would have wondered whether he had the godtouch of annoying people.

"Then Father let me help strategize on how to take back the east side of the river," Björn continued, his shoulders straight. "Helping me prepare for when I am leading the armies."

Jac kept his face carefully neutral. As the most skilled strategist of us all, he would have given his arm and leg to lead the armies to victory. Björn never wasted a moment shoving it in his face how Father had never invited Jac to a strategy meeting. It made my cheeks burn with fury.

There was nothing we could do, though. As Father was keen to remind us often, everyone had their place in our society, and as soon as one stepped out of line, it was only a matter of time before everything began to fall apart. If the people had rebelled against Father when he was crowned king, I have no doubt he would have used his fire to quell the insubordination in a heartbeat.

Thankfully, the people were thrilled when he won the Bloodshed Trials of his generation, slaughtering his two younger brothers without a second thought. The same way my four brothers were supposed to run swords through each other until only one was left alive—the one who would take the throne.

Only then would my father abdicate. He and my mother would become citizens like the rest of the population, albeit far wealthier than most. They would live peacefully as long as they didn't attempt to interfere with their successors' choices, in which case . . .

Well. Let's just say my own grandparents had been executed before I was born.

Erik spoke then. "We are successfully decimating Kryllian forces. If we are faithful and careful, we'll be able to take the war from our wastelands to their shores soon. The country will be ours for the taking."

Mother nodded, and I tightened my grip on my fork, knuckles going pale. Ours for the taking. I clenched my teeth and Frode shot me a warning look.

I know. I'm not stupid.

I'd voiced my opinions before, and they'd made it clear my thoughts weren't welcome. That didn't keep me from thinking the war was a waste of time.

My father sat back in his chair. "Victory is in sight," he said to my mother. She smiled at him, and I sent Frode an image of myself gagging.

Frode, who was mid-swallow, choked on his food. Jac had to thump him on the back for a moment before he could breathe again.

Björn shot me a suspicious look, as if he too could read my thoughts. I smiled at him.

"And what of the Hellbringer?" Mother asked.

Suddenly, I cared a lot more for the war talk than I had a moment ago. Frode sent me a strange look and I ran through my memory of the morning's chase, allowing him to observe it. He frowned and tapped his fingers against the table but didn't speak.

"He continues to wreak havoc on our armies," Father said. "He is the only thing standing between us and our victory. Now, though, there are rumors circulating about him. We've had intelligence return to us with news that he's away from the front more often than not. They say he's searching for something."

I was utterly absorbed and barely noticed myself asking, "What? What is he searching for?"

Everyone turned to me, expressions varying from surprise that I'd spoken to anger that I'd been listening. "Why do you care?" Father sneered. "The war is no concern of yours."

I swallowed hard and sat up straighter. "I am a citizen of Bhorglid. Of course the war is my concern. It's everyone's concern."

Björn glared. "The war is a matter for the godtouched. Not anyone as lowly as you."

Frode interrupted. "We don't know what he's searching for, only that he's looking for something that could win them the war."

The room fell into silence, Frode's support of my question hanging tense in the air.

Before I could return to my meager portion, my father spoke again. "Revna," he said. My name lingered in his voice, and I resisted the urge to cringe, immediately regretting bringing any attention to myself.

All eyes turned toward me. I fidgeted with the embroidery on my sleeve. "Yes?" I asked, raising my eyebrows. Everyone was staring at me, waiting for Father to strike.

My father crossed his arms. "Your mother informed me the new year ritual was disrupted this morning."

I tried to keep my face casual as I chewed another bite. "Really?"

Björn snorted and my mother's icy gaze narrowed on me.

"Yes," Father said. He intertwined his fingers and tilted his head to the side. "We've discussed the appropriate course of action thoroughly since my return."

I continued chewing methodically, though the bite now tasted like ash in my mouth. I refused to give in to what he wanted, which was to get a reaction out of me.

Father's voice grew stonier with every word he spoke. "For the sake of our country—the sake of our favor with the gods—I hope that infant perished the moment you snatched it from the sacrificial altar."

I stared straight ahead, not breaking eye contact with my father, though I desperately wanted to know what my brothers' faces looked like. Hopefully their shock at my crimes made my interruption of the ritual worth it.

My father clenched his fork so tightly, I wondered if it would break. Or whether, more likely, he would melt it. It wouldn't be the first time I'd caused him to damage property.

"You," he said, face turning red, "are a shame to this family. You dare disrespect the gods who protect us in battle?" His voice rose to a shout as he continued, "When we are so clearly losing the war? When we need the gods more than ever?"

Losing? Hadn't he said they were close to winning? The surprise lasted only a moment before it transformed, and anger coursed through me. I had tried to tell him over and over how terribly the godforsaken were being treated at the hands of the priests, but he wouldn't listen.

I slammed my palms on the table. "They have never been my gods," I cried. "You sacrifice the godforsaken, treat us as lesser beings, and refuse to listen to us!" I felt the blood rushing to my face. My heartbeat was loud in my ears.

The hand holding my father's fork erupted in flames. No one at the table flinched. The metal in his grasp began to wilt like a dying flower under the sun.

When he spoke again, his voice was terrifyingly soft. "You will not disrespect our country." His hand shook. "Or your gods. Or your family."

I glanced at my brothers and my rage evaporated from me like smoke drifting away in the wind. Björn grinned from ear to ear, watching with glee shining in his eyes. Jac stared at his plate, unmoving. Erik and Frode continued to eat, ignoring the argument entirely.

My father let his fire go out, wiping the liquid metal off his hands with a cloth napkin. "In six weeks, we will host the Bloodshed Trials. But before that, we will celebrate your wedding and your departure to Faste. In fact, the wedding delegation arrives tomorrow to begin planning. This is only one portion of your punishment." His cold blue eyes met mine. "I do not think either of us will be disappointed to part ways."

"Tomorrow," I said. My voice was as hollow as I felt. I forced the furious tears in my eyes not to move any farther. "You told me I had another month."

He shrugged. "We received word from Faste last week. There was a skirmish at their border and they are anxious to see their end of the alliance fulfilled in case Kryllian decides to bring the war to their territory. Besides, you're well-known for your antics. Why would I give you an opportunity to wreak havoc on your own engagement? It was more pertinent to keep the information from you."

Fury bubbled in my stomach, threatening to overflow.

"You're an absolute—"

Frode stood and put his hand around my wrist, clasping it tight enough to be a warning but light enough not to hurt. He raised an eyebrow, and I knew he was trying to calm me down.

He helped me stand and led me from the dining room. My father offered him a nod of encouragement and I hissed through my teeth, scowling.

Frode and I walked in silence. Having a brother who could read my thoughts was helpful when I didn't want to talk.

A skirmish at the border. Not even a real battle. That was all it had taken for Faste to renege on their original marriage date and come running to Father for help. If Kryllian truly was pushing at their borders, it made sense they'd want our soldiers occupying their country sooner.

But the logic of the situation didn't soothe my upended emotions.

When we reached my room, I sat on the edge of the bed, and Frode cleared his throat. "Are you okay?"

"Go away," I mumbled. There was no emotion in my voice. No thoughts in my head for him to steal.

He winced but nodded and stepped out, closing the door softly behind him.

I waited until his footsteps disappeared before slamming my fist into the wall, then watching the bruise bloom outward from underneath the skin of my knuckles. The pain was sour, but it felt better than the hole in my chest filled with disappointment, bitter about having to obey my father.

Again and again, my hand connected with the stone. I kept hitting until blood was smeared on the wall and I couldn't feel the pain anymore.

Only when I collapsed, my hand a destroyed mess of flesh, did I realize my father had never said what the rest of my punishment would be.

◆ ◆ ◆ ◆ ◆

THE HELLBRINGER VISITED ME IN MY DREAMS.

Beneath the haze of exhaustion weighing down my bones like lead, I knew I was asleep. The world swirled around me, colors and objects blending in impossible ways. The pain of my now-swollen hand was nearly forgotten, and the events of the day seemed laughable, not life altering.

I tilted my head to the left to study the dark figure who stared down at me. Despite his blurry form, I knew with a certainty who it was—the handcrafted mask was impossible not to recognize. And the loveliest thing about dreaming? The absence of fear. Where earlier the sight of him had made me freeze, now I found myself entirely neutral to his presence.

I tried to raise my hand to touch the helmet, discover what it was made of, but halfway up, a throb of pain shot through my fingers. Frowning, I muttered, "Ow."

The room was dim. The Hellbringer tilted his head slightly to study me.

The haze of dreaming refused to clear, my half-asleep state slurring my words and halting my movements. "You should just kill me. You know. If you're really so godtouched."

He stood silently and didn't reply.

I groaned, wishing I didn't have to talk to communicate. "Stupid.

I don't believe in gods. Why do they like you more than me, huh? Doesn't make sense. I'm great."

When was this dream going to fade to black? When would it transform into something wilder than Kryllian's most dangerous general standing in my childhood bedroom?

Without warning, a warm hand brushed against my bruised and bloodied one. I hissed and pulled it back, rousing slightly, but he ran a hand gently through my hair and my whole body relaxed. It had been so long since someone other than Arne had touched me kindly. Since I hadn't feared a hand on my face. My eyes shuttered closed as the Hellbringer's fingers combed carefully through my locks, brushing out the tangles there.

"'S nice," I muttered.

Eventually my injured hand lifted of its own accord and a steady, stable pressure replaced the throbbing pain. I blinked, vision hazy, to see my knuckles wrapped in thick white cloth.

I stared, my brain too sluggish to understand what it meant. How the bandage had arrived there. When I finally returned my gaze to the Hellbringer, though, he was gone.

And soon sleep dragged me fully under once more.

4

I DIDN'T MOVE FROM MY BED UNTIL THE MOON ROSE TO TAKE its place at the height of the sky. Once my anger had faded, leaving me an empty shell, I'd dozed on and off for several hours, only interrupted by my strange dream.

This late, the castle was silent outside my door. I stretched, waiting for the pain in my hand to wake me fully, but it never did. When I lifted it to my line of sight, my breath stopped in my throat.

Thick white bandages were wrapped tightly around the wounds, keeping the swelling down and my joints in place. It didn't take an expert to know the wrapping was medically sound—the dramatic decrease in angry throbbing told me my injuries were significantly improved.

It hadn't been a dream at all. The Hellbringer had been here, standing in my quarters. He'd managed to make his way into the castle without being detected and sneak into my room. He'd even treated my injuries.

The most miraculous part of it all was that I remained alive.

I took a shaky breath, flexing my hurt fingers, mind spinning. It made no sense. Why would the Hellbringer have any interest in me?

And more importantly, why wasn't he in the northern wastes, where he belonged?

If he was truly after something that would win Kryllian the war, he had no reason to be haunting my room in the dead of night.

Shoving the paranoia from my mind, I slid on a pair of warm pants and a simple blouse and tied the laces of my dancing shoes. It was dark, but I knew the pair better than my own reflection. When I finished, I began the familiar routine of quietly walking the halls to the front doors of the castle. Before the war, soldiers employed as guards had crawled through every nook and cranny of the castle, forcing me to take my late-night excursions by crawling out my bedroom window and scaling the walls down three stories. Now the building was empty and silent, but unfamiliar anxiety trailed my every step.

What if the Hellbringer hadn't left? What if he was still here, lingering in the shadowed corners, waiting for me to take my next step?

I shook my head and walked faster, trying to dislodge the thought. Maybe it wasn't the Hellbringer who'd bandaged my hand; maybe that part truly was a dream. Frode could have easily returned after I fell asleep. Maybe I was losing my lucidity. Maybe the realization that the Fastians were arriving in the morning had tipped me over an invisible edge. Either way, I would deal with it another time. Not on my last true night with my friends.

At the edge of the courtyard, I gazed at the descending path in front of me. The stone steps plunged for an eternity, and I took a deep breath as I began my trek to Halvar's.

The city was quiet below me, only a few lights flickering through windows in the distance. It took a few minutes to make my way down, finally stepping onto the stone path winding through the city.

The priests prowled the godforsaken end of town, using their authority to punish anyone breaking the rules they'd imposed upon the neighborhoods. They wouldn't dare cross me, not when the Fastians were arriving in the morning, but I avoided them all the same. It was easier to slip in and out of the shadows along the edges of buildings than have them all stare me down.

It would be a lie to say I wasn't on high alert for the flicker of a black cloak or the carved snout of a dangerous mask peeking from behind a building. But my walk was short and uneventful. Still, I hurried, anxious to avoid trouble. Arriving at the Sharpened Axe, roof sagging and door hanging half open on its hinges, I breathed deeply to steel myself for the crowd. Drunken laughter echoed through the street, and I hugged my arms to try and keep myself warm. Through the window I caught a glimpse of Arne and Freja dancing. When they stopped to breathe before the next song started, Freja poked him in the face and he laughed, an expression of happiness he reserved only for Freja and me.

Go in. You can do it.

In the end, I didn't have a choice. I opened the door slightly and a hand grabbed me by the wrist and tugged me into the fray, music twisting in my mind. The person who had dragged me inside pulled me into their grasp. I looked up to see Arne spinning me to the beat of the music.

I kept my footing only because I knew the steps by heart. I could do this jig in my sleep. Years of sneaking out after dark meant I had memorized all the dances, and as the tagelharpa player strummed, I lost myself in the music, shielding my injured hand from the throng.

The song ended and Arne offered me a mock bow and a raised eyebrow. I smirked at him, and he tugged on my unbandaged hand to draw me close for a kiss. Wolf whistles echoed around us, but he didn't care.

"You're late," he remarked, pulling back slightly to press his lips to my cheek.

When his gaze caught on my wrapped wounds, his expression

fell. He led me out of the dancing crowd to a table at the back of the tavern, where Freja sat waiting.

Arne nudged me toward a chair, and I sat, grabbing the frothing mug Freja shoved toward me. I took a long swig and winced at the taste of watered-down beer. Better than nothing; I was surprised there was beer of any kind left these days.

Arne grabbed my bandaged hand and held it up for Freja to examine. She gasped when she caught sight of the bruises blossoming around the edges of the wrapping. "You need to see a healer. Again."

"I don't want a healer," I said, voice monotone. I didn't look either of them in the eyes. A slow throb echoed through my hand. This injury wasn't one I'd earned through insurrection. It was a self-inflicted expression of my pain.

The pain I couldn't truly show anyone, even my friends. Not when they all had it far worse than I ever would.

Arne frowned. "Don't be an idiot. You need a healer. Get one yourself or I'll make you."

I lifted the mug to my lips and took another drink instead of answering. Arguing was pointless with Arne, the only person I knew who rivaled me for stubbornness. No matter how much I fought him, my hand would be healed whether I wanted it or not.

Before I came up with a way to effectively protest Arne's insistence that I see a healer, Halvar approached our table. His establishment was the center of life on the working side of town. A safe place for the godforsaken. The godtouched had no interest in a shabby tavern where the best drink offered was watered-down beer.

Us godforsaken, though? We cared far less about the drinks and far more about the camaraderie of our traditional dances and the lack of priests here.

Halvar grinned, offering us a gap-toothed smile. "Glad you made it," he said, clapping me on the back with a giant hand.

I returned the expression. "Thanks for letting me come by."

He rolled his eyes. "You're one of us. I'd never try to stop you."

Some godforsaken disagreed. They didn't realize I suffered too, albeit in a different way than they did because of my royal blood. It was hard to feel like I had anywhere I belonged.

But at Halvar's those feelings of loneliness and sense of loss disappeared. Halvar's was home.

Freja held up her mug. "To Halvar."

We echoed her sentiment and took a swig of the beer, letting it slide down our throats. I shook my head and ran my tongue across my teeth, casting a glance over the crowd. Familiar faces mixed with those I'd never seen before: I nodded to the cobbler whose shop was only a few buildings down, smiled at a middle-aged woman radiating nervousness, and watched a dark-haired man only a few years older than me run a finger through the condensation pooling on the wooden table in front of him.

Halvar glanced at Freja. "How was your morning?" he asked, focusing on the towel in his hands.

She shrugged. "I had work." Today had been her day off, but no one said anything in response to our usual code; she was letting us know the baby had been safely delivered to its parents, who were now on their way out of the country. I took a deep breath and relaxed slightly.

The codes were necessary for a reason. The last thing we needed was a gossip letting slip who was involved in my schemes. I was always more than happy to take the brunt of responsibility, especially knowing what would happen if my friends were caught. Freja leaned forward to rest her elbows on the table. "How's your storeroom looking?"

Halvar scanned the crowd around us for eavesdroppers before answering. "Storeroom's looking great."

Anyone in town could tell you where the storeroom was in the Sharpened Axe. But the trapdoor underneath was a secret we guarded with our lives. The place Freja, Halvar, and I had sat and talked this morning was where Halvar taught us how to fight.

Halvar fancied the idea of a revolution against the priests. Overthrowing my father and brothers would be his dream come true. Over the years, he'd worked in secret to set up his underground operation, gathering weapons and teaching non-magical people in the city how to fight. As the anomaly of a godforsaken with two godtouched parents, Halvar's mothers taught him everything he would have learned at the military academies. Determined to spread his knowledge and empower more of us, he took it upon himself to train those he trusted. By this point there were about fifty novice godforsaken swordfighters scattered throughout the city. In half an hour or so, Halvar would disappear for the night to help them keep learning, leaving his other manager in charge of the pub.

We knew it was risky to hide in plain sight, but Halvar's place was as close as we godforsaken got to having our own temple. Enough people gathered here daily to keep suspicion away from anyone in particular, and we worked together to keep the priests out. I'd caused a ruckus on the other side of the neighborhood a time or two to turn the suspicious red eyes away from the pub.

The biggest problem with preparing to revolt was how long it took Halvar to trust a person enough to invite them. It was understandable, considering the necessity of secrecy, but it also meant I had turned my friend down several times when he'd asked me to lead a rebellion against the throne. Against the might of the Bhorglid army, fifty godforsaken soldiers were nothing. They'd slaughter us in less than a minute.

The logic didn't disappoint or discourage him, though. He continued to train people, the hope of a revolution shining in his eyes. Arne, Freja, and I had been some of his first students.

The rebellion was why he pushed for me to try and join the Trials. "Just think," he'd told me again and again. "If we could win the throne fairly, the priests would be forced to uphold their own teachings and let you rule. They wouldn't be able to do anything about it."

Every time, I shook my head. "Even if I could hold my own against four of the most powerful godtouched in the country, they'd never let a godforsaken be queen. They'd cut me down in an instant, teachings be damned."

My mother's words from the morning had never felt more pointed. *You're many horrible things already, daughter mine. Queen will never be one of them.*

Halvar left to return to serving the rest of the godforsaken customers. Arne sipped his beer silently and adjusted his chair a few inches closer to me. He didn't necessarily approve of the things we did to disrupt the priests, but he didn't disapprove either. The only comment he'd ever made to me was regarding the time Freja and I had gathered buckets of dung straight from the fields of livestock and dumped them on the temple steps. Apparently he thought it was "childish and petty." After, we never asked him to participate, and in exchange he never bothered us about it.

He did worry, though.

Arne traced his finger through the ring of condensation his mug left on the table. "I did want to tell you," he began, voice strained, "I think your stunt this morning had more fallout than you two were expecting."

Freja and I exchanged glances. "What do you mean?" she asked.

Arne took a deep breath and his eyes flickered up to us. "I got a conscription letter this evening."

My heart dropped into my stomach.

Freja choked on her beer and Arne pounded her on the back while she coughed. When she could breathe again, she wiped the back of her hand over her mouth. "What the hell. You're not godtouched. They can't."

"She's right," I whispered. The rhetoric about why godforsaken were never conscripted changed every few months—the priests couldn't seem to decide if they kept us from the front lines due to our lack of magical abilities or because our very presence would taint the battlefield and summon the wrath of the gods. Whatever the reason, the godforsaken never fought, even if it was only to keep the economy moving while the rest of the population did the fighting.

In some ways it was a blessing. I had no doubt that, when the time came, Father would throw extra bodies in front of the enemy. The thought of my people being used as shields against the Hellbringer and an army of ruthless soldiers made my stomach turn.

If Arne was being conscripted, what would stop my father and the priests from pulling the rest of the godforsaken out to the front lines?

"How is this happening? Are all the godforsaken being conscripted?" Freja demanded.

He shook his head. "No. I've asked around. Only me."

I shook my head, unable to tear the image of Arne's lifeless body from my mind, my friend bleeding red into the snow as his eyes went glassy. *This is the other half of the punishment,* I realized. *They are using him against me.*

Freja pounded her fist on the table. "This is your father's doing," she spat. "Oh, I want to—"

I put a hand on her shoulder and she stopped talking. Looking around, I noticed a person or two gazing at our small group. Probably newcomers wondering what business the princess had here, but . . . it was always possible someone would overhear one of us get too zealous and take their news back to the king.

Freja's voice cracked when she spoke next. "Revna, can't you do anything?" The grief in her voice was palpable—as if she already mourned Arne, though he sat beside her. "Can't you talk to your father?"

I clenched my teeth. "I can't. He found out I was involved with this morning's events and . . . well, I knew they were going to marry me off, but I was supposed to have another month. The entourage from Faste arrives tomorrow. Kryllian has begun encroaching on their borders and they want the alliance to go through as soon as possible. I'll be gone by the end of the week."

Silence fell and Arne leaned his head back. It didn't fit—the music and the tapping of hard-soled shoes against the wood, the happy cries of the dancers stabbing sharply through the dull pain of knowing the three of us were about to part ways forever.

Freja, always upbeat, stared straight ahead at nothing.

"You can't both leave me," she muttered. Time snapped back to normal. She sniffed and rubbed a tear away, chugging the rest of her beer in one fell swoop. "It's rude."

She hid her pain behind a smile. Arne smiled back at her, albeit sadly.

"There's no guarantee it will end badly," he said. "I'm one of the few godforsaken lucky enough to have training with a sword."

"You've always wanted to be a fighter," Freja murmured, putting her hand on Arne's. "I'll see you again. If anyone can kill the Hellbringer, it's you."

I tried not to grimace at the thought of the Hellbringer. I didn't dare tell them of my strange dream, not so soon after I thought I'd seen him wandering our city streets. Especially when I wasn't sure if it was real or not.

We all had far more pressing matters to worry about.

I pushed the Hellbringer from my mind, turning my attention back to Arne. "You'll miss the Bloodshed Trials." I smirked. "Disappointed you won't get to see which of my brothers is alive at the end?"

Freja snorted. "Your brothers are assholes. Well, Björn and Erik are. And they'll be the last in the ring, so it'll be interesting to see who wins. I'll send you letters with a play-by-play of the action."

I would miss it too, I realized with a jolt. By then, I would be married to the Fastian Prince, whisked away from my home to become nothing but a symbol of unity between countries.

I tightened my hold on my mug, but I didn't say anything, keeping my mouth in a carefully preserved smile. How could I complain about my fate when Arne was going to war and Freja would be left alone? I'd be selfish to act as though marriage was nearly as bad.

"We should dance," I suggested. Maybe it would help us forget about our woes.

Neither friend responded. I sighed. The weight in my stomach had returned and I dreaded the thought of going home and closing my eyes. Tomorrow I would stop being Revna and start becoming the Princess of Faste.

To distract from my morbid train of thought, I stood from the table and threw myself into the music, spinning around and around to the tempo, letting my momentum take the weight off my shoulders. Nothing freed me the way dancing did.

I spotted Arne and Freja back at the table, their heads touching as they talked, worry lines between their brows. Did Arne's fathers mourn when they learned of his conscription? Was Freja planning to help care for his younger brother?

No, I told myself, *don't think about what happens if he doesn't come back from the front.*

Before my line of thinking could continue, the crash of the door being slammed open reverberated through the space. Many startled, hands flying to cover hearts. The music jolted to a discordant halt and those closest to the door gasped.

Catching sight of the newcomers, I scowled. Three priests stood in the doorway, filling the space so we could barely see the night behind them. They stepped in one at a time and the crowd fell silent. Their red eyes glared. A faint noise came from behind the priests. Finally, the last of them pushed through, dragging a cowering woman with him. She sobbed, trying desperately to shrink into the background.

My heart sank. The woman had a face I recognized too well. It was Freja's mother.

Freja pushed her way through the crowd until she stood face-to-face with the priests. They held their scythes loosely in their hands.

"Let go of her," she growled.

I moved forward to stand behind her, my head held high. I tried never to pull rank in front of my godforsaken friends, but now was worth the exception. "I command you to let go of her," I said. My voice shook.

The priests laughed and let go of Freja's mother, who immediately fell to the floor, shaking. Freja ran up to her and held her close, murmuring in her ear, but her mother would not allow it. "No," she whispered, trying to push her daughter away. "No, Freja get out of here, get out—"

But before things connected, before they made sense, one of the priests grabbed Freja's arms and wrists and placed a flat piece of metal along them. I watched as in one swift motion the metal bent, folding into perfect handcuffs.

"What the hell do you think you're doing?" I asked, stepping forward. I pulled my dagger from the sheath at my waist.

The crowd behind me was silent. One of the priests spoke. "I don't think you want to fight us, Your Highness," he said. He raised his hand, and the blade of my dagger bent in on itself, curving toward my exposed fingers. I dropped it, swearing. "We have the authority to arrest lawbreakers."

Arne stood next to me. I'd never been more thankful for his height—he towered over the priests, looking down on them like they were children.

"She hasn't broken the law," I snarled. My face flushed, only Arne's hand on my shoulder keeping me from lunging at them.

Another priest tilted his head. "Then who disrupted the new year ritual this morning?"

"I did," I said, but my voice shook. "You caught me this morning." I held my hands out, wrists exposed. "Take me instead."

They couldn't take Freja to prison. Not when her brother was on the front lines and her mother needed her. Not when prison was hell on earth. Not when she was everything, my best friend in the world.

The priest shook his head. "Your father only wants her," the priest said. "Besides, I wouldn't like to be the one to tell the king I arrested his daughter, would I?" As his voice turned sarcastic, I realized this was the priest who'd caught me this morning.

My throat burned. I stepped forward. "Freja—"

She shook her head wordlessly.

"Let her go," I protested, following them into the dark street. "Please. Don't do this."

Cruel laughter pierced the night sky as they mounted their horses, pulling Freja up to share a saddle with her captor, and galloped away. Freja didn't look back.

5

THE DAWN LIGHT WOKE ME FROM A RESTLESS SLEEP AND THE night rushed back in one swift memory.

Freja's hands, wrestled behind her back. Metal twisting around her wrists. Arne half dragging me up the mountainside and wrapping me in his arms to keep my body from shaking. He'd stayed until I fell asleep. I stretched a hand out next to me, but the bed was empty, my friend long gone.

I pulled my blanket back over my face and groaned. Not a dream. A real, living nightmare.

I needed to talk to my father and convince him he'd made a mistake.

All I could imagine was Freja, her cheerful demeanor dampened as she sat in the corner of a cold cell, chained to the wall. I shivered. I wouldn't wish prison on anyone, especially not in the winter.

This was entirely my fault. I would do anything to make it right.

When I opened my eyes again, I caught sight of a piece of paper on my nightstand with my name on it. I frowned and pulled it open.

Revna,

*I'm going to visit Freja tonight. Don't bother your father
about this; he'll only continue to take it out on her. Our first
priority must be keeping her safe.*

Arne

I swallowed hard, the knot in my throat sinking to the bottom of
my stomach. Arne was right—if I spoke out of turn to my father, he
would take it out on Freja. He already had; he was using her to get
back at me. My status was high enough that, despite the priests' dislike of me, they wouldn't imprison me without direct orders.

Freja was not so lucky.

I clenched my teeth. Father had found my weak spot.

The door opened and my mother entered, holding an elaborate
gown. "Get up. The Fastians will be here in half an hour."

I reached up to rub my forehead, where a pounding headache
had made its home. The image of Freja, shivering and cold, danced
through my mind again. I fought against a wave of nausea.

Meeting my fiancé was the last thing I wanted to do today.

My right hand twitched, and a throb of searing pain shot through
my fingers and up to my wrist. I grimaced. Somehow, in all the
chaos, I'd forgotten about my broken fingers.

"Could you send up the healer? I have a headache."

My mother's frown managed to deepen further as she kicked my
dirty clothes into a corner. On any other day, she would have pro-
cured a chunk of ice with her godtouch and that would have been
the only respite for my throbbing skull. Today, though, I knew she
wouldn't want to risk me being out of it when the entourage arrived.
"Out drinking again. Why am I not surprised?"

I rolled my eyes. "I can hear you."

"You were supposed to."

"Are you going to send Waddell or not?" I was already in a bad enough mood; this was making it worse.

"Fine. You'd better be outside when the delegation arrives."

She made sure to slam the door behind her.

Waddell arrived minutes later and did his job efficiently. Because my mother had sent him, he knew better than to demand a payment from me this time. I had to look away when he healed my broken knuckles; the loud crack of bones snapping into place was jarring. Watching the blood from the bruises flow back to my veins was fascinating, though. Ten minutes later my hand was good as new, my hangover was gone, and I was alone once more.

I glanced at the gown my mother had left on the chair. When I rose and picked it up, thick green fabric slid between my fingers. Intricate beadwork and endless jewels I couldn't identify cascaded down the layers of skirts. How was I supposed to wear something so heavy? Was it meant to be worn all day? It differed widely from my own wardrobe of simple linen dresses, casual pants, and tight shirts.

I hoped it was ceremonial. Surely the royal women in Faste didn't dress like this every day. If they did, no one would get any farming done.

Once dressed, I slipped my shoes on and headed out the door, holding back a groan when I realized the gown was longer than I had anticipated. The silky green fabric dragged on the ground behind me, and if I wasn't careful, falling down the stairs would become my legacy.

Twisting my hands in the fabric, I gathered it up enough not to risk an untimely demise on my way to the courtyard. I imagined Freja trying to stifle her laugh behind her hand at the sight of me in such finery.

I rubbed a hand over my chest. It hurt to breathe when I thought about her. I ignored another wave of nausea—vomiting on the prince probably wasn't the best way to start our relationship.

As I descended the stairs, I mulled over Arne's letter. To him, it wasn't worth the risk of talking to my father and trying to make a plea for Freja's freedom. But what if it was? My father wouldn't be cruel enough to keep her imprisoned, not after I'd been sent off to Faste . . . would he?

Panic settled over me and the pain in my chest sharpened. Would he keep her there after I was gone? Was Freja destined to live the rest of her life as a prisoner?

Her curls would flatten. Dark circles would find permanent homes beneath her eyes. Her dark skin would wither and the muscles she'd strengthened through the years with hours of training and swordfighting would atrophy. Her once cheerful voice would be hoarse and ragged from disuse.

I stopped walking and gulped in a breath. No. No. I wouldn't let that happen. I would find time to talk to my father. I had to.

To my left, voices echoed from behind a heavy wooden door, distracting me from my thoughts. The council was in session, which meant leaders from the six provinces of Bhorglid were gathered with the king to discuss the newest developments in the war and the impact it was having on their people. I frowned. The last council had been only a few months ago, and they typically only occurred twice a year. Why were they gathered now, especially with the Fastian royals arriving today?

A quick glance in either direction told me I was alone in the corridor. I kept my steps quiet as I leaned forward to press my ear against the closed door. The voices were easy to hear, something my brothers and I had discovered long ago when we were just children eager to be involved in our father's responsibilities.

The murmured words coalesced into a war report: "—finding the Hellbringer," my father was saying. I tensed, leaning closer. I still wasn't sure if the general in my room last night had been a dream, but I hadn't been able to shake the feeling of hands gently combing through my hair.

Noises of approval echoed through the room. Another voice asked, "What about these reports of the Hellbringer searching for something? And the suggestion that he's looking for it in our own cities?"

I sucked in a breath. They'd mentioned yesterday that the terrifying general was on the hunt for something, but to be looking for it *here*? This was new information entirely.

The king continued smoothly, "He may be searching for something, but if he is in our cities, he will be caught. Our priests are hallowed men, ordained by the pantheon themselves. They have the foresight needed to know where the Hellbringer will strike next."

I chewed my lip. This all but confirmed it: the man I'd seen yesterday was most certainly the Hellbringer. Was he following me? Why had he observed me as I slept instead of killing me outright? Was I connected to whatever he was looking for?

"And the alliance with Faste? Are those heathens still committed to helping us?" This voice was new, tinged with bitterness.

Father attempted to soothe them. "The alliance solidifies our next move. When the war is won, we will be Faste's trusted companions. It will provide the best chance for us to proceed with our conquest. Once we have Kryllian under our belt, we can move on to other pursuits."

A firm hand wrapped around my upper arm and hauled me to my feet. I started, turning, and was met with my mother's scowl. I winced when her nails dug into my soft flesh, her fingers cold as the ice she commanded with her magic.

"Eavesdropping?" she demanded. "I thought you knew better. Your father will have a word with you later. The delegation will be here any minute. Go wait outside with your brothers." She shoved me in their direction before opening the council room doors and walking in.

Huffing with indignance, I stomped to the front of the castle and stepped outside to take my place in line next to Björn. The sky was filled with gray clouds and my brothers stood stoically, waiting for the Fastians to arrive.

"You're late," Björn observed. "Run into priests on your way home from Halvar's?"

So he knew. I dug my fingernails into my palms, hoping the pain would distract me. It didn't work.

"You're such an ass," I muttered.

He laughed. "That's the best you've got? You're off your game today."

I scowled and forced my hands to my sides. For all I knew, he had been the one to suggest Freja's arrest. Where was a brutal god-touch when I needed one?

"Don't worry," he said. "Soon enough the prince will take you away to Faste and you'll never have to see any of us again." His smile was wicked.

I bared my teeth. "Good riddance."

Björn was suddenly yanked back by a firm hand. Erik. "If you two can't behave yourselves, then I suppose you need to be separated like children," he said, his voice dry and unamused. He dragged Björn to the other side of the line and shoved him into place.

I scooted over to make up for the space he'd left behind. Now I stood next to Frode.

He glanced at me out of the corner of his eye. "How's your hand?"

My lips tightened into a straight line. "Fine."

"Are you looking forward to meeting the prince?"

I rolled my eyes. "Drop the pleasantries, Frode. I'm not in the mood."

"I heard about Freja," he said. He kept his voice low so Björn wouldn't overhear. "When are you going to talk to Father?"

"I don't know," I said. Without warning, my eyes began to fill with tears. What if I didn't get the opportunity to talk to him before he rushed me away to be a bride?

Frode put a hand on my back. "Keep the tears in," he said softly. "Don't let him break you."

I took a shaky breath and steadied myself while Frode chatted on, trying to distract me. "I for one am not excited to see the delegation. Fastians don't know how to keep their thoughts to themselves. They're so *loud*. You'll fit right in." He rubbed his temple as if he could already hear them.

I chuckled through my shallow breaths. Frode always knew how to make me smile. "If you manage to get away from the fun, take me with you," I said.

He gave me a sidelong glance. "Not likely, but I'll do my best."

We fell silent. I wondered when I would see Arne again. He could tell me how Freja was doing.

Frode leaned toward me, evidently listening in on my thoughts. "Father told me they were conscripting him," he muttered, careful to keep his voice low. "I tried to talk them out of it, but . . . well, you know what happens to me when we get to the front lines. They don't exactly respect my opinion."

A chill that had nothing to do with the wind ran through me as I thought back to when we were younger. I was only eight when Frode came home from his first stint in the war, utterly broken. I found him in his room seconds before he slid a dull knife over his wrists. The voices were too loud in his mind at the battle sites, the unspoken pain of the dying and fearful soldiers wreaking havoc on my gentle brother. I'd begged Father to let him stay home, but to no avail. So, whether he wanted to or not, Frode had gotten used to it.

As used to it as a person could be, at least.

He shook his head. "Things were . . . worse this time around." He paused for a moment, and I resisted the urge to put a hand on his arm, wishing I could take the thoughts from him. "We are losing. Badly. The troops are growing weak. We lose soldiers in battles and we lose them from starvation. This alliance is the only thing that will save us."

I would have answered if I hadn't heard the sound of horses riding up the northern trail leading to the castle. Sure enough, the Fastian delegation appeared over the crest of the hill. Two carriages, both black, were pulled by majestic white horses. Soldiers in uniform were perched on the sides of each, keeping careful watch for enemies.

The carriage rolled to a halt in front of us and five people exited. I recognized two of them—the king and queen—from their former diplomatic visits to the castle. The younger man who stepped out behind them must have been the prince. He was dressed in finery and his ebony skin matched the king and queen's.

They dismounted and approached. The other two members of their party were guards—they wore Fastian green, the same shade as my dress. Weapons were sheathed discreetly at their hips.

I glanced at the prince, standing behind his parents. He nodded at me, and I returned the gesture. Might as well keep things friendly.

"Welcome," my father said, taking the queen's hand and pressing his lips to it. He'd stepped into the courtyard right as the carriages appeared. It was strange to see my father in his royal finery. Since the war started, he rarely put it on. The red coat made his shoulders look broader. A white sash with red leaves embroidered along it ran from his shoulder to his hip. "Thank you for coming."

The King of Faste wore a haughty expression. His long blue cloak was lined with fur and grazed the ground. He had a beard cropped close to his face, matching his dark, curly hair. "We are anxious to see our end of the deal come to fruition," he said, casting a look in my direction.

What an ass. I wanted to punch him in the face.

The prince chewed his lip. His face was nearly identical to his father's: same nose, same downward curve of the mouth. He was handsome, but I knew nothing about his personality. Did he wish this wasn't happening? Were his parents using him as a pawn the way mine were using me?

After enough pleasantries were exchanged, the royalty and their guards were invited into the sitting room to discuss politics. I was grateful—goose bumps ran up my arms and my teeth chattered in the morning air.

When we took our seats on the plush couches, I made sure to sit next to Frode. My mother scowled at me, obviously wishing I had chosen to sit next to the prince, but I ignored her look and settled in for the political talk.

Is the prince feeling as awkward about this as I am? I thought, hoping Frode was listening.

He was. Frode offered me a strained smile and nodded. The Fastians must be thinking louder than he expected—Frode looked like he was in physical pain.

"Headache," he whispered.

Across from us, the two kings discussed the war. "If you aren't careful to keep your army in control of the situation, you could end up with two fronts for this war," the King of Faste said. "We do not want Kryllian attacking our territory. This is your conquest, not ours."

My father leaned back in his chair before replying. "Kryllian will not risk splitting their troops, especially not when we have them cornered in the wastes. Their tactical choice to try and surprise us by coming from the north was only the first of many mistakes they've made. Rest assured, we have the advantage."

A servant arrived with cups of tea and Frode grabbed him by the arm, whispering something in his ear. The young man glanced at my father uncertainly, but Frode touched his chin lightly until the boy looked straight at him again. The boy nodded and left the room on whatever errand he'd been sent on.

"*Do* you have them cornered?" the Fastian King asked. "Last I heard, the Hellbringer was wreaking havoc on your armies. Will it be long before you're forced to enlist your non-magical people?"

The room fell silent. I wondered what silent conversations were happening between my father and my brothers. Surely they wouldn't admit to conscripting the first godforsaken in the ranks mere hours before the Fastians' arrival. I risked a glance at the prince. He was listening intently to the conversation, a clear frown on his face, chin propped up by his hand.

"We feel it is important for every citizen to have a chance to fight for their country," Erik said, his voice a deeper timbre than the Fastian King's. Something twisted uncomfortably in my stomach at the lie. "Godtouched or not, Bhorglid's citizens are united in the fight against our enemies."

It took every ounce of self-control to hold in my scoff. I was only successful because Frode reached over and put a hand on my knee, obviously aware of the fury building inside me. How dare they pretend we were a united people? How dare they pretend we were all equals?

To claim the godtouched and godforsaken were united in anything was as blasphemous as rejecting the pantheon itself.

"This war is one of magical proportions," the Fastian King countered. "Kryllian has the Hellbringer on their side. They will not hold back if Faste is left undefended. We have negotiated much of our alliance already, but in case it was not made clear"—he turned to stare directly at my father—"we expect any troops you send to protect our lands to be Lurae."

I glanced at Frode when the unfamiliar term was spoken. He leaned over and muttered, "That's what the rest of the world calls the godtouched. *Lurae.*"

Father's knuckles whitened almost imperceptibly, but I swallowed and sat up straighter. The King of Faste was no pushover. I wouldn't be surprised if an all-out brawl were to begin in front of us all.

But Father's cruel smile told another story. "Of course not. We are fully aware of how much we benefit from this alliance. My daughter could never be enough to make up for that on her own."

All eyes turned to me at the jab. I squared my shoulders and kept my face neutral. Father knew I was about to snap. The moment I did, he'd use it against me. Against Arne, against Freja. He had me right where he wanted me.

The prince frowned. I waited for the pity to appear, but it never did. His parents remained silent on either side of him, studying my expression.

The servant returned then with an empty glass and a tall bottle of wine, offering them to Frode. I glanced at my brother, my eyes widening. Alcohol was as rare and precious as food these days. Had my brother really sent this young servant to the cellars to retrieve a full bottle?

Frode smirked, answer enough to my unspoken question. "There won't be any need for the glass," he told the servant. The young boy nodded respectfully and took the cork from Frode once it was out of the bottle.

My father's mouth curled in disgust and Mother looked absolutely furious. Frode only offered them a charismatic grin.

What would I do without you around to keep things interesting? I asked Frode.

"Probably behave yourself," he muttered as he placed the bottle to his lips and began to chug, a small trickle of red spilling out the corner of his mouth.

The King of Faste snorted. I restrained the growl in my throat, leaping to defend Frode. A dizzy mind was the only way he could keep the voices at bay. "Apologies for my children," Father said, trying to draw the attention away from Frode and back to himself. "Let's save the war talk for later." Was it nervousness hiding at the edge of his words? The Fastians were discerning, and he was weak in the face of it.

I leaned back, my mind wandering as the conversation turned to purely political gossip. If I were in charge, there would be no war; instead, we'd have diplomatic relationships with all our neighbors. An alliance with Faste would be only for our countries' mutual benefit, not for survival. Arne wouldn't be risking his life as a godforsaken on the front lines. Freja wouldn't be in jail. Frode would stay home and do what he liked here instead of going to the front lines to be tortured by the screams and thoughts of the dying. Jac would be the general of the armies—he was good at what he did. And he would keep the peace much better than Björn could.

I almost snorted thinking of Björn in charge of the armies. In charge of the kingdom. I had no doubt the war would escalate as soon as he became king. Father had all but confirmed it to the council only an hour before—"Continue moving our conquest forward" had been his exact words.

When the conversation slipped into talk of the upcoming engagement party, it became clear the alcohol had gone straight to Frode's head. "Shut up," he groaned. The empty bottle of wine sat discarded at his feet and he pressed a shaking hand to his temple. "If you're going to think I'm a drunkard, you might as well say it." A wide, lopsided grin filled his face and he turned to look at Father. "After all, it's true."

I sighed. If Frode didn't ramble so much with alcohol in his system, it wouldn't matter, but . . .

"Björn, take your brother to his room," Father snarled. His fingernails dug into the fabric adorning the arms of the chair he sat in.

Björn stood, but I held out my hand. "I'll take him," I offered. "He says my thoughts are the easiest to deal with." Besides, I *had* asked Frode to take me with him if he found a way to get out of here.

Björn rolled his eyes and sat as I got to my feet and pulled one of Frode's arms over my shoulders. He was incredibly underweight, and lifting him didn't feel like even the slightest of burdens. The prince stood, too. "I'll help." Before I could give him permission, he stepped to Frode's other side.

I wanted to snap at him, tell him I could do it myself, but he had already started moving us toward the door. Frode hung limp in our arms, humming a tune I hadn't heard in years—a lullaby Mother used to sing me when she'd considered it worth pretending she loved us all equally. Pretending she wasn't disgusted by me, wasn't preparing my brothers to be part of the ritual sacrifice of heirs the moment they were grown.

I swallowed the lump forming in my throat.

"Third floor," I told the prince as we approached the staircase. He nodded and I sighed. "Look, I can carry him on my own. You should go back to the sitting room. Talk politics. I'm fine."

"You think I have any interest in being in there?" he said. "I would do anything to leave. Seems like you would, too."

I chuckled. "Was it that obvious?"

He grinned. "You're pretty easy to read."

"So I've been told," I said, shifting Frode's weight on my shoulder. My brother giggled and I rolled my eyes.

"I wanted to say I'm sorry," the prince continued. "In advance. I know it's not love, but our marriage will be good for both of our countries. I think we can manage to make it work and both be happy."

I digested his words for a moment. It was a straightforward way to begin our relationship; I couldn't fault him for that. "I hope you're right. What's your name?"

"Volkan."

"Nice to meet you. I'm Revna."

"Are you looking forward to our engagement party?"

I glanced at him, and his eyes were so sincere, I decided to be honest. "No. I'm nothing more than a pawn here."

He sighed. "That's a familiar sentiment." Volkan hesitated, dark eyes lingering on my face before he set his jaw. "Has anyone told you why my parents were so desperate to arrange a marriage for me?"

"No." Embarrassment gathered in my chest. I knew so little about my fiancé. "I assumed it was to ensure your people weren't targeted after Kryllian falls."

"Half right," Volkan informed me. "But there's another half to the story as well. My parents do their best to keep it a secret, so I don't blame you for not knowing." He glanced away, and I had the distinct impression he was nervous about meeting my gaze. "Romantic intentions between partners of the same sex have been outlawed in Faste for generations."

My brows flew up. We'd stopped walking, Frode hanging limply between us. Of all the scenarios I'd pictured, my fiancé being gay was not one of them. Especially when, despite all of Bhorglid's flaws, queer people were commonplace. Halvar liked men, Freja was asexual, and even I often eyed women with more than simple appreciation. One of Arne's fathers was transgender. "But . . . why would they force you to marry me?"

The prince's smile was sad. "When I was old enough to realize what it meant to like boys, I thought I could do the country a favor by speaking with my parents about it. Encouraging them to change their ways. You can see how my plan turned out."

"They forced you into an arranged marriage." Hiding the horror in my voice was impossible.

My fiancé shrugged. "I've come to terms with it. None of this is your fault. I only tell you this much because, first, I want to be upfront and honest about the nature of our future marriage, and second, because you're not the only pawn here. We're both being used."

I let out a shuddering breath. "Is that supposed to make me feel better?"

Volkan's laugh was surprisingly bright. "I certainly hope not."

We walked in silence until I pushed open Frode's bedroom door. The room itself was a mess, with clothes strewn everywhere. The bed was unmade, and the stench of vomit drifted from the bathroom. I pulled the neckline of my dress around my nose and Volkan took Frode from me.

As Volkan laid him down on the bed, Frode called out for me, his words slurred together.

I came to his bedside and squeezed his hand. "If you were trying to get out of all your responsibilities, you did a phenomenal job," I told him with a laugh. "Father will definitely leave you alone today."

Frode laughed, sounding like a child. "Hey," he said, tugging on my sleeve. I leaned in to hear what he mumbled. "You'd be a good queen. Way better than Björn."

Instantly, my brother fell into a deep sleep, and his snores reverberated around the closed room. I put my finger over my lips and Volkan followed me out. The door was silent as I latched it behind us.

You'd be a good queen.

"Your brother clearly cares deeply for you," Volkan mused as we began a slow return to the sitting room. Neither of us was anxious to get there quickly. "I hope one day you will be a good queen, when we rule Faste together."

I flicked my gaze at him briefly. His face was open and sincere, dark eyes warm—but disappointment pooled in my stomach at his words all the same. "No offense, Your Highness, but being queen of a country I don't belong to doesn't sound very enticing."

His throat bobbed with a swallow. "No," he murmured. "It doesn't, does it? Apologies."

I shrugged, rubbing the heavy fabric of my skirts between my fingers. "Seems we were both raised for higher purposes we don't agree with."

We reached the sitting room doors once more. Volkan's smile was sad now, emotions I couldn't interpret flickering over his expression. "It does seem that way."

We were quiet for a moment before he continued. "I know things won't ever be perfect between us," he said. "I won't lie to you and say I could love you—not in the way a marriage should entail. But you seem like a good person. I'm not going to keep you on a leash after we're married."

I turned to look at him, tilting my head. Of all the qualities I'd considered my fiancé having, kindness had never crossed my mind. The political world was ruthless, and I expected him to be the same. But maybe he was different.

"The same applies to you," I said, trying to act nonchalant about the matter. "If you have someone else you care for, I won't stand in the way."

I wanted him to tell me if there was someone else, but he sidestepped my unspoken question. "We'd better get back," he said, holding open the door to the sitting room.

I entered, and all eyes turned to me. As Volkan and I took our seats and the political chatter resumed, I couldn't help but feel a twist of guilt in my chest.

My marriage wouldn't be bad. I'd go on to live a life of near freedom. But in exchange I would have to leave Freja behind as a prisoner and Arne on the front lines as a sacrifice to the holy war.

I took a deep breath. There was no way to win; my father had
ensured it when he planned out my use.

My parents had invited the Fastian royalty to accompany us to our temple ceremonies, but it was a formality more than anything else. Fastians worshiped no gods, their people choosing to eschew the idea of religion after Callum and Arraya's initial attempt at taking power over the Fjordlands.

I didn't blame the king and queen for refusing the invitation. If staying home wouldn't incur the wrath of my mother, I would have done it in a heartbeat. Volkan, however, had chosen to come along. "Out of respect for my soon-to-be bride," he'd explained.

I'd nearly vomited at the word bride being used to describe me but accepted his generosity without comment. If he wanted to watch the priests berate me for my very existence, that was his choice.

The eight of us rode through a dusting of snow to the southern outskirts of the city, where a small temple had been built for our family. It looked nearly identical to the one in the square I'd been at yesterday morning. The only difference was the size. Where the temple in the square could host hundreds of people, our family's personal temple was only big enough for ten worshipers.

Despite its small size, the structure remained tall. If you climbed on top of it, you'd be tall enough to see the southern sea stretching between Bhorglid and Kryllian. I knew because I tried it when I was twelve. It took a priest with the godtouch of flying to get me back to ground level.

As the structure came into view, I leaned over to Volkan, who rode next to me. "You're godtouched, right?"

He frowned. "Godtouched?"

"Uh." I fumbled for the word his parents had used earlier, the one Frode had explained the rest of the world used to signify the godtouched. "Do you have magic?"

"Oh. Yes. Why do you ask?"

I sat back in my saddle with a breath of relief. "Because the priests would not treat you well otherwise."

After a few moments of silence, his tentative voice broke my concentration. "If those with magic are called godtouched, then how are those without magic referred to?"

"You didn't pick it up during the talk at the castle?" I asked. "We're godforsaken. Abandoned by the pantheon long ago."

I held my breath, uncertain if he already knew I was without magic. This moment might sear itself forever in my mind as the one where Volkan's budding regard for me turned to disgust.

I waited for the scathing look and its accompanying words. Instead, he simply said, "That feels dramatic."

The laugh escaped me without permission. Volkan's expression brightened at the sound. "Dramatic is certainly an accurate way to describe it."

"Your people don't half-ass anything," he mused. "Is it true the heirs to the throne fight to the death to see who will be the next ruler?"

"Ah, you've heard of the Bloodshed Trials."

"But you won't be competing, right? Since we're to be married."

My rising mood fell just as abruptly. "I am not permitted to compete because I am godforsaken. If I wasn't worthy of magic, why would I be worthy to take the throne?"

"But you are worthy to be used as a bargaining chip." Volkan ran a hand through his hair. "That's incredibly unfair."

I'd expected to hate Volkan. He represented everything about my life that I despised. It was stranger to realize I'd be disappointed if he was as cruel and callous as the godtouched I knew.

"It's nowhere near the same, but my family was disappointed when I came into my magic. I'm a healer. My father's magic bonds him with water and my mother can conjure lightning on a cloudless day." He smiled to himself and shook his head. "And here was their only son, with the most common Lurae of all."

I said nothing, but Volkan didn't push the matter. As we rode in silence, I studied him. I'd wondered what my future husband might be like for months, ever since I'd first been informed of the engagement. Never had it occurred to me that he might be a stalwart ally.

Were the godtouched and the godforsaken treated equally in Faste? If they were, I'd need to bring him to meet Halvar before we left for his homeland. Perhaps the two could discuss politics, make a plan in case the next generation of rebels had the power and capability of making a move against the priests and the royal family.

A priest waited outside the temple for us. The red eye on his forehead stared at me as our horses approached, looking like blood. Part of me expected it to start dripping, trailing over the clean fabric. Not for the first time, I wondered whether it was true they could see through the sewn-on markings. It was said their devotion to the gods was so high the priests were given the gift of sight in their minds as an additional ability when they swore their oaths to the Holy Order. They were certainly able to chase me through the streets with deadly accuracy yesterday. But part of me always thought it was just a trick—that the fabric must be thin enough for them to see through.

Even if they couldn't see me, I glared anyway. They all deserved to feel my ire. Especially as the memory of Freja's arrest continued to play in the back of my mind, fresh as a bleeding wound.

The priest bowed to my father and then Björn as we approached, ignoring the rest of us. They had taken my volatile brother under their wings years ago, encouraging him to become more blood-thirsty as time passed. Now Björn was filled with an appreciation for the gods and the desire to do what they wished—in as violent a way as possible.

I glanced at Frode. *I want to go home.*

My brother shot me a look telling me to be quiet. He had a fierce hangover from his drunken escapades in the sitting room earlier.

Peeking over the foothills of the mountains in the west was the top of the prison, with its tall watchtowers. I glanced at my family. Would they notice if I left? Not to break her out—only see her. Tell her I was working on it. I could take Volkan with me, save him from the priests' boring speeches and rituals.

"Don't be stupid," Frode muttered.

My father was the first to dismount from his horse and greet the priest. We followed suit, lining up behind him. I stayed as far back as possible, directly next to Volkan.

"Thank you for having us today." Father's voice was quiet but managed to echo through the stone pillars holding up the temple.

I crossed my arms to protect them from the cold. We were still in our finery, and while this dress was pretty, it was not intended for warmth. The chill seeped through my heavy cloak. My mother glared at me until I rolled my eyes and stepped forward, in line with my brothers.

The priest's voice was muffled through the fabric. "Thank you for being here, Your Majesty." He turned to look at me—I thought. The embroidered eye appeared to stare straight through me. "I see your daughter and her fiancé decided to join us."

My father frowned. "She didn't have a choice."

I stared at my shoes, boots pressing deep prints into the snow covering the cobblestones. On a normal day, I'd exhaust my best excuses to get out of going to temple. But I knew better than to make a scene in front of other royalty. Father would never hesitate to discipline me in private and then send Waddell to seal the wounds. If it didn't leave scars, then to him it was fair game.

With healers at our disposal, not much was capable of leaving a permanent scar.

"Well, we are delighted to have her." The priest tilted his head and the white fabric covering his face shifted to the side a bit. I clenched my teeth and didn't look up. His voice was strange, and I wondered, not for the first time, if there was something inhuman under the cloth. "And you as well, Your Highness."

Volkan inclined his head slightly. "Thank you for allowing me to witness your ceremonies."

I wondered what he would think of our ceremonies by the time we were finished.

The priest led the way through the wooden doors of the temple. My parents followed and then the rest of us ascended the stairs. I hesitated on the bottom step.

Erik put a hand on my back and pushed me gently but firmly toward the door. Reluctantly, I allowed him to move me forward. Father would say it was my duty, and Erik would doubtlessly agree.

Once I left for Faste, I wouldn't have to attend temple again. The thought managed to comfort me.

At least the inside of the temple was warmer. On my left, several acolytes warmed their hands by a burning hearth. The acolytes, still in training to the Holy Order, were almost more eerie than their superiors. Their uniforms were the same, but they had not taken their vows yet, and therefore had no eyes embroidered on their veils.

The acolytes turned at our entrance and bowed, pressing their palms together in front of their chests. "Rise," my father commanded. They obeyed silently.

Nine chairs were arranged in a circle in front of us and along the wall were seven closed doors. They led to individual prayer rooms for each of the gods in the pantheon.

The priest sat at the head of the circle of chairs. My parents sat on either side of him and then my brothers took the chairs closest, leaving me and Volkan to sit directly across from the priest.

I stifled a groan. This was my absolute least favorite spot for temple and my brothers knew it. When I was young, I would beg them to trade chairs with me so I didn't have to stare straight at the priest the entire time.

Björn smirked at me from his seat next to my mother. I took a deep breath and settled into the hard wooden chair.

"Let us begin," the priest said. The acolytes moved from their places by the fire to sit on the ground behind the priest. I grimaced at the sight of all of them. They couldn't be older than I was, and yet they'd given their lives and free will to the Order.

In one fluid motion, each member of my family reached out to grasp the hands of the two people on either side of them. Together, we formed one huge circle. I reached out for Frode's hand on my left. Volkan, understanding the expectations, took my right. The sooner we started, the sooner it would be over.

The priest began the calling of the gods. "Aloisa, goddess of the soul, bless us with your presence. Aksel, god of air, bless us with your presence. Hjalmar, god of fire, bless us with your presence. Viggo, god of water . . ." The chant continued until all the gods had been mentioned by name.

I laid no claim to the gods, but if I had, Aloisa would be my favorite. She was the only woman in a household of men, overlooked by those meant to be her subjects. They rarely spoke of her despite her abilities being incredibly sought-after. Whether or not she was real, I knew how she felt.

When the priest finished, he reached into his pocket and scattered a handful of ash onto the dirt in front of us. It was burnt grass, but it always made me cringe regardless. It represented the final state of bodily decay, indicating our powerlessness before the gods who watched over us and decided when it was time for a person to die.

"Tell me the troubles of this country," the priest murmured.

That was my father's cue. We released our hands and he began to speak.

"We seek a blessing on the union of Bhorglid and Faste, to be sealed with marriage," he began. "We seek guidance in our war efforts, to know how we may win the holy battle against the Kryllian nation. We seek strength for my sons as they prepare to compete for the throne."

The priest tilted his head back as if listening for something. I used every ounce of self-control not to roll my eyes.

After a moment he spoke. "The gods tell me the future of your kingdom hangs in the balance," the priest said. He knelt and drew a line through the scattered ash with his finger. "Your daughter and her friend sabotaged the new year ritual. This does not bode well for the coming year. The gods are angry."

I chewed the inside of my cheek and folded my hands in my lap. Everyone in my family looked at me. Mother, Father, and Björn glared. Erik and Jac were more concerned than anything else, and Frode . . . well, his eyes gazed in my direction, but they were both unfocused. Volkan, on the other hand, appeared curious.

The priest needed to shut his mouth before he got me in serious trouble.

"Do not fear. There is hope yet. Under the guidance of your youngest son, the kingdom will thrive. But the alliance with Faste is necessary to win the war." He looked up so the embroidered eye gazed at me again.

The priests had started this war in the first place, whispering in Father's ear how we "deserved" what was rightfully Kryllian's; they would take any opportunity to blame it on me when things started going wrong.

The priest turned to my father. "Continue to fight the holy war," he said. "The gods desire for your bloodline to lead Kryllian. The next ruler must listen carefully to the words the gods have to offer them."

Björn straightened his back and tilted his chin up. The priest was clearly addressing him, though no one was bold enough to say it.

I saw Erik cast a glance in Björn's direction, taking in our brother's haughty expression. Erik didn't look thrilled. What was he thinking? Did he lust for the throne the way Björn did? And what did Jac think?

My father bowed his head slightly. "Thank you."

I closed my eyes and dug my fingernails into my palms. More war meant Arne's death. The preaching about Bhorglid's fate hanging in the balance practically guaranteed Freja would be stuck in prison until I left. My father would hold her over me for the remainder of my time here.

I rubbed my hand across my forehead, my headache returning in full force.

At least the first ritual was over. The priest stood and dusted the ash from his hands. Acolytes scrambled off to continue doing their chores or warming their hands. My family all stood, and I stretched my arms over my head. Volkan moved to examine the symbols on the doors of each prayer room, leaving me alone with the head priest.

The priest moved to stand beside me. "Be careful with your choices," he murmured. "You may hold more than your own fate in your hands."

"This is coming from the person who conscripted one of my friends and arrested the other yesterday," I said with a saccharine smile. "Forgive me if I don't trust your intuition."

He chuckled, shoulders shaking. "I pity the Fastian Prince. He doesn't know what he's in for, does he?"

My vision clouded with red, but as my hands tightened, another wrapped around my arm and pulled me away from the conflict. Frode—hungover but managing to look out for me regardless. I huffed and shook my wrist from his grasp, wishing the priest's words didn't follow me.

But as I watched Jac, Björn, and my mother move to enter individual prayer rooms, a hand fell on my shoulder, fingers digging in just shy of too tight. Erik stepped up beside me. "Do not anger the gods," he warned. "There is far more at stake here than your personal vendetta. Bhorglid is the land of the gods' true will. If we anger them, they may choose to lend their favor to more faithful worshipers."

I stifled a groan. Of course Erik was most concerned about the gods—they were all he cared about. Before I had the chance to think of a retort, he sauntered off to a prayer room, leaving me behind.

Frode sat backward in his chair. He rested his arms across the top of the wooden backing. When I leaned closer, I heard him humming the same lilting melody from this morning. The lullaby Mother used to sing us.

I patted Frode gently on the shoulder. He didn't acknowledge it. I hoped his brain rested in blissful silence.

My father stood by the entrance, arms crossed over his chest. He towered over the tallest acolyte, and his build was large enough to be frightening—to me, at least.

Before I let myself think it through, I moved across the room to stand in front of him.

"Father," I said, bowing my head slightly. Asking a favor meant remembering my manners.

He stared over my head, but I saw annoyance cloud his eyes. His red hair brushed against his shoulders when he sighed. "What?"

I took a shaky breath and lowered my voice. "What happened

yesterday was my fault and it was a mistake. I didn't realize it was going to cause so many problems for so many people." *Lie.* "Please, let Freja go. This wasn't her fault; I dragged her along"—*another lie*—"and she shouldn't be held responsible for what I did. Please."

I felt eyes on me and turned to see the acolytes sightlessly staring at us. I ignored them, trying to think of anything but the heat rushing to my face.

Father put his hand on my shoulder, and I winced. To any casual observer, it appeared he was being kind, but I knew better. His hand was trembling with how tightly he held me, and heat from his Lurae surged through his palm. Any hotter and he would singe my dress. I bit my lip to keep from letting out a whimper.

He leaned forward. "What makes you think you deserve another chance?" he growled. He kept his voice quiet, and I was grateful. "You heard the priest. If our kingdom falls, it is because of you and your ignorance. You have been nothing but disrespectful since the day you learned to speak and you're lucky I haven't had you thrown out of our household for insubordination. Freja will not be released. Ever. The only reason you're not in a cell is because this alliance will secure our fates."

He released his grip, and I stumbled back. The joint throbbed and I knew there would be dark bruises there when I changed that night.

Hot tears filled my eyes and I glanced toward the acolytes—all staring.

I glared at my father, wishing I could channel all my rage and fury into fire, like he and Björn could. Then he would know what I truly thought of him.

But no magic flowed through my veins. So instead, I stormed out the door.

The priest who led the ceremony tried to grab my wrist and pull me back. "Princess, you're forgetting the end ceremony—"

I threw off his grasp. "Don't touch me." If I spent another moment in the temple, I'd begin tearing it down brick by brick.

My mother appeared in the doorway as I fled and mounted my horse. "Revna!" she shouted. Fury coated her features. "Get back in here!"

With a click of my heels, we were off. Only the wind in my face kept me from screaming.

◆ ◆ ◆ ◆ ◆

THE PRISON WAS SETTLED IN THE LOW FOOTHILLS TO THE WEST OF the city. Behind it rested the mountain range, which continued far north into the wastelands. The peaks were covered in thick snow, and white flakes fell from dark skies, dampening my hair.

I rode hard, the fury within me building and burning as the tall, dark structure grew closer. I wished it would break like a wave reaching its peak. The longer it twisted, the more hopelessness climbed to meet it. Soon my anger would morph to despair.

Tears stung my eyes, and I chose to believe they were from the wind whipping against my face. I had to keep fighting, keep trying to come up with a way to help Freja escape, to keep Arne alive.

But how, when I was being rapidly stripped of all my autonomy?

The thundering of my horse's hooves against the path was matched by another rider, gaining speed until they pulled aside me. I took a moment to steady myself before I looked up. Who had followed me from the temple? My mother, keen to give me another lecture on how useless I was?

When I finally turned my head to the side, my eyes were met with a dark mask.

Startled, I sat up straighter in the saddle, continuing to urge my horse on at a steady pace. The Hellbringer—gods above, that was really him—stared at me when I pulled my sword from the sheath buckled at my waist.

My heart thundered. Was he here to kill me?

I had no experience fighting on horseback. My first swipe with my blade was too wide, and he only had to lean slightly to avoid it. Wrist shaking from the effort of fighting one-handed, I readjusted my grip and swung again.

Another sorry attempt.

Anger had festered beneath my rib cage all morning, but now it erupted to a boil. "I hate you!" I screamed over the wind, knowing he was close enough to hear me. "Get it over with and kill me already!"

The dead-eyed mask only stared back at me, his mount keeping pace with mine. I pulled on the reins, bringing my horse to a sudden halt.

The Hellbringer continued on, his cloak billowing behind him, revealing the dark plated armor covering every part of his body. He didn't slow or even glance back at me.

My nails dug into my palms, and I let out a scream, the only way I knew to release the emotions mounting in me. I panted as I watched him grow smaller in the distance, turning slightly north. No interest in going to the prison, then. So why had he been on the same path as me in the first place? Why dare show himself when he knew I would try to kill him?

More thundering hooves echoed from behind me and I whirled, sword still drawn, to see Volkan ride into view. When he arrived at my side, he was gasping for air. "Was that you screaming? Are you all right?"

I shook my head. "I'm fine. I saw—"

When I turned to point out the Hellbringer, he was gone. Vanished as if he'd never been there. I frowned. He hadn't been riding nearly fast enough to make it past one of the other foothills and out of sight.

"What did you see?" Volkan's voice was concerned.

"Nothing, I guess." I turned and proceeded on my ride to the prison. No matter what, I would see Freja today. Only death would stop me, and it seemed the Hellbringer had no interest in killing me for now.

Assuming I hadn't hallucinated him, of course.

I clenched my jaw. Impossible.

Your entire life is turning upside down, my thoughts whispered. *Maybe you did imagine it. And if you didn't, who would believe you?*

When I arrived at the prison, tying my horse's reins to the post out front, Volkan was still with me.

"You can go back," I told him.

He shrugged and climbed down effortlessly. "I wasn't attending the temple ceremony to appease your family. I was trying to get to know you better. If you'd rather be here, then I'll join you."

I regarded him for a long, silent moment, all too aware of the guards' curious stares burning holes in my back. I took a step closer to him until there were mere inches between us and lowered my voice. "What is this?"

His eyes flicked to the guards, then back to me. "What do you mean?"

I wanted to shove him. "We aren't in love. We're getting married to fulfill a contract, nothing more. Stop pretending to care about me."

Volkan studied me, crossing his arms as he did. "Revna. We might not love each other, but we'll be spending the rest of our lives together. Doesn't it sound better to be friends? I'm here because I don't want my wife to be a stranger. Even if she's my wife only in name."

Anyone else I would have doubted. But everything about Volkan screamed *genuine.* Each movement he made, every word he spoke, was with the intent to heal wherever he could. I clenched my teeth. I didn't want to believe him, not when my experience with the godtouched told me at most they were capable of indifference.

He chuckled at my silence, placing a hand on my shoulder. I tensed under his touch and he sighed, letting his arm fall at his side.

Was he raised to be like this—kind to a fault? Or was he the exception to a rule?

The question burst from me without warning. "Are the godtouched and the godforsaken equal in your country?"

Volkan raised an eyebrow, clearly surprised. "Mostly, yes. Those with Lurae—magical abilities—are given jobs where they can use their gifts to better the world around them. We're an agricultural nation, I'm sure you know. You don't need a Lurae to farm." He shrugged. "There are occasional skirmishes. But there are also no gods—and no religious leaders to insist our abilities mean something about our worth."

Equal enough. Far more than here, at least.

I nodded firmly. He wasn't trying to get under my skin, worm his way into my trust until I caved. Godforsaken and godtouched were the same where he came from. He was unlike the rest of us, predisposed to our prejudices by the priests.

Freja would want to meet him. And despite my general attitude toward the godtouched, I trusted him. "Then come with me."

He followed obediently when I approached the guards. "I'm here to see someone," I told them. The prison's location was so isolated, their jobs required little effort. Any escapees would struggle to make it out of the valley quickly enough to avoid capture.

The first guard tilted his head. "Leave your weapons. And make it quick."

They unlocked the door, pushing it open enough for me and Volkan to squeeze through. We stepped into the darkness and the entrance closed behind us, leaving us to let our eyes adjust.

"Only two guards?" Volkan asked, looking back over his shoulder. The whites of his eyes shone in the dim light. I didn't miss his hands curling tightly in the fabric of his shirt.

"Silencers," I explained as we began our trek. The layout of the prison was simple, with a single winding hallway making up each floor. My ancestors designed the layout purposefully, with only one way in and out. I beckoned for Volkan to continue following me and we walked through the first level, lit dimly by lamps. Guards stood watch every so often. I nodded to the first one I saw, but he ignored me completely. "That's what we call them, at least."

Volkan hummed. "We call them silencers, too. I've always thought it was strange that some people were given the magic to . . . well, prevent magic from being used."

My eyes adjusted slowly. Cell after cell lined the walls and a horrid groaning floated through the tunnel, the sound of something inhuman crying out in pain.

I walked a little faster. Volkan's footsteps sped up behind me.

"Maybe the gods were trying to even the playing field," I suggested. My voice dropped to barely a whisper. I peered briefly into each of the lower cells looking for Freja. The winding hallway went on forever before we reached the staircase. Part of me wanted to call out her name, but the silence of the prison felt too reverent to break. In other ways, it was suffocating, as if any speech would be drowned out under the weight of it.

"You do believe in the gods, then?" Volkan's voice was tinged with curiosity.

The staircase spiraled and I focused on watching every step. "No. Even if they are real, for them to create a world like this would be horribly cruel, don't you think?"

He didn't answer. I had the sense he agreed but was lost in thought.

Iron bars stretched to the ceiling, only a couple of inches apart. The dirt floor was rough beneath my boots. We were almost all the way down the hall when I finally spotted her, crouched in the corner of a tiny cell as if huddling against herself might provide enough warmth to be comfortable.

"Freja." I slid to my knees in front of the metal bars, wishing I had a godtouch that would let me bend the metal to reach her.

She crawled forward, a flicker of hope lighting her face. "Revna? Is that you?"

I reached my hand through the gap in the bars and she took it, our palms pressed together. Only when she squeezed my hand did I realize it trembled.

"Volkan is here, too." My fiancé stepped forward into the dim light, nodding at Freja.

She gasped, clutching a hand to her chest and glaring at me. "The Prince of Faste! Why would you bring him here? This is not how I wanted to meet my best friend's future husband for the first time."

He chuckled and sat cross-legged beside me. "I wasn't invited, don't worry. I tagged along against Revna's will."

Her smile was exhausted but genuine. "I bet she loved that."

I rolled my eyes. "Enough about us. How are you?" My voice remained low; I didn't know who else was in the nearby cells and I didn't want to find out.

I took in her now limp curls, the shadows taking residence under her dark eyes. Her clothes were covered in a layer of dirt. "Alive."

It was the first time I'd ever heard Freja speak without a spark of laughter in the back of her throat. Something inside me wilted and shriveled in on itself.

"I'm so sorry," I said. I couldn't—wouldn't—release her hand. "This is my fault and I'm going to get you out of here."

"Did you talk to your father?"

"He won't help."

She let out a sigh and tried to tuck her hair behind her ear, to no avail. "I figured. We've done our fair share of mischief over the years, but stepping in to stop a ritual . . . I can't say I blame him."

I rubbed a hand over my pounding forehead. "We'll figure something out. There are a few days before the wedding. I'll make sure you're free before then."

"You can't actually think your father would let me go."

"He won't. But I'll get you out."

"To do what?" she scoffed. "Leave Bhorglid? Leave my mother behind? Never see my brother again? I'd rather be here than separated from my family."

Bitterness welled within me. She would turn down her freedom—not just from this prison but from her life as a godforsaken. I wanted to take my own offer, run and be free without ever having to see my family again. It took all my discipline to swallow the anger.

"How is Arne?" she asked, breaking the silence. Her tone was too stiff, too forced. She'd always been able to read my moods.

I shrugged, thinking of his expression at the Sharpened Axe last night when I'd mentioned the early arrival of the Fastians. Stony and cold. "I haven't seen him at all today. But I don't think he's happy." A pang echoed through my chest. "What I wouldn't give for things to go back to normal."

"It isn't your fault," she said. "I agreed to help. I was the one who planned it all. I wouldn't have gotten involved if it wasn't a cause I believed in. In the end, we just sped up the timeline a bit."

We fidgeted in silence, Volkan's presence keeping us from divulging all our feelings. He didn't know about my history with Arne, and I didn't want to tell him before I knew what he would think.

Freja and I wholeheartedly believed in our cause. But believing it and accepting the consequences for it looked different for the two of us.

"You were never supposed to end up in prison," I finally protested. "I'm sorry, Freja. I shouldn't have asked you to be a part of this."

For a moment, her eyes lit with fire. "Stop apologizing. We did the right thing. I've been willing to accept my fate since we started this. You should be, too."

"Willing to accept my fate?"

"No. Willing to accept mine."

"You want me to leave you here?" My voice broke. "I won't."

She reached through the bars, her face set, and grabbed the collar of my dress. Her voice lowered to a raspy whisper. "No. You'll ruin everything. Just because I have to rot in a prison cell doesn't mean you need to martyr yourself. You have a future to think about."

Lowering my voice to match hers, I didn't hesitate to let my anger show through. "I'm not going to leave you here. I'd never forgive myself."

She frowned and released me, crawling back to the dark corner of the cell. "You should go."

I stood and Volkan followed suit. My fingernails dug into my palms, and I struggled to keep my voice steady. "I would do anything to get you out of here, Freja. I *will* do anything. I hope you know that."

She nodded, expression sour. "I know."

Exiting the prison felt like walking to the gallows.

The scenery around the isolated building was unchanged from when we entered—flakes of snow drifted down around us, pure against the background of scattered pines that dotted the hillside.

Just before I lost myself in the sorrow of accepting my fate, Volkan placed a hand on my shoulder. "Revna," he said slowly, "I think I have an idea."

VOLKAN PACED BACK AND FORTH ACROSS HALVAR'S SECRET basement room, anxiety radiating off him in waves.

"Are you going to tell me what's going on?" I griped, not for the first time. "Or are we going to continue like this?"

After having what he claimed was a brilliant idea, Volkan had asked if there was a safe place we could go to discuss it. Truthfully, I wasn't sure anywhere but here counted as safe—not when there were godtouched everywhere who wouldn't hesitate to take any overheard information back to the king. Halvar may have given me a strange look when we showed up but he hadn't turned us away.

"I'm just—" He sighed, ran a hand roughly through his hair. "I need to make sure I've thought of everything. And I don't know if I have."

The hatch in the ceiling thudded open and closed again, and Halvar descended the ladder. He glared at me. "You brought a god-touched here?"

"He's trustworthy," I promised.

Halvar glanced at Volkan. My fiancé looked at me. "You need to compete in the Bloodshed Trials," Volkan said without preamble.

I blinked, then sighed. "*That's* your plan? Halvar and I have been over this a million times. Even if I could convince them to let me compete, I would never win."

"And that's where I think you're wrong." Volkan's face was alight with fervor. "Especially because you don't *have* to win. At least, not in the traditional sense."

Halvar hummed. "What do you mean, boy?"

"Your brother thinks you would be a good queen." Volkan looked at me and I conceded with a nod. "Why does everyone have to die? If the two of you team up to compete together, you can choose to stop the fighting when you're the last ones left. Then Frode could hand over the crown to you."

I opened my mouth to protest. There were so many holes in the idea, so many places for things to go horribly wrong. And saying you thought someone would make a good ruler didn't mean you'd kill your brothers to prove it.

But before I could speak, Halvar chimed in. "Think of the chaos, Rev," he muttered. "The perfect opportunity. The priests would be utterly defenseless, and if we got all of the godforsaken willing to fight to be there, they could—"

"No."

They both fell quiet and I stood from my chair to glare at Halvar. "You would lose lives. You understand that, right? And if we failed, then they would kill us all. There would be no going back.

"Besides"—I turned to Volkan now—"if you think my father would let me compete in the Trials, then you're delusional. This alliance keeps the war going. It keeps us from losing. If we don't follow through with it, if your parents back out, we will be starved and then overrun by Kryllian in a matter of weeks."

My thoughts swirled like a storm, and I wished they would stop. I closed my eyes, the reality of the situation overwhelming. Why did my father get to have so much power over me? Over my life?

When would I have the chance to take back the power?

Freja's smile and Arne's laugh pranced through my head. A lump settled in my throat. The words from dinner last night echoed through my skull, reverberating like the beat of a drum. *We are losing the war, losing the war, losing the war.*

The alliance before us, the marriage behind it—my father desperately needed both to keep our people alive. If I didn't marry Volkan, Faste would pull their food shares. The Hellbringer would wreak havoc on our weakened armies, decimating Bhorglid's godtouched population beyond repair. And with the majority of our stores going to the front, any soldiers who managed to return would find nothing and no one left.

The silence in the basement room seemed to echo, tension stretched tight between the three of us. I didn't want to look at either of their faces, didn't want to be persuaded.

"Revna." Halvar's voice was gentle. "Think about what would happen if the alliance didn't go through. Who would suffer?"

"Everyone," I protested. "We would all starve."

"Yes," he conceded, "unless the war ended before we could starve."

"Impossible. Björn will continue the war when he becomes king—it won't end anytime soon. We could be dying in the streets of hunger and they wouldn't stop their march against Kryllian."

"Björn would continue the war," Volkan said. "But would you?"

My head snapped up at the thought, the realization hitting me hard. Father *needed* me. Needed the alliance with Faste in order to keep fighting, needed the marriage to secure the deal. Otherwise the plan unraveled at the seams, the war lost before a victor ever stepped off the battlefield.

For the first time, my father needed the pawn to make his final move.

For the first time, I had the advantage.

I could save Freja. Save Arne.

You would make a great queen.

The fate of my country lay on my back. The power to damn our nation rested in my palms.

But if I can take the throne, I mused, *then perhaps our salvation lies in my hands instead.*

I would have to compete in the Bloodshed Trials.

It would be nearly impossible. A death sentence. But wasn't walking into this marriage the same thing? The only difference was whether my soul would wither away slowly or my throat would be slashed open by my brother, ending my life in an instant.

I knew which I preferred.

Seized with a sudden rush of confidence, I looked at Volkan. My heart pounded against my rib cage, measuring the seconds as they vanished into silence. Could I do it? Could I destroy the fragile strings keeping me tied to my father, my brothers?

You would make a great queen.

Volkan had been watching, waiting for something in my expression to change. I knew he'd seen it when he stepped closer to me, determined. "If they don't have food, morale on the front lines will decline. The king will lose the favor of the citizens, the soldiers. He will be utterly desperate—and it will make him sloppy. Without the alliance, Bhorglid is nothing. And the alliance depends on *us.* If we refuse to go through with the marriage, then we hold the upper hand."

I hesitated. "What about the people here? Won't they starve before the soldiers?"

"No," Halvar reassured me. "Food stores are low, but we have enough to last us through the Trials. Win the throne, pull the soldiers back home; if we're not sending everything to the front lines, we'll have plenty."

I bit my lip, still not reassured. "So we do what? Tell them we won't get married unless I'm allowed to compete?"

"Yes." Volkan was growing excited again. "You tell your father you won't marry me unless you get a chance, just like your brothers. If you lose or forfeit, then they can send you home with me. Otherwise, you won't do it."

I chewed my lip. "It might work. But we need input from some other parties first."

◆ ◆ ◆ ◆ ◆

THE EARLY GLAZE OF SNOW ON THE ROADS WAS DISTURBED ONLY by my footprints. Was it possible to both relish in my triumph and languish at the idea of my impending death? Because unless one of the gods themselves dropped from the sky, I was as good as dead.

Halvar, Volkan, and I had decided to meet up the following morning to discuss more details of our plan. It had potential; even I could admit that. But I didn't want to commit unless we had Frode fully on board. Especially with how difficult his godtouch could make combat. If he was unwilling, then I wouldn't move forward.

Besides, it was one thing to say I'd make a good queen; it was an entirely different beast to put your words into action.

As I took a less conspicuous route to the Sharpened Axe, I considered the thoughts that plagued me the night before. Thoughts of my own likely imminent death.

Forcing my father to let me compete would be difficult, but Volkan's reasoning made sense. Even if I managed it, though, I would still have to stay alive in the arena. And I had the suspicion that if my other brothers discovered Frode and I had teamed up, they wouldn't hesitate to do the same.

When Björn's feet touched the sand of the arena, I had no doubt he would send his fire straight for me.

As the huge, expensively made homes of the godtouched slowly gave way to the ramshackle houses the godforsaken occupied, I wondered whether I would see the Hellbringer again today. Something in my stomach swooped dangerously at the thought of drawing my weapon to face off against him, the fierce hand of the Kryllian Queen. Despite all the stories about him, curiosity overwhelmed me at the thought of his godtouch.

Better a swift death at his hand than a long, drawn-out one at Björn's.

I shook the thought from my head and pretended I wasn't disappointed the streets were emptier than ever as I slipped through the back door to the Sharpened Axe, grabbing a lantern from its post as I lifted the hatch leading belowground. Descending the ladder was second nature, and I was in the secret training room within seconds.

The flickering light illuminated the space, and an unexpected wave of sorrow rushed through me.

Arne and Freja should be here. We should be celebrating whoever's birthday had passed most recently with drinks and a knife-throwing contest Freja would undoubtedly win. Making jokes about the priests and planning how to disrupt the next ritual.

Instead, I stood alone, shadows my only companions.

I forced myself to move, to set up one of the straw targets for throwing knives or a bow and arrow while I waited for the rest of the party to arrive. Instead of losing myself in the what-ifs, I worked at honing my skills. Something about practicing until sweat soaked my clothes kept me pieced together. Kept me from slamming my fist into walls or breaking glass decorations at the castle.

It could have been minutes or hours when I heard another person descending the ladder behind me. I'd given up on lobbing knives at the target. Despite my strength, they missed the bull's-eye too many times to ease my frustration. Instead, I'd taken to punching a bag filled with straw.

I whirled on my intruder, unsheathing the sword at my waist and pointing it at them as I stepped swiftly forward.

Halvar stood there, dark circles beneath his eyes, his hands raised in surrender. I lowered and sheathed my weapon, nodding at him.

"The others should be here soon," he said, taking a seat on one of the benches. "So long as they're punctual."

I sat down across from him, waiting for my heartbeat to return to normal. "You think he'll show up?"

Halvar shrugged, twisting the cigar in his hands. "You would know better than I would. How did Frode seem to take it when you asked him?"

My thoughts drifted back to the evening before and I rubbed my wrists. The burns there had healed, but it would take another day or so for the fresh scarring to fade with the rest. Father had been furious when I returned from the prison, not hesitating to take his punishment out on me the moment Volkan had returned to his rooms. I hadn't had the chance to catch Frode alone before we were all assembled at dinner.

Frode, seated on my right side, had given me a strange look. I knew my thoughts were chaotic. I'd glanced at him, wondering how much to reveal about our plan in that moment, then decided to make things simple.

Can you meet me at Halvar's tomorrow morning at dawn?

He'd replied with a raised eyebrow and a nod. The rest of dinner had continued without a hitch.

"Frode will be here," I told Halvar. "I'm hoping Volkan hasn't backed out."

"He seemed the most motivated between the three of us, if we're being honest," Halvar said with a chuckle. "That boy *really* does not want to marry you."

I smacked him on the shoulder, then burst into laughter. "I wonder if he has someone waiting for him back home."

The trapdoor squeaked on its hinges and another person descended into the space as Halvar griped about oiling the metal parts of the hatch again. When Frode stepped into the light, followed closely by Volkan, my shoulders sank with relief.

"Who's going to tell me what's happening here?" Frode asked without preamble. He sauntered through the room, hands in his pockets, observing the weaponry stacked carefully on all sides. He glanced at Halvar curiously. "Is this an assassination attempt?"

"What?" I asked as Halvar sputtered. "Why would I have asked you here to assassinate you?"

Frode shrugged and gestured to the weapons. "You've been incredibly vague about this, even in your thoughts, so I made an assumption based on all of these swords and knives."

Volkan snorted and took a seat across from me on the other bench. "You seem to be the only decent member of your family besides Revna. I'd hate to kill you."

"If you think I wouldn't at least try to eliminate Björn first, then you clearly don't know me as well as you thought you did," I added.

Frode was examining the knife selection Halvar had displayed on the wall. My brother's own long, curved knives were sheathed at either hip. "Excellent. Well, since we've established that no one is being murdered today, give me one moment." Frode walked back to the ladder, clambering to the top and knocking three times on the hatch. The rest of us frowned.

Then the trapdoor opened again and Jac hopped down, boots sending a cloud of dust into the air from where they hit the ground.

Halvar stood. "Why is he here?"

Jac adjusted his cloak, pulling down the hood and moving to sit next to a surprised Volkan. "Because I followed a very suspicious-looking Frode."

I glared at Frode, who shrugged. "I've never been good at secrecy; you know that. He demanded to know where I was going, so I told him."

With a heavy sigh, I pressed two fingers to the bridge of my nose.

Having Jac here complicated things. Frode could be trusted, but Jac—quiet, soft-spoken Jac—was far more of an enigma.

Frode put a hand on my shoulder. "Jac is trustworthy. Whatever you're planning, he'll keep your secrets from Father."

I took a steadying breath. "Well, then . . . how do the two of you feel about having a godforsaken queen?"

◆ ◆ ◆ ◆ ◆

MOST GIRLS WOULD SWOON OVER THE THOUGHT OF ATTENDING their own engagement party. Instead, I stared at the wooden doors leading to the ballroom, dread and anxiety creating a noxious mix in my stomach.

My dress swept across the floor, silk the color of emeralds winding around my arms. It hugged my torso, flattering my curves, and fell straight along my sides to brush against my ankles. My dark hair was pulled into braids, loose curls from the long ends of the braids falling around my shoulders.

I never had reason to look this nice, and on the one night I did, I couldn't enjoy it. I huffed at the inconvenience.

I chewed my red-painted lips and ignored the curious glances of the servants posted at each door. I'd arrived late on purpose, worried my anxiety about the plan Volkan and I had concocted would be utterly obvious on my face. Would Father sense it the instant I walked through the doors? Or would I be able to hide the deception beneath my made-over appearance?

Music drifted through the hall and I took a shuddering inhale. Was walking toward your engagement supposed to feel like walking toward inevitable death?

One of the doormen raised an eyebrow at me and reached for the door handle, but I held up a hand to stop him.

"Not yet," I said. Someone tapped on my shoulder, pulling me back to the present, and I turned to see Jac standing just behind me. I was so lost in my own thoughts I hadn't heard him approach.

He looked impassive as ever, but the red of his formal military uniform added another level of stoicism to him.

Jac held out his arm to me. "May I escort you in?"

If I didn't move, I was going to puke. I nodded and took a deep breath, winding my arm through Jac's. This time the servants opened the doors to the ballroom without hesitation.

And I stared into a room full of godtouched who hated me.

Partygoers waltzed across the dance floor; others watched from the sidelines. Guests were dressed in long gowns, necks adorned with precious gems. Some wore dark suits with red sashes marking them as military. There were banquet tables set up around the perimeter, filled with more food than I'd seen in months. Had the Fastian royals brought it with them? The Fastian colors were draped across every available surface, emerald green creating a sea of color around the room.

When the audience saw me, hushed murmurs spread across the room, winding their way through every nook and cranny. I fought every instinct and tilted my chin high. I might be out of my element in this ballroom, but the pantheon would fall before the godtouched saw me cower.

My father sat on his favorite throne, adorned to look like gold. As a child, I found him most intimidating there. Now I only saw his insatiable lust for power, his desperation to seize control however he could—over Kryllian, over the godforsaken, over me.

Loathing crept through me at the sight of him. Tonight I would take the upper hand.

The rest of the royalty were no less imposing. On my father's left was my mother, seated on a smaller, black throne. On his right, the Fastian King and Queen had each been offered white thrones, both smaller than my mother's. The white accented their emerald green finery and dark skin. They were easily the most beautiful people in the room. Jac kept me pressed tight to his side as we were announced, then began a winding path through the room.

"Where are we going?" I asked.

My brother's expression didn't change. "As far away from Father as possible. If we have to be here, the least we can do is avoid the formality of it all for as long as we can."

I raised an eyebrow, smiling. I'd never been as close to Jac as I was Frode, but he had surprised me today.

"Thank you."

He frowned, steering me away from an aristocrat who eyed us with too much interest. "For what?"

I shrugged. "For supporting me. For agreeing to this scheme."

Jac chuckled under his breath. "The war has kept us apart. If I'd known you were doing more than performing petty acts of rebellion, I would have joined you in your endeavors long ago. The efforts to overtake Kryllian have continued for far too long."

I smiled, grateful he'd snuck his way into our plans.

With so many unknown godtouched surrounding us, we kept our conversation generalized. Curious eyes followed our every movement, and I had no doubt ears were fine-tuned to listen in on our exchange. Still, Jac steered me clear of sycophantic conversations with those who sought to belittle me. I was under no impression that any guest was here to offer their blessings on my impending nuptials.

We turned our conversation to the war. "Do you fight with a bow and arrow on the front?" I asked, realizing for the first time I didn't know the answer. "Or do you use your godtouch and transform into a beast?"

"Depends on the day," he said. "If it's a larger battle, I'll use my godtouch. For little skirmishes, though, a bow and arrow do fine."

"Tell me about the Hellbringer." It had been over twenty-four hours since I thought I saw the masked Kryllian general outside the prison, but he haunted my thoughts. I wondered if he watched me from hidden places—if he knew what we were planning to do tonight.

If he was even real. It was entirely possible I was losing my hold on reality.

"What is there to say?" Jac's voice was gruff. "He's a terror in a mask. A monster in human skin. It's hard to believe people see him and live to tell the tale."

The description warred with the glamour of the ballroom around us, just as the beauty of the party warred with the unsubtle glances and vicious stares of the attendees. The Hellbringer was a monster in human skin and I was a privileged royal daughter dressed in finery I didn't deserve. A pawn in a ballgown.

Though if everything went right tonight, that wouldn't be the case for much longer.

Frode approached us, parting the crowd like a wave. The god-touched were disgusted by me, but they didn't love Frode either. He had a reputation as a drunkard, a shameful addition to the royal family. The two of us originally bonded over our shared notoriety, black sheep left to their own devices.

Tonight he looked royal as ever in his finery. "It's time," he told me. I couldn't read minds, but it was easy to see the nervousness on his face. He smiled slightly when he heard that thought. "I'm not as nervous as Volkan. Though I'm not sure what he has to be nervous about—you're the one who will suffer if this doesn't work."

I glanced around, grateful none of the partygoers seemed to be paying us much attention. I released Jac's arm and took Frode's instead, the older brother guiding me to the dais where the thrones awaited.

Volkan waited for me on the dais and I stepped up to stand

beside him. Frode gave me an encouraging nod before stepping down to stand in line next to the thrones with my mother and other brothers.

When my fiancé took my hand in his, I was surprised but not ungrateful. There was a gentleness about Volkan I appreciated. It bolstered my strength.

I bowed low to my father. He smiled, but I knew not a soul in the room fell for it. Each person in attendance tonight was godtouched. They each had their own magic. And they'd all whispered to each other on the day I turned nine what a disgrace it must be to father a godforsaken child when magic supposedly ran so strongly in one's bloodline.

I wondered what they said now. Anger burned in my blood.

My father placed a hand on my shoulder. I kept a straight face, even as he hissed under his breath, "Be on your best behavior." Heat flared from his palm. I tightened my jaw, pulling away from his grasp.

"It is time for the engagement ceremony to begin." My father's voice boomed over the crowd, which immediately fell silent. "Revna."

My thoughts swirled like a storm, and I wished they would stop. The crowd stared me as if I had a contagious disease. The golden buttons on my father's long red coat glinted in the light. All attention was on us.

"Tonight," he bellowed, "we are here to celebrate the union of two nations."

I closed my eyes. This was going to work. I was going to take back my power. My father had made a mistake when he decided to use me as a pawn, and this would prove it.

"My daughter is to be engaged to the Prince of Faste," he continued.

"No."

My voice echoed through the silent room, and for a long moment time stood still. Then the whispers began in a flurry, gasps bursting through the crowd. The satisfaction flowing freely through my veins felt better than when I'd slammed my fist against a wall two nights ago. It was a high unlike any I'd experienced before. I turned to face my father.

His face was the same shade of dark red as his hair. "Revna," he growled, "you will do what you promised."

I dug my nails into my palms, a wicked smile slashing its mark across my features. "I didn't promise anything. You did. You tried to steal my life to fight a war we don't deserve to win. But you made a mistake when you chose to stake your plans on me. I have the upper hand now. And I will not marry Volkan."

Without any warning, my mother collapsed. Erik stepped forward in time to catch her and place her down gently, unconscious. Against the light stone floor, she looked like a ghost, her hair fanning out in stark contrast.

The King and Queen of Faste grabbed Volkan by the arms to pull him away from me. He kept his eyes on me, his face carefully neutral.

"You've caused too much trouble," my father hissed, and the blade of a knife gleamed, hidden in his closed fist. He would kill me for this—he truly would.

But I raised a hand and he stopped. "Kill me and there is no alliance," I reminded him. Hesitation gleamed like fire in his eyes. "Here's my offer: let me compete for the throne in the Bloodshed Trials. If I yield, then I lose, and I will marry Volkan. But if I win . . ." I shrugged. "The crown will be mine."

The crowd was eerily silent for a heartbeat.

My father erupted. "*Out!*" he screamed, and the crowd jumped. "*Everyone out!*"

People forced their way toward the exit in a giant mass. I stood on the dais surrounded by my family but completely alone as the crowd departed.

When the giant doors swung closed, my father turned to me again. "You," he hissed. "How *dare* you question my authority. How dare you presume you have the power to break an alliance. You are *nothing* and you will do as I say."

The King of Faste interrupted. "You dare slight us this way, girl?" His voice was cold as he turned to my father. "We agreed to take your daughter and feed your people despite her being Nilurae and your war being nothing but a petty religious crusade. Our son is not a beggar to be spurned. He is a prince."

I swallowed the lump rising in my throat, the panic tightening in my chest. No alliance meant no leverage against my father. It meant if I didn't win the Trials, then Kryllian would win the war.

Frode shot me a look, and I wished I knew what he was thinking. I pretended I did, inserting the words I wanted to hear: *No alliance is a good thing. It will work in our favor. Press your advantage while you have it.*

The King of Faste continued. "If you wish to continue our alliance, then renegotiations are in order. Swiftly, too. I will not keep feeding a nation that offers us nothing."

"Father," Volkan muttered, visibly uncomfortable. "It's fine. We need their troops, remember?"

"It's not fine," his mother snapped. "We need protection, yes. What's to keep us from forming an alliance with our eastern neighbors instead? Surely they have more to offer than an ungrateful brat for our son." She glared at my father. "We will return in the morning for renegotiations. You better have something of greater value to offer us than this farce of a marriage deal." The queen inclined her head at me, then turned, her dress fanning out behind her. She and her husband dragged their son off the dais.

Volkan managed to glance back at me as he was pulled away. The determination in his eyes was clear as day—the closest he could get to wishing me luck.

We waited in silence until the ballroom doors slammed shut behind the retreating royals, the sound echoing through the room.

My father let out a guttural scream and lunged, his hands aimed at my throat.

I tried to run, scrambling not to trip in my dress. My feet tangled in it regardless, and I stumbled off the dais, falling face-first toward the ground.

The shock of my weight landing on my palms sent a jolt through my forearms, but nothing seemed damaged. My father scrambled to try to get around Jac, who had transformed into a huge wolf covered in fur and sporting teeth sharp enough to slice through bone.

Erik went to my father, who thrashed attempting to get past Jac, and took his arm. Despite his natural strength, my father was no match for Erik. As the king continued to spit curses at me, my oldest brother attempted to defuse the situation. "Calm yourself, Father. What will the people say if they know a godforsaken has managed to derail your plans so easily? There must be a way to recover from this."

The beast slowly shrank back into Jac once more, but Erik's words had accomplished little. My father might not be reaching for me anymore, but he still looked like he wanted to throttle me. He continued to scream, spittle flying from his mouth.

From one of the Fastian thrones Björn studied me, twirling a dagger between his fingers while he lounged. "Father, perhaps this is an opportunity for us."

Panting, my father grew quiet. His fine clothing smoked along the edges. I was amazed the entire room wasn't on fire.

"If the Fastians are disappointed with little Revvy this quick, an alliance with her as the glue wouldn't have lasted long anyway. Besides, it's easy to see how much they fear Kryllian. They're desperate for protection, and while they might claim to have allies in the east, it's unlikely another country will have interest in entering our conflict. I have no doubt we'll manage to secure their cooperation when we renegotiate tomorrow."

Björn leaned forward, elbows on his knees as he studied me, his gaze like a predator's. "But now we have a chance to get rid of the pesky blot on our family tree once and for all. And all we have to do is let her compete like she asked." Björn's grin was feral.

I forced myself to think of Freja as dread filled my stomach like lead.

My father's breathing began to slow. Jac and Frode moved to stand on either side of me, offering silent support.

Then my father began to laugh, the sound coming from deep in his throat. It echoed through the empty ballroom, a chorus of nightmares, before he finally stopped to breathe.

"Yes," he said, pointing at me. "You think you have the upper hand? You're godforsaken. The pantheon looks down on you, and they will show it.

"You may compete. Yielding in the Bloodshed Trials is forbidden. Either you win or you die." He paused. "And for the sake of the gods and the future of Bhorglid, you'll perish a horrible, painful death."

I forced my mouth to stay shut, pushing away my snarky retort. I'd won. They were going to let me compete.

"Tomorrow morning you will report to the war front with the rest of your brothers," he continued. I felt the blood drain from my face. "That's right. You want to compete? Then you must prove yourself capable of leading our armies, fighting our battles. I suspect you will not have what it takes. We will see whether you are fit to be a queen.

"Now get out of my sight." My father waved his hand with a disgusted look, then turned to lift my mother.

There was nothing left in me to speak, to acknowledge my victory, to do anything but leave the way the rest of the crowd had gone until I was once again alone under the stars.

What the hell had I done?

I KNELT ON THE DAMP GRASS IN DESPAIR UNTIL MY BONES FELT frozen enough to crumble under a single touch. My teeth chattered, but the events of the night wouldn't stop repeating in my mind over and over.

The guests had finished departing long ago. Now the courtyard was empty aside from the few priests who watched me warily from their guard posts.

"This would be so much easier if Freja were here," I muttered. I'd expected to cry until my tears froze to my cheeks, but instead I was numb all over. The stars were out in their full glory, and I gazed at them, wishing they could help me disappear. Wondering if I'd made a mistake in agreeing to the Trials.

No, I reminded myself. *Even sacrificing your own life wouldn't be enough to repay Freja for all she's done for you.*

"Revna?" I turned and spotted a lone figure moving toward me in the dark. From a distance, all I recognized was the pressed military uniform. But the only person who would call me by my name instead of my title tonight was . . .

"Arne?" I straightened.

He moved closer and I nearly gasped; the black fabric of his formal coat stretched across his shoulders, gold buttons shining on the collar and the wrists. A red sash draped from his left shoulder to his right hip.

He looked handsome. Regal. Like a prince himself.

"You look . . ." My voice trailed off as I pushed to my feet. For a moment the despair sitting in my chest vanished, distracted by the unexpected visitor. "I'm amazed they gave you a formal uniform."

"I didn't think they would either," he said, fingers fidgeting with the buttons on his sleeves. "They seemed unsure, but I'm the first godforsaken they've enlisted, so there's no rule in place."

He glanced over his shoulder at the two white-robed priests standing guard at the top of the mountain path. Arne's conscription had elevated him enough for the priests to let him in the gates. Odd that the very thing meant to punish him—punish *me*—had raised his status. Their embroidered eyes kept careful watch on the two of us, waiting to report back to my father.

Suppressing a shiver, I studied him as he ran a nervous hand through his hair. "Are you ready?"

"To try and survive?" He shrugged. "Ready as I'll ever be. I've trained as much as I was able. I said goodbye to my dads before I came over."

My mind was drowning with the events of the past two days. Volkan, so much kinder and far more trustworthy than I'd anticipated; Freja, asking me to leave her in prison; Arne, ready to go to war; me, putting my life on the line for my friends. "When do you report?"

"First thing in the morning. Are you . . ." He glanced at his feet, cleared his throat. A tinge of red brushed his cheeks. "How was the engagement ceremony? What are you doing out here so late?"

I opened my mouth, then closed it again wordlessly. My thoughts swarmed like insects. Arne didn't know I had turned down the proposal and secured a place in the Trials; when it had come time to formulate the plan, including him hadn't crossed my mind. He was leaving, after all. There was nothing he could do from the front.

There was nothing I would be able to do from the front either.

The words were on the tip of my tongue, but at the last moment I held them back. I didn't want him to know. I wanted him to treat me the same for a moment. Especially when I knew he would never forgive me for my decision. Where Volkan, Halvar, and Frode were proud of me for standing up to Father, for making a change that would benefit the godforsaken, Arne would only be upset.

"I was . . . trying to clear my head. Take everything in." The words weren't even a lie.

He pulled me into a hug. I pressed my face into the wool coat, inhaling the scent of new fabric, trying to hold back tears. Arne and Freja were the only good things I had. And in the morning, they would both be gone forever unless I managed to win the Trials.

Memories bombarded me. Arne and me stargazing in our secret clearing while he whispered his fears to me; how his fathers loved him but he wasn't sure why they should if his birth parents gave him up willingly; clutching each other a little tighter after my own father had beaten me particularly badly; the very first time we met, when we were both eleven and his big, dark eyes had taken me in with curiosity and not the disgust I was used to. His departure marked the end of whatever flame had flickered between us. It was hard to feel grateful while I feared for his life.

His breath ghosted over the shell of my ear and I shivered. "What if we ran?" he whispered. "What if we left—right now? Stole two horses and disappeared."

I stiffened, pulling back. "We can't leave."

Arne blinked. "But we could be together. Don't you want that?" His next words shone on his face before he said them. "Revna, I love you."

My mouth went dry.

My worst fear was confirmed. His love was like a flame against the pure snow covering Bhorglid all year: bright and hot and impossible to deny. He'd shown it in every dance, every brush of hands, every kiss, every moment of intimacy we'd shared. And yet I'd clung to him selfishly, only wishing for something to keep for myself, someone to be safe with while I waited to meet my inevitable fate.

A chasm opened in my chest, threatening to swallow me whole. Arne stood reaching for me on the other side, but no matter how desperately I attempted to bridge the gap, I knew futility when I saw it. I longed to wrench my heart in his direction, force it to obey. I wanted to want him. Why couldn't I? Who gave my foolish heart the right to deny him and me what we both deserved?

It certainly wasn't me.

Arne swallowed. "Do you love me?"

The words took their time coming. Telling him the truth . . . could mean losing him forever. A loss more permanent than physical separation: bitterness. The end of our friendship. I pulled my hands from his warm grasp, unable to meet his eyes.

Silence fell like an ocean between us.

As the seconds ticked by, something changed in his face. Was it the excitement blinking out of his eyes? The subtle hardening of his mouth? The way his next exhale made him shudder, like the cold was seeping through his coat?

"I can't leave," I protested. "Not when Freja is still here. Not when my father would kill her if I disappeared."

He took a step back. "I understand." There was a hollow note in his voice.

I reached out a hand. "Arne, please—"

"No." His bright blue eyes were like daggers. "No. It's better if this is the end. I know what you're doing. I know you're trying to spare me the pain."

I wanted to groan, wanted to shake his shoulders until he understood. Arne deserved a woman who'd drive a blade through the heart of all who threatened him. Not me, unable to give him everything when my heart still rested in other places—Freja's safety, the freedom of the godforsaken, and the Trials were barriers I couldn't tear down even if I wanted to.

But instead of arguing, I used my hands on his shoulders to pull him in for a blistering kiss.

Our mouths collided and it wasn't sweet or gentle, not the way it had been every other time before. Yet it was so incredibly Arne— exposing the depths of his emotions that he would always say but never express.

We kissed and kissed and I waited, hoping desperately for some spark. Some proof that maybe I did love him after all.

It never came.

But what did was the familiar press of him, hard against me through his pants and my dress. His hands shook slightly as he pushed my hair away from my neck to press his lips there. "One last night?" Arne's voice was hesitant, his eyes pleading when they met mine.

After all the firsts we'd fumbled through together, he was an intrinsic part of me. I might not feel the same way about him, but his soft-spoken words still made me long for him.

I wanted to say yes. Wanted to welcome him into my bed and my body one more time before we were separated forever. But I didn't want to lead him on. I knew I didn't love him. I knew we'd been growing distant as the looming presence of my engagement encroached upon our peaceful hiding place.

Except we both wanted one last night together. And if it meant different things to each of us, then so be it. After tonight, he would be off to the front lines of the holy war and I would be a dead woman walking. He would be the only person I'd ever shared so much of myself with—even if only as a friend. If after my death he thought I'd loved him back, surely there would be no harm. Surely it would be better to leave his memories of me intact, rose-colored with love instead of the bitterness that would surge if he knew his affections weren't reciprocated.

I grabbed his hand and pulled him with me into the castle. We ascended the stairs quickly and I let myself think of it as an escape from the torturous night I'd had. At least I could forget everything that had happened when we sank into the heat of our bodies together.

Before I opened my door, Arne pulled me back, his face nervous. "You're not . . ." He scratched at the back of his neck. "The Fastian Prince isn't in there?"

I blinked. "Why in the world would I have brought you up if that was going to be a problem?"

Even in the darkness I knew he was turning bright red. "Right. Right, yeah."

He pushed the door open himself, and when I shut it behind me, twisting the knob on the lamp to light the room, he unceremoniously stripped until he was bare. In the past, I'd always taken a moment to drink him in with my eyes. I might not have loved him, but I knew how to recognize beauty when I saw it. Arne's tall frame, lean muscle, and dark hair were the picture of perfection.

But tonight, hands shaking, I turned around. "Help me with my dress?" I asked.

Arne, ever the gentle lover, obliged, his fingers soft against my back as they undid each button with care. He bent to press the occasional kiss to my spine as he worked, and I was grateful my wandering thoughts and rising guilt didn't prevent the shiver that raced through me at his touch.

Finished with his task, he pushed the dress lightly so the sleeves fell off of my arms. I stepped out of the skirt and my underthings and turned to face him once more.

His eyes raked over me darkly. "You're beautiful," he murmured.

It was the only time besides the first that I'd ever felt nervous under his watchful gaze. Then he pulled me closer, and we kissed once more. Our lips danced as he pushed me back onto the bed, falling over top of me and hiking my leg up and around his hip without preamble.

Gods, why couldn't I relax?

I clamped my eyes shut in a desperate attempt to focus on everything I was feeling—Arne's hot breath in my ear, the way he sucked on my collarbone and pressed his fingers between my thighs—but it was to no avail. Instead, the memory of Freja's arrest formed beneath my eyelids as vividly as if I were seeing it for the first time again. My father's feral scream when I refused the engagement echoed in my ears.

My panting breaths had nothing to do with pleasure. "I can't do this," I gasped, pushing Arne off me and moving to the bathroom. I dunked my face into the bucket of clean, cold water I kept there. The shock to my system was enough to drag me back to reality, despite my shaking limbs.

He was there behind me in an instant. "What's wrong? Did I hurt you?"

I choked out a bitter laugh. "No, that's not—that's not it, I just—I can't do this."

Silence sat so heavily in the room, it was almost like a third person was there. After a moment, I felt him retreat and the rustling of fabric informed me he was dressing again. It was easy to sense what he wanted—but asking him to stay felt beyond my scope of capability, especially knowing I'd spend the evening staring at his closed eyes and pushing myself to feel something—*anything*—more for him.

It took everything I had to shutter my wild thoughts behind closed doors. When I could breathe once more, I dried my face on a towel and went back into the room. My hands still shook, trembles I couldn't force away echoing through my fingers.

Arne was lacing his boots, his new uniform now wrinkled from its time spent on my floor. "I'm sorry," I said. "It isn't you, I swear."

He nodded, standing, and pressed a gentle kiss to my cheek. "I'll go home," he said. "You're right. It would be torture to say goodbye tomorrow. This will be farewell, Revna. I hope to see you again someday."

Tears shone in his eyes, and I cried too as he turned and made his way out of the room. Not for our love—or, rather, his love for me—but for the last look at our inseparable friendship. The three of us, Arne, Freja, and I, would never be in the same room again.

I T WAS THE DEAD OF NIGHT, AND VOLKAN WAS SITTING IN THE hallway outside my bedroom.

I paused in pulling my cloak over my shoulders and whispered, "What are you doing here?"

He stood, tilting his head back and forth to get a crick out of his neck. "I wanted to check in on you after the party, but I only barely managed to get away. Thought you might be sleeping. Couldn't let you leave for the war front without saying goodbye, though."

Cloak fastened, I rushed forward to wrap my arms around him. He seemed surprised but hesitantly returned the gesture. "What happens to you?" I asked. "Will your parents continue negotiations with my mother?"

"Most likely," he said. "Though they're no closer to deciding tonight. We'll presumably stay a few more days until your mother finds something valuable enough to satisfy my parents and then head back home. With Kryllian skirting closer to our borders . . ." His voice trailed off and he shook his head, stepping back from my embrace. "They're terrified of the Hellbringer. Everyone is. I don't blame them."

"I don't either." I bit my lip, thinking of the masked figure I'd seen three times now. Even if he was a figment of my imagination, he felt utterly real and overwhelmingly terrifying.

Instead of voicing my thoughts aloud, I turned to the other point Volkan had mentioned. "If you finish negotiations soon, we likely won't see each other again." I tried to hide the sadness in my voice. A few days earlier, Volkan had been the last person in the world I wanted in Bhorglid. Now I was mourning his loss. In that short time, our worlds had been upended.

Together, we'd changed our futures.

"I'm planning to travel back to watch the Trials, at least," he said. "In the interest of strengthening the relationship between our countries, I think my parents will agree it's a good move. When the monarchy changes hands, they'll want to make sure the new ruler has every intention of upholding the agreement."

I hummed. "If Björn is the successor . . . watch your back." The words felt loaded, and I glanced over my shoulder in the direction of my brothers' closed doors, as if they might be able to hear me.

"I have every faith the crown will land on your head," he said. "Write to me from the front if there's anything I can do, understand?"

"Of course."

Volkan seemed to suddenly realize I was preparing to leave. "Where are you headed?"

"To Halvar's. I can't leave without saying goodbye."

Volkan nodded. "Tell him farewell from me, too."

◆ ◆ ◆ ◆ ◆

WHEN I REACHED THE SHARPENED AXE, ALL WAS QUIET. EVEN THE late-night crowd had departed. In the east, the sky was swiftly lightening from inky darkness to navy. I had to hurry if I was going to make time to tell Freja I was leaving, too.

Halvar was asleep when I arrived, but I didn't hesitate to let myself in and rouse him from slumber. Despite his age, he moved as swiftly as ever, and I sighed when I found a knife pressed to my throat.

When his eyes adjusted to the dark, he relaxed. "What are you doing here? It's the middle of the night."

"I'm going to the war front tomorrow," I said, rubbing the nick he'd left on my jugular. A tiny drop of blood smeared on my finger. "Can you take care of Freja while I'm gone?"

"The war front?" He sat down heavy on the bed. "Why? Did they not let you into the Trials?"

I grimaced. "Oh, they did. But now I have to prove I can endure the war if I want to be queen. Father is insisting; I'm not sure why."

"Probably wants to get you killed before you end up competing." He rubbed a hand over his face. "I'll keep tabs on Freja, visit her as often as I can. But in the meantime, you stay safe out there. The war front is not kind to godforsaken."

"I know." The hilt of my sword was comforting in my fingers. I rubbed the worn leather wrapped around it, wishing I wasn't so damn frazzled. The night's events ran through my brain over and over, the constant loop keeping my heartbeat elevated. I wouldn't have been able to sleep even if I tried. "And you'll work on things with the rebellion, too? Have the godforsaken ready to fight by the time the Trials roll around?"

"You can trust me." Halvar put a fist over his heart. "The godforsaken will be ready for you. Ready for their queen."

I relaxed slightly. "In that case, I'm off to say goodbye to Freja."

◆ ◆ ◆ ◆ ◆

I STEPPED BACK OUT INTO THE STREET, THE WIND SCRAPING COLD fingers against my skin. I forced myself to think of Freja and Arne. Every move I made since the night of Freja's arrest was to help my friends.

Arne was likely on his way to the front already. The soldiers left in the dead of night, the darkness keeping knowledge of our regiment's full numbers out of Kryllian hands. He could be halfway there, entirely unknowing that I'd be joining him shortly.

I exhaled. He was going to be furious if we ran into each other out there. I wondered how the army was split up; maybe we'd be stationed in different camps. If I was lucky, he wouldn't find out what I'd done until it was too late.

I steeled myself, preparing to continue to my next stop, but when I looked up, a pair of dark, wood-carved eyes stared back at me from down the road. I stilled.

His dark clothes stood out starkly against the pale snow. The carved wolf skull mask, stained so dark it was almost black, bared its teeth menacingly. But the Hellbringer didn't move. He didn't strike, or pull out a weapon, or even take a step toward me. He simply stared.

A glance told me all the priests who usually patrolled this area were nowhere to be found, despite claiming they did their jobs at all hours of the day. And yet, I couldn't believe I was the only one seeing this. Surely someone would peer through their curtains and acknowledge Kryllian's deadliest general standing in the middle of Bhorglid's capital city. Surely someone would walk out of a nearby shop and let out a scream of fear.

The most surprising thing of all was how calm I felt. No panic rose inside of me, no wariness. Even the anger I'd lashed out at him with yesterday lay dormant. Only a mild fascination stirred in my chest, as if the part of my brain controlling my fear response had turned off.

"Is this real?" I muttered. "What could you possibly be looking for that would make you hound *me* so relentlessly?"

He didn't answer. I peered at the eyes carved into the mask, wondering how well he could see me. Wondering if he realized covering his body from head to toe with fabric was a very priestly thing to do.

I sighed. Every part of me was tired. "If you're going to kill me, get it over with," I continued. "I'm the least interesting person here."

"Are you?"

I startled slightly at his response. Three times I'd seen him before, but this was the first I'd heard him speak.

By the gods, this was . . . definitely real. His boots sank slightly into the snow where he stood, proof of his existence, and my eyes widened. There was no imagining the low, distorted voice emerging from the helmet.

I took a step back. My face had to be as pale as the snow around me. Where yesterday I'd been fearless, explosive emotions pushing past the logic screaming at me to cower from him, now I was all too conscious of how swiftly he could end my life.

"Yes," I whispered, aware my hands were shaking. Placing one on the hilt of my sword did nothing to calm my nerves. "Leave me alone."

He tilted his head but didn't move. "Very well," he said finally. "I'll be seeing you soon."

With that, he turned and walked away. I gaped after him. Striding down the streets of the city like he belonged here.

"This isn't real," I said, pressing my palms to my eyes and rubbing hard. "This *can't* be real."

I opened my eyes and reached out a hand, prepared to call him to a stop and ask him why he was following *me* of all people, but he was gone. The street was empty.

But when I looked closer, the snow where he'd been standing was still pressed down into the shape of two boot soles.

Real.

A priest stepped out from an alleyway to stand at his usual post. When he noticed me staring, he twirled his scythe menacingly. It was enough to spur me into action, and I walked toward the path leading to the prison, my thoughts swirling.

What the hell was happening?

♦ ♦ ♦ ♦ ♦

A LIGHT DUSTING OF SNOW WAS STREWN ACROSS THE GROUND, AS though the gods had considered coating it but given up halfway through. Thoughts of the Hellbringer plagued me, but I forced them away when I passed through the prison's front doors. Freja was worried about enough—I didn't need to tell her the most dangerous man in Kryllian was haunting me.

Though I couldn't fathom why, especially when he was supposedly here on a far more important mission for his country.

The guards let me in without a word. I was grateful not to have to search every nook and cranny for Freja this time around. Instead, I went straight to her cell and sat cross-legged in front of it.

"Revna." She sounded exhausted but smiled when she moved into the light. "It's nice to see a familiar face. The walls are getting boring."

I grinned, and when she sat across from me, I reached a hand through the bars to grasp hers. "I have good news," I said. "I've come up with a plan to get you out of here."

She shook her head. "I already told you, I'm not running."

I took a deep breath. "I declined the engagement. I'm competing in the Bloodshed Trials."

Freja's mouth opened and then closed again. Finally, she managed to get a word out. "How?"

I told her about the engagement party, about the Fastians threatening to revoke their support, and the plan Volkan, Halvar, Frode, Jac, and I had come up with. When I finally finished speaking, she had her face in her hands.

I took a deep breath. The prison was still and silent, and I knew there must be other inmates and guards listening. For a moment my only thought was gratitude that the prison itself was impenetrable. Even if it meant I couldn't break Freja out, it also meant no one here could tell Father of my plan to ally with Frode and Jac.

"You're an idiot," Freja said at last, voice muffled. She lifted her head out of her hands to glare at me. "I cannot believe you could be so stupid."

Stung, I raised an eyebrow. "Doing what I can to rescue you and free the godforsaken is stupid?"

"Yes!" she exploded. "Yes, Revna! You're going to die, do you understand? What the hell am I supposed to do then? When you and Arne are both bodies in caskets?"

I pushed myself back, withdrawing my hand from between the bars. I didn't try to hide my hurt—Freja knew me well enough to pick up on it regardless. "You don't know that. With Frode and Jac on my side, we stand a good chance of winning."

"Against Erik?" she argued. "Björn? Your brothers are ruthless. They are *powerful*. They will corner you and show no mercy."

"Have a little faith." Why had I come here? My best friend couldn't even offer me her support when I was doing all of this— every bit—for her. I'd been foolish to hope she'd be happy about this; to hope she would encourage me, be proud of my efforts. "Jac and Frode are powerful, too."

"And what happens if they turn against you?" She stood and paced, irate. "Are they sincere in wanting you as queen? What happens if the three of you are left standing and the priests kill you all in an instant?"

My nails dug into my palms as I resisted the urge to hit something— anything. "Do you think I haven't thought this through?"

"Yes!" she cried, throwing her hands in the air. "I know you, Revna. You have dreams of a better world, but you don't seem to realize the cost. And most of the time you act without thinking. I love that about you; don't get me wrong. But to sign up for your own death on the slight chance you'll win the throne? What would you even do if you became queen?"

"Make a fucking difference." My temper, steadily heating to a boil beneath my skin, finally bubbled to the surface. "You think half the people in this prison are here because they actually committed crimes? You think the godforsaken deserve to be killed by the priests again and again, helpless against the godtouched? I know you're scared. So am I. But I'm tired of letting fear rule my every decision. For the first time I have the chance to make a change for the better. And gods be damned if I don't take it."

I pushed to my feet, brushing sand and dirt from my clothing. "I came here hoping you would be excited for me. That this might bring you a bit of hope, knowing I'm doing what I can to get you out of here, to keep you from rotting in prison until you die. I likely won't be visiting you again until after the Trials—Father is bringing me to the front lines, since I'm competing now." I swallowed thickly. "This is goodbye."

"I didn't ask you to do this," she whispered. "I don't want you to die for me. But it seems I don't get a say in the matter anymore."

Each footstep felt heavy as I took my leave.

10

T HE SUNRISE IN THE EAST TINTED THE SKY A PERFECT PINK, matching the tip of Frode's nose. My sword was strapped to my hip and a small bag of my clothes was hooked to my horse's saddle.

I couldn't decide if my pounding heartbeat was from excitement or lingering fear. Probably both.

When we headed south, into the city, I was confused. The war front was several hours' journey in the other direction.

I turned to Erik, riding next to me. "Where are we going?"

He didn't look at me when he responded. "The temple. We always go for a blessing before we leave for the front."

I tried not to groan. Would Father let me stay outside and wait? Or would he insist I join them?

My stomach sank as the pillars of the temple appeared in front of me. The inside of my mouth tasted sour. I would rather face the Hellbringer alone in battle than be here.

Despite the enemy general's claims that he would see me soon, he was nowhere to be found this morning. As we rode through the streets, my eyes searched every shadowed alley and concealed corner for any evidence of the man who'd been following me. But if he was watching, he'd found a hiding place I hadn't thought to search.

I'd tossed and turned for the single hour of rest I'd had after returning from my visit with Freja, desperate to parse out why he'd been tracking me. The Hellbringer was an enigma—no one understood why he allowed the war to continue, why he didn't simply kill us all and put a stop to it. Now I knew he spent his precious time following a godforsaken royal who meant nothing in the grand scheme of things.

It didn't make sense.

We came to a stop in front of the temple steps and my father instructed the servants to keep careful watch over the horses.

Inside, fires blazed on every wall, both for light and warmth. The priest at the front of the room saw me enter and inclined his head. I didn't acknowledge him, moving forward to stand next to the rest of my family. The red embroidered eye on his forehead kept careful watch as he spoke to my father.

"Your daughter will be accompanying you?" the priest asked.

My father nodded. "She does not truly understand the war, like most of the godforsaken. I believe her experiences in the northern wastes will serve to change her feelings about the Holy Order of Priests and help her rethink her decision to compete in the Bloodshed Trials."

My hands tightened into fists.

"Each of you may come forward to receive a blessing and a marking," the priest said. My brothers moved toward him.

A small thrill replaced my resentment for a moment. I loved seeing my brothers in the traditional war paint of our ancestors, wearing it proudly into battle. It reminded me of victory. Bhorglid wasn't perfect, but I would represent my forebearers as I made an attempt to change it for the better.

Callum and Arraya founded Bhorglid on the principle of the godtouched being superior because they were gifted magic by the gods. But for there to be a hierarchy in the first place, the godforsaken had been subjugated—the first of our kind forced to believe they were less-than. I considered them to be my true ancestors. I would don my war paint with hope of a future that past generations would be proud of.

Once, our ancestors had performed all religious rituals with the blood of animals, including applying the symbols they wore when preparing for battle. After a bad winter several generations back that killed most of the livestock, the priests of the time considered it more prudent to switch to paint instead of blood. I was glad for the change.

After Jac went to the front for the first time, he'd explained the changes made to the symbols themselves over time as well. I wished I remembered what he'd taught me.

Erik stepped forward first. The priest muttered something under his breath and then raised a brush to Erik's forehead. When he finished and Erik turned to face me once more, I had to hold in a gasp at the bright red marking on his forehead.

There were two lines across each of his cheekbones and another two lines extended from either of his temples to form a point in the center of his forehead. He noticed me staring, and while Frode stepped forward, Erik leaned close to explain the markings.

"The ones on my cheeks are for leadership," he said softly. "And the marks on my forehead are for strength. Those are the blessings the gods saw fit to give me today. When it's your turn, you'll receive your own."

Frode stepped away from the priest with a line of dots across his forehead in a straight line. "Focus," he explained in response to my curious thought. He rolled his eyes. "They give it to me every time."

Did I truly believe the paint offered any additional power? No, not really. But perhaps the markings would one day symbolize peace between the godtouched and the godforsaken once more.

Jac received a line from the top of his forehead, over his nose, and to the base of his chin. Frode remained beside me, so he helped translate. "Perseverance," he said. When I raised an eyebrow at the three jagged lines Björn was given on his forehead, I could hear the exasperation in Frode's voice. "Power," he grumbled. "That one is consistent, too."

My father received two lines across his forehead; Frode explained they symbolized truth. I had to hold in a scoff at that. Then it was my turn. I stepped forward, wondering what the priests could possibly see fit to bless me with as I went to battle.

The priest was silent for a long time before he finally spoke again. The scythe in his hand glinted in the flickering firelight. He leaned forward, his voice practically a whisper. "The gods are most disappointed in you, Princess," he said.

I stiffened. "Are you going to bless me or not?"

The priest shook his head but put his paintbrush to my face. The paint was cold and sticky. He drew two lines on my face, each diagonal, intersecting to form an X across the bridge of my nose.

I froze. I didn't understand many of the symbols the godtouched claimed, especially those involved in the temple ceremonies, but this was one I knew intimately.

I turned to face my brothers. Frode had paled. Jac looked at his shoes. Björn burst into gleeful laughter and my father turned away, striding out the doors.

Death. The X on my face meant I'd been chosen by Aloisa, goddess of the soul. Marked to die, like the symbol was a target for my enemies.

I turned back to the priest. "You disgust me," I spat. "If Aloisa sees fit to claim me, I will do anything I must to stay alive."

"I only repeat what the gods tell me," the priest said.

"Liar," I said. "You use the gods for your own gain."

Frode grabbed my arm. "Let's go."

He pulled me out the door, into the cold again. The wind swept up the strands of hair falling from my tight braid, obscuring my vision slightly. A storm was coming in. I mounted my horse, trying not to think about the paint on my face.

Frode leaned over to me from where he sat on his own horse. "Take the paint off," he said. "It doesn't have to mean anything. Not if you don't want it to."

I shook my head. "No. It stays. If they're damning me, I want the whole world to see it."

Frode sighed. "Come on, then. Let's catch up with the others."

◆ ◆ ◆ ◆ ◆

I HEARD THE SCREAMS AND EXPLOSIONS BEFORE THE FRONT LINE came into view.

The mountains towered above us, jagged like monstrous teeth covered in snow, and with every blast the whole world shook.

Eyes wide, I turned to Frode. *Is this it?*

He nodded, mouth set in a grim line, and pulled a flask out of his saddlebag. I watched him tip his head back and drain the entire container in one swig. "They're mid-battle, through the canyon pass."

A man I'd never seen before pulled his horse up to ride next to mine and I jumped at the sight. He looked vaguely familiar, but I couldn't place the big nose turned up at the end and the brown hair with a white streak through it. "You ready for this?" he asked.

My expression clearly showed everything going through my head. The man laughed and shook his head until his hair transformed to red, facial features familiar again. Jac had already taken another form to prepare for battle. "Makes me less conspicuous," he explained. "Be ready for anything; it's only a matter of time before we run into some Kryllians. They'll see you as easy prey if they recognize you."

Another explosion echoed through the canyon pass and the mountains themselves shuddered, snow threatening to topple into an avalanche at any moment. I set my jaw and dragged my sword from its sheath. Would there be time to dismount and get my feet under me before I was forced to parry an inevitable blow? I'd never regretted more not mastering a ranged weapon.

My father, brothers, and the rest of our group slid helmets over their faces. I copied them, wishing mine didn't block out my peripheral vision.

"Ready your—"

Before my father could finish his sentence, someone let out a wild cry. Figures cloaked in black emerged from ahead on the trail, brandishing weapons I'd never seen before. Cruel blades curved and glimmered in the snowy sunlight.

Crouched in the middle of the canyon pass was a masked figure I recognized. A carved wooden helmet covered his whole head. The leering smile of a predator's skull unearthed a feeling I'd never had before, even when I'd seen him in the streets of the city. There, he'd been frightening but out of place, like a boy dressed as a monster. Now, there was no doubt in my mind what he would do to achieve his goals.

This is what it feels like to be prey.

As the thought struck me, I remembered the Hellbringer's promise from this morning, before the dawn broke.

Fear overtook each of my limbs and I went stiff. Was this it? Was he finally going to strike me down? Were we going to die before we reached the front lines?

We'd walked straight into an ambush.

My father swore. I heard Erik muttering a prayer to the gods under his breath. Jac nudged his horse in front of mine, his bow and arrow drawn.

Frode leaned over the side of his horse and vomited his breakfast into the snow.

My father screamed at his men to charge, and the horses galloped toward the ambush, soldiers with their weapons drawn. I watched the Hellbringer stand and tilt his head.

Panic wrapped its cold hands around my throat. In one glance, the Hellbringer could annihilate everyone here. The entire royal family would be gone and Kryllian would have the freedom to waltz in and take Bhorglid, killing anyone who opposed their reign.

"Come on." Jac pulled the reins of my horse toward a grove of trees lining the edge of the canyon. "Get out of sight. Don't let him see you."

But my eyes fell on a body several meters away, lying slack in the snow. A horse snorted unhappily, breath fogging into the air, stomping hooves narrowly avoiding its prone rider. Frode.

"Wait." I slid off my horse and took off through the chaos toward my brother, discarding my helmet.

The shriek of metal on metal was mostly above Frode on the trail, but a few of the Kryllian soldiers had made their way to his position. One raised his sword, swinging the blade toward my face. Jac swore and I watched as an arrow whizzed from behind me and skewered one of the soldiers through the eye. The man collapsed, another carcass in the snow.

"Thank you, Jac," I whispered. The dead soldier's blood stained the white powder, and through the chaos and screaming, a voice hummed a familiar tune—the same lullaby Frode had sung the past few days while he was drunk. I knelt in the snow next to Frode, wondering how he was managing to vocalize while he was unconscious, but forced the thought away as the battlefield noise escalated once more.

Wake up! I rolled him over and slapped him hard across the face.

His eyes flew open, snow matted in his lashes. "Get up, get up," I muttered, tugging his arm. He pushed himself to his elbows and his eyes widened.

I turned with my sword in time to parry a blow from another Kryllian soldier. Our blades connected and a thrill rushed through me. Finally, *finally*, I would get to put some of my skills to use.

Adrenaline pumped through my veins as I lunged for a weak spot in his defenses—but the soldier was too fast, and with a sharp twist of his weapon my blade fell from my hand. I sprawled helpless on the ground next to Frode.

The soldier reached to grab me, and I scrambled backward in time for another arrow to land, this time skewering his neck through a small gap in his armor. He collapsed to the ground in front of us, his warm blood staining the snow. I looked away, refusing to watch the life leave his eyes.

Frode groaned and put his hand over his mouth. I didn't want to think about hearing a dying man's last thoughts, so I grabbed him with one hand and my sword with the other as I pulled him to his feet. "Get over here," I growled, dragging him back toward where Jac waited in the trees.

A glance behind me confirmed we had the upper hand. Björn breathed fire, burning them all to a crisp, and Father's flames licked over his great axe, charring anyone who came within reach of his blade. Erik crushed skulls in his bare hands.

The Hellbringer, however, had disappeared. I turned to Jac, who had shifted into his alternate form. "Where did the Hellbringer go?"

Jac pushed me aside to peer between the trees. "I don't know," he said, panic at the edge of his voice. "I didn't see him go anywhere."

Discarding my helmet, I moved over to Frode and pulled a blanket from one of my saddlebags. He was on his knees in the snow, hands over his ears, teeth chattering. I wrapped the blanket around him and patted him on the back.

"We should be safe here," Jac said. "Frode can warn us if anyone is coming."

"I don't think he's in the best mental state to read minds right now," I said, glancing at Frode, who curled into the fetal position on the ground. "Climb a tree to give you a vantage point. I'll stay with Frode. If anyone tries to attack us, it'll be impossible for you not to hear it."

Jac shifted his weight in the snow but finally nodded. As he grabbed the bottom branch of the nearest pine, he turned to point a finger at me. "Don't you dare die," he ordered.

I smirked as he ascended to the top.

Frode was shivering on the ground. "Are you okay?" I whispered, moving closer to help him sit up.

He shook his head, and I was surprised to see tear tracks on his face. *Is it like this every time?*

A solemn nod was his only reply.

I put a hand on his shoulder. "It should be over soon," I murmured, pulling his helmet off to brush the snow out of his hair. He was paler than usual, and the few freckles that had stayed on his nose over the winter stood out. "We're going to wait it out. Only a few more minutes."

Hopefully. As long as they weren't all dead at the Hellbringer's hand. I shuddered at the thought of everyone lying slack-jawed in the canyon pass.

Frode made a strangled sort of noise and I was pulled back to the present. "What's wrong?" I asked, examining him for injury.

Then I realized—he was laughing.

"You can't stand to imagine them all dead out there," he managed to say, "and yet you didn't hesitate to invite yourself to the Trials. To war. Now is not the time to grow soft, Rev."

I clenched my jaw and decided it would be better not to say anything. Then I heard the crunch of a footstep behind me.

Whirling, I pulled my sword from the sheath to point it straight at the Hellbringer.

11

MY EYES WIDENED, PULSE FROZEN IN MY VEINS. MY SWORD wavered. Something in me had enough space to feel shame at my fear.

The mask was more terrifying up close. I couldn't see his eyes through the mask, and I didn't want to. Nothing to humanize a monster.

Especially a monster who might be hunting me. And now he wanted to hurt my brothers.

A rumbling laugh, deep and dark, echoed from beneath the mask. "What exactly do you plan to do with that?" the Hellbringer asked, gesturing toward my blade.

Every second I wasn't dead was precious time now, a chance for my two brothers to escape. I lunged without thinking, swinging my sword in a way that felt relieving and final. He was unarmed; maybe I could wound him enough for Jac and Frode to have time to run before he could get to them.

My sword hissed through the air. He moved so fast, I didn't see him until he spoke again. "Are you done yet?" Though his voice had become quiet, it rumbled through my bones. There must be some kind of voice modulator under the helmet, deepening his voice so it was unrecognizable.

I whirled to my left, where he was now positioned, and sliced my blade through the air again. But once more it made no connection. He hadn't unsheathed the blade at his hip.

"Too cowardly to fight me?" I raised my sword and faced him.

He tilted his head. "Why bother? My Lurae can accomplish the same results in mere moments."

I scowled. "Kill us, then."

Before he could respond, Jac dropped from the pine tree, landing steadily on the ground. His bow was drawn, an arrow pointed straight at the Hellbringer's heart. I'd never seen Jac's eyes wild like they were now. "I'll shoot."

The Hellbringer surveyed my brother, hands behind his back. "Then I will kill you." The masked general turned to me and extended a beckoning hand. "I am only here for you, Princess. Will you come willingly or by force?"

I paled. "Come with you?"

He nodded. The puzzle pieces clicked into place. He hadn't been looking for something in Bhorglid but *someone*. Me.

But why? Did he think I knew information about the war effort that Kryllian could use against us? I imagined all the ways he could kill me. His godtouch was only one of them.

"No," Frode croaked. I turned to find him clinging to the tree as he pushed himself to his feet. "No, take me instead. You don't need her. She's godforsaken. She's of no use to you." It looked like he might collapse at any second. I wondered what he discerned from the Hellbringer's thoughts.

"Sit," I snapped. His face was devoid of all color and Jac extended a hand to steady Frode while shooting me a fearful glance.

"I will not ask again," the Hellbringer said. "Come. *Now.*"

"Why?" I demanded. "Frode is right. I have no magic. I'm useless to you."

He stepped forward until he towered directly over me, inches from my face. "Is your imagination so dull? To think I would take you and try to wield you as a weapon on my behalf?" He let out a barking laugh. "If this war were to be won by power alone, I would have slaughtered your forces years ago."

Standing this close, could he feel me trembling? I clenched my teeth. If he didn't want me for power, then he must want me for information. Or leverage.

The picture was clear as day in my mind's eye: tied to a chair in the center of a Kryllian war camp, I would writhe in pain while their most powerful godtouched general tortured me, trying to get information I didn't have. And when they finally found a truthteller among their ranks to confirm I had no knowledge, the Hellbringer would stretch out his hand and clench it into a fist, ending my life.

The commotion from the fight outside of the grove of trees was dying down. I heard Erik calling out for Jac. Maybe if I stalled for a moment, I could get away; maybe then I wouldn't have to walk to my death.

"What will it be, Princess?" The deadly voice reverberated through the crisp air. "Willingly or by force?"

Instead of answering, I shot back another question. "Why don't you just kill us all?"

The Hellbringer paused, his long cloak floating behind him in the breeze. "I can change my mind if you'd like."

I didn't answer. Erik's calls were growing louder.

"And if we aren't out of sight before your Father and your other brothers return, then I *will* change my mind," he said softly. "That is what bringing you by force looks like."

He reached out his black-gloved hand. I refused to let myself think about it. I barely heard Frode's protests as I grabbed the Hellbringer's hand.

I swore the masked general relaxed a little. But before I could make any assessment of him, a soldier clothed in black dropped from the trees, placed a hand on our clasped arms, and teleported us away from my family.

◆ ◆ ◆ ◆ ◆

FOR A MOMENT THERE WAS ONLY DARKNESS, THE FEELING OF HIS gloved hand clasped around my wrist, and a rush of wind whipping my braids back. Then my feet touched solid ground.

I stumbled against rugged stone and fell on my hands and knees, hissing as my palms slapped against the floor. Nausea swarmed for a moment, threatening the loss of my breakfast, but gradually subsided. It was impossible to see through the thick darkness surrounding me.

Footsteps sounded, and I heard the switch of a match against something. A flicker of light slowly grew until a lantern cast a shadow against the Hellbringer's engraved mask. Before I had the chance to say anything, the soldier who had transported us grabbed the Hellbringer by the arm once more and they were gone again.

I pushed myself onto my knees. Where was I?

The lantern swung slightly from a peg in the stone wall. I took it and held it up as I turned, taking in my surroundings.

I was in a dark, damp hallway. Despite the barrier between me and the outside world, the cold sank in, wrapping itself around me and making me shiver. When I reached out to brush my hand against the wall, the below-freezing temperature seeped through my gloves. I frowned. Who would make a structure out of metal in the wastelands?

The hallway continued in both directions, the lamplight illuminating only a few feet each way before being swallowed by utter darkness. The ground was smooth beneath my feet but covered in a thick film of dust. I wondered how long it had been since this place was inhabited.

I turned in a circle. Surely one of these directions would lead me out—but how far were we from the front? My breath, crystallizing in front of my face with every exhale, told me we were still in Bhorglid, but without being able to look around, I couldn't be sure. Maybe I'd been transported to another place with equally frigid weather. Maybe this was Faste or even Kryllian. Maybe I wasn't even in the Fjordlands anymore.

My body shook and I pulled my coat tighter around my shoulders. My family would assume I was dead. I didn't blame them; it was only a matter of time before the Hellbringer returned and finished me off in the blink of an eye.

I clenched my teeth from both the cold and the determination flowing through me. If I didn't find a way out, a way back to my family, then Freja would rot in prison. Björn would become king. The godforsaken would never have a place in the world.

If the Hellbringer had dropped me here and left without any guards or soldiers to watch me, it must mean escape was nearly impossible. But I had to try. For Freja. And at the least, walking would keep my blood flowing and my body temperature up. This metal structure was somehow colder than the snow-covered mountaintop.

The only question remaining was: Left or right?

Freja's voice popped into my head, with its razor-sharp spark of glee at the thought of an adventure. *When in doubt, always go right. Then you can't be wrong.*

I tried to smile to myself, but my lips were so cold it became a grimace. I turned to my right and started walking.

◆ ◆ ◆ ◆ ◆

IT MUST HAVE BEEN HOURS LATER—IT *FELT* LIKE HOURS LATER— when the lamp started sputtering. I swore. Navigating the rest of this structure in the dark would be a nightmare.

My walking had revealed more than I wanted to know. This place wasn't simply an old, abandoned building—it was an old, abandoned *prison*. Thankfully, the cells I'd noticed as I explored were empty save for a few bones that looked suspiciously human. I'd hurried away from them. Knowing what remained in the cells wasn't necessary.

The layout of the prison was utterly baffling. There were endless twists and turns. Making my way back to where I started would be impossible. I scowled. Why would the Hellbringer drop me off in an abandoned prison? What was the point?

My one useful discovery was two heavy doors with more locks than I could count. After careful examination, they appeared to be thicker than the other doors, which opened easily. I assumed these unique doors led to the outside, providing a possible means of escape. If I managed to open them, that is. Without any tools to provide leverage, picking the locks would be hopeless.

Going back the way I had come felt futile, so I took the next branching hall, starting in the other direction. The candle within the lantern sputtered again, clinging to its last bit of life. Seconds later the wick made a popping sound and the light went out.

"Damn it," I muttered. There was no way I could go anywhere now. I reached for my sword, hoping the hilt would bring me comfort, but instead it reminded me that the Hellbringer hadn't bothered to disarm me before taking me captive.

My eyes adjusted slowly to the dark. Some of the indentations and imperfections along the walls came into a shadowy focus. Ahead, the glow of another lamp beckoned me.

I squinted. Was I imagining it? There had been no light before.

I moved toward it. I had walked only a few feet before the passage widened into a large room.

This had clearly been a communal space at some point. Maybe a mess hall for the prisoners? But now it was curated into cozy living quarters. Most of the room was empty, but lanterns lit the entire perimeter. I walked to the back, where there was a long dining table made of dark wood with a single chair on each end. Shelves lined the walls, and a small bed was pushed against one side of the room.

To the right of the bed was a firepit. It extended into an opening in the wall, funneling smoke out through a chimney, and the crackling flames spread warmth into my bones. An involuntary gasp escaped me, and I ran toward the blaze, peeling off my cloak as I went. My knees hit the ground hard enough to bruise and I stretched my fingers toward the heat, paying no regard for how close the sparks jumped. Being burned was nothing unusual growing up as the only godforsaken child in the king's household.

Soon my frozen extremities regained feeling. I relished the warmth. I'd been riding in the frigid air for hours, and my face had gone numb far too early in the journey. Hours spent navigating this hellhole hadn't helped either.

With my body temperature slowly adjusting, I began wondering what I'd left behind. Was the battle over? Had Bhorglid been victorious? Or were the Kryllians taking my family prisoner right now?

No. If my father had managed to evade defeat for this long, one ambush would not be enough to tip the scales.

Comforted by the thought, I scooted to the side of the fire and rested my forehead against the wall. I told myself to check if the chimney was a feasible escape route once the fire was extinguished. Now, still shivering, I didn't have the heart to even consider embracing the cold for such a meager chance at freedom. In the meantime, I'd take my chances and hope the Hellbringer would return.

I settled in for a long morning.

◆ ◆ ◆ ◆ ◆

"GET UP."

The dark, distorted voice was becoming far too familiar for my liking. I started and turned, using my feet to scoot myself back against the wall. I must have dozed off in the fire's warmth.

My eyes scanned him from toes to head, taking him in. On second, closer look, he appeared more terrifying than I had first thought. His black boots had soles two inches thick and were laced up his calves to protect him from the snow. Dark plated armor covered his legs, arms, and torso, glinting dangerously in the light of the fire. Gloves covered his hands, and the neck of his shirt concealed any skin that could potentially be exposed between the armor and the mask.

I swallowed. The mask. The skull had wide, gaping hollows where the eyes should be, two carved nostrils, and teeth bared in a wide, hideous grin. When I'd seen him on streets that were familiar and not in his domain, the helmet hadn't felt nearly as grotesque. But here, it was my worst nightmare come to life.

He crossed his arms over his chest. The thick cloak fastened across his collarbone shifted along with his feet as he took another step toward me. "Get. Up."

I pushed down my dread, forcing it to lie still in the pit of my stomach long enough for me to stand. He wouldn't see me cower.

At my full height, my eyes barely reached his chin. I copied his stance, crossing my own arms and widening the space between my feet to stabilize myself. Everything in me wanted to fight, but with his godtouch there was no point.

"Kill me fast," I said. I couldn't tell where his eyes were, but I stared into the eyes of the carved skull. I held back a shiver. I clenched my shaking hands into fists to hide my trembling. Dying wasn't what I wanted, but I knew it would be better than the alternative: torture, ridicule, starvation. I could only imagine the horrors in store for me at the Hellbringer's hands.

There was a swift beat of silence that felt like an eternity. "I am not going to kill you," he said.

I furrowed my brow. "Well, why not?"

"My queen has other plans for you, Princess," he said. "Your cooperation is necessary for her success. Killing you now would be foolish."

My thoughts raced. Maybe this was why he'd been searching for me. "Plans?" I asked.

He didn't respond, and after a moment I realized he was taking me in the same way I had looked him over upon waking. I wondered what he assumed, who he thought I was. Why he'd been looking for me when there were far more powerful people who could accomplish his purposes.

He turned toward the small table I'd noticed when I first walked into the room. "Come eat."

I didn't move. This man was responsible for the deaths of hundreds if not thousands of my people.

Any fascination I once felt regarding him was gone. Anger coursed through me until I burned with it. He had slaughtered my people but not me. Gods be damned if he thought I would sit and eat anything he provided.

I had to be quick. Taking him out would require my life, but I'd willingly give it to pay him back for his crimes. His back was turned, and as he moved to sit at the table, I pulled my sword from the sheath at my hip and lunged for him.

There wasn't time to blink before his own blade parried mine. I twisted, lunging out of his sword's range before attempting to strike again. The sound of metal on metal filled my ears.

I scowled. But before I could move, he pushed his full strength against my sword, bending me backward until my wrists shook with the effort of staying upright.

The sunken eyes of the mask bored into my own. I swallowed. At least when I died it would be fighting. There was no greater honor.

He spoke, his voice eerily soft. "Did you think it would be easy?" he asked quietly. "Did you presume I couldn't wield a weapon? That my Lurae was my only skill? That you're the first one to attempt my assassination?"

A bead of sweat dripped past my eyes. Gods, he was *strong*. I gritted my teeth, trying to summon the effort to keep my wrists from snapping under the pressure. My spine was beginning to ache from bending backward at such an unnatural angle.

Without warning, he dropped his stance, sheathing his blade once more. My breath came in ragged gasps and the point of my sword hit the ground. But I refused to lower my eyes.

He wouldn't even kill me.

"Coward," I growled.

He didn't dignify me with a response. Instead, he turned to the shelves behind him and began pulling out containers, placing them on the table.

My anger surged again. He would leave me alive to be tortured and used for ransom. I swung my sword again, heaving with all my might.

The Hellbringer didn't turn; he raised a gloved hand and caught my blade in his palm, clenching his fingers around the sharp edges. The connection of my weapon against his flesh resonated like a music note.

My eyes widened. Blood ran down the silver, tinging my reflection with red.

"Put your weapon away," he said. "There will be no wars won here. Not tonight."

With my breathing ragged and tears blurring my eyes, I let out a guttural scream raging with agony from somewhere deep in my chest. I wished I had a godtouch to end him on sight.

But I didn't.

He shook his head. Gravity pulled my sword until the blade clanked against the floor. The Hellbringer gestured to the container he had placed on the table. "Eat."

I didn't bother to place my sword back in its sheath. There was no point. I released the hilt and left it to clatter, discarded. Silence throbbed through my mind, pain building behind my eyes.

Prisoner. I was a prisoner. There was no telling how long I would be here, kept in isolation.

The worst part was knowing the truth: no one was coming for me.

I moved to the table and glanced into the wooden box. It was full of nuts and berries I didn't recognize. Maybe they were from Kryllian.

At a sound behind me, I turned. The Hellbringer was taking off his cloak to hang it on a set of hooks set into the stone. I watched him remove his sheath and sword, placing them on the hooks as well.

Without turning around, he peeled off his right glove, the blood-soaked fabric already drying. It surprised me to see pale white skin appear, drenched with thick red. Two long, gaping lines of flesh were scored across his palm. He gazed at the hand, flexing his fingers, as if he enjoyed the pain.

I hoped he hated every moment of it.

The cloak had masked his form. His shoulders were broad, but while he was strong, he was also wiry, as if he hadn't eaten a proper meal in several months.

He grabbed the corner of his cloak and wiped at the blood on his hand.

"You'll want to have a healer look at that," I muttered.

He turned back to face the wall, pulling his stained glove over his hand again. "Eat."

"No."

"Then be silent," he growled, whirling to face me. "You are standing, all your limbs attached, because I decided it would be so. But be warned: Her Highness needs you alive, nothing more."

I clenched my jaw.

But the anger melted from his tone when he spoke again. "If you wish to sleep, the bed is yours," he said, gesturing to it.

I didn't move. He walked over and took a seat at the table but didn't eat; he simply stared at the crackling fire.

Despair made my hands shake. How long would I be here? What could the Queen of Kryllian possibly want with me? How much time did I have before they realized I was useless and got rid of me?

I shook my head. If they thought I had information, they were wrong—but I bore no disillusion that they would believe me. Torture was likely in my near future. Then death when they realized I was useless. Guess I wouldn't have to worry about competing against my brothers after all.

I stormed to the bed and buried myself under the blankets. To my surprise, they were warmer than I'd imagined. The bed itself was comfortable, too. I hated how everything was designed to make me forget I was a prisoner.

Well, everything except the tall figure, clad in black, sitting stoic and silent at the table.

12

THERE WAS NO MORNING LIGHT TO WAKE ME, SO I HAD NO clue how long I'd slept. But when I sat up, the Hellbringer was in the same spot he'd been in when I fell asleep. The fire, however, was barely embers. Torches on the walls had been lit to make up for the missing light source.

For a minute the Hellbringer didn't move. Perhaps he was sleeping, his eyes closed beneath the mask. I shut my eyes tight and opened them again, half hoping the scene around me would dissolve, replaced by snow-covered mountains and green pines.

It was useless. I swallowed the sour taste of anguish in my mouth, the memory of the day before. Had it only been one day?

"Good, you're awake." The deep voice echoed against the walls and the masked, black-clad figure stood and turned to face me. "Are you ready to begin?"

Sitting up, I glanced at him, then began re-braiding my hair tightly to my scalp. One stray lock, too short to stay back, fell in front of my eyes. "Begin what, exactly?"

He strolled to the hooks on the wall. I watched with morbid curiosity as he drew his sword from its sheath. Holding it up in the torchlight, the Hellbringer studied the flame reflected back at him. "Training."

"Training? What training?"

He extended his sword to point to where mine rested next to me on the bed. I'd kept my hand tight around the hilt while I slept, in case he tried anything. Not that I could do much against his god-touch. Surprisingly enough, he kept true to his word—he hadn't attempted to kill me so far.

"*Combat* training?"

He nodded once, beckoning me to stand. I didn't move. Surely there was an ulterior motive here. Until I understood his endgame, I wasn't willing to play along.

"Why would you train me?" I asked, folding my arms across my chest. "We're on different sides of the war."

He chuckled, and the sound reverberated through my bones. "Not for much longer," he said. "My queen hopes to make a truce with your nation."

Good luck.

"A truce? Your queen must be foolish if she thinks my father will consider anything but her surrender."

He nodded. "Tell you what. If you train with me today, I'll tell you why I brought you here. And everything else you want to know."

Everything?

I frowned, wishing I wasn't tempted by the offer. "How do I know I can trust you?"

The mask was impassive, but I swore I heard something catch in his voice as he said, "You will hear no lies from me. I promise you."

My stomach soured at the prospect of caving to his demands, but I was too curious to remain on the bed. Despite my predicament as his captive, the Hellbringer's words rang with sincerity. I stood, grabbing the hilt of my sword as I went.

"What is your weapon of choice?" he asked, moving forward to examine my sword more closely. He gestured with one hand and I obliged, holding up the blade for him to study.

"Sword, I guess? Never fought with anything else."

"May I?" I handed him the sword, hoping he didn't kill me with it. His gloved hand dwarfed the dull steel, and I was reminded viscerally of the night before, when I'd watched his blood run down the metal. Some of it still stained the weapon, now a dull rust red. "Your blade is subpar at best. A strong strike in the right place would shatter the metal. We'll need to find you a more suitable weapon. What do your brothers fight with?"

I swallowed down the irritation pushing to the surface. We hadn't been at it for a whole minute and he'd already insulted the weapon I'd learned on. The one I'd chosen myself and guarded with my life. "I'll have you know that subpar blade has saved my life on more than one occasion."

"I don't doubt it." He tilted his head slightly, and I knew his focus had been drawn from the blade to me. I crossed my arms. "In many situations, the weapon matters far less than the one wielding it."

Was that . . . a compliment?

It was too soon to tell. I pursed my lips, knowing my suspicion was clearly written across my face. I hadn't answered his question, though. Eager to change the subject, I considered each of my brothers.

"Erik uses a greatsword." I ticked them off on my fingers. "Frode has two long knives—not exactly daggers. I'm not sure what they're called. Jac is best with a bow and arrow, but in close-range fighting he prefers to transform into a beast and use his claws as his weapons. And Björn uses a sword like mine. I think he throws daggers on occasion, too."

I watched closely as he twisted my sword and studied the hilt. He ran a careful gloved hand over the worn leather, which had warped slightly from my years of practice with it. "We could forge you another kind of weapon if you'd like, but since you already have a sword, I assume you're probably most comfortable with it."

It wasn't a question, but I knew he was waiting for an answer regardless. "Hard to say. I can't imagine fighting with anything else. I know how to use the sword, though. If I needed to learn another weapon, I'd be starting from the beginning."

He wrapped a hand around the blade again and extended the sword to me, hilt first. I took it, wondering what a newer version would look like in my hands. Whether the familiar grip of this one would be something I missed. "A sword is versatile. I think it will be your best option, considering your brothers' weapons of choice," he said.

"My best option for the Trials." I rubbed a thumb against the hilt of my sword. "You know I'm competing."

The Hellbringer's chuckle was dark. "The whole world knows by now, Princess. Now, prepare to spar."

I took a deep breath. He was trying to bait me by calling me *princess*, and it was effective. He didn't say it like a fact, even though it was. He said it like an insult.

The worst part was that I didn't blame him.

"I've already been trained, you know," I said, facing him and planting my feet in position. My words were meant to give me confidence but had no effect. "I'm not bad."

"Who taught you?" he asked, observing my stance. "Your feet are all wrong."

When I knew my death was not imminent, he was much less frightening. Just annoying. "My friends."

"Not your brothers?" He moved close to me, sheathing his sword so he could readjust my stance.

I flinched as his gloved fingers touched me. He could sense it—he stilled for a moment and the mask tilted toward me, as if to ask permission before continuing. I nodded, refusing to look at his visage, ignoring the whiff of pine that strayed from him. "No. Why would my brothers teach me anything?"

He must have heard the bitter note in my voice. I was grateful he was focused on my feet so I couldn't look at the mask's blank stare. "Your family is different than most."

I grunted an affirmation, too annoyed to be grateful for his gentle touch. The Hellbringer stood straight again and stepped back to survey my stance. The room was significantly colder when he stood far away. "Better," he said.

"I don't like it," I muttered. "It feels weird."

"It feels *right*," he corrected.

I rolled my eyes.

"Your hands are fine," he conceded. He spread his arms. "Now come and get me."

I relaxed. "Is this a joke? You don't have your weapon out. And you're wearing no armor."

"You would refuse the chance to run a blade through my heart?"

Yeah, right. He'd proven already that he wouldn't let me kill him no matter how hard I tried. But I sensed a smirk under the mask and my irritation made me clench my jaw.

I lunged forward, swinging my blade with my momentum. To my surprise, it failed to connect with flesh.

He had *dodged* my swipe. Flustered, I turned. *Fine. Faster, then.*

I moved, nimble on my feet, my blade sailing through the air, catching the torchlight as it flew. At no point did the Hellbringer see fit to parry, much less to unsheathe his own weapon. Instead, he stepped lightly away from each attempt I made to wound him. Like a shadow slipping between flickering flames, he moved with the ease and grace of a wolf.

With every missed swing, a heavy anger formed in the pit of my stomach. After ten minutes of no success, I finally screamed wordlessly and hurled my sword at him.

He stepped to the side. The blade clattered against the wall.

I turned away, grinding my nails into my hair.

"You need work," he commented. "But you're better than I expected."

I lunged blindly, this time with my hand pulled into a fist.

His own gloved hand reached out and caught my wrist. The strength of his hand was like iron; try as I might, I couldn't pull away.

"First rule," he growled, his mechanical voice echoing slightly off the wall. "Never fight angry."

I tugged my hand and he let go, leaving me to pick up my blade and pull a lantern from its hook.

"Where are you going?"

"I'm leaving." I stormed out the door, back into the corridors winding through the building.

He didn't follow me.

◆ ◆ ◆ ◆ ◆

THE HALLWAYS BLURRED TOGETHER IN A SWIRL OF BLACK AND gray, shadows and dark metal. My boots pounded a constant echo against the floor. I tried to keep my breathing steady, but as thoughts ran through my mind, it turned more ragged.

Anger built in my stomach, pounding to the beating of my heart. Sweat collected on my brow despite the frigid cold, and I reached a hand to wipe it out of my eyes. I took another left.

Better than I expected. The Hellbringer's comment, made with no sarcasm or jest, only pure logic, made me seethe.

When I turned too fast, my foot caught on a corner and I flew forward, the heels of my hands landing roughly on the metal floor. The lantern clattered to the ground and rolled away from me.

The anger heated to boiling in me and I screamed.

The sound wrenched itself from me. I had no control over it; it bounced off every wall, containing every ounce of what I felt.

You are in a prison with a madman and no one is coming for you.

Father had brought me to the front lines in the hopes I'd be killed. We hadn't even made it there before I was taken. Every day, I was one step closer to my demise, but the cruelest part of being with the Hellbringer was never knowing when it was coming.

Any plans the Kryllian Queen had for me would end in my death. To keep me alive would be a child's mistake.

No one is coming for you.

Finally, the echo of my scream faded into silence, and I clenched my jaw until pain radiated through my face. I looked up at where the light of the lantern flowed to the top of the ceiling. In front of me, the hallway extended into darkness so thick, it could have been a dead end. The place was a maze, impossible to navigate. And I was only on the bottom floor—I'd ignored the ascending stairs I'd passed while I ran.

"What are you doing?"

I wasn't surprised to hear the Hellbringer behind me, but when the grinding voice softened slightly through its distortion, I stiffened.

Sympathy from a monster?

"Trying to get away from you." I didn't turn to face him, but the lantern caught his shadow and threw it against the wall. I could see my own shadow, reflecting where I sat on my knees, shaking from the cold burrowing deep into my bones. He towered over me.

Something inside of me broke; I couldn't define it, but I felt every ounce of will leave me. I had been wandering the endless hallways for what must have been an hour. I was no closer to escape.

You are in a prison with a madman and no one is coming for you.

"All of the exits in this prison have been sealed entirely," the Hellbringer said. "Doors that used to open have been welded shut. The locks on the few doors with functioning mechanisms are impossible to pick. I've seen to it myself."

I stared at the ground, unmoving.

"The only way in or out is for my soldier to take us. This location is hidden from all but her."

Frode would look. So would Jac. If they could get away from Father for long enough to search. But if what my captor said was true—and I suspected it was—then they would have no success.

I took the shaking part of me and forced it back into the pit of my stomach. Pushed the image of Frode's and Freja's faces far into the recesses of my mind. "It doesn't matter," I whispered. "It wouldn't make a difference anyway."

There was a long beat of silence, broken only by the crackling of the lantern's fire.

"Go away," I said. It would be better to die of starvation in the darkness.

His lantern was held outstretched as he stared at me. There was nothing behind the eyes of the mask.

What did he see when he looked at me? A broken princess, desperate to free her people and impossibly far from achieving that goal?

Did he pity me?

I was too numb to care.

He didn't speak. When I looked up again, I was alone.

◆ ◆ ◆ ◆ ◆

KEEPING TIME WAS IMPOSSIBLE WITHIN THE PRISON, BUT I ASSUMED several hours had passed. And I'd spent all of them wandering, hoping to find a shred of evidence the Hellbringer had been lying, and there was a way to escape. I'd come upon several doors, many of which appeared to lead outside, but they wouldn't budge. Many of them were melted along the edges, the frames indeed welded shut.

Only one door had seemed usable in any way. I made a mental note to come back with tools to try picking the lock. Assuming I could find tools, of course.

I clutched my arms around myself. My teeth had been chattering long enough my jaw hurt, but I wasn't going back to him. I couldn't. I would rather die here in the dark and the cold than face the Hellbringer again.

Because then I'd have to admit I needed him to save me.

The lantern light danced in front of me as I forced step after step into the gray darkness. Shivers overtook my every movement. Occasionally the metal was dulled and dented where something heavy had swung into the walls. The prison told a visual story, like scars on skin.

If I could escape, then it wouldn't matter if no one was coming to find me. I would save myself. The way I always had before.

Step after step I continued walking, finding several dead ends and turning back around to locate the next available path. I knew I was hopelessly lost, but the moment I admitted it to myself, fear would come creeping in. So instead I kept walking.

That is, until the cold sank far enough into my bones that my knees groaned and gave out.

I let out a grunt as I fell. The lantern's delicate glass covering shattered into pieces as it hit the ground again, and I felt a shard sink into my palm. My tongue was numb from the frigidity, so I couldn't swear.

Darkness. It soothed me. I faded in and out, in and out of consciousness.

I was dying.

The fear I'd expected didn't come. Instead, a sigh of relief covered me like a blanket, and my body relaxed. *Finally.*

I slipped into the dark.

13

THOUSANDS OF NEEDLES PUNCTURED MY SKIN.

My mouth was frozen shut, making releasing a string of curses impossible. A whimper escaped me, and I scowled. The god-forsaken princess didn't *whimper*.

I opened my eyes, only to be blinded, so I slammed them shut again. Every part of me ached.

Memory of my last moments of consciousness came flooding back, and shock pulled my jaw open. "Why aren't I dead?"

I opened my eyes again and put a frigid hand over my mouth. The sound that had emerged was not my own voice. It sounded like it belonged to a creature from someone's nightmares.

When my eyes finally adjusted, I saw the tall figure in black moving around the room. "That would be my fault," the Hellbringer confirmed. "Did you think you weren't being followed?"

There was no anger left in me, only cold. And resignation. I swallowed, trying to wet my dry throat, but only succeeded in launching myself into a fit of coughing that made my lungs hurt.

The Hellbringer came over to me and held out my gloves. Reluctant as I was to accept his favors, he'd put them by the fire, so they were warm. I pulled them on and then took the mug he offered me, filled with steaming-hot tea.

"Thanks," I muttered.

"You're an idiot," he replied. "And I should have let you die."

I scowled. "Why didn't you? I'd rather be dead than used as a bargaining chip." The first sip of tea burned my lips, but I forced myself to swallow it. I felt it travel all the way down my throat.

The Hellbringer sat at the table and gazed at the fire for several minutes while I continued to sip the tea. Soon enough, the pins and needles began to fade from my skin and I sighed, grateful to be warm again.

Finally he spoke. "We made a bargain," he said. "And you fulfilled your end of the deal. So now I'll tell you why you're here."

I crossed my arms over my chest and set the mug on the bed next to me.

"I told you my queen is looking to secure a truce," he began. "This is true. But she does not want to broach the matter with your father. That would be a fool's errand. Instead, she hopes to sign a treaty with you."

It startled me enough that I sat up. "With *me*?" I frowned. "For that to work, I would have to be . . ."

He nodded curtly. "Queen of Bhorglid. Yes."

Everything came to a standstill. "You want to instate me as queen," I breathed. "You're training me to win the Trials." I stared at him, mind blank. "I don't understand. She could find a more powerful ally with one of my brothers. Frode, or Jac. They're god-touched, but they want to end the war, too. It doesn't make sense to choose me."

He shrugged, staring at the flickering flames. "You're right," he said. "And I told her as much. But she refused to listen. She has her heart set on you."

Set . . . on me? A godforsaken? I frowned. "This doesn't make sense."

Finally he glanced over. "I of all people should know. The best course of action would be ending the war by taking Bhorglid and installing me on that throne. It accomplishes the same purpose of forming an alliance, and at least I'd have earned the position. But instead she insists it be you."

My heart skipped a beat. The Hellbringer was jealous of *me*. "Why wouldn't she give it to you?"

He slammed his fists on the table. I flinched back. "I don't *know*!" His voice was twisted with distortion.

I stared at him, heart pounding, wondering if I should flee into the maze of halls. Who knew what the Hellbringer would do when he was angry? All he had to do was think about killing me and I would be dead. That part was terrifying enough. But imagining his gloved hands around my throat?

I shivered, and not from the cold.

He stood to pace, and I pulled the blanket up to my shoulders. The smaller I appeared, the better. But curiosity burned at my lips, and I spoke, though every instinct screamed at me not to.

"Why do you want to be king? And in Bhorglid of all places?"

He didn't answer, merely paced in silence for a long time. My eyes traced his path back and forth in front of the fireplace.

Seemed I wasn't getting an answer to that question. "Is this why you were following me?" I asked. His head snapped around to face me. "In Bhorglid?" He was silent for a moment, so I pressed on. "You could have taken me then. Why did you wait until now?"

He shrugged. "The queen expected you to make your way into the Trials, but she couldn't be entirely sure. She asked me to wait until you were in the competition for certain before approaching you. Until then, my orders were to observe. Nothing more."

I resisted the urge to roll my eyes. "At any point, did it cross your mind that it would have been far more effective to spy on me without your whole"—I made a sweeping gesture to encompass him from head to toe—"costume?"

He growled, and with the voice distortion it was a menacing sound. But I refused to shrink back. I was determined to get answers. One answer in particular.

Why would the Queen of Kryllian want me to win the throne?

The question danced in front of me as if to taunt me. I couldn't begin to imagine the queen's motives. I'd never learned anything about her, much less met her. My father openly hated her, which only guaranteed the things he'd said about her in passing probably weren't true. The Hellbringer seemed reluctant to elaborate on the queen's specific plans for me, but perhaps with time he would tell me more.

More importantly, the Hellbringer had unknowingly confirmed what he told me earlier: he wasn't going to kill me. At least, he wasn't *supposed* to kill me.

It didn't mean I trusted him, though. My desire to escape wasn't waning, despite his admission of a bigger plan. Ending the war would be a good thing, but did I really need the help of our most notorious adversary in order to do it? Was peace worth becoming a pawn in another ruler's hand when the Trials were over?

"What about when you're done training me?" I asked. "How do you plan to return me to Bhorglid without getting caught?"

His pacing slowed while he replied. "I will leave you with your family before they return home."

My face twisted into an expression of distaste. "Father will be mad you didn't kill me."

The Hellbringer paused, glancing at me, before continuing his steady march. "Why would he want you dead?"

I lay back and propped my hands behind my head. "The better question is: Why *wouldn't* he want me dead? That one has a shorter answer."

Before I could continue, there was a loud pop and a cloaked Kryllian soldier appeared in front of the Hellbringer. I started, sitting up and pulling my sword closer to me.

I frowned at the weapon. I hadn't noticed my captor had left it there, easily within my grasp. My jaw tightened when I realized he didn't see me as a threat.

"Her Highness requests your presence," a feminine voice said from beneath the hood of the cloak. Her features were well hidden.

This must be the same soldier who had transported us here from the forest.

The Hellbringer's fist clenched, and I wondered for a moment if he would hit her. I cringed, waiting for the blow to come, but then he relaxed.

"Very well." He turned to me. "If you wander and get lost again, I may not be back in time to find you before you freeze."

I opened my mouth, a fiery retort on my tongue, but he extended his arm to the soldier, and they disappeared in a blink.

"Well . . ."

My voice trailed off. I looked around the space, slowly taking in everything I could see. The fireplace on my left; the entrance to the rest of the prison directly in front of me, nothing more than a spot of darkness against the flickering lanterns; to the right, the table with its two chairs and the wall shelves.

He was gone.

I glanced toward the room's exit and pondered whether to try the maze of hallways again. It didn't appear to be a promising endeavor. Either the Hellbringer was telling the truth and there honestly wasn't an accessible exit, or the winding interior was so convoluted, he didn't think I'd ever find my way out.

I sighed. My limbs were weak from my earlier attempt. Trying again would kill me.

My stomach gurgled and I realized how hungry I was. When was the last time I had eaten? Had I been here for a whole day?

With no captor to keep a watchful eye on me, I got up from the bed to explore the shelves of containers. Maybe one of them would have something familiar I could snack on.

When I put all of my weight on my knees, they buckled without warning, sending me to the ground. I groaned, my head and wrists throbbing where they had connected with solid rock. "Stupid knees," I muttered. I forced myself to rise again, keeping a hand on the bed, and was able to support my own weight this time, albeit shakily.

"You can do this," I said through gritted teeth. Several steps later, with a hand on the wall supporting me, I was close enough to pull one of the chairs toward me and sit.

I'd barely moved six feet, and yet my breath was ragged. I groaned. Where was Waddell when I needed him? The sad truth was I couldn't determine whether my inability to stand came from my earlier excursion or from hunger.

Keep going. I pushed myself up and grabbed as many jars as I could, placing them all on the table. When only four or five remained on the shelf, I sat back down, unable to support my own weight any longer.

These would do for now. I opened each one, looking for something I recognized. Each was filled with a different food: dried fruit slices, berries, nuts, seeds, oats. Nothing incredibly filling and nothing familiar, but it would have to be enough.

When the jars were empty and my hunger satiated, my energy had returned enough to look around the rest of the room. While the Hellbringer was gone, I could do some snooping. Maybe there were tools hidden somewhere. I still needed to pick the lock on the door I'd found while wandering earlier.

The space between the entrance and the furniture—where we had sparred that morning—was huge and empty. I turned my focus to the small armoire next to the bed.

I wasn't sure what to expect, but I flung the doors open, sword in one hand at the ready. I lowered my weapon when extra cloaks on hangers, folded shirts and pants, an extra pair of boots, and another warm blanket came into view.

Boring. I clicked my tongue. Not even a weapon to toy with. I closed the doors and peered under the bed.

A box. My arm was barely long enough for my fingers to graze it and pull it out, but I managed. Surely there was something incriminating in here: a severed body part or a bloody knife.

I threw the lid open to find pots and pans.

With a groan, I slid the box back underneath the bed.

Then I considered the bed itself.

I tilted my head and stared. It was a bigger bed than the one I had at home, taking up several feet with its width. Only one blanket and two pillows sat atop it—nothing extravagant. Yet the bed frame itself was dark, beautiful wood. When I glanced at the bedposts, I noticed they were carved with different designs.

Sitting up, I scooted over to the nearest one. It was adorned with a delicate carving of the seaside, a sunrise peeking over the horizon. The others were slightly familiar: a forest of pines, falling snow, a mountain range. They'd clearly been done by a careful hand, the scenes filled with a sentimentality I hadn't expected to find in a prison.

For the first time, I found myself wondering if he always lived here. Did he sleep separately from his legion? Or was this place only for prisoners?

No. It was too nice to be used for just prisoners. And the carvings were too sentimental to be left behind. These had to be his living quarters.

But . . . if I was the one being held captive, why did he allow me to sleep on the bed?

It didn't take long to go through everything in the room. The space was big but mostly empty, filled only with necessities. No incriminating secrets or interesting things for me to bother the Hellbringer about when he returned. Only more questions and no answers.

I sighed and fell back onto the bed. It was going to be a long day.

◆ ◆ ◆ ◆ ◆

"FINALLY!" I SHOUTED WHEN THE HELLBRINGER RETURNED. "IT'S been *hours*. I've been bored out of my mind."

The teleporting soldier vanished as quickly as she had appeared, not sparing me a glance as she left my captor there. The hideous mask turned to face me, and I tried to keep my face blank. There was something about the carvings in the wood—the teeth and the hollow eye sockets—that made me squirm.

"You could have been practicing." The dark voice was calmer than it had been when he left, and I relaxed. I hadn't known what kind of mood the Hellbringer would offer when he returned. So far, his anger hadn't scared me, but only because I wasn't afraid of death. Now knowing he couldn't kill me, I feared other forms of torture awaited me.

"I could barely stand for several hours," I pointed out.

He shrugged and caught sight of the table, strewn with the now-empty jars. "Hungry?" he asked.

Was there a hint of sarcasm in his voice? I tried not to turn red. "Clearly."

"Good. I brought dinner." He pulled a package wrapped in papery canvas out from beneath his cloak. Wet spots soaked the wrapping, obviously not made by water. He strode over to the bed and kicked out the box I'd been rummaging through earlier to grab a heavy cast iron skillet and set it in the fireplace, on a metal shelf I hadn't noticed until then.

He peeled off his black gloves to unwrap two bright red steaks, which he tossed onto the pan. They sizzled and my stomach growled at the scent. When he wiped his hands on a cloth, I noticed his palm bore the wounds from where he had grabbed my sword. Had he not seen a Healer?

I curled my legs underneath me on the bed. "I have to say, I'm glad we aren't going to be eating nuts and berries the entire time I'm here."

The Hellbringer didn't respond, simply replaced his gloves with a pair from the armoire and grabbed some spices from the shelves, seasoning the meat profusely.

You're a prisoner, I reminded myself. *Not a guest or a friend. Not even an acquaintance.*

I savored every bite of the meal when it was ready. Steak was a rarity in Bhorglid, with cows being such a precious commodity. The last time I'd eaten steak had been almost ten years ago, for Erik's eighteenth birthday. I dreamed about it frequently.

When I finished my meal, the Hellbringer stood. "Take your weapon," he ordered. "We keep training."

I did as he asked. "How long is this whole training program supposed to be?" I stood in the ready stance, immediately on guard.

He sighed, dropped his own stance, and came over to adjust my feet again. "If it were up to me," he said as his warm hands moved my boots and legs, "you would already be gone."

◆ ◆ ◆ ◆ ◆

SLEEP EVADED ME. THE HELLBRINGER AND I HAD TRAINED IN near silence for the rest of the evening, speaking only when he needed to adjust my form or instruct me to swing differently. I had the feeling my time in captivity was going to be long, arduous, and lonely.

No matter. I was used to being ignored at home. This should be no different.

So why couldn't I stop thinking about my captor?

Reaching a hand beneath my pillow, I rubbed my thumb against the crowbar I'd discovered when I searched the room earlier. The closest thing to a lockpick. It would have to do. Next time I had the chance to wander, I'd make my way back to the locked door and try to get out that way. If my limited sense of direction was correct, the door wasn't too far from this room.

My mind conjured an image of being caught breaking out—of being brought back here and tied to a chair, tortured in some nameless way that left me screaming.

I rolled over in the bed, now facing away from the Hellbringer, and pushed the thought away.

There. If I couldn't see him, that would help.

The events of the day simmered in my mind: Kryllian royalty helping me succeed to the throne of Bhorglid. I'd tried to find a loophole, hoping to discover the trick proving it was a trap, but I couldn't. At least, not yet.

The Queen of Kryllian wanted to help me win the Bloodshed Trials. All because she wanted me on the throne so we could negotiate a truce. It was too good to be true.

I didn't know anything about Kryllian politics. Did they want to end the war? Or did she believe by putting a godforsaken ruler in place, she would be able to conquer Bhorglid more easily?

I wouldn't become a pawn for a power-hungry ruler again.

Stuck here, investigating the queen's true motives was impossible. I had no clue what things were like in Kryllian. My father's judgments couldn't be trusted and the Hellbringer wasn't exactly unbiased.

If she was so desperate for me to win the Trials, why did the Hellbringer have to be the one who trained me? Surely she had dozens of soldiers good enough. And instead of sending a capable one, she sent one who was utterly deadly.

And incredibly irritating.

Could he teach me to be anything but a murderer? Or was this going to turn me into a monster, too?

I did believe one thing he said, though—he was not going to kill me. He'd had the chance plenty of times and yet here I was. Why would he have waited this long if the plan was to murder me?

I glanced at where he sat next to the fire, his back against the wall, head tilted down. Was he asleep? Or was he watching me look him over?

Our game of cat and mouse, captor and captive, was merely a tug-of-war with a thread of power. Not magic, no—control.

My eyes fluttered closed as exhaustion sank its claws deep. I knew, as dread mounted within me, that the next five weeks until the Trials began were going to be utter hell.

"YOU COULD BE SLEEPING, YOU KNOW."

I jumped and whirled to see the Hellbringer studying me, his entire visage obscured by the darkness. My racing heartbeat began to slow slightly, fear replaced with annoyance. "Can't a girl at least make a decent escape attempt without being rudely interrupted?"

The crowbar I found yesterday had thus far been of absolutely no use in trying to unlatch the mysterious door at the end of the long hallway. This abandoned prison shouldn't have been so difficult to escape, and yet the Hellbringer hadn't truly interrupted any real progress.

"Normally, yes. But we have places to be this morning."

I frowned. If my calculations were correct, it was still far too early for the sun to have risen—not that either of us would know if it did. Maybe the lack of light was messing with my brain. "It's too early to be training."

Did I catch the hint of a laugh in his next words? "If it's too early to be training, then it's too early for an escape attempt."

I threw the crowbar at the Hellbringer half-heartedly. He caught it in one hand. "Then what is so urgent it needs to be done right now?"

"Traveling to the nearest forge to make you a better blade." He motioned for me to stand.

Exhaustion, sore knees, and my unsuccessful escape attempt had made me irritable. I didn't move. "Neither of us wants to be here. Can't you take me back to the front?"

"No." He stepped forward and nudged me with the toe of his boot. "Get up."

Groaning, I obeyed. My joints ached with stiffness from kneeling in such an awkward position for so long in the frigid cold. At least I'd been smart enough to bring my cloak this time around.

"Come on." The Hellbringer turned and began walking toward the dim glow of the main room. "Mira is waiting for us."

The teleporter glared at me from beneath her hood when we stepped back into the firelight. The Hellbringer adjusted the pack slung over his shoulder. "Make sure you have everything. We'll be gone for a few days."

I grabbed my gloves and buckled my sheath and sword back onto my belt. "Ready."

"Then let's go. Give Mira your wrist."

Mira's blond hair shone in the firelight and she extended her hand to me. I tried to hide my grimace—teleporting had been bad enough the first time and I wasn't keen to do it again. But the Hellbringer nodded and in a flash we were off.

It was impossible to tell whether I lost my balance landing in two feet of snow or if Mira pushed me slightly upon landing. Either way, I landed face-first in the ice-cold powder. "Fuck this," I snarled, pushing back to my feet to scowl at the Hellbringer. His companion was already gone. "Where's the damn forge?"

I looked around, hoping to see something, anything, recognizable. The landscape was all familiar, but not in the way I wanted. The same pine trees and thick blanket of snow that covered the northern half of Bhorglid surrounded us on all sides. To my left stood the foothills of a mountain range that towered over us, the peaks breaking up the gray clouds dominating the sky and allowing an occasional rising sunray to peek through.

The northern wastelands stretched out for miles in either direction. Gusts of wind whistled, tossing loose snow up and around us. A good weather day, all things considered. I suspected the Hellbringer had taken me farther north when he kidnapped me from the battlefield, but we could be anywhere now. It was all indistinguishable when the cities fell from view.

He pointed to the mountain in the distance. "That way. I hope you're prepared—we have a long hike ahead of us."

I followed the sound of his boots in the snow. Hiking in these conditions was not going to be enjoyable. "Your soldier couldn't have dropped us off any closer?"

"No."

My breath fogged out in front of me in the dawn when I huffed. I'd spent most of the night awake in the dim firelight, my frustration growing in my chest. He didn't want to be here, training me. He was only doing it because he'd been ordered to. And now it seemed he was trying to make it as difficult as possible for both of us.

"I really hate you," I told him, allowing the venom in my voice to seep through. It radiated over the snow, echoing slightly and catching in the next gust of wind. I wanted him to feel it, wanted the words to find the chink in his armor and pierce straight through the heart.

But I wasn't surprised when his only reply was "You and everyone else, Princess."

◆ ◆ ◆ ◆ ◆

THREE HOURS OF WALKING LATER, THE MOUNTAINS APPEARED just as far as when we'd started. There was no telling how far the trail of footprints we left behind extended. It could be miles for all I knew. But it certainly didn't feel like we'd made any progress, and the exhaustion of not sleeping was catching up to me.

I gnawed on a stick of dried meat the Hellbringer had broken out of his pack a while ago. My nose was utterly numb and I was shocked my ears hadn't fallen off, abandoned in the snow behind us somewhere. And since my companion wasn't keen on conversation, I felt like a petulant child when every half an hour I asked, "How much farther?"

He responded to my current inquiry the same way he had all the others. "A ways."

I slowed my pace, the piece of dried meat finished, and glared at his back. "That doesn't answer my question."

My retort was met with silence. I don't know what I expected. The Hellbringer had shown me exactly who he was and exactly what he thought of me. I'd spent most of the night tossing and turning, wishing that if he hated me so much, he would have refused this job. Or even left me stranded in the snow. Because discovering a formidable ally shouldn't have felt the same as dealing with the worst of my brothers.

My patience snapped, worn thin by the cold, the hunger gnawing at my stomach, and the uncertainty of knowing when this trek would end. I stopped walking. I'd been taken from the front no more than two days ago and I was already at my wit's end with my captor. "What is the point of this?"

The Hellbringer glanced back over his shoulder, but didn't stop or fully turn around. "To make you a weapon. One that actually has a chance of defeating your brothers." The rest of his words remained unspoken, but I heard them clear as day regardless. *Are you daft?*

My captivity was wearing on me, but I was confident I knew what I was doing when I retorted, "If you think you deserve Bhorglid's throne so badly, then kill me." I held my arms out.

At this, he did turn, surveying my position with no readable emotion in his voice. "Believe me, I wish I could."

"You can. Pretend it was an accident," I snarled, snow crackling beneath my boots as I moved toward him. He stilled, like a prey animal hiding from a predator, aware it had been seen but unable to overcome its basest instincts. When I reached him, I pulled my sword from its sheath in one fluid movement, pressing the hilt to his chest. With only inches between us, I lowered my voice to a whisper. "Tell them I fell on my own damn weapon."

I stared into the eye sockets of the wolf skull, wondering what he saw in my face. I hoped it was the fury of my helplessness at being his prisoner, the rage of being treated by my enemy as if I were less-than. The Hellbringer made it clear he had no interest in helping me; he did it because his queen had ordered him to. I couldn't change that.

He made no move to take the weapon from me.

"I'm more than aware you don't want to be here." I said every word slowly, deliberately. There would be no misunderstandings on my watch. "I don't either, in case my escape attempt at the crack of dawn didn't make that utterly clear to you. But I'm not going to stand for you treating me like mud under your boot. If you can't manage to act like we're equals despite your godtouch and my complete lack of magic, then this is where we part ways."

For a moment we stood there, the only sound the wind in my ears. I didn't move my weapon, leaving the hilt there, ready for him to take. He didn't need it to kill me. But his queen had given orders to keep me alive, and the Hellbringer appeared to be her obedient servant, so I wasn't truly worried.

"You'd die on your own out here." His murmur, distorted through the mask, was still gentle somehow. "I estimate you'd make it an hour before you came crawling back."

I shrugged. "You think I'm going to die in the Trials. So does it matter whether I die now—by your hand or the wastes'—or later?"

His shoulders stiffened, and despite the many layers he was wearing, I saw it. He'd tried to call my bluff, tried to make me admit

I wanted to live more than I wanted to be rid of his sorry attitude. And in return I'd called his bluff right back.

Still, my heart sank a bit knowing the truth. He thought his task was useless, that training me was for naught. At the end of it all, he expected me to be nothing more than a lifeless body on the arena floor.

I smiled without humor. He was much taller than me, and at this close range I had to tilt my head back to look into the skull eyes of the mask. Was he afraid to move because he worried he would kill me if he did? It was entirely possible. With only a twist of his wrist, the blade would plunge through me irrevocably. There would be no time to get me to a healer before I bled out in the cold. And yet I felt like I'd pinned a moth by the wings with only my gaze.

He was listening. Caught in the truth. It made me all the more powerful.

"Here's how this is going to work." Gods be damned if he thought I was going to sit patiently and let him act superior when my life was the one on the line in the first place. "If you want me to continue on with you, there are two requirements. The first is that you convince yourself—even if you believe it's a lie—that I am going to win the Trials. No matter what happens in the future, you have to pretend. Understand?"

I was met with only the rush of wind in my ears, and I took it for an answer.

"Good. Next, I need you to understand that you're being an absolute asshole. I know it's part of your natural charm, but I'm sick of it. So, Hellbringer"—I pulled my arm away from him, ignoring the warmth in my fingers and wishing the memory of his heartbeat wasn't pressed permanently into my knuckles—"tell me something true."

My last command seemed to bring him back to himself. For a long moment there was only stillness and silence.

"Something true?"

I nodded. "Don't fling an insult at me. Don't say something vague just to get under my skin. If this is going to work, then you need to be honest with me. So tell me something true."

I waited with bated breath. The next moments would decide whether I followed him the rest of the way to the forge willingly or if he'd have to drag me kicking and screaming.

"Mira dropped us off so far because no one knows the true location of this forge but me." His hands flexed at his sides. I wasn't sure what it meant or what he was feeling beneath his monotone voice. "It's abandoned."

Not just any truth, but the one I so desperately needed to hear. The one that eased my suspicions. He wasn't trying to kill me and leave me for dead out here, wasn't trying to make things harder on me than they needed to be. There was a legitimate reason for our long trek.

My next thought soured my relief. *He hates you so much, he couldn't even tell you that until you gave him the chance to kill you and make it look like an accident.*

I stepped forward, smiling thinly, and clapped a palm across his chest. "See?" I raised an eyebrow. "That wasn't so bad, was it?"

I might have been imagining it, but I could have sworn a shiver ran up his spine before he turned and walked onward. "An hour and a half before we arrive," he said gruffly.

Readjusting my gloves, I followed. If I'd known telling him to kill me would change his attitude so significantly, I'd have done it the moment I met him.

◆ ◆ ◆ ◆ ◆

TRUE TO HIS WORD, WE ARRIVED AT THE FORGE AFTER NINETY more minutes of trudging through the snow.

It reminded me of the prison we were staying in. The architecture was obviously from the same time period—the slate-gray metal of the prison also made up the walls of the forge. The biggest difference was that the forge was built into the side of the mountain, woven into cave walls so seamlessly that, without studying them closely, the melding of metal and stone might have gone unnoticed.

We stepped through the open entrance, stretched wide like a gash against the mountain, and the world dimmed. I didn't realize how loud the wind whistling in my ears was until it vanished. I could hear my own breathing again, the sound of my own thoughts like music.

There were no doors to close behind us and snow followed our footsteps inside. The ceilings were tall, held up by strong beams of wood reinforced with metal in some places. I wondered how the material survived the damp weather.

The Hellbringer moved to the wall and lit a lantern, pulling it from where it hung and handing it to me. When his gloved hand brushed against my own, a fresh patch of goose bumps appeared on my arm—and not from the cold. I staunchly ignored it. He gave himself his own light before gesturing for me to follow him.

I obliged without complaint. We hadn't spoken any more on our trek here, but he'd at least glanced back every few minutes to make sure I hadn't died in the snow behind him. *Generous of him*, I thought now as we continued further into the cave lined with evidence of man's conquering. The pathways twisted and turned and I wondered how much of the cavern was man-made, carved away from the rock by godtouched.

"How long has this forge been here?" I asked as we moved into a bigger, more open part of the cavern. The ceiling was higher here and the temperature dropped. A quick glance upward explained it—there was a giant hole in the ceiling, exposing the clouded sky. A few flakes of falling snow drifted down through it, landing in a small pile on top of a giant firepit positioned in the center of the room.

The Hellbringer grabbed a broom leaning against one of the walls and began using it to brush the snow off the firepit. "Not sure. I found it ten years ago or so, long after it was abandoned."

Why would there be a fully functional forge abandoned in the northern wastes of Bhorglid? I frowned and walked a circle around the edge of the room, studying the dusty equipment. The Hellbringer had obviously made improvements to what he found all those years ago—the wall had an impressive number of hammers and anvils hung on it, obviously curated by a careful hand. But the existence of the structure itself bothered me.

Especially because the Hellbringer had no reason to be wandering the Bhorglid wastes ten years ago, before the war even started.

"We're in Bhorglid still, right?" I asked, glancing over at him. Faste was the only country touching ours, but their northern border didn't extend as far. When the Fjordlands were first divided, no one had wanted to claim the desolate land. Callum and Arraya eventually brought it into Bhorglid, thinking the extended territory would increase their power. If we weren't in Bhorglid, we had to be outside of the Fjordlands for it to be this cold.

He continued to clean off the firepit. "Where else in the world is this damn cold? Yes, we're still in Bhorglid."

It was difficult not to imagine a Hellbringer of ten years ago stumbling upon this place. It was impossible to tell his age now, but he couldn't be much older than Erik. Was he a gangly teenager, taking shelter from a blizzard in the nearest cave he could find? Had the helmet been too big for his features back then?

A crackle made known the fire in the center of the forge was coming back to life. The Hellbringer retreated from the tiny flame he'd coaxed to grab larger logs off a pile behind him, carefully adjusting them with no regard for the heat.

"You're a dancer."

I jumped when he spoke, startled gaze shifting to his face. I'd been utterly absorbed by the fire, wondering what my brothers might be up to now that I was gone. "What?"

He didn't look at me, merely continued working. "You're a dancer. What kind?"

"How do you know that?"

He sat back on his heels and brushed soot and wood shavings off his gloves. "I spent a long time watching you. I was there in the tavern when you found out your friend had been conscripted. And when the other one was arrested."

My mouth twisted at the realization. How many of my private moments had he observed with me none the wiser? "Without the mask, I assume," I said drily, stepping forward to observe the preparations he was making.

The Hellbringer had swept the snow from the firepit into a large bucket earlier. Now, he moved it next to the fire, keeping it far enough away that it wouldn't melt easily. It was obvious he knew this space well. None of his movements revealed uncertainty. Something unfamiliar swooped in my stomach at his confidence, his competence. "Good assumption."

"Why even bother with the mask?" I asked. His next acquisition was a table on which he placed a large . . . anvil? I wasn't sure what to call it. I forced my eyes to remain on his hands, nimbly arranging tools. If I looked at his face, he would notice the flush of my cheeks. A flush I didn't want to think about or rationalize.

"So that I can do things like spy on you without being noticed. You think your bartender friend would have let the Hellbringer walk into his tavern without a fuss otherwise?"

"You do a lot of reconnaissance work, then."

The Hellbringer shrugged as he took off his cloak and tossed it to the edge of the room. "Enough."

"Why ask about my dancing if you already knew?"

He assembled materials on the table. I moved forward, curious. Hammers and long metal tongs. A small assortment of broken sword blades. I wondered who had taught him to forge in the first place. "I asked because it might help your fighting if you think of it as a dance. Many of the steps to some dances are similar to the footwork and positions. Like dancing, swordfighting uses every muscle. Both are underappreciated arts. As part of your training, we could dance a bit."

I choked on a laugh. "Are you serious?"

He moved a strange contraption over to the fire, hooked a cast-iron bucket onto it, and then placed the broken blades inside. "I'm always serious."

The inside of the cave was beginning to grow warm, and I discarded my own cloak, trying to decipher his new motive. The thought of teaching the Hellbringer to dance was utterly ridiculous—but then again, the man flowed like water when I tried to nick him with my sword yesterday. Maybe he wouldn't be half bad.

"I don't think that's a good idea," I finally answered him. I gestured to the pot of melting steel. "Can you explain what you're doing? I'd like to have an idea of what I'm getting into before I handle scorching-hot metal."

He twisted sharply to look at me. "You'll only be watching. I'll be doing the forging."

I scowled. "Nice try. If this is the blade I'll be using to kill my brothers, then it will be made with my own two hands—no one else's."

"You think I'd sabotage you? There are far easier ways to do so than by tampering with your sword, especially since I'll be spending the next month teaching you how to use it properly."

"I don't think you're going to sabotage it." Now, I frowned. Should I be worried about treachery? "I want to learn. I want to forge my own weapon. I don't want you doing it for me."

For a long, unbreakable moment, he was silent. Finally, he nodded. "Fine. But it's backbreaking work. You can do all of it or none of it. No in-between."

I smiled. "Let's do this, then."

◆   ◆   ◆   ◆   ◆

HE WASN'T WRONG ABOUT IT BEING BACKBREAKING.

In truth, it was the most physically strenuous thing I'd ever done. But the budding truce hovering between us made it bearable. The once-aggravating Hellbringer turned patient in the face of a challenge, especially one that could be hammered into submission.

"Is this the secret to controlling aggression?" I panted, lifting the mallet in my hand to bring it down again on the newborn blade held in the tongs.

The Hellbringer, who was shaping a dagger on another anvil he'd brought over to the working area, huffed a laugh. "I suppose."

My limbs shook and sweat poured down my face as I hit the metal over and over, the clang drowning out my thoughts. There was only the weapon in front of me, beginning to take shape, and the finished version I saw in my head. Each time the metal cooled, unmalleable once more, I returned it to the fire. The Hellbringer had kept it burning all day, steadily adding more logs to keep it hot.

I had no idea how long I worked before I needed a short rest. My clothing was damp with sweat, and while the smoke rose and drifted out the hole in the cave ceiling, I wanted to lie down in the snow and take a nap there. I put down the tools and stripped the heavy protective gloves from my hands. "I'm going to step outside for a minute to cool off."

The Hellbringer grunted in response. I rummaged through his pack for more dried meat, snagging a couple of pieces and taking the waterskin. I could refill it with snow outside, leave it to melt by the fire so we'd have enough for the rest of the day.

The path to the entrance was winding but solitary. Impossible to get lost on my way back. I wondered whether I should be offended that he didn't insist on coming with me. He truly believed I had no chance of escaping on my own.

As the late-afternoon sky came into view, I remembered again why he was right. The lightly falling snow must have continued through the day, settling into a thick crust over the powder. The mountains stretched for miles. The howl of a wolf echoed in the distance, and I sighed.

There was no war front here. Nor anywhere remotely close to here.

I relished the cold air on my face, though. My sweat froze quickly and I felt the hairs escaping from my braid stiffening. Best to be quick, then.

After draining the last of the water and refilling the flask with snow, I stepped into the shadow of a tree to relieve myself. By then I was ready to be out of the cold once more.

Without hammering steel resounding in my ears, my worries returned with a vengeance. Was Freja suffering in the prison? Was she still angry with me?

Was I still angry with her?

I sighed as I walked, uncertain of the answer. We'd both said things we didn't mean, all because our lives were falling apart around us. I didn't blame her for lashing out. I hoped she knew my reaction had been purely emotional, not vindictive.

I hoped I'd have the chance to tell her.

The light dimmed as I entered the forge and I traced a hand

along the wall to keep from tripping. Were Frode and Jac worried sick about me? Or were they grateful they didn't have to worry about keeping me alive in the arena anymore?

One question was louder than the rest: Would training with the Hellbringer honestly help me win the Trials? Or was I wasting time here when I could be planning with Frode and Jac to ensure we were united in our strategy for victory?

Every question vanished from my mind when I stepped back into the largest cavern and saw the Hellbringer—utterly shirtless.

My breath caught in my throat. I desperately hoped the flush warming my cheeks was from the heat of the fire and not a blush. Thank the gods he had his back turned—though whether I was more grateful to have a moment to compose myself or to get a good look at him unobserved, I couldn't say.

Wouldn't say.

He still wore the mask, but the expanse of pale skin that was his back glistened with sweat in the firelight. A jagged scar traveled over his right shoulder, carving into the flesh. A few moles stood out, landmarks on a map I found myself wanting to explore. Trace. Connect the dots.

I'd never *really* appreciated a torso before now. Not like this.

As he slammed down the hammer on the dagger blade he was shaping, muscles rippled in his arms and back. He was strong, but not in a way that boasted. It was honed strength, the kind derived from a life of hard work.

I was struck with the realization that Arne was a boy. The Hellbringer, on the other hand, was a man.

What if I . . .

I took a half step forward. An image appeared in my head as desire formed like a hunger deep within my gut. It would be so easy to trace a finger down the length of his spine—to make him shudder beneath my touch, to feel the bump of every vertebra and memorize it.

I blinked back to the matter at hand, shaking my head. Where had that thought emerged from? The Hellbringer was physically attractive, but he was also my captor. He represented everything I hated.

It's your subconscious, I told myself, waiting for my racing heart to slow. *You don't know when you'll get laid next, now that you're not with Arne, so you're redirecting your desire elsewhere. He just happens to be closest.*

I shrugged the unwelcome thoughts away and returned to my own working space, hefting the tongs and returning the steel to the fire for another round of shaping. The blade was nearing completion, the closeness spurring me on.

We worked in silence for another hour or two. My focus stayed mostly on my own weapon, but occasionally my disobedient eyes wandered to the Hellbringer, unable to keep from tracing the lines of his chest or studying the trail of dark hair disappearing beneath the waistband of his pants.

I suppressed a grumble and turned back to my task. For someone who claimed his identity was his closest-kept secret, he certainly didn't seem too concerned about revealing his body.

"You have a natural talent for this."

I blinked back into the moment at hand to see the Hellbringer studying me. When I didn't say anything, he nodded toward the metal clasped in my tongs, steadily cooling. "Your new weapon is coming along nicely."

"It's close," I said. "I can't get it to the exact width I want, though. I'm worried I'll make it too thin and it will break."

He set down his own equipment and ambled toward me. I swallowed thickly, begging my eyes to move upward to his face. The last thing I needed was to study him like a piece of artwork, a living sculpture, without a mask to hide my own expression.

I turned my gaze back to the metal in front of me as he stepped closer, examining it. "Here," he said, reaching for the hammer I was holding. "Try this."

But when I tried to hand him the tool, he shook his head. "No. Let me show you."

Before I knew what was happening, he crowded behind me, far too close for comfort, and wrapped his hand around mine over the hammer.

I understood how forearms could be muscled. But how was it possible his hands, so much larger than mine, seemed to exude strength?

I inhaled sharply, trying to focus on the logistics of what he was explaining and not the hard planes of his body pressed against my back. He pulled my hands into a new placement, changed the angle, and murmured, "There. Now try shaping it like this." He guided my hand, and together we began hammering on the sword once more.

The scent of pine, fresh snow, and smoke filled my senses. He radiated heat. Could he hear the thud of my heartbeat in my ears? Was he as acutely aware of the flush in my cheeks as I was? Or was this—being so close to another person you found terribly attractive—a normal occurrence for him?

He doesn't find you attractive, my thoughts whispered. *He can barely stand to be here with you. He's only following orders.*

I shrugged them away. That was fine. He was my captor, nothing more. And I'd seen a naked man before. This was nothing new. Not to mention he still smelled good after working for hours in the heat. I'm sure I smelled terrible.

And if he was affected by our closeness, I'd never know. Not with the mask on.

"Good." He surveyed my work, releasing my hand and allowing

me to continue on my own. "Keep doing that and you'll be done in an hour. Then we can break for dinner."

I examined my blade, which looked more refined from the technique he'd shown me. A hint of pride shone through my distraction. I was crafting a weapon with my own two hands. I didn't have to be godtouched to make something new, something *good*.

I lost myself in the sword and my thoughts, but only for a few precious moments. Soon the memory of the Hellbringer pressing against me reared its head once more. The reasoning for his actions, for removing his shirt and encroaching on my personal space, was impossible to parse. Was he testing me? Trying to get a reaction from the prim and proper princess he'd been stuck with? Or perhaps he was making fun of me. The confidence in his voice when instructing me how to work the sword . . .

Gods, the number of innuendos interspersed with my lustful thoughts was absurd.

The knowledge didn't keep me from wondering whether he'd be just as commanding—just as confident, just as capable, just as careful—in bed.

You hate him! I reminded myself. The refrain was on steady repeat in my mind for the rest of the afternoon.

♦ ♦ ♦ ♦ ♦

THE HELLBRINGER TWISTED THE MAKESHIFT SPIT, EVENLY ROAST-ing the meat cooking over the fire. The too-big eye sockets of the skull mask made him an enigma in the dying light of day. A creature of the night, preparing to rejoin its brethren in the dark.

The finished blade lay next to me in the snow. It wasn't sharp yet—he'd explained I'd need to grind the edges down in the morning, after we rested through the night—but I was too proud of it to let it sit in the forge, in the dark.

My blade deserved to see the light of day before it slept. It would stay by my side, this creation of mine, until it was ready to spill blood. Until it was sharpened and honed along with me, ready to win freedom for my people.

The Hellbringer didn't agree.

"Leave the blade in the forge," he'd argued when I picked it up, cradling it in my arms as we cleared the room, putting out the forge's fire and preparing to move to the cave entrance for our meal.

"No," I'd snapped. Maybe he didn't understand the beauty of making something with your own two hands when they'd done nothing but destroy in the past. But I knew the blade was precious, and I wasn't letting it go.

Now, he handed me a skewer of cooked rabbit, steaming in the cool air. I breathed in the smell, my growling stomach eager to begin. But I paused with my mouth open when he took his own portion and rose.

"What are you doing?"

The mask was impassive as always, but I could hear the raised eyebrow in his voice. "Going to eat."

He trudged off, presumably to find a private spot to take off the mask and have his own meal. I chewed thoughtfully on a bite of my own dinner as I watched him disappear into the trees, then stood up to follow him.

I wasn't certain of much, not when I didn't know whether I'd live to see more than the next month and a half, but I did know the Hellbringer had a distinct advantage over me. He was the captor—the one with all the knowledge and all the power.

Seeing his face would more than level the playing field.

I stayed as far back and out of sight as I could, stepping in his footprints where possible. His stride was long enough that in some places my legs wouldn't stretch far enough. But I figured it was more important to get to him without being noticed. I'd worry about returning to the fire after the fact.

The trees kept me hidden, shielding me with their shadows, and I crept along in near silence as the Hellbringer took his leave. About a quarter of a mile from the entrance to the cave, he stopped and sat, his back against the trunk of the nearest pine.

I remained unseen but wouldn't for long. Carefully, I reached for the nearest weight-bearing branch and hauled myself up, climbing the tree until I was confident he wouldn't see me. Frode and I had spent hours playing hide and seek as children, his godtouch forcing me to find more unique places to hide throughout the years. The tops of trees were among my favorites because they presented a convenient loophole: if Frode could hear my thoughts but couldn't *see* me, then I technically hadn't been found. I'd leap from pine to pine, forcing him to chase me down to win the game.

The skill would come in handy now. The Hellbringer was still far enough from me that I wouldn't be able to get a good look at his face, though. I inched to the edge of the branch I was perched on, grateful the trees grew as thickly as they did, and clambered onto the neighboring pine. I repeated the motion again and again until I could see the mask from a distance. He still wore it: Why hadn't he started eating?

I settled in, waiting for the precise moment.

The Hellbringer pulled one of the freshly made daggers from the sheath at his waist, flipping it over and over in his hand. I waited for him to cut the meat off the stick, use it as a makeshift utensil.

Instead, he flicked his wrist, sending it hurtling through the air straight toward me, to bury itself up to the hilt in the bark of the pine. Right next to my face.

The impact startled me, my sudden flinch sending a pile of snow from the branch to the ground below. I gritted my teeth, barely holding onto the branch. If I had spent any less time perfecting the skill of balancing in trees, I'd have fallen ten feet to the ground. "Fuck you!"

"Can I eat in peace, or will you force me to starve through the night?" he called, ignoring my expletives.

I wrenched the blade from the trunk and swung down from the branch, landing nimbly on my feet in the powder. "Why won't you eat in front of me?" I demanded, brandishing the knife as I approached him.

"I'd happily eat in front of you if I could. But I won't remove my mask."

"Why not?" I resisted the urge to throw my hands in the air with exasperation. "Are you secretly hideous? Or do you truly believe you're so important that your identity must remain a secret?"

He leaned back, and without being able to track his eyes, it was impossible to know whether he was looking at me or the green needles stretching out above him. "I have no idea whether you'd think I'm ugly."

I pursed my lips to keep from interrupting. With a body like his, I highly doubted he was an eyesore. Then again, stranger things had happened.

"Can you imagine trying to live any kind of normal life having a Lurae like mine?" His voice was quieter now, almost pensive. "I kill people, Princess. Not just the bad ones. And not just when my country is at war."

"You're the perfect weapon." Bitterness seeped into my voice, uncontrollable. I couldn't stop it if I tried. "You could show up anywhere, anytime, kill them all. Leave no one the wiser. If all the witnesses are dead, why protect your face? If you're the most powerful man in the world, why hide?"

Freja's father had been one of the bodies left in the Hellbringer's wake. She rarely spoke of it, preferring to grieve in her own time, in her own way. But I never forgot.

He stood, retracing his footprints in the snow. The sun sank further below the horizon, casting long shadows over the blanket of white. "Is the most powerful man in the world the one who can kill without a second thought?" he asked, looking away from me. "Or is it the one who holds his leash? The one who knows his weakness and holds it at knifepoint?"

When he set off for the cave in silence, I followed.

15

I STOOD ON ONE FOOT, THE OTHER LEG EXTENDED BEHIND ME in a straight line, wobbling and desperately trying not to fall on my face in the snow.

"What is the point of this, again?" I asked through gritted teeth.

Beside me, the Hellbringer executed the same pose in perfect stillness, utterly content to watch me struggle. "Fighting requires use of every muscle, even the ones you aren't thinking about. If you're going to stand a chance at defeating your brothers, you need to develop those muscles." He paused for half a heartbeat before adding, "Though right now, we're simply working your core."

I bit my lip as I teetered. "Are you insulting me?"

There was a hint of humor in his voice, a sly note I'd never heard before. "You seem to think I'm insulting you no matter what I do, so I won't be answering that question."

I laughed unexpectedly, then lost my balance and toppled over. When I pushed up on my hands with a grumbled "Shit," I swore I caught the end of a chuckle from him.

We'd spent the morning running through a series of exercises designed to help me prepare for training with him. Running a mile through two feet of snow was not my ideal way to begin a day, but I was determined to win the Trials and I had admitted by now that the Hellbringer was a far more experienced warrior than I. At the end of the day, we both wanted the same thing. His methods were unusual, but I would oblige—for now.

The early hours of the morning were spent in silence. The heaviness of our evening conversation weighed on me. But the run warmed more than my out-of-shape muscles, and soon enough we'd returned to our natural state of constant arguing.

Our conversation from the night before remained fresh in my mind, though.

Between losing myself in the push and pull of my muscles, attempting to contort my body into absurd poses that required far more effort than they should have, and scowling at the Hellbringer, I wondered at the implications of his comments. The insinuation of a leash being held by a higher power had kept me up half the night.

Several hours from waking, I was no closer to determining what it meant.

Now I stood sore and shivering from falling in the snow. Pushing to my feet, I attempted to brush the powder off my clothes, succeeding only in melting it slightly and growing damp. Whatever.

"Are we going to finish the sword?" I asked, unable to keep the question contained any longer. I'd been thinking of the blade all morning. When I had trouble sleeping on the rough cave floor, I'd considered searching for a whetstone so I could sharpen the metal until I grew tired. In the end, I hadn't. It was impossible to tell if the Hellbringer was sleeping or not, and I didn't want to wake him and risk his wrath.

"Yes." He returned to the cave and I followed, excitement sparking like a new flame in my chest. "You'll need to shape the hilt today.

Carve it from wood, attach it to the blade, and wrap it in leather. Then we'll be done with the hardest parts."

✦ ✦ ✦ ✦ ✦

THE SUN HAD RISEN HIGH IN THE SKY WHEN THE HELLBRINGER AP-proached me to examine the hilt I'd carved.

"Good," he said, and I hoped he couldn't see the pride on my face, blossoming in my chest at his words. "Your weapon will need a name."

I thought for a moment. "Aloisa."

Let them cower before the soul goddess in that arena. She may have been a figment of a zealot's imagination, made real only by the thousands who worshiped her, but she was a symbol of something real. Power.

Power was tangible. Power was a crown on my head, the snowy path to it soaked in Erik's and Björn's blood. It was my unwilling father relinquishing his hold on the godforsaken; whether he let it go willingly or at the point of my blade mattered not.

When we attached the hilt to the blade, wrapping it with leather, I held it and marveled. I had created it from nothing. Brought it to life under the Hellbringer's watchful eye.

Aloisa. Goddess of the soul. Blade of the godforsaken princess. Symbol of the revolution.

It was perfect.

✦ ✦ ✦ ✦ ✦

THE TREK BACK TO WHERE MIRA HAD DROPPED US ORIGINALLY felt significantly shorter the second time around. Maybe because of the new lightness between the Hellbringer and me.

My new sword was sheathed at my waist, and even I could admit my former blade paled in comparison. It still needed a good sharpening, but the Hellbringer assured me there was a whetstone back at the prison I could use.

"Why don't we stay at the cave?" I asked, rubbing my thumb along Aloisa's leather hilt. "Seems nicer than the prison."

The Hellbringer glanced back over his shoulder from where he walked a few paces ahead of me. "It is nicer. But the prison keeps us safer from the elements. Just wait until the first storm of the year really hits. You'll be glad there's no hole in the ceiling then."

I sighed and kicked at the powder in front of me, knowing he was right. A week or two after the new year began was always when the first storms hit the cities in Bhorglid; out in the wilderness, it likely occurred far sooner.

"Blizzards are nothing new to me," I remarked, "but as much as I hate Björn and my father, growing up around two men with powerful fire godtouches was more of a luxury than most godforsaken had. I hate not being able to see the sun every day, but you're right—the prison will be safer."

We walked in silence for a few more steps before he asked, a note of puzzlement in his voice, "Why do you call yourself 'godforsaken'? And those with power 'godtouched'? Are the terms not 'Nilurae' and 'Lurae'?"

I shrugged. "So I've been informed. But not in Bhorglid. I'd never known there were other words until I met Volkan earlier this week."

My steady gait faltered. Had it really been only a few days since I first met Volkan? It felt like a lifetime ago.

"Do you prefer Bhorglid's language?" The Hellbringer sounded genuinely curious. "Words are powerful. As a Nilurae yourself, you're intimately aware of such."

I considered the thought as we tromped through the snow. A few flakes descended from the skies, the white spindles stark against the dark end of my braid. Halvar, Freja, and I had always focused on the bigger things, the ones we felt would make the most difference.

But the Hellbringer had a point. Words had the ability to change thoughts, change reality. I considered the way Bhorglid's citizens talked about him: the descriptions and stories painted a horrifying tale of an irredeemable monster, something inhuman behind a carved mask. And maybe some of them—*most* even—were true.

He was more irritating than terrifying, though.

I'd never thought of how calling ourselves godforsaken would reinforce the literal meaning of the term. Those of us without magic weren't cursed or forgotten by any pretend gods. We were simply different.

"Nilurae," I said softly, testing the feel of it on my tongue. There was something right about it, and I made no effort to suppress a small smile. "Nilurae."

"I don't know the origin of the word, but I believe it's older than the terms used in Bhorglid," the Hellbringer said. His long cloak billowed behind him in a sudden gust of wind. "It wouldn't surprise me if your priests were the ones to coin the . . . less pleasant terms."

I rolled my eyes. "Don't get me started on the priests."

He hummed. "They're the driving force behind the war. Behind everything. I've never interacted with them, only watched from afar, but . . . I often can't help but wish . . ." His hand squeezed into a fist by his side.

I knew exactly what he meant. And, truthfully, I didn't think I'd mind if he used his godtouch—his *Lurae*—on the priests to exterminate them either.

"You dislike the war, then?" I asked. "Don't you want to keep your country safe?"

He waved a hand dismissively, the black glove like a stain against the perfectly unbroken picture of white surrounding us. "I care about the people of Kryllian, but it's hard to feel like they're *my* people."

I furrowed my brows. "You're from Kryllian, though. Aren't you?"

"Yes."

"I don't understand. Why wouldn't they be your people, then?"

We were interrupted by Mira's arrival. She appeared out of nowhere, landing on both feet in the snow. I glanced back toward the mountains in the distance, where the forge lay. Had we really walked the entire distance in such a short amount of time?

The Hellbringer noticed me looking. "Almost like stewing about how much you hate a person makes the trip feel longer."

I ignored him and grasped Mira's extended wrist. Her expressions were difficult to read, especially since she never spoke more than a word or two in my presence. But her slight scowl radiated dislike. I wondered what imagined slight I'd inflicted on her.

We were back at the prison in an instant, the cold, gray walls glaring down at me. I let go of Mira and held back a sigh. I missed the sun already. At least outside, the cold was accompanied by snow. In this depressing place, it was simply frigid and dim. The fire had been put out before we left, meaning it would take ages to warm up again.

I turned to ask the Hellbringer where he kept the kindling, but he and Mira were both gone. Once again I was alone.

The wary camaraderie I felt for the Hellbringer disappeared in an instant.

You have been kidnapped by a madman and no one is coming for you.

I began to search for kindling and firewood.

16

WHEN THE HELLBRINGER REAPPEARED ONE EVENING—OR what I assumed was evening—I knew I'd been in the prison for several days. He held out his hand to silence me before I could speak.

"It's been four days since we returned from the forge. And if you ask me again how long you've been here, I'll make you do another hundred push-ups."

I frowned from my perch on the bed. "Don't I have the right to know?"

He snorted, but it sounded strange through the voice distortion. "You're a prisoner. Prisoners don't have rights."

I bit back a retort. At least he'd brought me something to read while he was gone during the day. I couldn't do much while he was out and about on the surface because I was so sore from our rigid training regimen, but I always managed to stretch out my aching muscles, eat whatever was in the jars, and read some of the book. It was an excruciatingly dull piece on the strategy of war and the history of the Fjordlands.

Better than nothing, I supposed.

We'd fallen into a routine so quickly, it surprised me. Each morning, or what I assumed was morning, the Hellbringer would train me in combat. Most often it was swordplay, but occasionally he spent an hour or two teaching me hand-to-hand attacks and defenses as well.

Then we would spar.

Aloisa was a far better sword than the one I had previously, but I had yet to touch him, much less defeat him. It was both belittling and annoying how quickly he could move. Each morning training session ended with me fighting in a blind rage until I threw my weapon to the ground, swearing.

At that point Mira would arrive and transport him away, giving me time to sulk until the heat of my anger died and I could stretch my taut muscles.

He would be gone for hours. I spent the time reading, exploring the winding halls of the prison, and—begrudgingly—thinking about him.

I wasn't sure if I'd suffered a head injury with uncommon symptoms or I was losing my sanity after so much time without seeing the sun, but thoughts of the Hellbringer invaded my mind at almost all times. If I wasn't wondering what he was up to on the war front, worrying about whether he'd killed the brothers I'd allied with, then I was forcing myself away from thoughts of his hands wrapped around the hilt of his blade, the press of his body behind mine when he helped me shape Aloisa, the ridges of muscle I'd seen when he took his shirt off.

It was distracting. And extremely frustrating.

He was incredibly aggravating and ridiculously attractive. An unfortunate combination.

Fortunately, he hadn't removed any more clothing in front of me since we returned. I found myself wondering sometimes whether I'd imagined the whole thing, my mental faculties damaged by the unwavering heat of the forge.

My thoughts also drifted to Freja, though. My friend was not forgotten, not when everything I did was for her freedom. I wondered if she was surviving, managing to stay warm despite the steadily encroaching winter weather. Surely Halvar had brought her something to keep her from freezing.

When the Hellbringer returned each evening, he would bring something to cook for dinner, usually meat or stew, and then we would train again before I collapsed into bed, exhausted. We rarely spoke, so most of my days were spent in silence.

Over the past three days, I'd bothered him for information on the war. "What's happening? Who won the battle where you kidnapped me? Is my family alive?"

The first time, he'd studiously ignored me until I gave up. But I tried again the next day with another tactic.

"Shouldn't the future Queen of Bhorglid at least be aware of the political climate outside this prison?" While he cooked, I paced along the open stretch of wall. At my assertion, he stilled, and I pushed on. "At least tell me if there have been any major developments in the last few days."

He'd sighed. "War is slow, Princess. Strategy is the foremost game here, despite the insinuation by everyone close to you that it should be slaughter. As much as your father might enjoy decimating Kryllian troops, our goal is to end this with as little bloodshed as possible."

I narrowed my eyes. "You didn't answer my question."

He muttered something under his breath that sounded like "pain in the ass" before saying, "Nothing has happened. And if it does, I'll tell you. Satisfied?"

"Not particularly."

He'd stomped over to me and stared me down, close enough that, without the mask, I would have felt his breath on my face. "I. Am. Not. Your. Personal. Informant," he growled. "Pick up your sword. Sparring seems to be the only way to keep you from talking my ear off."

However, when he returned the next day, the first words from his mouth were "No changes today. Only a brief border skirmish."

I'd paused practicing the sword stances he'd taught me and now raised an eyebrow. "A border skirmish? This land is all Bhorglid."

"'Border' isn't exactly the right word," he said with a shrug as he prepared dinner. "Not border of the country. More like there was a skirmish where Kryllian soldiers attempted to force the Bhorglid army back south. I assume they're hoping to move the fighting out of the wastelands and into the populated area soon."

My blade glinted in the light of the lamps around the edge of the room as I let it drop. "Into the populated area?" Anyone could have heard the strangled way my voice tightened at his statement.

"Don't worry. You'll be on the throne long before they make any real progress. And then the queen will work on a treaty with you." He'd gone back to focusing on dinner, but my thoughts didn't stop whirling.

If I didn't win the Trials, didn't become queen, didn't arrange a truce . . . what would happen to the godforsaken people in Bhorglid? They'd be defenseless against the Kryllian armies, especially if Halvar was successful in starting any kind of rebellion and threw the country into chaos—

"Stop," the Hellbringer said. His tone told me behind his mask he was rolling his eyes.

I blinked and turned to him. "Stop what?"

"Thinking. It's loud."

He sounded exactly like Frode, and it made my chest ache. I already hated the Hellbringer, but his snide comment solidified my feelings.

Tonight's meal was beef. It cooked quickly and I scarfed it down quicker. As soon as it was gone, I bounced to my feet and hefted my sword. The day's report had left me on edge and I buzzed with pent-up energy. "Fight me, Hellbringer. Let's get this over with."

He stood and walked to where I waited. He didn't draw his weapon. "It's not exactly a fight if you can't hit me."

When I pursed my lips, his ensuing laugh caught me by surprise. It wasn't derisive or cynical, as his laughs before had been. It was genuine, and it startled me how much I enjoyed knowing I'd caused it.

I schooled my features into a scowl. "What?"

"Your face is easy to read. It's amusing," he chuckled. "You don't hide anything, do you?"

"Oh, please." I rolled my eyes. "Like you'd know how to socialize properly if you tried."

"At least I'm not trying to kill you. You can't say that about your own family."

"Are we sparring or not?"

He didn't answer my question. Instead, he returned to the table and started clearing away the remains of dinner. "Your turn, Princess. Tell me something true. Do you truly believe your father would have murdered you?" he asked. There was a strange hollowness in his voice, and I hesitated. Why the sudden interest?

The callback to our moment in the wastes threw me off. It was the only reason to explain why I obliged his request and answered him honestly.

"My father has been trying to get rid of me my whole life. This is nothing new." I sheathed my weapon. Apparently, tonight's training had been canceled. "It would have been more surprising if he *wasn't* trying to murder me."

"Why don't you murder him first?"

I raised an eyebrow. "Do you think murder is the solution to all of life's problems?"

He shrugged from where he scraped the remains of the food into the fire. "It's always been the solution to mine."

I tried to hold my laugh in, but it burst out of me. "Do you hear yourself?" I asked. "You sound ridiculous."

"I was joking." He might have been lying, but without a facial expression to read, I couldn't be sure.

I felt myself grinning and managed to wipe it off my face. *He is your enemy. Do not let him take advantage of you.*

I stopped laughing and forced myself to replace it with irritation. For some reason I couldn't summon anger no matter how badly I wanted to. Annoyance would have to be enough for the time being.

The Hellbringer was quiet for a moment. "Would your father be punished if he murdered you?" he asked. "He is king, after all."

"Probably not, but if he were, then the priests would be the ones to execute him," I explained. "My father holds the ultimate authority in Bhorglid, but their influence on the crown is strong. It's been that way for generations."

I watched as a shudder moved through the Hellbringer. "I hate your priests," he muttered. "Their uniforms are . . . eerie at best."

Another laugh fell from my lips.

"What?" he asked.

"Have you ever looked in a mirror while you're wearing"—I gestured at him—"*that*?"

I waited for him to chuckle, the response I was expecting. But he didn't speak. Silence followed him like a dark shroud. It was fitting, with the shadows dancing across the walls from the lanterns. My amusement turned sour in my stomach.

When a long moment passed without a response, I realized he was done talking. More than that, he was ignoring me now.

For the briefest moment I allowed myself to wonder where the man I was coming to expect had disappeared to. This was no longer the Hellbringer who plied me with requests to tell him something true. Who was endlessly patient when I didn't master a new form with instant perfection during training.

No. That man had disappeared in a swift instant, replaced by the general who had kidnapped me.

After returning to my place on the bed, I cursed myself in the silence. I'd begun to let my guard down as I eased into routine with him. He'd been warm, inviting, even friendly at times. I had started thinking of him as human. I shook my head. That was a mistake. I was a captive here.

You are in a prison with a madman and no one is coming for you.

This time the words did not come unwillingly but as a reminder.

I ran them through my head over and over again until dinner was cleaned up and the Hellbringer ordered me to run laps around the space.

◆ ◆ ◆ ◆ ◆

SPARRING WAS QUICKLY BECOMING MY LEAST FAVORITE PART OF the day.

Frustration wrapped its strangling hand around my throat—again—and I forced myself to breathe deeply in an attempt to sate it. My limbs shook with a dangerous combination of exhaustion and anger. When the Hellbringer readjusted his stance and ordered, "Again," I shook my head.

"No." The word tasted like bile. "I won't. I'm done with this."

I laid Aloisa down—after the lecture he'd given me two days before about throwing my brand-new sword on the unforgiving metal floor, I was begrudgingly gentler with the weapon—and moved to begin kicking the toe of my boot against the wall. It was nothing like the way I'd ravaged my hand back home before my last night at Halvar's. This was a softer motion, because even if I was done, even if I did demand the Hellbringer take me back to Bhorglid that very minute, I still had to compete in the Trials. And I had my suspicions that no gift would be enough for Waddell now that I was a contender for the throne.

Still, the repetitive motion and the sensation of impact on my foot soothed me. My thoughts, a deep spiral unafraid to dive further into darkness, settled slightly. I swallowed the lump in my throat at the thought of Frode, who would wrap me in an embrace whenever he sensed my thoughts turning morbid.

Gods, I missed him. And Jac, too.

A rustling pulled me back to the present and I turned to see the Hellbringer discarding his cloak against the wall. "What are you doing?" I asked, my voice far softer than I wanted it to be.

He sighed, and I could sense his reluctance before he spoke. "Teach me the dance."

For a long moment we stared at each other. "What?"

"I said teach me the dance. The one you were doing in the tavern that night when they took your friend to prison." Through the distortion of his voice, I could tell he was gritting his teeth as he spoke. He waved a hand dismissively, as if it would make the request any less absurd. "Show me how to do it."

I leaned my forehead against the wall. "You're making fun of me."

He snorted, and it sounded strange through the mask's voice distortion. "If I was going to make fun of you, Princess, there are far easier ways to do it. Most of which don't involve humiliating myself. So, no, I'm not teasing. I'm trying to show you this doesn't have to be entirely miserable."

I stood and faced him, arms crossed. "How does dancing have anything to do with my training?"

"It keeps you nimble, quick on your feet. Gets your blood pumping. You'll have to dodge plenty of attacks during the Trials. This will help." He moved a hand in the direction of the mask before it twitched and returned to his side, a motion I'd begun noticing over the past few days. If I ever managed to see his face, I bet he'd run that same hand through his hair whenever he was nervous—which, apparently, he was now. "Think about your brothers—the ones you'll be fighting. Their methods of fighting will be the same because they learned from all the same people. But you? Your background in swordsmanship comes from entirely different sources. And as a dancer, you have a sense of movement few others possess."

I looked at my feet, unwilling to answer him. Then the Hellbringer, Kryllian's most feared general and possibly the most powerful man to ever live, extended a hand to me. His voice was soft around the edges when he said, "Please?"

In a trancelike state, I reached back. I stared at our hands, clasped together the way Arne's and mine had been that night, and decided to untangle the strange cacophony of emotions whirling around in my head later.

I focused in on his request. The Hellbringer wanted to dance? Then we would dance.

I cleared my throat and focused on my feet, wishing for my dancing shoes. The line dance he'd watched was fairly simple, and it started with a classic step, one that wasn't too difficult. I'd begin there. "Have you ever heard of a grapevine?"

"The plant? Sure."

He was . . . entirely serious. My mouth fell open slightly, and for a moment I wondered whether to laugh. Instead, I forced myself to shake my head. "Different kind of grapevine. We'll start there. Stand behind me and copy what I do."

The Hellbringer was a painstakingly precise teacher, unwilling to accept anything less than perfection, unfailingly diligent in correcting any small mistakes I made. As I instructed him how to step to the side, then behind, then to the side again, it became clear he was listening closely to every word I said, determined to get it right.

"And then when you step together again, you bring your hands up and clap," I said.

I didn't need to see his face to know he was rolling his eyes. He brought his hands up and together so lightly, it didn't make a sound.

I smirked. "I don't think so. You don't get to half-ass this, not when it's my turn."

He exhaled slowly. "You're right." His next attempt was loud enough to echo in the wide space.

"Excellent. After the two grapevines, partners turn to face each other." He obliged, and I tried not to look into the gruesome eyes of the mask, gaping and empty. Focusing on his chest was easier.

Except my traitorous thoughts immediately began reminding me exactly what that chest looked like unclothed. My cheeks heated and my brain stuttered. For a half second too long I was incapable of human speech, my mind far too invested in the thought of him stepping forward into my space, forcing me to look up at him as he ran a gloved finger down the column of my throat and—

"Are we going to stand here all evening, Princess?"

There was a wry note of humor in his voice and I jumped, shaking my head. I cleared my throat, hoping my thoughts weren't clear as day on my face. "Then we link arms and skip in a circle."

His aggravated sigh lifted my spirits, and I couldn't hold in a snort of amusement. "What? Is the fierce Hellbringer too afraid to spin like he means it?"

He chuckled. "Never."

Teaching him the rest was fairly easy. He threw himself into it and I managed to keep my imagination away from thoughts of his torso for a while. It was refreshing to be the expert for once, even if it was only for a short time. For the first time since the night of my failed engagement party, my mind was unoccupied.

I relished it.

When we reached the second half of the dance, the complicated footwork started. I wasn't surprised when the Hellbringer had trouble mastering it—I'd practically been born doing traditional Bhor-glid dances, and even I hadn't perfected this one until my later teenage years.

"Why would anyone think this is fun," he muttered under his breath.

I suppressed a smile. "Do you need me to go over it again?"

"Yes." His hands rested at his sides, but his fingers were curled into tight fists.

"It's a step-ball-change and then a series of twisting steps," I began, turning to face away from him so he could watch and mimic. "So you start by stepping out with your left foot—yes, good, just like that—and then while that foot is planted, you'll step directly behind it with only the ball of your right foot touching the ground." I continued to observe him, craning my neck to watch over my shoulder. "Oh, I see. You're trying to do it more like a box step, so your right foot is going too far past your left when you step back. Freeze just like that."

Obediently, he stopped moving and I jogged behind him, dropping down to my knees next to him. Only when I landed there did tension drop a heavy hand over me, a reminder of everything floating between us.

I swallowed. No, I wasn't going to think harder than necessary about being on my knees before the Hellbringer. There were so many ways that could go wrong. So many ways I could imagine this going under any other circumstance.

Was I imagining tenseness overtaking his whole body in a way I'd never seen before? Was his breathing heavy because we'd been dancing for almost an hour, or did it have something to do with my proximity to him?

I inhaled and forced myself back to the present. I was the only one feeling the tension stretched taut in the room; that was certain.

This was hands-on learning, nothing more. I rested a hand on his right ankle and pushed gently, forcing his foot back toward his center of gravity. "When your feet are aligned, it's a lot easier to balance."

If the gods were watching, they had a cruel sense of humor. Keeping my hands light proved to be a challenge with the massive snow boots the Hellbringer had failed to remove when he arrived back at the prison, and just a little too much force ruined the very balance I'd been trying to help him achieve.

He lost his footing and tumbled.

I sucked in a gasp, flailing my hands automatically to try and catch him. But the Hellbringer was not a twig. Our sparring sessions had proven he was built of pure muscle, and this only confirmed it as his shoulder caught mine, pushing me to my back.

He managed to catch himself before his entire weight slammed into my body, an arm pressed into the floor next to my head. My left arm was outstretched, the right clutched to my chest and now pinned between myself and the Hellbringer. I was keenly aware of every inch of our bodies that was touching, from our stomachs to our thighs.

He smelled like pine and fresh snow. The scent filled my lungs the way the warmth of him filled the rest of me. Cautiously, I flicked my gaze to the mask.

The Hellbringer was staring at me. Or at least it looked like he was. The eye sockets of the mask were focused directly on me. How did he see out of it? Was there magic involved?

For the first time I noticed the subtle imperfections of the wooden features. It was a strikingly accurate wolf's skull, but there were occasional nicks on the surface, evidence it had been made by human hands.

The connection was instant: the carvings on the bedposts, the way the Hellbringer had so expertly fashioned me a hilt for Aloisa from nothing but a block of wood. "You carved your helmet."

The visage tilted slightly. "Yes."

For an endless moment we were both unnaturally still, incapable or unwilling to move as we caught our breaths. As I relished the weight and warmth of him atop me.

My free arm moved and I reached slowly, slowly, for the helmet. He didn't stop me, but I felt him tense. I licked my lips, nerves thrumming beneath my skin.

I brushed two gentle fingertips against the wood. It was smooth and soft—sanded and polished to perfection. How old was he when he carved this? A boy on the cusp of manhood, perhaps?

Abruptly, my thoughts scattered as he rolled off me, pushing to stand and leaving me behind, the chill air rushing in to fill the void left by his heat.

"Sorry." The word escaped me like a curse. "Sorry. I didn't mean to push you off-balance."

He didn't answer. Instead, he fastened his cloak and adjusted his scabbard. Then, without a word, he strode out of the room and into the maze of hallways.

I only stared after him.

Hours later, when sleep eventually claimed me, the Hellbringer still had not returned.

◆ ◆ ◆ ◆ ◆

WHEN THE HELLBRINGER'S WEIGHT PRESSED INTO THE MATTRESS against me, I knew I was dreaming. But the haze of consciousness was too dense for me to care, and the fuzzy reality my brain summoned was peaceful.

I craved it.

Dimly, I registered that the mask was gone. But as my dream eyes fluttered open, it didn't matter, because the Hellbringer was rolling over to me, pulling the blankets over us both to calm my shivering. His face was the last of my worries. "It's cold. Let me keep you warm."

I sighed. It was all I was capable of as the smell of him flooded my mind. "How do you always smell like that?"

His voice was still distorted even though the mask was gone. He chuckled, and the sound rumbled through my body. My toes curled beneath the blanket, a shiver of pleasure traveling up my spine with the sound. "Like what?"

"Like a forest." I pressed my face to his chest, nuzzled there, content in his warmth. Here, there was no forced animosity hovering its angry head over us. Here, we were just two people enjoying each other's company. "Like the wastelands."

He placed his hand on the small of my back and rubbed gentle circles there. "Probably has to do with how much time I spend out there."

The first press of his lips fell on my forehead. Gentle, sweet. The brush of his nose against my cheekbone sped the beating of my heart, and when one of the hands wrapped around me and ventured lower, over my ass with a squeeze, my cheeks heated. A harsh breath left me in a rush, my own hands coming to clutch the fabric over his chest.

He hummed, the vibration beneath my fingers sending a thrill through my stomach. Full lips dragged up and down my jawline. "You like that?"

I nodded. He was warm and inviting, the hard planes of his chest unyielding under my fingers.

"Say it," he demanded, and in a half thought our clothes had disappeared, leaving us bare beneath the blankets. His weight pressed into me, and the lips at my throat turned to teeth scraping. "Tell me you like it, Princess."

I couldn't keep my legs from stretching out, reaching for what I desperately needed—him, in the soft place between my legs. Desire throbbed dangerously. My head was cloudy with the dream, foggy with *want*, but I managed to gasp, "I like it. More? Please?"

"Good." The approval in his voice was intoxicating, and I threw my head back. He shifted his weight downward until his cheek was resting on my sternum, giving his mouth access to the underside of my breast. The Hellbringer sucked a mark there, one hand reaching up to cradle my cheek and the other sliding down my body to find solace at my damp center. Softly, almost sweetly, he ran a fingertip over my entrance and swore. "Fuck. Never imagined you'd be wet for me."

The dream blurred in a haze of pleasure then, my body conscious only of the imagined intrusion of his finger, a pair of dark eyes focusing on my face as the too-familiar voice went husky. "Gods, you're beautiful. Love the way your mouth falls open when I push into you, like you can't believe it. Like you're afraid it's going to break you."

My breath came in ragged gasps, a shudder coursing over my spine. The pad of his thumb began coaxing my pleasure from me. A dark head of hair entered my vision as he bent over my chest, teeth closing carefully around the stiff peak of my nipple. My toes curled. I wanted him to bite harder, to take me closer to the edge of where pain and pleasure blurred. But words were impossible in this dream, especially as my body reacted to his every imagined touch.

"Can I watch?" he asked. "While you fall apart? Can I look into those pretty eyes while you clench around my fingers until you're soft and pliable for me? Ready for my—"

Consciousness fell over me like a bucket of ice water.

I blinked back to awareness, my body tense beneath the blankets. For a long moment I was still and silent, unsure what to do. A shuddering breath left me, the pent-up desire fading slightly. I held back my curse, clenched my teeth, forced myself to inhale slowly and acknowledge the truth.

I'd just had a sex dream about the Hellbringer.

With my fists squeezing so tightly that I knew my nails were leaving imprints on my palms, I lifted my head slightly to peer at the man himself. The Hellbringer was where he usually was: sleeping next to the fireplace, his head against the stone wall. For a second, my mind addled with inexplicable lust and frustration, I imagined myself walking over to him and pulling the mask off in one smooth motion. What face would I see, softened in sleep before it sparked into rage?

Was he handsome under the mask?

He'd better be. Otherwise that dream was pointless, I grumbled inwardly. I was still far from regaining my self-control, and I shook my head, trying to bring myself back. What the hell was I thinking?

I had no business dreaming of the Hellbringer maskless, naked, body pressed tightly against mine. Fingers in places they didn't belong.

I shivered. Forcing the dream from my mind was nearly impossible when the thought of his dark voice whispering in my ear had me half undone. I hadn't even touched myself, hadn't even been touched by him.

When I moved to roll over, grumbling at the release I so desperately craved being so close and yet so far, I finally realized—more than a blanket covered me.

I slid the fabric of the Hellbringer's long cloak between my fingers. It was finely made, the material thick enough to hold in heat and sturdy enough not to rip despite endless treks and what must have been years of wear. My hand grazed a few threads that were thicker than the others, a repair where the war had left a mark of damage. But the patch was so well done, it would never be noticed without a fine eye. It was clear the hand that had mended it was loving.

This cape meant a lot to someone. And in the winter mountains, during the heaviest snow season, giving up your source of warmth was foolish at best.

Deadly at worst.

If the Hellbringer was asking for a death sentence, it wasn't my business to do anything about it. I shrugged off the gnawing unease and allowed myself to enjoy the warmth. Maybe I would wake in the morning to find a dead body keeping watch over me.

I chewed my lip, confused as to why a killer would offer me not only survival but comfort. There was no one else around to witness such an act of kindness. No one to impress.

Did the Hellbringer care what I thought about him?

No, I told myself, pushing down the part of me that desperately wanted the opposite to be true. *Mass murderers don't care what their enemies think of them.*

I pulled the thick fabric of his cloak to my face and breathed in deeply. The scent of pine and fresh snow was intoxicating, straight from my dreams. It must have been what triggered my lustful subconscious. It reminded me of home. And beneath it was a smell I couldn't identify—something unique to the Hellbringer. Rubbing my thighs together offered me no relief, and I refused to do anything in front of him that would come back to bite me. Muttering curses under my breath, I settled in. It was going to be a long night.

◆ ◆ ◆ ◆ ◆

THE MUSCLES IN MY ARMS BURNED AND MY BREATHS RATTLED IN my lungs. Painstakingly, I lowered myself to a position parallel with the ground before pushing myself back up into a plank again.

I dropped to the ground, exhausted. The cold stone felt amazing on my burning skin. Push-ups were cruel—probably the reason the Hellbringer kept making me do them.

"You complain too much," he'd told me that morning. His order before he left for the day was "Do one hundred push-ups in silence."

He didn't vanish in time to miss the obscene gesture I threw him.

I rolled onto my back and stared at the ceiling. Two nights ago I'd taught the Hellbringer a traditional line dance. The same one I'd learned at Halvar's when I was barely a teenager, finally learning what it meant to be Nilurae and royalty, despised by my family. The Hellbringer would never know how much those simple steps meant to me.

Two nights ago I'd had a highly inappropriate dream about the man, too. And now I couldn't stop thinking about it.

The dream served to confuse me more than anything, and over the past few days my frustration had only built. My body made certain to remind me I hadn't found release that night, and it made my stomach far too eager to swoop at even a hint of decency from my captor.

The only thing keeping me sane was allowing myself permission to reminisce as I fell asleep. Knowing I'd be able to imagine him touching me brought a perverse sense of relief that allowed me to focus during the day. I hated it but accepted it grudgingly. There was no other way to keep my head on straight.

Between snatches of lustful imaginings, I began to wonder what more lay beneath the general's mask. I hadn't forgotten my determination to level the playing field between him and me; despite our few moments of camaraderie, I still knew next to nothing about what made him tick. But I had no clue where to even begin my search for answers.

Prone on the floor, cheek pressed against the cool ground, I made a list in my mind: Lurae of death. Powerful general. That was all I knew.

Terrible sense of humor. Rude and bossy.

I smirked. Couldn't forget to add those to the list.

Glancing around the room, I carefully took everything in again, hunting for some clue about the Hellbringer's origins. I'd already searched the place, but then I'd been looking for any means of escape. Now I was looking for signs of life. My eyes traveled over the lanterns, armoire, fireplace, shelves. Nothing here spoke of his identity.

It was like my thoughts had summoned him. He appeared without warning and the soldier with him disappeared instantly, leaving me alone with my captor once more. "I brought you dinner from camp," he said, holding up a basket of something.

In a matter of minutes I was enjoying a bowl of stew while the Hellbringer sat across from me. My mental list returned to the front of my mind. Time to add to it. Without preamble I spoke. "Tell me something true, Hellbringer."

He stilled in his chair, tension lining the set of his shoulders. Before he had the chance to derail my line of questioning with whatever fact he deemed most worthy of sharing, I asked a question. "Do you live here?"

Did I sense a flicker of emotion in the silence, hidden behind the skull mask? "When I am participating in the war, yes."

"Why don't you stay with your legions?"

I waited for him to answer, but as the quiet dragged on for a minute, I moved on. "If this is your home, don't you want the bed? Why do you let me sleep there?"

He shrugged. "The bed is simply a formality. I'm used to sleeping on the floor."

Used to sleeping on the floor? Was that from being at war for so long, or some kind of ruthless upbringing? To be the cause of mass homicide . . . surely something in his childhood must have gone horribly wrong to put him in such a terror-worthy position.

"How old are you?" I fired the question at him in between bites of stew.

"How old do you think I am?"

"I don't know. It's impossible to guess with your whole . . ." I gestured to him, trying to indicate his armor and the mask. "You could be an old man for all I know."

There was a hint of amusement in his voice. "I'm twenty-two."

My spoon froze in midair on its way to my mouth. "You're only *twenty-two*?" I gaped. Arne was twenty-two. Freja and I would be turning twenty-two in the next year.

What was it like to be so young and have the fate of two countries at war on your shoulders? I clenched my teeth as my thoughts reminded me. *You already* do *know what it's like. You're in the same position.*

"Now it's your turn," he said, not acknowledging my disbelief. "Tell me something true. Why did you turn down your proposal?"

The callback to when I'd demanded he kill me in the snow made my cheeks heat. "Oh, I see how it is," I said with an eye roll, hoping he didn't notice the flush on my face. "No superficial facts from me, then."

He shrugged, crossing his arms and leaning back in his chair. "I already know the basics about you. A symptom of being royalty—you've never gone unnoticed. I know you just turned twenty-one. I know you are the only daughter in your family. I know you only get along with your two middle brothers. And I know someone taught you how to wield a sword wrong." Was he *smirking* underneath that mask? "Did I miss anything?"

I glared at him and swallowed the bite I was chewing. "If you must know, I refused the proposal because I didn't want to marry Volkan."

"You would rather die than be married to someone you don't love? Volkan is kind; he would have left you your freedom."

I raised an eyebrow. "How would you know?"

He sighed. "Volkan is . . . a friend."

My eyes widened and my spoon clattered in the dish. "Gods above. You dated *Volkan*?"

He whipped his head around sharply. "How the hell did you know that? Did he tell you?"

"No, you just did! You should have heard your voice when you said he was your *friend*." I laughed, then stopped abruptly. "Wait, you're not still dating him, are you?"

"No. We broke things off amicably years ago."

I picked up my spoon and resumed eating. "How did you even meet him?"

He tilted his chair back, balancing it on only the back two legs. I resisted the urge to snap at him to sit properly. "We attended many of the same diplomatic events as children. This was long before I was the Hellbringer. None of the adults wanted anything to do with us, so we got into trouble on our own."

The Hellbringer had aristocratic blood, then. If he attended the same events as Volkan, presumably when the Queen of Kryllian and the royalty of Faste got together, then he was high in station. Perhaps the queen's son? But, no, the Queen of Kryllian had no children. I tacked the knowledge onto the end of my list of facts about him.

If things had been different—if Bhorglid had been open to diplomacy—would the three of us have been friends as children? Would I have met the Hellbringer before the mask defined him?

"You're queer too, then." I raised an inquisitive eyebrow as I took my next bite.

I had no doubt he was rolling his eyes at me behind the mask. "Not that it's any of your business, but yes. Bisexual, if you want to get specific."

"Me too," I said. "It's not outlawed to be queer in Kryllian, is it?"

He shook his head. "No. I'm surprised Bhorglid doesn't make a big deal of it."

I snorted. "We make a big deal of so many other things. I'm sure we would have added queerness into the mix too if we weren't so busy policing every other aspect of people's identities."

"True. But you never answered my question: Why did you turn down the proposal?"

I scraped the bottom of the bowl with my spoon. "I rejected the proposal because I was tired of only doing what I was forced to do," I admitted. "And because I realized when my father uses me as a pawn, he gives me power to destroy his plans. In this case he believed my marriage would be the key to ending the war; all I had to do was demand what I wanted in exchange."

"And what did you want?" the Hellbringer asked.

I glanced up at him. Considered telling him about Freja for a moment, how I needed to free her. But he'd admitted to being there when she was taken prisoner. He likely already knew she was part of my motivation. Besides, if he got to keep secrets, then so did I. "You know the answer. A chance to compete for the throne."

There was a pause. "Do you think you can win?" he asked. His voice was quiet.

An ounce of the panic I'd held back for days threatened to spill over its dam. "Probably not," I said. During a sparring session a few days earlier, I'd explained the plan my brothers and I had concocted. It seemed pertinent to the Hellbringer's mission to train me. "With Frode and Jac on my side, I at least have a chance. So I'm going to try."

He nodded. "I understand. To be nothing more than a pawn in someone's game is less than ideal."

The mask hid his face and the voice distortion kept me from hearing any hint of emotion in his words as he said, "Sometimes you make sacrifices for the things you care most about. Even when the sacrifice is becoming a weapon."

We sat in the shared quiet until the fire burned to embers and I was left to wonder what—or who—the Hellbringer cared enough about to kill entire legions.

17

"AGAIN."

"But I'm tired," I gasped, sweat making my palms slick.

The Hellbringer was making me work at hand-to-hand combat. I hated it. It was evident he had been training for years and I had only been training for days. It didn't take me long to learn beneath the dark leathers was a man built of pure muscle. Every hit he allowed me to land felt like my fist was connecting with solid rock.

"Will your brothers care?" he asked, easily dodging my next sloppy punch.

I could see the smirk Björn would level at me if I said I was tired while he pummeled me with his fists. He wouldn't stop; he would light his knuckles on fire before he swung again.

The thought of my brother's flames ignited a blaze within me. I gritted my teeth and lunged again.

My fist connected with nothing but air and my center of balance lost its hold, sending me stumbling toward him. The air left my lungs in a moment of panic and I stretched my hands out to catch myself. But before my palms connected, a hand wrapped around my shoulder, catching me mid-fall and wrenching me back to my feet.

My jaw shook a bit as I realized the Hellbringer had kept me from face-planting. "This is embarrassing," I hissed under my breath. I half hoped he wouldn't hear.

He did. "You have no reason to be embarrassed. I am your teacher. The point is for you to get better. That won't happen immediately." He took his defensive stance once more. "Again."

As I squared my shoulders, I cursed myself silently for caring what he thought. He was right—he was my captor, nothing more.

So why did he make me nervous?

Don't be an idiot. He makes you nervous because you want *to hear him call you* princess *these days. If falling for him is your worst nightmare, you're standing on the edge of a precipice.*

The thought made me want to cry or hit something. Either would do.

I centered myself, drawing in the virulent emotions raging around me. Drawing a steadying breath, grinding my boots into the floor. *Never fight angry.* Maybe there was truth in his words.

Left, right, step, step, duck, turn, right, left. I almost laughed aloud when the flurry of a step-ball-change aided me in keeping up with his breakneck pace. My movements flowed like water through a river and suddenly I knew why it was so apparent the Hellbringer loved doing this, loved fighting. Because when my fists connected with his abdomen, one after the other, the pain and exhaustion didn't matter anymore. Only the dance.

My success surprised me enough that I pulled back from him, from the exercise. I stared at my hands. "I did it," I said. I glanced up at him, wide-eyed. "I did it."

He nodded. "You did."

Was he smiling behind the mask?

Why do you care if he's smiling?

I stifled the thoughts that came next. I didn't want to hear them.

He sheathed his sword and removed his gloves, tucking them into a pocket while he undid the fastenings of his armor. But I reached out and grabbed his arm, pulling his now bare hand toward me.

He stilled, and I felt the flush creeping up my cheeks as I examined his palm. "Why didn't you have a healer look at this?"

The two lines from where he'd caught my sword on our first night together were still there, an angry red. The wounds were sealed, but as I traced my thumb absentmindedly along the lines of his palm, he flinched and pulled back from me. Maybe they still hurt.

He curled his hand into a fist. "Haven't had time."

The reality of what I'd done—caressing the Hellbringer's hand—hit me. The memory of my dream resurfaced with full force once again, and for a moment I was caught up in wishing his hands would wrap around my waist and draw me closer to him.

I chewed my lip, turning away to remove my own armor, now that we were apparently finished sparring for the night. Ignoring the way my own hand tingled, like I'd been zapped by one of the harmless jellyfish in the southern sea.

I didn't ask about his hand again.

◆ ◆ ◆ ◆ ◆

THE NEXT TWO DAYS PASSED WITHOUT EVENT. TRUTHFULLY, I WAS more relaxed than ever. My dream about the Hellbringer seemed to lose its edge in the wake of my pride at being able to keep up with him when we fought now. I'd nearly forgotten it by the time the next storm arrived.

Nearly.

Running circles around the main room of the prison was my least favorite aspect of training, a fact the Hellbringer recognized and seemed determined to use against me. Even now, despite sweating profusely, I noticed the temperature dropping steadily. Goose bumps snaked across my arms when I shivered.

The Hellbringer, who was whittling away at a block of wood,

didn't look up from his task. "The weather will be dangerous tonight," he said. "There's a bad storm blowing in. We must do everything we can to keep ourselves warm."

I ran my tongue over my lips where they stuck together with dryness and wiped sweat from my forehead. "What are you proposing?" I asked, slowing to a stop. "A trip somewhere warmer?"

"No," he said, and I felt a twinge of disappointment. Although the smoke filtered out through the tunnels above the fireplace, I still smelled like the unceasing fire. My desire for fresh air was as poignant as hunger pains. I hadn't expected how cooped up I would feel without access to the outdoors.

"We will share the bed tonight."

My face burned bright red at his words, my once-clear thoughts immediately filled with memories of what I'd dreamt in that same bed mere nights before. There was no way I would be sleeping next to the man whose imagined voice had nearly made me come. "Excuse me?" I sputtered. "Absolutely not."

He didn't look up at me. The mask obscured any emotion on his face, and I glowered, knowing my expressions betrayed my feelings. "Do you not want to live through the night?"

I bristled. "I'm not the one who was stupid enough to pick an abandoned prison in the middle of the northern wastelands as my hideout. Can't your soldier teleport us? Why don't we spend the night in Bhorglid?" It was a stupid question—he would be found and captured in an instant. But, for the briefest second, I found myself missing my own bed and the way the snow fell in flurries at home instead of blizzards.

There was no acknowledgment of my question. The fire flashed sparks as he threw another log into it. "What, exactly, do you find so reprehensible about sleeping next to me?" I heard a note of wry sarcasm in his voice despite the distortion.

I rubbed a hand across my forehead. He didn't know, *couldn't* know. The whole thing had happened in my head. But the thought of the Hellbringer crooning, "Tell me you like it, Princess," had me flushing from head to toe. And that wasn't even the dirtiest thing my subconscious had made him say. "Perhaps the number of people you've slaughtered in cold blood. Will I get any sleep or spend the whole night wondering if you'll stick a knife in my back?"

"Oh, Princess. I have much more efficient ways of killing you than with a knife." He finished tending to the fire and stood, turning to face me. Within moments he was mere inches away. I had to tilt my head back to keep eye contact with the carved helmet. I staunchly ignored the thrill that ran down my spine. When had his very presence become so magnetic?

"If only you knew," he murmured, "the pleasure of feeling your magic set free to take what it pleases." He reached out and fingered a strand of hair that fell against my shoulder. Every muscle in my body tensed.

His next words were soft. "Do you know what it is like to be not a man but a weapon?"

He stepped back, releasing my hair, and gazed at the fire. I hated the red flushing my cheeks. Hated the way heat flared in my belly, between my thighs. Of all the people I could have been craving, why did it have to be the worst one?

It's physical, I reminded myself. *Nothing more.*

But something about it made me wonder. Arne and I had been physically intimate, but it had felt different; straightforward and purposeful, a means to an end. The way I was curious about the Hellbringer was a new sort of wanting.

I refused to acknowledge it. "Fine," I said. "But I won't sleep next to someone who is dressed in a full suit of armor."

He looked at himself as if realizing he was armored for the first time that evening. But he glanced at me and nodded. His hands reached up to his throat, where a chain clasped his cloak around him, and unfastened it, tossing it onto the bed.

Slowly, one piece at a time, he unstrapped his dark metal armor, revealing his casual black shirt and pants underneath. I couldn't see any of his skin, and yet I blushed like I was watching someone undress entirely.

It was too intimate. His casual clothes hugged his body, showing off lean muscle. I knew he was strong—had even seen his bare torso before—but it was another feeling entirely to *see* the strength of him on display, his shirt clinging to his biceps and his pants tight around his thighs. Every movement declared his intentions: he wanted me to watch him, to drink him in with my eyes.

I turned to hide my face from him. "Well," I said, unceremoniously. "I guess I'm . . . going to bed. If you want to join me."

He laughed then, and despite the voice modulator, the sound was lovely. "No one has ever invited me to bed with so little enthusiasm," he said, and I heard his footsteps following behind me.

I looked over my shoulder. "Don't flatter yourself." It was easy to imagine the kinds of people who must throw themselves at him in Kryllian: wealthy, charming individuals with little ambition for anything other than a life of ease. Was he allowed to maintain relationships as the Hellbringer? I opened my mouth to ask, then thought better of it and shut it promptly.

I took the left side of the bed, drawing the blanket over myself and turning to face outward. I felt the other side of the mattress sink when he sat. Both of his boots clunked against the floor as he pulled them off.

He could be ugly, I reminded myself, trying not to tense as he brushed against me. Could he hear the way my heart thundered violently?

He didn't ask, merely turned on his side to face me and wrapped an arm around me, pulling me close. He draped his cloak over both of us.

I tried to hate it. But, by the gods, he was *warm*.

Over the next several minutes my shivering slowed to a stop and my jaw relaxed. The anxiousness I'd felt about being so close to him had subsided. His arm draped casually over my stomach, the maw of the mask tilted up so his head rested above mine. The palm pressed over my belly was too much like the hand from my dream, the one that had reached down between my legs.

But beneath the layer of tension was a measure of unfamiliar comfort. I'd never been . . . held this way. Arne knew I didn't like to be touched and respected my wishes. But my hesitancy evaporated at the feeling of the Hellbringer clutching me to him.

I waited for his breathing to slow, but it remained quick. Quick from the cold or . . .

No, I scolded myself. *Don't start.*

I glanced at his hand. His glove was still torn from where he had caught my blade the very first night we'd spent together. The slices in the fabric were jagged. He must have seen a healer after I mentioned the markings on his palm, because there was no longer any trace of a scar. But his blood stained the edges of the fabric. I wondered why he didn't replace it.

I didn't realize I'd reached out to touch him until I felt the stiffness of the bloodstains on the fabric. My eyes widened and I pulled back immediately. I waited to feel another breath from him, but he was utterly still.

"Sorry," I whispered. I clutched my hand to myself.

He exhaled. "Go to sleep." I'd expected his voice to be harsh through the distortion, but it wasn't. It sounded raw, like his throat had gone dry.

Thinking about it was too much to bear. I needed to sleep. Needed to push away my feelings for the Hellbringer.

A wave of dread rolled over me. *Feelings for the Hellbringer.* Did I have feelings for him? Or was it intrigue at the mystery of it all?

No matter—soon enough we would be on opposite sides of the war again. Thinking of him this way was pointless. Besides, he'd never feel the same. He was a cold-blooded killer. Mass murder didn't leave a person untouched.

This was the wrong topic of thought for someone trying to drift off to sleep.

"You're anxious," he murmured. I tensed. "I can feel your heartbeat." He tapped with two fingers where his hand brushed against the bottom of my rib cage. "Right there."

I pushed away from him to stand up. "Don't touch me," I snarled, embarrassed at the heat coiling in my stomach from the contact. My feet were freezing to the floor, but I stood my ground, arms crossed over my chest, glaring at him.

He propped himself up on one elbow. "You'd rather freeze to death?"

I clenched my jaw. "Than be touched by a monster? Yes."

The heartbeat of silence was long enough for him to rise and stand in front of me, and I tilted my head back to look into the eyes of his mask. The reminder of our height difference made warmth pool in my belly. "Are you aware the *true* best way to share body heat is naked?" He took a step closer to me. If I moved my hand, it would've touched him.

I tried to stubbornly wish the red out of my cheeks. My imagination was taking on a life of its own, replaying the vivid dream I'd had only a few nights ago: his fingers pushing into me, his dark voice murmuring in my ear, telling me exactly what he wanted. Praising me, calling me good. How did I tell my sworn enemy I really wouldn't mind doing this naked?

The next shiver coursing through me had nothing to do with the temperature.

"Get. Back. In. Bed." The command was no more than a hardened whisper.

"No," I said through chattering teeth.

He stared at me through his helmet. "What are you afraid of? Do you feel something when I touch you?"

My eyes widened.

I watched, frozen, as he lifted a gloved hand to my face and brushed it against my cheek. "Does it scare you?"

Silence.

He shrugged. "If you'd like to freeze to death, be my guest. If not, you know where to find me." He turned and lay back on the bed, pulling the blanket around himself, facing away from me.

I knew the bitterness I felt was not as sharp as the cold enveloping me. My arms were numb. Another minute or two and I wouldn't be able to feel my legs either. If I didn't get in the bed and get close to him, I would die tonight. The crackling flames in the fireplace wouldn't be enough to prevent that.

But would climbing back into the bed be admitting defeat?

I let out a shuddering breath, watching it crystallize in front of me, and moved back to the bed. The Hellbringer lifted the side of his cloak so I could clamber under it.

Now I curled against him. Shame coiled in my stomach. Shame that he'd clearly won the advantage over me. Shame that the tentative peace I'd made with him would be ruined in the morning. And shame that I wanted to hold him close and embrace the murderer who chipped away at every barrier I put up.

Slumber took its time coming to claim me.

◆ ◆ ◆ ◆ ◆

WHEN I WOKE UP, THE COLD HAD SUBSIDED A BIT. I WAS WARM UNder the blankets and goose bumps weren't trailing telltale lines over my arms and legs. It was a relief—I'd shivered through the night despite the Hellbringer's warmth next to me.

That warmth was strikingly absent now, though. I sat up and

looked around, but I was alone. I yawned and stretched. Maybe his soldier had come to get him and take him away for a mission of some kind.

It was probably best he wasn't there, I thought while I braided my hair. It would save us both from the awkwardness. Besides, he was my enemy.

But . . . did enemies make comments to each other about sleeping naked together? Did enemies stroke each other's faces and ask what they were afraid of? Did enemies think about each other while getting themselves off?

My thoughts were abuzz.

Boots sounded on the metal floor, distracting me. Mira gave me a perfunctory glance from where she'd landed. The Hellbringer, dressed in his armor once more, stepped back into the room. He was the picture of power. Looking at him, ready for war, sent the same kind of thrill through me as when he'd been close last night, asking what I felt for him.

"Get ready," he said, adjusting his gloves. I wondered if he had just put them on. "We're leaving."

Ten minutes and a dozen questions later, my boots crunched in white snow as Mira disappeared. Afternoon sun reached down between the pines to brush against my palms.

"Oh." I stretched out my arms, looking at the green canopy of needles above me and watching my exhaled breath crystallize in the air. It tasted crisp in my lungs, fresher than the air I'd breathed all week. I felt my nose turning pink. "I've missed this."

"Stretch your legs while you can," the Hellbringer instructed. "We can't stay here for long."

I turned in a circle, trying to see if I recognized anything. Considering the entire northern half of Bhorglid looked identical, the place was unfamiliar to me. I pulled my hood over my head to warm my ears. "What are we doing here?" The trees stretched for miles. I could see no clearing in any direction. Not five minutes before, my captor had instructed me to grab my cloak and my sword. The next thing I knew, Mira whisked both of us aboveground. I was confused but not upset at the turn of events.

"I thought you could use a break from our rigorous training schedule," he said. "And I wondered if you might be interested in spying on your brothers and father for a moment."

I blinked at him. A moment of silence passed. "Spying on my family?"

"Yes."

I shook my head. He couldn't be serious. "Why? Surely you have more important things to do."

"Gathering information is what I've been ordered to do."

The thought of seeing my family again was equal parts exciting and repugnant. While I longed to see Frode and Jac and reassure them I was okay, the thought of laying eyes on my father or Björn made me shiver with dread.

I crossed my arms over my chest. "Why would you ask me to come with you?"

He sighed. "What did I say about petulant questions? Are you coming, or should I have Mira take you back?"

The threat silenced me. "Let's go," I said.

We walked for about an hour while I mulled over the Hellbringer's proposal. Was this a test? Was he waiting to see if I would run? Neither of us had reason to trust the other.

And yet . . . here we were.

If the chance came to escape, would I take it?

Part of me wanted to. It was the part of me that hated seeing only prison walls every day and despised losing every time we sparred. The part that missed Frode and Freja like cut-off limbs and longed to change things back to the way they'd been before.

The freezing wetness seeped into my socks through the tops of my boots with every step. My toes would be numb soon. The Hell-bringer's pace kept my circulation up, though, and we continued on our march.

The only way forward was through.

I smelled the smoke of a fire and heard the low rumble of an army chattering in the distance. Longing thrummed through my veins with my heartbeat. The war front wasn't home, the Lurae soldiers weren't my family, but the colors of Bhorglid and the scent of stew floating to me was like an anchor for my soul. Finally, I was going to get to see my brothers. And they would be none the wiser. *I wonder if they've missed me.*

Then a thought struck me and I froze.

"Wait," I said, grabbing the Hellbringer's arm. Nausea seized my stomach.

I must have surprised him, because my touch caused him to stop. He turned to face me. "What?"

I took a deep breath and swallowed. My voice shook. "Are you leading me into a trap? Are you going to force me to watch while you kill everyone in camp?" Tears flooded my eyes as anger did my stomach, thinking about the scene he could leave.

He didn't move or speak for a moment. I tried to keep my hold on his arm, but every muscle failed me. My other arm twitched toward the hilt of my sword.

I would kill him if I had to or die trying. Trials be damned. My people would live to see another day. Even the Lurae.

Even my family.

The breath he let out made a strange sound through whatever device altered his voice. He shook his head slowly. "We are not here to kill anyone. We are here to eavesdrop; that's it." When I didn't move, he held up his hands as if surrendering. I hadn't noticed that my hold on his arm had gone slack. "I promise." He placed his hand over his heart. "I will not kill anyone today."

"How can I trust you," I demanded through clenched teeth, "when you've killed so many already?" My hand was clutching the hilt now, ready to draw my weapon.

"I kill only when I'm ordered to," he replied, lowering his hand. "I don't know what else to tell you."

He peered into the distance where the voices were coming from. I could hear the hum through the trees. A laugh echoed above the rest of the thrum.

"What if you go on your own?" he suggested. "This trip is for you, not me. Go, eavesdrop, and return with what you learn. I will wait here for you."

I stared, stunned. "You want me to go spy on my brothers alone?"

He nodded.

Was he an idiot? Was this part of a larger plot I didn't understand?

"I'm your prisoner," I said slowly, "and you would let me go? Why?"

He sighed. "I have yet to tell you a single lie. If you choose not to believe me, then you can stay here while I go, but I must return with an update on the workings of your family. I mean them no harm. So go." The Hellbringer gestured ahead. "I won't stop you."

I was starting to feel like I had missed something. What would prevent me from lying to him about the things I heard? Kryllian might be trying to put me on the throne, but it didn't mean I was willing to hand over information willingly.

"I don't trust you," I said finally, shaking my head. "What are you trying to take from me?"

He leaned against the pine tree closest to him. "I can't make you trust me. If you don't want to go, then stay here. I have no problem doing this myself."

A sense of unease gnawed at my stomach. Frode's grin flashed against the backdrop of my mind. Catching a glimpse of him from the trees would be enough.

I hesitated, but when the Hellbringer sat cross-legged in the snow, I took a step forward. Then another. And another.

Until finally I was running, sprinting as fast as I could toward the camp, desperate to see someone, anyone familiar, to tell them to take me away from the Hellbringer.

A few minutes later I dared to look back. He had disappeared, hopefully moved out of sight. I slowed, my breathing heavy.

What would he do when I didn't come back?

My breath fogged out in front of me. Would he care? Would the Queen of Kryllian still move to make an alliance if I won the Trials after I'd ditched her most loyal hound?

But then again, why bother thinking about the long term when surviving the Trials themselves was still an uncertainty?

If you stay, he will keep helping you. My thoughts were more reasonable than usual today. *You'll have a better chance of saving Freja.*

I chewed my lip as I thought it over. That was true. And there was always a chance he would renege on his promise not to kill anyone if I didn't return.

But . . . no. He had been oddly sincere when he promised he wasn't going to use his Lurae. And it was true he hadn't lied to me, at least as far as I could tell. Maybe I could take him at his word.

I *hoped* I could take him at his word.

Maybe it would be better if I returned to the prison after getting the information the Hellbringer wanted. While the thought of Frode and Jac enduring my father alone pained me, they needed me to win the Trials more than they needed my presence on the war front.

I gritted my teeth. I didn't want to return. But I would if it meant having a better chance to make a difference.

When I was close enough to the camp, I climbed a tree and leapt from branch to branch. Soon I settled above a busy path between two large tents.

I made myself comfortable on the powdered perch, thankful for my waterproof cloak. Without it, I would have been soaked from sitting in snow. Below me, small figures swarmed the fire in the center of camp. Canvas tents were pitched around it from every side.

The Hellbringer had only said he wanted information; he hadn't specified *what* information. Hopefully that meant I could get away with saying nothing of importance when I returned. I wasn't about to give him the advantage he needed to win the war.

The Queen of Kryllian could send as many messengers as she wanted to convince me she intended to negotiate a truce with us after I became Queen of Bhorglid. But until a treaty had been signed, I refused to trust her fully.

I waited for half an hour, watching the crowds come and go, their chatter merely a hum from my vantage point, before a face I recognized appeared: Erik, walking purposefully toward the tent closest to me. He didn't look up, and if he did, he probably wouldn't have seen me. The trees were good cover.

He pushed through the entrance and disappeared into the tent.

Were they going to do all the talking inside? I frowned. There must be a way to get closer without arousing suspicion.

A hand brushed my shoulder. Without thinking, I grabbed it, whirled around, and delivered a solid punch directly to my attacker's nose. There was a crack as my fist connected with bone, and I moved to push the person off the branch.

A grunt of pain. "Shit, Rev, why'd you do that?"

I froze and took in the face in front of me, covered with blood. "Frode?" I pulled him back up to balance on the branch. "Oh, gods. I didn't realize it was you!" I pulled my sleeve over my hand and used it to wipe the blood dripping from his nostrils. "How did you—"

He cut me off with a look. I sighed. "Right. My thoughts are loud. I remember."

He chuckled, but it was muffled beneath his blood-soaked glove. "I shouldn't have startled you. What are you doing here? Everyone thinks you're dead. How did you get away from the Hellbringer?"

For a moment, I considered lying—but even that made Frode raise an eyebrow. I groaned. "I'll tell you everything, but first we need to find somewhere we won't risk being overheard. The whole camp is probably wondering what that ungodly screech was."

My brother raised an eyebrow. "Are you talking about my cry of *pain* from when you *broke my nose*?"

I couldn't smother my grin. The events of the last week felt like they'd happened years ago, but Frode managed to be the person I was most myself around.

How would I possibly live in a world without him if we didn't win the Trials?

"Come on," he said, beckoning for me to follow him. "And get those thoughts out of your head."

I did my best to empty my mind as we leapt a few trees over and clambered down. Frode led the way as we shuffled through the snow to a patch of forest with fewer trees. It wasn't a clearing, but sunlight glittered through the spaces between the pines.

Frode sighed with relief, stretched out his arms, and fell backward until he landed in the snow's soft embrace. "This is where I come when it all gets too loud," he explained. I moved to sit cross-legged next to him. "It's far enough away that I can barely hear anyone at camp. Jac knows how to shout for me if they're under attack, but since we moved so recently, it's unlikely we'll be ambushed again." I watched as he grabbed a handful of snow and pressed it to his swollen nose.

A momentary echo of music floated in from the distance. I frowned. "Is anyone nearby?"

Frode shook his head, and the red of his hair looked like flame against the whiteness. The music faded into frozen silence once more. I must have imagined it.

"They say the forest is haunted now," he replied to my thoughts. "That it's Aloisa-touched. Full of wandering souls killed by the Hellbringer."

"And you believe that?" I asked, raising my eyebrow. "I didn't take you for the superstitious type."

He shrugged. "I don't know. I've just wondered lately if my own soul might be better suited for this place than any kind of afterlife."

I stiffened, the lack of feeling in his words like a knife between my ribs. He shouldn't be thinking about his own death, not when our plan was laid out in stone. Why the sudden morbidity?

I wanted to press the matter, but I told myself there would be time later. Instead, I changed the subject.

"Well, the Kryllians do know the location of your current camp," I said, "so don't get your hopes up about avoiding another ambush."

"Are you going to tell me how you know or keep being mysterious?"

I let out a breath and watched it fog in front of me. "You have to swear to me you won't tell anyone. Even Jac. The only reason I'm telling you is because eventually you'll read my thoughts and figure it out anyway."

His solemn face didn't match the mischief in his eyes as he put his hand over his heart. "You have my word."

Gods, I'd missed him.

"The Hellbringer has been training me. Teaching me how to fight. Kryllian wants to help me win the throne so they can negotiate a truce once I'm queen and end the war." I glanced at him and let my thoughts drift through the last week. It was easier to remember than it was to explain.

I was careful to keep my thoughts far from . . . certain events, though. Namely two involving the Hellbringer's bed. Frode didn't need to know about those.

Frode's eyebrows shot up, and I knew he was observing my memories. "That's . . . a lot to take in," he said. "We've been waiting for a ransom letter. Father was confused when one never came, but now it makes sense. He assumed they'd killed you when they realized you didn't know anything."

"Wouldn't that be lucky." I rolled my eyes. "Let him keep thinking I'm dead. Things are probably easier that way."

"Well, yes and no," he said. "When Father decided it had been long enough and you weren't coming back, he was thrilled of course. But now he won't stop talking about what the battle between his 'two great sons' will be like. In case it wasn't obvious, neither I nor Jac are included on the list of said great sons."

"Aren't you glad about that, though?" I spread my cloak out and laid next to him.

He shrugged and rubbed a hand over his forehead. "I hate Father. It's impossible not to. You know that. He deserves to be despised more than anyone I've ever known. And yet . . ." Frode let his voice trail off for a moment, wincing as he examined his broken nose with his fingers. "Sometimes I look at him and wish he would be proud of me instead of disappointed."

I reached for his hand. "I'm sorry."

He laughed bitterly. "Don't be. I'm not hurting anyone but myself with those expectations."

"It isn't the same, but I'm proud of you," I whispered. "I would be lost without you."

He turned to look at me and smiled. Though his face was covered in dried blood and his expression was full of sorrow, I saw gratitude in his eyes. "I haven't forgotten the time you saved me, right after I came back from the front the first time," he said. "Even when things are hard, I'm always grateful you found me in time and stopped me. You've given me reason to keep living."

I squeezed his hand. "I miss you, Frode," I said. "I'm staying in an abandoned prison. It's freezing cold. Most of my days are spent alone. I want to come home."

"No, you don't." When I shot him a puzzled look, he continued, "Or at least, you shouldn't. I see how difficult it is for you to weather this training, but if Kryllian truly does want to end the war, you *must* win the throne. And the Hellbringer might be a terrible companion, but it's only been three weeks and I can already see more confidence in your eyes."

I'd known he was going to encourage me to stay, but for a moment disappointment tore through me. Part of me wished he would beg me to come back with him.

Frode stood and reached down to pull me to my feet. Then he wrapped me in a hug. "I miss you more than words could ever say," he murmured, "but we need you to be strong. For me and Jac. For Freja. For the godforsaken."

"I will," I said, though the tears leaking from the corners of my eyes begged me to say otherwise. "Oh, wait, before you go—I was supposed to be spying. I need some sort of information to bring back to the Hellbringer."

"Father has no plans except to find the Hellbringer, but he's no closer than before." Frode pulled away and brushed the tears from my face. "We have no leads. Now go, and tell him I said if he lets anything happen to you, I'll kill him where he stands." He offered me a lopsided grin.

I rolled my eyes. "Yeah, just threaten the most dangerous man in the world."

"I have no doubt you beat me to that opportunity the moment he took you." He winked. "Now go. We'll be okay. And so will you."

✦ ✦ ◆ ✦ ✦

WHEN THE AFTERNOON WAS TURNING TO DUSK, PAINTING THE sky bright orange, I arrived back where the Hellbringer and I had parted ways. There was no one around. The snow itself appeared untouched. Had he abandoned me?

I glanced up and my eyes found him then, sitting on a low-hanging branch in the dimming light, his back to the tree's trunk. "I suppose wearing all black does help camouflage you when it's dark," I called. "Care to come down?"

In one smooth motion, he tilted and let himself fall into a back-flip, landing expertly on his feet. *Show-off.*

"You're back sooner than I expected." He dusted snow off his gloves as he came toward me, then paused. "Part of me thought you might not return at all."

I stared at his feet. Was I supposed to tell him I hadn't wanted to? I debated for a moment before deciding to keep my conflicted feelings to myself. I'd returned, and that was what mattered.

"What information did you gather?" he asked.

"No progress," I said, my voice hoarse from the crying I had done earlier. "They are no closer to finding you."

Before I could continue, he replied, "Excellent. Let's go. Mira will be waiting for us." The Hellbringer turned and began walking away.

"That's . . . that's it?" I asked uncertainly. "Nothing else you wanted to know?"

He glanced over his shoulder. "This journey was not for me, Princess. It was for you. If only for you to realize you are not my prisoner but my guest. And to learn I am always a man of my word."

I considered his words as I followed several steps behind him. "Did you know they say this forest is haunted now?" I ventured. "By all of your victims?"

He didn't turn to face me, simply kept walking. "And what do *you* think?"

"Well, my people wonder if you're Aloisa-touched. It wouldn't surprise me they also think the forest might be."

"I'm not goddess-touched," he said. "Or so I hope. If your gods are real, then they're foolish."

I chuckled. "Yes, they are. You don't believe in any gods?"

He shook his head. "No god would be foolish enough to entrust a power like this to me. A god turning a human into a weapon? It's more than nonsensical. It's cruel."

He took two more steps forward before a Bhorglid sentry, clothed in forest colors to keep himself hidden, moved out from behind the trees and fired an arrow straight into the Hellbringer's arm.

The scarlet on the snow made me gasp. My hand flew to my mouth and I reached out—though I wasn't sure if it was to comfort his pain or stop his retaliation—but the world had slowed and I was frozen in place.

A scream stuck in my throat, my eyes locked on the scene as the Hellbringer gave no reaction to the pain except to face the sentry and raise his hand, palm out, then close it into a fist.

And the Bhorglid soldier fell dead in the snow.

18

THE NEXT MINUTES BLURRED TOGETHER.

The Hellbringer moved quickly, shoving the arrow through his arm with a growl of pain. He broke the shaft and pulled both halves out, leaving the projectile to stain the snow a slick red. Then he grabbed my arm and pulled me forward.

"You . . . you . . . you *killed* him," I gasped.

He said nothing, only moved faster, blood dripping behind him. With a *crack*, Mira appeared in front of us. She took one look at the Hellbringer's arm and said, "Healer?"

"Not until you take her back."

I moved to pull my arm from his grasp, but Mira took my other wrist and left me stumbling to the floor in the flickering light of the prison. Then she disappeared, presumably to take the Hellbringer to be healed.

◆ ◆ ◆ ◆

WHEN THE HELLBRINGER RETURNED TEN MINUTES LATER, I WAS in the same place Mira had left me: on my hands and knees, shivering.

I didn't look at him. He didn't speak.

It had been instinct, nothing more, when he clenched his fist, ripping the life from the young sentry. The boy had shot him; what did I expect? It was self-defense.

But was it really? With the odds so far in his favor?

He had to kill the boy. No one could know the Hellbringer was there.

He promised you he wouldn't. He said your people would be safe.

I couldn't get the image out of my head: the young boy, no older than sixteen, dark hair speckled with snow, trying to hide the fear on his face as he fired an arrow. He must have known what would happen to him. And yet he took his shot anyway, like his superiors would have instructed him.

His eyes going glassy. The way he crumpled to the ground like a rag doll.

I'd never witnessed the Hellbringer's destructive power with my own eyes. Until now, he'd behaved like a Nilurae—like me. It made the soldier's death all the more startling, because at some point over the last three weeks I'd stopped believing he was capable of murdering innocents. Of annihilating my people.

Despite my harsh return to reality, no fear slithered through me. Only anger, hot as Björn's fire, curling in my stomach and my shoulders and my hands. I forced myself to my feet, trembling, and shoved the Hellbringer with all my might, half hoping to push him into the flames. He didn't stumble but took a step back.

"Revna, I—"

"Shut up!" I screamed. My fingers tangled in my damp hair, pulling at it frantically. "How could you? You *promised* me you wouldn't!" I took my fighting stance and threw blow after blow, hitting him as hard as I possibly could.

He stood still and took each one.

When my arms had no strength left and tears stained my cheeks, grief flowing from me for a boy whose name I didn't know, I fell to my knees.

"*There is no greater death than to die in service to Bhorglid.*" My father's voice echoed through my head.

"No," I moaned. "No, no, no."

A pair of arms wrapped around me, pulling me in. I sobbed into the Hellbringer's shirt until my mind was empty.

❖ ❖ ❖ ❖ ❖

WHEN I WOKE UP, THE HELLBRINGER WAS GONE.

At some point, while he rocked me softly against his chest, I must have fallen asleep. And then . . . he moved me to the bed. It was the only explanation. Every muscle hurt, as if the soreness resulting from each training session had held back until now, the well-earned pain demanding to be remembered. I groaned. My voice was hoarse, my eyes swollen.

I rolled over and pulled my cloak over my face. Why did I have to be awake? Why couldn't I sleep and forget it all?

It was impossible to tell whether I'd slept till the afternoon, missing our morning training, or if the Hellbringer had left early to give me space. I didn't particularly care either way.

I added another thing to my list of what I knew about him: *liar.*

He had promised me he wouldn't hurt anyone, wouldn't kill anyone while we were visiting the camp, and he had lied. Even though the boy had shot him, even though retaliation was instinctual, he had taken an innocent life.

You know he didn't mean to.

I pushed the thought out of my head. Why did it matter? The Lurae were all the same. They saw everyone around them as bodies to do their bidding and nothing more.

The boy was Lurae, too.

Tears welled in my eyes again at the thought, emotion clawing at my chest. One day he would have been exactly like the Hellbringer.

Maybe that made his sacrifice a worthy one. To keep another Lurae from terrorizing Bhorglid.

That was when I heard it. Coming from somewhere deep inside the prison, a haunting, eerie noise like a wail.

I scrambled for my sword. There was someone else here. How had they gotten in?

Grabbing a lantern, sword in my other hand, I peered into the darkness. The noise was quiet, as if it were nothing but a distant memory echoing through the halls. If there was someone here, they were far away.

I took a step into the darkness and frowned. The echoes made it difficult to discern which direction the noise came from, but after a moment of hesitation, I turned left. I had to start somewhere.

I followed a twisting path for ten minutes, the sound slowly growing louder as my fingers went numb. The noise was strange and animallike, almost unrecognizable. How had something living managed to work its way into this underground sanctuary?

I turned the corner, and my lantern cast a too-familiar shadow on a distant wall. Panic hit me like a punch to the stomach and I stepped back fast, hiding behind the corner, shielding the lamp with my cloak to hide the light.

The Hellbringer hadn't seen me. I relaxed slightly, tilting my head to listen.

He was crying.

No, not simply crying. He rested on his knees, face in his hands, and shaking sobs echoed back to me. Despair resounded around us, each of his shaking breaths punctuating his anguished lament. But most startling was my eyes adjusting to the darkness just enough to see his helmet resting next to him. He faced away from me, any details of his face obscured in the darkness. Long dark hair covered the back of his head, appearing in the dim light almost the same color as his mask, which stared at me now with wide, unseeing eyes.

As I stood frozen, he spoke.

"Forgive me." His voice trembled, thick with emotion. "Please forgive me."

A shiver shook me, and I didn't know if it was the cold or the realization that I was eavesdropping on something personal. Even sacred. Was he praying? He'd said he didn't believe in any gods. What higher power could possibly grant him forgiveness?

What could make the Hellbringer sound broken?

My hands shook. I rushed back down the hallway, keeping my footsteps as quiet as I could, hoping he wouldn't hear me.

With each step, thoughts flooded my mind. One stuck out more than the others: Did he . . . feel *guilty* for the young boy he had killed?

Upon returning to our room, I hung the lantern in its place and sat cross-legged in front of the fire, letting the flames warm my cold fingers, wondering when he would return.

I wasn't sure what I'd say when he did.

The part of me burning with hatred and mistrust had been replaced with acceptance and understanding when Frode told me to stay with him. For all of the Hellbringer's anger during the first several days of my captivity, he'd slowly softened. I'd wondered as we spoke after I returned from talking with Frode if a tentative understanding was building between us.

I stared at the dancing flames and sighed. Just this morning I wanted to leave and never come back. Now I was convincing myself the Hellbringer's intentions were good, even when they resulted in death. Never had my morals been so complicated; until now, the only dilemmas I'd had to face involved the priests and their foolish philosophies.

This . . . was entirely different.

Are you any better than him? My treacherous thoughts betrayed me. *The only reason you're here is so you can kill your own brothers and steal a crown you don't deserve. At least the boy he killed posed a real threat.*

I swallowed. I didn't want to be like the Hellbringer. But I'd have to continue deeper and deeper down the path of a killer if I wanted to survive the Trials.

Not everyone wept when they ended a life, though. Forgiving him felt impossible, even though I knew it made me a hypocrite to hold today against him. Maybe it was enough to move forward and hope for the best. Allow his actions to show me his true intentions.

The sound of boots on the metal floors announced his return. When he walked in, I stood in the open area and pointed my sword at him. "Draw your weapon," I said. "It's sparring time."

19

FOUR DAYS LATER I LOOKED DOWN AT MYSELF AND WISHED— not for the first time—for a change of clothes. I'd been wearing the same ones since I departed Bhorglid. I spent all day sweating or shivering in them and they reeked. It had been almost three weeks now since I first arrived in the prison. How much longer would I be living in my own filth?

When I expressed my need to bathe, I expected the Hellbringer to decline, rudely reminding me that I didn't get to ask for anything as long as I was here. Instead, whatever torment he'd felt earlier this week seemed to be forgotten as he displayed his usual, straight-to-the-point attitude. "Come with me," he demanded. He turned on his heel and stalked out of the room.

I hurried to grab my sword and follow him. Maybe we were training in the enclosed spaces of the prison hallways today.

He moved quickly, never looking back to see if I followed him. I worked up a sweat keeping up. Did he know I was there, or was it up to me to avoid getting lost?

We walked for about fifteen minutes before reaching the door I'd tried to make my escape through. The same crowbar I'd used to try and pick the lock lay discarded on the floor, exactly where I'd dropped it when he startled me that early morning, demanding I travel to the forge with him. Had it really only been two weeks since then?

Now he removed a chain from around his neck with a key on it. I frowned, stretching up on my tiptoes to examine it more closely. He hadn't been wearing it when he had his shirt off in the forge, and I'd never seen so much as a glimmer of light catching on the artifact when we were sparring.

He reached to unlock the door. "If you're still entertaining thoughts of escaping, then be warned: I rarely have the key on me."

I wasn't sure if the Hellbringer or I was more surprised when I softly said, "I'm not. Entertaining thoughts of escape, that is."

It was impossible to decipher my own thoughts or untangle the web of emotions inside me, but the words weren't false. While sparring together after I'd seen him weeping, I'd decided to set aside my complaints and remain here willingly. This was where I needed to be; I was done fighting it.

For a moment he stilled. The time around us froze like the winter landscape when the door swung open to reveal an opening filled with snow up to my chest. But he didn't comment on it, instead saying, "You know, this is one of the few times I wish we were working to get that fire Lurae brother of yours on the throne."

I shoved him, and he laughed, an unexpected sound that echoed in the wild, snow-covered wastes.

Half an hour and a lot of swearing later, we'd managed to hike to a body of water nearby. Steam curled off the surface, tendrils reaching for the trees around them like wanting hands.

"Oh," I sighed as a bit of warmth drifted over me. "A hot spring." I couldn't hide the surprise in my voice.

"Yes," he confirmed. "I figured it was time I brought you here to wash your clothes and have a bath. You reek."

I rolled my eyes. "The stories don't lie when they speak of your pleasant demeanor, do they?" I remarked drily. I couldn't deny the truth of his words, though. "I do need to bathe."

He reached into the bag slung over his shoulder and set a neatly folded pile of black clothing on a dry rock near the shoreline. "I had an extra set of clothes stored. While you wait for yours to dry, change into these. Wash yourself and your clothes. When you're dressed, call for me and I will return."

"Thank you." This show of kindness was . . . unexpected to say the least. In the time since we'd returned from my family's camp, the Hellbringer had been different. A bit softer around the edges.

It was new. It was nice. And sometimes I found myself opening my mouth to tell him I didn't begrudge him the sharpness he'd held before—in fact, maybe I even understood his need to keep me at a careful distance—but I never allowed the words to leave my mouth.

Now he hesitated a moment, then nodded before walking away.

I waited until his silhouette disappeared between the trees, then sprinted into the water fully clothed. I sighed as I felt the silt and grime washing away. The water soaked through the fabric of my clothes and left them to fall heavy on me.

I dunked my head under the hot water, letting it burn my skin. While I was submerged, I took the tie off the end of my braid, letting my hair fall loose around my shoulders. It floated, unearthly, like a shadow beneath the water's surface.

I wanted to strip my clothes off so I could scrub at my skin, but I glanced toward the path we'd carved through the snow, where the Hellbringer had retreated. Unease gnawed at me. Was it safe? Was he out of sight?

He had disappeared into the thick copse of trees. No dark figure stared back at me.

And if it did, I realized I didn't particularly care. The coat of grime over my body itched enough that it would be worth it.

I pulled my clothes off, one item at a time, and scrubbed them before tossing them toward the nearest dry rock. I then proceeded to wash myself more thoroughly than I'd ever done before.

When I scrubbed my face, I was surprised to feel traces of the paint the priests had marked me with stuck to my skin. I'd forgotten about it once I'd been captured. As I washed it off, I smirked at the irony of being branded by Aloisa—marked for death. The Hell-bringer was about as close to death as a person could get, and yet here I was, unclaimed by it.

Guess the priests aren't as prophetic as they like to think they are. The thought was as satisfying as submerging myself in the water.

Time moved faster than I wanted, and when I finished washing, I let myself float on my back, savoring the heat. I hummed with contentment.

A song my mother used to sing—the same one Frode had been humming that fateful day when I met Volkan for the first time—drifted through my memory. It was instinct to let my voice carry the tune over the slowly moving water, the soft drifts of snow on the bank of the hot spring. I couldn't remember the words, but the tune had stayed with me throughout the years. And now, I realized happily, the notes reminded me of my brother and not my selfish, bitter queen.

The tune echoed slightly through the trees, somehow managing to touch each flake of snow on the ground. As I sang, I realized that for the first time in a long time, I wasn't angry. I wasn't thinking about my father or my brothers; the looming Bloodshed Trials hadn't crossed my mind in hours; and the constant fury bubbling under my skin at being treated like godforsaken trash had cooled.

It was peaceful.

Eventually the song came to an end, and I relished the silence for a moment longer, loath to leave. The sooner I got out of the hot spring, the sooner I had to endure the frigid temperatures on the hike back to the prison.

I couldn't stay forever, though. I wrung my hair out as I stepped onto the shore, rocks digging into the soles of my feet, and grabbed the pile of clothes the Hellbringer had left for me. There was a towel on top that I used to dry off, then wrapped around my sopping hair.

The pants went on first, then the long-sleeved black shirt. The material was soft, much better than the travel garb I'd been wearing for . . . was it twenty-five days now? The waistband of the pants draped loosely on my hips, threatening to fall if I wasn't careful. Likewise, the shirt was too big but tight around my chest. Clearly made for a man.

Then it hit me—these were the Hellbringer's clothes. He hadn't brought back a set of women's clothing when he went aboveground. He had found an extra pair of his own clothes and left them here for me.

A smile flickered across my face. He didn't have to show me the hot spring. Didn't have to lend me clean clothes. But he did anyway.

For a murderer, there was certainly some kindness behind the mask. I wondered how much he did under orders, and not of his own will. It confused me.

Maybe it confused him, too.

Either way, a sort of intimacy came with wearing another person's clothing. I didn't mind. I doubted the Hellbringer intended anything other than basic decency.

When I'd put on my cloak and boots, among my other warm outer layers, I gathered my wet clothes in the towel and called out. "Hellbringer? Are you there?"

I glimpsed the shadow of a man in the distance. He faced away from me. "Are you . . . decent?"

I snorted and began trekking over to him. The pants, too big around my ankles despite being rolled up several times, allowed some of the snow in and I winced at the sensation. The Hellbringer turned to face me, then froze, still as a rabbit realizing it was a wolf's next meal. "Yes. Can we go back now?"

For a moment he merely looked at me, hands balled into fists. I tilted my head. "Hellbringer?"

His name brought him back to reality. He nodded, and we began to walk. His distorted voice floated back to where I walked behind him. I thought I heard a slight tremor in his voice when he said, "You sing beautifully."

Red stained my cheeks. "You heard that?"

He glanced over his shoulder. "Yes."

How close had he stayed? Within earshot, clearly. "You didn't . . . I mean you weren't . . ." I paused, letting the question hang unspoken in the air.

He stopped abruptly and I nearly ran into him. "*No*," he said forcefully. "I stayed out of sight. I would never have dreamed of . . ." He shook his head and resumed walking. Then he muttered, "I know what you must think of me. It's true I am a monster, but there are lines I will not cross. You are safe with me here. And not only because those are my orders."

I couldn't explain why, but I believed him. The nervousness in me settled, and we kept moving.

The question had brewed in my mind for days, ever since our return from Bhorglid's camp. Since the sentry boy was killed. I'd kept the curiosity clutched to my chest since then, but the hot water had loosened not only my limbs but my tongue, too. "When you kill on the battlefield with your Lurae . . . do you do it because you want to or because you're ordered to?"

He didn't seem fazed; he only chuckled, the sound cold as darkness. "Trying to find my humanity?"

I didn't answer. I *was* trying to find his humanity. Truthfully, I enjoyed being with the Hellbringer more than my own family. He made me feel like myself—here I was Revna, not the godforsaken princess.

And didn't it make me as much of a monster, to care for the man who murdered my people for sport?

"I hate to disappoint you, Princess, but it doesn't matter. I'm the one behind the blade—metaphorically speaking, of course. I am a monster either way."

I bit back the disappointment slicing through me, and we walked in silence the rest of the way. But it didn't keep my thoughts from spinning. There was something beneath the mask I wanted to discover. What was it?

A memory came unbidden. The summer I was twelve, a delegate from Faste had come to the castle. She had dark hair that fell in dreadlocks and gold piercings peppering her brown skin. There was a tattoo on her forehead she'd explained to me, though that part of the memory was fuzzy. But I did remember her peculiar Lurae—she could taste the emotions of the people around her.

"Imagine the bittersweet taste of a lemon," she'd whispered to me at dinner. "That is what it tastes like to dream of what you can never have."

I held back a sigh. The memory of lemons lingered in my mouth. I couldn't deny it—I wished the Hellbringer might feel I was worth something. That I was important enough to make a difference. That he wouldn't be disappointed or disgusted with the lack of potential in me, not the way others were.

And I supposed, deep down, I wished he would take me away from it all.

◆　◆　◆　◆　◆

"WHAT IS THE QUEEN OF KRYLLIAN LIKE?"

The sound of a knife scraping shreds off a block of wood stopped instantly, and I looked up from where I sat at the table, pretending to read the book on war strategy. I rubbed the thin pages between my fingers, anxiously awaiting his reply.

He was in the middle of carving something, though I wasn't sure what. I'd tried several times to steal glances, but it was too early to tell what the finished product would be. Perhaps another hilt for a weapon. The other day, he'd presented me with two of the daggers he forged while I was busy shaping Aloisa.

I'd accepted the gifts reverently, uncertain how to feel about the gesture. But considering I was training for battle, I wasn't about to turn down a weapon.

"I only ask because surely she and I will be working closely after the war is over," I hurriedly explained, not entirely certain why I was so nervous about having this conversation with him. "I want to make sure allying with her is the best choice—the right choice."

"Of course it's the right choice," he scoffed. "You don't have another one. The only reason this war isn't already over is because the queen doesn't want it to be. If she did, your family would be dead at my hand long ago."

"And that's what I don't understand. Why are we still fighting? If she could easily destroy us and take Bhorglid in a few days, then why hasn't she?"

The Hellbringer sighed and set down his project. "I wish I knew. The citizens are becoming tired of the war, from what I can tell. There is no public interest in taking over Bhorglid, only in stopping the violence. Many people are frustrated with the queen for not ending things when she easily has the power to."

"Through you," I pointed out. "Does she really have any power other than what you offer her?"

"Yes." His response was instant and gravely serious. "I'm nothing more than a weapon to her. A powerful one, to be sure, but if I weren't here, she still could have conquered your country in just a few weeks."

"A few weeks?" I gaped. "This war has been constant for the past seven *years*."

"I know." He moved a hand toward his mask, then seemed to catch himself, closing his fingers into a fist before bringing it back down. I wondered if he had wanted to run his hand through his hair or rub it along his jawline. "This is bigger to her, for some reason. I have the same question you do: Why does she want to end the war now, when you have the potential to sit on the throne? It's not out of any desire to spare your people, I can assure you."

"What is her Lurae?"

"No one knows. She's never used it in any recognizable way."

I stared, uncertain what to say. "She sounds . . . as bad as my father."

He shrugged. "Maybe. I don't know your father well enough to say."

I swallowed. If I won the Trials and became queen, would it only be possible to end the war by becoming a pawn again?

"Hellbringer?" He looked up. "Why do you stay? Why do you kill for her?"

His gloved fingers began to drum against the table. The quiet, bated breaths escaping me while I waited to see if he would answer felt like anvils against my chest. This woman, this queen I would have to bargain with for the safety of my people . . . was she hurting him? What did she hold against him to make him do these things?

The Hellbringer cleared his throat and stared into the fire. "I have a sister."

I was afraid to ask, but I had to. "Is the queen . . ."

"Torturing her? No. Holding her captive? Also no. Sonja probably thinks I'm dead, truth be told. I have no idea where she is, only that she's safe and healthy enough. But the queen knows. And she will have Sonja killed the instant I step out of line."

My heart sank. This was the knifepoint he'd hinted at when I confronted him at the forge. A sister. One who clearly meant a lot to the Hellbringer.

The question of his parents flitted across my mind. They were aristocrats, surely—to date Volkan, the Hellbringer would have been running in upper circles. Was the Queen of Kryllian threatening the daughter of her staunchest supporters? Or was there more to the general's history I wasn't picking up on from the basics he chose to share?

It struck me then that the Hellbringer and I were far more alike than I'd ever wanted to believe. Two pawns of our respective monarchs, the lives of our siblings strangely tied to our freedom.

"Death is a strange concept in my family," I offered quietly. "My brothers were raised knowing it followed their every footstep. Each year the Trials grew closer and their fates more certain, especially as our parents began to show favoritism toward the more powerful of them. When I planned to involve myself in the Trials, I knew it would mean killing some of them. And yet, I still can't imagine it."

The soulless gaze of the mask was fixed unwaveringly on me. I wondered what expression he wore beneath it—whether the conversation was as raw for him. I continued. "If someone was holding Frode captive, I would do the exact same thing as you."

"Become a monster? I doubt that."

"You're more human than you think." I kept my voice soft. The feeling that he would shut down if I pushed him too far was instinctual, innate.

Something had changed between us, but I didn't mind. The Hellbringer was gentler, more careful with me. And now the secrets between us thinned with every passing minute as he bared pieces of his soul. Told me of his sister and the atrocities he committed in her name.

The trust he placed in me felt like the most tender of gifts. And while maybe once I'd believed him to be a monster, I wasn't sure he truly was—not anymore.

I wanted to see his face. To lean over and pull the mask off, to look into his eyes and memorize the sadness there. To do everything in my power to make sure he never felt like that again.

Instead, I stood from the table and held out a hand, palm open. "Dance with me, Hellbringer."

I watched his throat work for a moment before he tentatively reached out and took my hand. Tugging him from his seat reminded me of the last time, when I'd only been his prisoner for a week and a half. For a man who moved like a shadow in battle, he had two left feet on the dance floor. It hadn't taken long for him to become the frustrated one.

This time he was marginally better. I called out the steps to the line dance in a rhythm. The Hellbringer was consistently half a beat behind, needing to watch my every move before he made his own. And when he tripped and fell on his ass trying to do the step-ball-change, I cackled, tears streaming down my face from laughter.

Grumbling, he pushed to his feet. "We're doing this my way now."

The next thing I knew, we were so close our heaving breaths brought our chests mere centimeters apart. One of the Hellbringer's hands was wrapped tight around my waist and the other grasped my own, lifting our joined palms up in the air. My free hand found his shoulder, resting there lightly.

The laughter faded into silence. The only sound was the crackle of the fire, which cast shadows over the mask.

It was terrifying. But I was not afraid.

"This is a far different kind of dance." My voice was hoarse, my throat full of something I couldn't name.

The fingers on my waist tightened briefly, then relaxed as he replied, "This is the only kind of dancing I'm familiar with."

He stepped backward and I followed, his movement so certain, I didn't fear missing a step. The Hellbringer would guide me.

"You were raised an aristocrat, then?"

Why was my voice so breathy? Why was my heart pounding so loudly? Why was I so acutely aware of every inch of skin touching the fabric of his borrowed clothing?

Why did I wish I knew what his lips looked like?

"Yes and no." His response was the only warning he gave before he spun me, sending me away from his warmth for a brief second before pulling me back in.

When our bodies reconnected, touching all the way down, my breath left me in a whoosh. This, nothing more than the barest connection, was even more electric than my dream of him had been. I wanted to kiss him or bite him; I wasn't sure which. Neither felt adequate to express what was happening inside me right now, the way I wanted to meld myself with him. We understood each other so precisely, so intrinsically. Surely there was a way to commemorate it, to force the knowledge on the world, ensure no one forgot.

My next inhale was filled with him. The pine and snow scent he carried everywhere, the faint trace of smoke from our living quarters. Did his skin smell like this, too? If I ran my tongue over the planes of his stomach, would my mouth taste of the northern wastes?

Slowly, ever so slowly, he leaned forward until the forehead of the mask was pressed to mine. I couldn't hold in the sound that escaped me.

"Something true." My voice trembled under the magnitude of what I couldn't hold back any longer. "I want to see your face. I want to take off your mask."

"I know," he murmured, a hand coming up to caress my cheek. "I know. But we can't."

I swallowed. "Don't you trust me?"

"Revna." He sounded pained, his hold on my hand tightening. "I can't."

The disappointment brought me back to myself. The elation of being so close, reveling in our newfound trust, evaporated in an instant. I cleared my throat and took a step back, removing myself from his embrace.

"You're right." I couldn't look at him. "I won't ask again."

The prison was colder and quieter than usual when we separated, each of us heading to our respective sleeping places.

20

THE DAYS FOLLOWING WERE HEAVY WITH TENSION.

Things had changed between us again in another unspoken way—far too similar to when we'd first returned from spying on my family's camp. Then I hadn't been sure what to make of his kindness, the way he'd softened around me. Now, when every interaction turned into a spat, it was easy.

The Hellbringer was frustrated.

Our tender moment of dancing had been electrifying. But when he reminded me of the barrier between us, his hidden identity, the duties we both needed to put first . . . he might as well have dumped a bucket of ice water over me.

I refused to become tangled in something so messy. Not now, when my complete focus had to be on the Trials. And especially not when the person I wanted wouldn't even show me his face.

I understood his reasoning. But it wasn't enough.

He seemed determined to punish me for it. Or perhaps he was punishing himself; there was no way to be certain.

Sparring against the Hellbringer was nothing like sparring with Halvar. The pub owner had been precise but slow—something I didn't realize until the Hellbringer began to spar against me with a speed and intensity I'd never seen before.

The past two nights I'd gone to bed sore, my muscles aching so badly that I woke multiple times. Yesterday, I demanded he take me to the hot springs again for a long soak. He didn't seem inclined to acquiesce, but I knew my facial expression conveyed what my words didn't: if he didn't take me to the gods-damned hot springs that instant, I would use the sword he had helped me make to end his sorry life.

The water helped my muscles recover. I no longer felt like every part of my body was swollen. Visiting the hot springs had the added benefit of giving me the chance to wash the set of clothing the Hellbringer lent me the last time we were there. I was sad to see it go—it was ridiculously comfortable—but it was more satisfying to see his hands clench at his sides when I returned the sopping-wet pile of fabric to him.

If he wanted to fight dirty, I would fight right back.

There was no morning sun to shine over us as we sparred today. Only flickering firelight that reminded me too much of our dance together.

Sweat poured down my forehead, forcing me to blink it out of my eyes or risk giving the Hellbringer an opening. I couldn't stand to let him win—not today. Not when he was acting like an ass.

After a particularly rough clash of our swords, my thin patience fractured. "What the fuck is your problem?" He pretended not to hear me.

The next strikes came with enough blunt force behind them to make me stagger. More than once I had to leap out of reach of his blade. Even parrying took all my energy. Before long, I was exhausted once more.

My hands twisted along the leather covering Aloisa's hilt and I swore. "Why are you acting like such a man-child right now? If you have something to say, then say it!"

"*No*," he snapped, finally stopping. I followed his lead, lowering my guard slightly. Was he going to finally explain what was happening in his head?

If only. "Your hands are wrong." He stepped over to me and I wordlessly held out my hands, wrapped around the hilt of my sword. It took all my willpower not to snap at him for his rough readjustment.

"There," he said finally. "Again."

"You were the one who told me never to fight angry."

"*Again.*"

I planted my feet and raised my blade. As I adjusted, grit scraped beneath the soles of my boots.

We fell into the rhythm of war once more.

Fury fueled each of his movements—I knew because the Hellbringer's swings became sloppy and wild, the way mine had been when we first started training.

For the first time since we'd started training together, I was afraid of him.

Was this battle real? Was my life in danger?

He lunged, plunging the sword down from above his shoulder. I swung mine up to meet it. They connected with a clang and I shifted my weight to the left, kicking out with my right foot to try and connect with his ribs.

He stepped back, lithe as a wildcat, and moved toward me again, twisting with his strike. Adrenaline pumped through my veins. But my core tension slipped enough to take me off-balance, and a wave of panic surged through me. I exhaled in a whoosh as pain erupted across the top of my arm and veered into my shoulder, the impact of his blade in my flesh pushing me to the ground.

The world blurred around me as my shoulder connected with the floor. An uncontrollable spasm wracked my body and I let out a cry. My right hand went to my injured shoulder on instinct, but I didn't feel the touch—only the blood seeping through my fingers.

"Shit." The Hellbringer was on his knees at my side in seconds, lifting me into his arms. "Shit, I didn't— I'm so sorry."

The world blurred. I struggled to keep my eyes open. A fuzzy figure approached me, humming a familiar melody. Frode? I cringed when my arm moved. My mind buzzed with questions fueled by panic. How bad was the wound? How much blood had I lost?

I slammed my eyes closed as a wave of nausea washed over me. I would *not* throw up on the Hellbringer; it would haunt me for the rest of my life.

"Take us," I heard him say, and before I knew what had happened, my stomach lurched again, the way it had when I was first transported to the prison—like I'd been flipped upside down and turned inside out.

A gust of cold wind hit my face and I curled into the Hellbringer's chest to shield myself from it. Through the pain, one thought reverberated: *Outside. I'm outside.*

I heard noises I couldn't identify: shuffling and thudding and murmuring. But I did hear the Hellbringer shout, "I need a healer *now!*"

I tried opening my eyes, but nausea swept over me once more and I had to turn my head to vomit in the snow. Dizzy. I was so dizzy.

Clinging to consciousness with everything I had wasn't enough. Moments after emptying my stomach, the darkness swept me away.

◆   ◆   ◆   ◆   ◆

I FADED IN AND OUT FOR WHAT MUST HAVE BEEN SEVERAL HOURS, the whole time dreaming of a melody I couldn't escape. It repeated itself over and over until I was lost in the jumble of notes and sounds.

The first time I dared open my eyes, a familiar face hovered over me.

"Volkan?" I whispered, tilting my head. I must be hallucinating.

But he offered me a grim smile. "Nice to see you, Revna. How about we get this healed up for you?" He muttered something under his breath and reached out to touch my wound.

I couldn't feel a difference through the pain.

He laid a hand on the gash and I looked over. A giant chunk of my flesh was missing. Strange, to look at your own body and see brokenness. Every falling drop of blood rang in my ears, played the next note in the song hovering just close enough for me to hear.

As soon as he touched my arm, the pain began to subside. I sighed with relief. Slowly, the muscle and blood vessels started weaving their way back together, prompted by Volkan's magic. It itched and burned, but as tears filled my eyes, I was grateful.

"What are you doing here?" I asked, my voice raspy. I must have screamed even while I was unconscious.

"We'll talk about that later," he said with a gentle smile. He pressed something against my lips. "Now chew. It'll help with the pain."

I obeyed, and then I swam in stars again.

◆ ◆ ◆ ◆ ◆

I DRIFTED AWAKE IN THE DARKNESS. NIGHT ENVELOPED MY SUR-roundings like a lover's embrace.

With a gasp, I reached for my shoulder. There was nothing but smooth skin where there had once been a gaping wound. I looked around but couldn't see anything. "Where am I?" I mumbled, rubbing sleep from my eyes.

"You're awake." One of the lanterns was lit and the Hellbringer was revealed, sitting in a chair on my left, watching over me with his mask on.

He looked like an omen of death. Fitting. In my hazy state of mind, I giggled.

"What's so funny?"

I shook my head. He wouldn't get it. "I don't like your mask. Take it off." My brain swam in dizziness and a part of me knew I wouldn't remember this in the morning. What had Volkan given me?

He was silent for a moment. "I can't."

I groaned. "But I want to see your face." I turned to lie on my side, curling up under the warm blankets. "Will you come lie next to me?"

Several seconds passed before I heard him stand and then slide into the bed next to me. But he didn't curl up against me like he had when we shared the bed during the storm; this time he lay flat on his back, arms folded over his chest.

I rolled my eyes, moving closer to him and laying my head on his chest. I carefully moved my now healed arm over his abdomen and hooked our ankles together. He stiffened but I didn't care.

My brain was mush. Before I had the chance to say another word, I drifted to sleep once more.

◆　◆　◆　◆　◆

THE NEXT TIME I AWOKE, I HEARD MURMURS OF VOICES I RECOG-nized.

"Thank you for coming." The Hellbringer.

"Yeah, about that." Volkan. There was the sound of a glass being set on a table. "What the hell do you think you're doing, asking me to come here? Sending your soldier into Faste? To the palace, no less. You're lucky the teleporter isn't dead. Scared the shit out of my guards."

There was silence. I cracked my eyes open to see the inside of the dimly lit tent. The Hellbringer and Volkan sat at a small table facing the entrance, looking out to where the stars shone and a fire flick-ered in the middle of camp. The masked general looked out of place next to Volkan—so open and easy to smile. I spied a layer of snow on the ground, but somehow the bed was warm.

"I wasn't thinking," the Hellbringer said, his voice quiet. "I panicked. It was my fault and . . ." He cleared his throat. "I couldn't watch her die. You were the only one I trusted. You're the best healer the Fjordlands has ever seen."

I watched Volkan take a long sip of a drink. He sighed and ran a hand over his short curls. "Please tell me this isn't what I think it is."

"What?"

"Don't play dumb with me."

Sleep fogged the edges of my mind, but I was startled to hear Volkan snap. I'd only known him as kind and empathetic, never harsh.

"I'm not." The Hellbringer clenched his fists where they rested on the arms of his chair.

"You have feelings for her," Volkan said. "Don't deny it."

Shock coursed through me. What was Volkan saying?

But the Hellbringer's words startled me more. "I couldn't deny it if I wanted to."

My eyes widened. I lay quietly, careful not to make a sound.

"Why is she with you, anyway?" Volkan asked. "I thought she was at the front."

"I kidnapped her."

"Of course you did." Volkan rubbed his temples with his fingers. "Why are you like this?"

The Hellbringer turned his head so fast, I worried he would snap his own neck. "You know damn well why I'm like this."

Volkan stood. "I need to go. If anyone notices I'm missing, there will be panic. The king and queen will raise an alarm."

The Hellbringer stood and left the tent, presumably to find Mira. Volkan glanced back at me.

I shut my eyes, but not fast enough. "You're awake."

When I cracked my eyes open, he was at my side.

"What are you doing here?" I whispered. "I thought you weren't dating him anymore."

A shocked laugh escaped him. "He told you we used to date? He's more gone for you than I realized." He rested a hand on my cheek and gave me a soft smile. "Come home and we will talk. I'll be in Bhorglid for the Trials. For now, I have to go." He glanced toward the tent flap. No movement there. "You'll be safe with him. There's no need to worry, despite how much he wants you to. Don't let him intimidate you."

I raised an eyebrow. "Don't let the murderer intimidate me. Great advice."

Volkan rolled his eyes. "I see kidnapping has done nothing to dampen your shimmering personality. Let me see your shoulder one more time before I go."

I moved the tunic to the side, and he ran gentle fingers over where the slice had been. There was nothing—no shadow of pain or injury. "I must say, that's some of my best work," he murmured. "You'll be good as new in the morning. Get a good night's sleep and it shouldn't bother you at all. Next time you're training, be more careful."

Volkan moved toward the entrance of the tent, ducking out and leaving me alone in the dim light.

I sat up, wrapping my arms around myself. Perhaps I was reading into things, but it seemed like a rash move to send Mira into foreign territory simply to bring Volkan here. But my thoughts didn't dwell on the matter for long before they drifted to the Hellbringer.

Volkan had said the Hellbringer had feelings for me.

And he hadn't denied it.

I lay back on the bed, one pillow behind my head and another in my arms. Behind my closed eyelids, I saw a faint memory—my head nestled against the Hellbringer's chest, my arm draped over him.

My eyes flew open again. Shit. Had I honestly been so delirious I'd asked him to stay with me while I slept?

The tent flap opened to reveal the Hellbringer and I sat up again, my heart beating too fast. For a moment he just stood there, the two of us staring at each other.

"I want to apologize," he said finally, stepping to the side of the bed and sitting in the chair next to it. I wondered how long I'd been unconscious—whether the chair had been occupied for most of that time. Something within me already knew the answer. "For injuring you. I was careless and angry, and you suffered for it."

My cheeks flushed. I pushed myself up to a sitting position, leaning against the makeshift headboard. For a war front tent, these were nice accommodations. "It's fine."

"No, it isn't." He shook his head. "I've spent days stewing over everything. You asked me for something I wanted to give you and, not being able to acquiesce . . ." I watched his throat bob. "It's been eating away at me. It was easier to blame you, to be angry, to convince myself you were asking too much. And then we were sparring and you were . . ." The Hellbringer huffed a laugh. "Everything. You asked what the fuck my problem was and I wanted to toss my weapon down and pin you against the wall and just . . ."

A loaded silence fell over the tent. Before I had any inkling of how to respond, how to feel in the wake of his confession—*Pin me against the wall and* what? my thoughts demanded—he continued. "Even when I'm not using my Lurae, people are in danger from me. It's no wonder they're all afraid."

I didn't know what possessed me, but something in his voice sounded like longing, despite the distortion. I reached out and laid my hand on top of his. He lifted his head.

"I am not afraid of you," I whispered.

"Don't lie," he said bitterly. "I could have killed you at any point. I saw the fear in your eyes from the moment I arrived on the battlefield. You've heard the stories."

"I didn't say I've *never* been afraid of you," I chuckled. "Only that I'm not anymore. And besides, everyone has heard the stories."

He tilted his head and shrugged. "I suppose some of them are true."

Honesty burst from me despite my instincts. "I don't want you to take me back when you're done training me."

"What? Why not?"

"Because I'm enjoying my time with you," I said hurriedly. Meeting the eyes of the mask was an impossible task, so I continued staring at my hands. "Here I'm your equal. Not your pawn, the way I am my father's. And if I do win, the corruption in Bhorglid runs deep. Becoming queen is the beginning. We would have a long road ahead of us."

There was a pause. "'Us'?"

I felt my face turn red. "No, I didn't mean—not like that. I'm sorry."

"There is nothing to be sorry for."

I glanced at him. There were things I missed about seeing the sun every day, but I had meant what I said. If the choice were up to me, I would stay with the Hellbringer. I wondered if he would want to stay with me.

If I were to become queen, could we be together?

"Tell me something true?" I asked tentatively. He nodded, and I continued: "What will your life look like? When the war is over. When you don't have to be the Hellbringer anymore."

He tilted his head. "Will that time ever come?" he asked. "If I am not a war machine, then I am an assassin. Another tool in the queen's pocket. I will remain in Kryllian as her weapon until she sees fit to let me go. If that ever occurs."

I swallowed a lump in my throat. When this ended, he would remain under the control of another. Still the most powerful man in the Fjordlands. Still a weapon to be wielded.

"I don't envy you," I said.

"Well, I don't envy *you*," he replied. "Trying to kill your most powerful brothers with only a month of training under your belt. The odds aren't good."

"Would you go back?" I whispered. "If you were me?"

"I don't know," he said. "But I think you should. You're a good person."

"I have no interest in being a good person," I scoffed. "I only have interest in liberating my people."

"Some of your people," he corrected. I glared at him. He chuckled.

"You're joking." I smiled. "You hardly ever joke with me."

"I want to. But this"—he gestured at his helmet—"dictates I shouldn't . . . get attached. To anyone."

I raised an eyebrow. "You're attached to me?"

He looked at the floor. "Yes."

My eyes widened.

"I know you were awake," the Hellbringer said. "You don't need to deny it. You heard what I said to Volkan. What he accused me of."

I swallowed. My pulse pounded incredibly fast, want curling in my stomach. The question of what he'd wanted to do after he pinned me to the wall was back in full force.

He sighed, and for a moment honesty overwhelmed his barriers, too. "I know I am not the kind of person you would ever feel for. It would be stupid of you to pretend. But, Revna, you fascinate me. I dream of being good enough for you."

I stared at him, silent.

He cleared his throat, as if suddenly realizing what he'd admitted. "I've treated you poorly. You didn't deserve that. Fear has been holding me back."

"Holding you back?" My voice was breathless, a faint thing against the warmth of the firelight. "From what?"

The next moments seemed to pass in slow motion.

He stood, stepping over to close the tent flaps, making sure they were secure. Once he'd returned to his chair, the Hellbringer ran a hand over the front of the wolf skull mask, then slid the other hand down the side and pressed a latch. It clicked, loud against the back-drop of silence, and then he pulled it off to reveal his bare face be-neath.

The first thing I noticed was his hair, a chestnut-dark mop he had to brush off his forehead. This revealed his eyes, dark gray and penetrating, even as they flitted away from my own, as if nervous to make contact. To acknowledge the vulnerability laid out in front of us.

Heartbeat in my throat, I traced every one of his features with my eyes like a starving woman. Gods, I wanted to touch him. His cheekbones, high and sharp, contrasted with the softness of his plush lips. Dark brows furrowed against his forehead. I resisted the urge to smooth the lines there.

"I trust you, Revna." He still wasn't looking at me. His lower lip trembled slightly, and I knew his knuckles were white beneath his gloves from how tightly he clutched the mask. The distortion in his voice was gone; he sounded like a man now, not a monster. "And what I feel for you . . . it's brighter than the sun in the sky. I don't be-lieve in gods, but I would if it meant I could deserve you."

Here his eyes finally flicked up to mine. "Maybe we can never be together. Maybe you'll never want me back, not the way I want you. Because, fuck, I can't explain how much I think about you. Nothing has ever torn me apart the way you do. And—"

I leapt from the bed to stand between his knees, pressing my hands to his shoulders. My injured arm let out a ghostlike throb, but I ignored it, sliding my fingers up his neck and over his sharp jaw-line. There was a hint of stubble there, scratching my palm. His eyes were full of something intangible—longing, or maybe anticipation.

Bending down, I pressed my lips to his.

Gods, they were just as soft as I hoped they'd be. His hands, which had been frozen to the helmet, seemed to thaw, moving to push the mask to the ground, wrap around my waist, and pull me closer, tug me down until I had no choice but to clamber onto his lap.

Soft, exploratory brushes of our lips turned hungry with an unfamiliar swiftness. I scraped my nails against his scalp gently, gently, and the answering groan set me alight.

The Hellbringer kissed like he sparred—the moment I seemed to have the upper hand, he retaliated, teeth nipping at my lower lip and making me gasp.

"*Fuck.*" He moved his mouth to my jaw, my throat, and I arched against him. "I refuse to have you for the first time in a tent where anyone in camp can hear us. But please know I desperately want to."

I sighed, unsure whether it was from the pleasure of succumbing to my desire or frustration from knowing this was as far as we would be going tonight. Petty, I ground against him, and the satisfaction of feeling him hard beneath me, straining against his pants, was perfection.

"Unfair," he gasped, and in response I chuckled.

"No part of this has been fair," I murmured, pulling back to look into his eyes. There was the barest hint of a smile beneath the contentment on his face, and it made me want to kiss him again.

"I know." He brushed a stray lock of hair from my face. "I hope this is enough to make up for it. Now get back into bed. That shoulder of yours still needs rest."

I obliged, clambering off him to return to the mattress but tugging at his hand until he acquiesced and joined me there, curling up next to me under the blankets. We faced each other and I drank him in. It was intoxicating, seeing him without the mask. The slope of his nose, the flush in his cheeks, the flutter of his lashes—it all painted a picture of him I'd never seen before.

Then I realized something. "What's your name?"

His smile was soft. I wondered if this would feel like nothing more than a dream tomorrow. "Søren."

I hummed. "It suits you." Deep within me, I heard a chastising voice. *What are you thinking? He is the Hellbringer. You have no future with him.*

As I rolled over, I shoved the voice away. And as we settled on our sides, his arm around my waist, I intertwined my fingers with his and decided I would care about the consequences tomorrow.

21

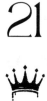

THE NEXT DAY FOUND ME PACING BACK AND FORTH AS IF TRY-ing to wear a hole in the prison floor.

The Hellbringer—*Søren*, I had to keep reminding myself—was gone, on another mission for the queen. After the life-changing moment we'd shared in the tent the night before, I was expected to return to normal. We'd returned and he'd left, and was I supposed to slip back into our routine? Impossible.

Hence the pacing. All the while, my thoughts flooded like the tide, rising and then receding, only to be replaced by another.

The kiss. There was no denying what we felt anymore. We'd done things, said things, that couldn't be taken back. And I liked it that way.

The press of our mouths, our breaths becoming one, our heartbeats synchronizing. His firm grip on my waist, the desperation in his hungry eyes. My own desire for him reaching a new high.

I couldn't chase it from my mind. I wasn't sure I wanted to either.

His face was engraved into my memory as well. The Hellbringer was Kryllian's most vicious general, but Søren . . . Søren was beauty incarnate. A work of art in human form. I blushed as the memory of his smile returned to me, his eyes heady enough to get drunk on.

And he'd shared his true identity with me. His face and his name both. I wasn't sure what to make of it. What to do with it. Because, despite the trust he'd given me, the way I cared for him, he *was* my people's most feared enemy. The general who could eliminate us all in a heartbeat. Who would to save his sister.

The worst part was understanding him. My feet, bare against the cold metal floor, began to grow numb. I sat down on the bed momentarily to wrestle my thick socks and boots back on. Before, when he'd been a faceless monster, it was easy to hate him. Without a name, he was nothing more than a curse, a scourge on my people. Regardless of whether I believed the war was holy or a mistake.

"Søren." I whispered his name like a prayer, running the feel of it over my tongue.

Would a monster care for me so openly? He wasn't just pretty words and promises; the Hellbringer was action, confidence, power. He'd declared his feelings and I believed him. It wasn't in his nature to lie.

Where did that leave me? Caught between my country and my heart.

I stood once more and pulled a target from where it stood against the wall. A week back, the Hellbringer had brought it for me to practice on with throwing knives. We hadn't used it much, but he taught me the basics. Now I hoped using the knives he'd gifted me would help me clear my mind.

With the first throw, my thoughts drifted to Freja. My best friend, my anchor. Stuck freezing in a prison against her will, all because we'd defied my father and the priests. This was for her. Everything was for her. If my arms trembled and gave out, if I took a knife or a sword to the gut, if I lost my life in the arena, it was for her.

But it was also for me. For the Nilurae in Bhorglid, who suffered under my father's rule. Who would suffer just the same, if not worse, under Björn's.

Freja had started me on this path, but even if she were free this very moment, I would continue. This was more than a campaign for one person's justice now; it was a true rebellion. It had been an uprising from the beginning for everyone else, but not for me.

The realization steadied me. When my first two throws missed, I jogged over to pick them back up and start again.

When the Hellbringer returned late in the evening, I was still there, limbs trembling with exhaustion, preparing to throw the knife again. His steps were quiet, but I heard them beneath the roaring of blood in my ears.

My churning thoughts and endless repetitive movements had worn me down. Despite it, I was happy he was back. Alone, my thoughts were overwhelming. Now we could talk. I could make sure I hadn't hallucinated the kiss, dreamt his face.

Warm hands landed on my shoulders, squeezing gently, and his voice—not distorted from the mask but entirely his own—murmured in my ear, "Your footing is likely causing some issues." His touch migrated down to my shoulder blades, my waist, landing on my hips. I shivered when his breath brushed against the shell of my ear. "Try this." He turned my hips until my footing was aligned the way he wanted. "Good."

And, gods, if that didn't send a thrill of longing through my stomach . . .

"Now," he said, placing his hand over mine on the dagger, "do you feel how the knife balances? Right here? When you release it, you want to be sure you stay relaxed. Tensing up can make your aim worse. Go on, try it."

He stepped back, chill air replacing the heat of his touch. I missed the warmth immediately but took a deep breath and focused on performing the best throw I possibly could.

It landed one ring away from the bull's-eye, and I threw a fist in the air, reenergized with triumph. "Did you see that?"

I turned to ask the Hellbringer, but he was already there, fire in his eyes as he placed his palms on either side of my face to pull me in for a blistering kiss. The dagger in my other hand clattered to the floor as I relaxed into him, our bodies melding along every curve and plane to fit like puzzle pieces.

"Perfect," he murmured between kisses, bending his knees and placing his palms on the backs of my thighs. I understood his silent request and jumped, wrapping my legs around his waist. The end-less neediness clawing at my rib cage for him was new. I took a steadying breath, trying not to become overwhelmed.

He walked me to the table and set me down on it. I ran my nails through his hair, tugging lightly on the dark strands, and he groaned.

I hummed and tried to pull him back in for another kiss, but his hands on my wrists stopped me. "No more tonight," he said softly.

I wanted to scoff. A pair of pretty gray eyes was apparently all it took for me to lose myself to lust. Propping my feet up on the dis-carded chair closest to me, I nodded and placed my chin on my knees, wrapping my arms around my shins.

The Hellbringer—no, Søren—brushed a stray lock of hair be-hind my ear before leaning over with his hands on the table on ei-ther side of me, bringing us almost to the same eye level. "You're beautiful," he said. "I've never told you before, I don't think."

We stared at each other for a long moment. I didn't know what to say. Should I tell him I thought he was beautiful, too? It was the truth, but I worried he might think I was growing soft. Instead, I let the words hang in the air for a while before answering with a quiet "Thank you."

He blinked and seemed to return to himself. Clearing his throat, he stepped away from the table and began assembling ingredients from the shelves surrounding us. "Tell me what's on your mind, Princess."

I hid a smile. His previous iterations of the nickname were disparaging, condescending; when I'd dreamed of him using it differently, it had still been a command. The thought of it being sweet, endearing, had never crossed my mind. But my smile faded as I considered what to say. "Everything."

He hummed his understanding and I closed my eyes, letting the darkness soothe me with the sounds of his cooking. "The war. The Trials. I'm a different person now than I was when you first stole me away. I feel so much responsibility for my people. I would save them all if I could—even the Lurae. But none of that is possible if I don't win. My brothers were all raised knowing they'd kill each other one day. I knew it would happen. Still, it's going to be the hardest thing I've ever done, watching the life drain from Erik and Björn. Even if I hate them both."

The smell of cooking meat filled the room and my stomach grumbled loudly. "Also, I'm hungry, apparently," I added.

Søren laughed. "You look like you haven't eaten all day. I'm not surprised."

Tilting my head to the side so that my cheek rested on my knees, I watched him. "I can't save everyone I want to."

His back was turned, unaware of my watchful eye. His shoulders stiffened slightly at my statement. Perhaps he read through the lines—realized I wanted to save him, too.

"You'll save as many as you can." Søren's reply was calm as he stirred and added fragrant spices to the meal. "Not everyone wants to be saved. Not everyone can be. It's unfortunate, but it's reality. You can't spend your life hating yourself for the choices you make. You won't save anyone that way."

"It's just . . ." I toyed with the words, wondering whether I should voice them. "Is there any point to being together? When we'll have to go our separate ways soon?"

The thought had been wandering in and out of my consciousness all day, but I'd refused to acknowledge it, forcing it back until now, when it slithered forward to curl insidiously in my mind. Especially because I couldn't stop wondering if this was exactly how Arne had felt.

And if I were Arne in this situation, with the Hellbringer in my place—accepting affection but never *truly* returning it—it would be unbearable. I wouldn't make a fool of myself that way. Better to know now.

The instant the question left my mouth, the clatter of cooking stopped abruptly. Before I knew it, Søren was in front of me again, hand under my chin, tipping my face up to meet his gaze. I swallowed thickly.

"Revna," he said, voice low. "If you don't want to do this, if our uncertain future is too much, then I understand. But to me? This is more than worthwhile. I would trade everything for a single day with you. If you disappeared tomorrow, I'd still see your face every time I made a decision for the rest of my life."

Why was my vision blurring slightly? Was I tearing up?

He leaned down and pressed his forehead to mine. "If you want this, then so do I. And if you don't, say it now—I swear to you I'll never mention it again."

I let out a shaky breath. "Yes," I whispered. "Yes, of course I want this. I want *you*."

His smile could have ended the war and melted the wastes, it was that radiant.

◆ ◆ ◆ ◆ ◆

THAT NIGHT, WE SPARRED.

I was grateful, despite my injury, that Søren didn't hold back. We fought as vigorously as always, and tonight it was easy to see my form was improving. I could go for longer before begging for a break, and he needed significantly more strength to overpower me.

"Good," he said as we finished for the evening. "I'm impressed."

I smiled as we hung up our weapons. I hadn't slept with Aloisa in the bed for several days now.

"I do have a question, though," Søren continued.

My eyes skittered to him, then narrowed. He sounded odd. Wouldn't meet my eyes. "What?"

"There's only so much time left before you have to go back." He glanced at me, trepidation in his look that swiftly transformed to earnestness. He approached me until we stood face-to-face, only a step apart. "If I am going to train you to use your Lurae, we have to start now."

For a long moment, his words didn't register. "My Lurae? I don't have one."

He pursed his lips. "I thought you trusted me now."

I frowned. "I do. What does this have to do with trust?"

"Everything." Patience, his new normal now, was swiftly descending into irritation. His hand closed into a fist at his side and I wanted to step back, put distance between us. "You can tell me the truth. I want you to tell me the truth."

I put a hand on my forehead. "What in the gods' names are you talking about? Do you hear yourself?"

"You have a Lurae," he growled. He took a deep breath, made a concerted effort to calm himself. "I know it. I know it's powerful and that you've hidden it for far too long. I know you're probably scared. But I have taught you how to wield a weapon. And I can teach you how to wield your power as well."

Søren stepped forward and reached for my hand, but I pulled back. This was the Hellbringer standing in front of me, not the unmasked man I'd come to care for. And despite his wounded eyes, I would not budge. "You think I'm lying?" My voice quivered, the anger barely contained. "You think somehow I've hidden a Lurae for the last twelve years?"

He only watched me.

I screamed. A wordless, feral thing. "How *dare* you?" I howled. "You think I survived on scraps, claimed an entire people as my own, and it was a lie? I would never have let my father and brothers abuse me if I had the power to fight back. I am *nothing*. I clawed my way into the Trials, and if I lose, it will cost me everything. Do you understand?"

Søren stood expressionless, the only crack in his façade an almost imperceptible downward twitch of his mouth.

And then it hit me.

"The queen only wanted me because she thought I had a secret Lurae." The words sounded ludicrous, absurd even, but they sent dread coursing through me like ice water poured over my head. "Gods. This is fucked. And you don't even believe me."

A muscle ticked in his jaw. "I want to believe you. Really, I do. But the queen . . . she is convinced. And she is never, ever wrong."

"What evidence does she have?" I demanded. "There is not a drop of magical blood in my veins. Believe me, my father has seen enough of it to know."

He winced—finally. "I don't know. You think she would tell me? I'm a tool in her arsenal. She trusts me as far as she can use me; that's it. I wish I knew more."

I took another purposeful step back from him. "And that's why you've been trying so hard to get me to trust you, isn't it? So I would show you my Lurae." I snarled the words, hoping the devastation wasn't visible through the cracks in my façade.

I channeled the burning behind my eyes into fuel for my fire. "You're despicable."

"No. I wouldn't do that." He was adamant, but I didn't care.

Summoning everything left in me, I steeled myself. "Who am I even talking to right now? Søren? Or the Hellbringer? Because the Hellbringer would. He would do anything if it meant pleasing his damn queen."

The hurt in his eyes was overwhelming. Instinctively, part of me wanted to take the words back, deny them. I wasn't sure if they were true. But the thought that they might be was ripping me to shreds. If I voiced the words, then surely they would hurt less.

I turned away from him. The longer I looked, the more I wanted to melt against him, to seek comfort from him despite his betrayal. And I wouldn't give in—I wouldn't show him weakness now.

When I dared to glance back over my shoulder again, he was gone.

22

WHEN A WEIGHT SANK THE OTHER SIDE OF THE MATTRESS enough to wake me, I acted entirely on instinct. In a millisecond, a dagger occupied my dominant hand and I rolled onto my side, kicking off the blankets to knee my attacker in the stomach. They let out an *"Oof"* and lost their balance, the perfect opportunity for me to launch myself onto them. The momentum carried us off the bed and they landed hard, flat on their back.

My eyes adjusted to the semidarkness as we sat there, both breathing heavily, my knees rammed into the Hellbringer's rib cage, my dagger at his throat.

Søren studied me, not nearly as surprised as he should have been. By some instinct, his hand had moved to palm the back of my thigh. I hated it. "I didn't mean to wake you."

I rolled my eyes and rolled off him. "I wish you hadn't."

"Wait, Revna. Please."

Ignoring him and crawling back into bed was easy. Until he clambered in after me, hastily discarding his armor piece by piece with loud clangs. "Please, Princess. Give me a chance to explain."

"No."

He groaned, and when I peered briefly over my shoulder, he was on his knees, head hung, hair falling over his face. "I fucked it all up. I'm sorry. I was trying to do my duty, all right? Same as you. To serve my queen." His throat worked as he swept a palm over his forehead. "I believe you. I hope you know I do."

I sat up grudgingly, wrapping my arms around my knees. The prison was warmer than usual tonight, but I had no doubt the cold would seep back in sooner rather than later. "How do I know you're telling the truth? How do I know you're not using me—or, worse, that you'll discard me the moment I prove to be as powerless as I always have been?"

He stretched his long frame out along the bed, his face in front of me. "I'm not sure how to prove it to you. But asking was stupid. Insisting was even worse. I made a mistake. I don't care whether you have a Lurae—regardless, you're winning those Trials and taking the throne. You have enough grit and determination to make you far more dangerous than anyone with a Lurae."

There was raw honesty in his eyes. And more than that, I *wanted* him to be telling the truth.

After spending so long in no one's company but his, I felt we were finally coming to understand each other. What kind of person would I be if I faulted him for attempting to fulfill his obligation to the queen? Was I not here because of a commitment to my own people? Did I not know *exactly* what it was to disregard my own feelings in favor of something bigger?

We both deserved to trust each other for a while longer before I returned to reality.

"I'm not the only one whose future is being determined right now," I said softly, rubbing the edge of the blanket between my fingers. The sensation was a comfort against the storm of emotion flooding me—emotion I didn't want to even begin deciphering. "There are people counting on me. Not just Freja but . . ." I hesitated, then decided to prove I had forgiven him. "There's a rebellion. A small one, but they need me. If I win, we might stand a chance of decimating the priests. Rooting out the corruption. Killing every head at once, so no new ones can grow back."

Søren's brow creased. "Winning the Trials is all-or-nothing, then."

I nodded. "I know you said you believe me. But what about the queen? What will she do when she discovers I have no magic? Will this be over before it's even had the chance to begin?"

He sat up, swinging his legs to stretch them out on either side of me, then took my hands in his. "No. I won't let it. I'll make her see reason—understand you still have a chance at winning. You said you're allied with your brothers, right? There's no way the three of you together can be defeated. Not when you're this strong even without a Lurae."

I tackled him to the bed and kissed him.

It was the same as our other kisses—hot, heated, passionate—and different at the same time—slow, heady, filled with words we couldn't say aloud. He wrapped his arms around my waist and twisted us onto our sides, legs intertwined, and we kissed like we were lovesick.

Maybe we were.

I ignored the hot tears burning behind my closed eyelids. "I won't let her hurt you," Søren promised, his nose nuzzling beside mine. "I won't."

We both pretended we didn't know the truth: the Queen of Kryllian could do whatever she wanted; Søren had a sister to protect who mattered infinitely more than the woman he'd never see again after this war ended; and if by some miracle the queen decided not to kill me, I had two brothers waiting in line to do the deed themselves.

"What would this be like," I whispered against his mouth between kisses, "if we were both entirely different people?"

He hummed quietly, chest rumbling with the sound. Twisting

strands of my hair in his fingers, he mused, "We'd have met in an equally hostile way but doing something utterly domestic. Like buying fruit."

I snorted, picturing the image in perfect clarity. "You'd have demanded a bad price for something and refused when I tried to haggle. So I would have picked up the nearest tomato and hurled it at your head."

We both burst into laughter, and it felt even better wrapped in each other's arms. Like the joy of the moment multiplied because of our nearness.

Søren was always beautiful, but laughing? He lit up like a sky full of stars. I wanted to bottle up the moment and make it last forever.

"But we'd find ourselves together regardless," he continued. "Maybe we'd live in a cottage on a beach somewhere."

"You like the ocean?" I scrunched my nose.

"Sure. Don't you?"

I shook my head. "That much water in one place isn't natural."

"It's the very definition of natural."

"You know what I mean." I shoved him half-heartedly, immediately pulling him back into my embrace. "I'd rather live in a forest. Maybe near a mountain."

His eyes lit up. "That sounds lovely."

We basked in each other's gaze for a long while before he added, "And there would be no war. No Lurae. No corrupt rulers, no duties, no people to save."

"No mask," I interrupted. "No death. Just . . . *this*." I tightened my hold on his hands.

Søren leaned in to press his lips to mine, hard. "Maybe one day all of this will end and we can have that."

I smiled sadly. "It's nice to pretend."

◆ ◆ ◆ ◆ ◆

THE NEXT WEEK PASSED IN A BLUR.

The topic of my Lurae wasn't brought up again. We returned to our normal routine of training and sparring, with additional time spent learning to throw the daggers the Hellbringer had given me. He said it was better to walk into the arena with both a close-range and a long-range weapon, to be safe. I agreed. During the days, I trained alone while he put on the mask and continued whatever missions the queen sent him on before he returned in the evenings to teach me.

Søren had shown even more trust in me by presenting me with the key to the prison door. "In case you want to hike to the hot springs or train outside while I'm gone," he'd explained, running a hand sheepishly over the hair on the back of his head. "You haven't been a true prisoner for a while, but, honestly, if you tried to escape, you'd die in the snow long before you made it—"

I cut him off when I wrapped my arms so tightly around his middle that he couldn't breathe.

Seeing the sun every day cheered me up significantly, though the Hellbringer had asked me to make sure I was inside with the door locked in the evenings, when Mira arrived to transport him back. "No one can know," he'd said. "This thing between us . . . if the queen found out, she would use it against us both. And I don't want that."

My hands clenched in anger, my nails biting into my palms at the thought. Søren was *afraid* of the queen. He'd never admit it, but the way she coerced him, held the knowledge of his sister's safety and whereabouts from him in case he protested an order . . . it made me furious. And yet there was nothing I could do about it, especially if I was plotting to win the Trials so I could enter into a treaty with her.

One step at a time, I told myself. *Maybe when everything has settled you can free him from her hold.*

To Søren, I'd simply said, "Of course. I understand."

Whatever remaining time we had left was spent talking, laughing, and kissing. We hadn't gone further, despite ending up in compromising positions several times. I'd stopped us on multiple occasions, afraid we would break an unspoken pact of keeping enough distance to not be *too* hurt when the time came to part ways.

Part of me didn't care, though.

One morning Søren declared he didn't have duties from the queen, and we were heading out to train in the snow. Eager to put the skills I was honing to use, I readily agreed.

Three hours in, my ankles were killing me. We were still in the same sparring session that we first started, our skills so evenly matched now, it was difficult to determine a winner.

Søren made a swipe at me with his sword, but I saw it coming and parried in time. Then I lunged at him, aiming for his leg. He blocked it, but I shifted my weight and leveled a kick to his ribs.

As he moved to slice my face, I brought my blade up to deflect his. We were inches from each other, and he pushed against my defensive position with all his might. My hands trembled under the pressure. I gritted my teeth and swung my leg upward, aiming for his crotch.

He leapt back and I pulled a dagger from a sheath on my arm, throwing it straight at him with my non-dominant hand. It spun end over end, and he stepped to the side to avoid it. But the distraction was enough. I had him pinned in the same moment.

I stopped the blade right before it sliced his throat.

Breathing hard, we stared at each other. A triumphant smile lit my face. I had beaten the Hellbringer in battle.

"You're ready," he declared. "You are ready to win the Bloodshed Trials."

✦ ✦ ◆ ✦ ✦

WE RELAXED IN THE SILENCE, ON OUR BACKS IN THE SNOW. SØREN had laid our cloaks down for us to rest on. He'd shot and cooked a deer for our midday meal, and for once he wasn't pushing me to keep training, keep practicing. Instead, we were sharing stories of our youths, my head nestled on his chest.

It was blissful. Peaceful.

Only for a moment, though.

He inhaled deeply. "I'll be taking you back tomorrow."

I sat up. "Tomorrow?"

His expression was grave. "The Trials . . . they're in four days. We have to make sure you are able to depart the front and go back to the city with your family."

I swallowed, refusing to let him know how the tender spot beneath my rib cage ached. "I lost track of the time."

Four days until my life changed irreparably. Until my fate was decided.

Until Bhorglid's future was set in stone.

Where had the time gone? Five weeks had disappeared in a blink. Closing my eyes, I lay back down, wishing I could stay here with Søren forever. Wishing this wasn't going to be our final night together. Wishing it didn't make my throat and eyes sting to think about never seeing him again.

The sun began to sink below the horizon, preparing to rise over the mountains again the next morning. Wordlessly, he wound his fingers through mine.

My duty and his. We were inexplicably bound together, but our paths would more than likely end here.

His thumb caressed my palm, the touch sending a spark of heat through me. I'd spent the whole week holding back despite how desperately I wanted him. But I was tired of being afraid. And if I was going back to my death, never to see him again even if I did live, then surely it was fair to take part of him with me.

"Come to the hot springs with me." I stood up, pulling my cloak from the snow and shaking the powdery flakes off it. Every beat of my heart ricocheted against my bones in anticipation of what I was planning. I held out a hand to him.

He looked it for a moment, gray eyes keen, and I knew he was reading my mind. I wondered how his magic worked. Did killing with a flick of his wrist mean he could hear my pulse beating beneath my skin? I wasn't subtle. He had to know what I wanted. How I wanted *him*.

The tension between us grew thicker, and I worried it would snap. Worried he would turn me down. But instead he reached out and accepted it, tugging me back down until I tumbled, collapsing with my knees on either side of his hips.

"We shouldn't." His voice was rougher than usual, a few notes deeper. "I'm already too attached to you. And once we start . . ." He swallowed. "I don't know if I'll be able to stop. I've been dreaming about you for weeks."

My blood heated, and I leaned forward, my forearms resting on his chest. Already he was growing hard, and the feel of him beneath me, between my thighs, sent a thrill down my spine. "Who says we have to stop? Haven't we earned this?" Slowly, I rubbed myself up and down his body. His head tilted backward, his eyes fluttering closed. I summoned every ounce of boldness I could muster and continued. "Don't I deserve to make you come?"

"Keep talking like that and you might make me before we've even taken our clothes off." He opened his eyes, his gaze traveling over my face before pausing on my neck, where he'd sucked a blooming bruise into the tender skin just the day before. "I don't want you to regret this."

I shook my head. "I won't. I was afraid of being too attached, of not wanting to leave. But that was all going to happen anyway."

Something solidified in his eyes. "Then let's go."

Evening was falling in earnest when we arrived at the hot springs, the steam misting in the air and reaching like whisper-thin fingers. I was shivering from the cold, my cloak too wet to truly keep me warm, so I stripped and rushed into the water, splashing a bit as I went before relaxing in the heat.

When I turned around, Søren was watching me, hunger in his eyes.

"Well?" I said, my confidence building as he surveyed my bare skin. "Care to join me, Hellbringer?"

He began to take his armor off, one piece at a time. The plates landed in the snow with a thud, and when he was standing in only his black leather, he began moving toward the shoreline. He removed his shirt with little thought, focused like a predator on me.

I waded back until only my face was above the water, watching him with wide eyes. I'd dreamed of his bare torso more times than I could count by now, and yet I still hadn't managed to remember every detail of his pale skin. His muscles were defined in a way that bore testament to how long he spent training every day and working as a soldier. Søren was not the product of a life of ease, and I was glad. It made us all the more evenly matched.

He tugged off his pants with an impatient huff and I laughed. He rolled his eyes and stripped off his underwear, leaving him naked for a flash before he splashed into the water to meet me.

I couldn't tear my gaze from his body even as it slipped beneath the surface. When he reached me and noticed my line of sight, he chuckled.

My cheeks heated and I wrapped my arms around myself, suddenly conscious of my body on display for such an attractive man. But he sank into the water and gathered me in his arms, skin against skin in the warmth, and pressed a kiss to my temple before leaning close to murmur, "Look at you. A body like yours might be enough to make me believe in the gods."

I flushed, tracing the tips of my fingers over his stomach, brushing against the swollen head of his cock. He shivered and I grinned. "You're not half bad yourself."

He nipped at my earlobe playfully. "Rude."

"I'm joking," I reassured him. "I've been imagining you naked ever since you took your shirt off in the forge."

He laughed, a full-bodied, full-throated sound. "I can't believe that was only a few weeks ago. I was gone for you even then." Before I had time to question him, he slid me down his body a bit, enough for me to feel his cock hard against my stomach. I let out my breath in a rush, suddenly desperate for his hands and his mouth and his thickness in the soft place between my legs.

Søren's eyes gleamed in the evening light. He placed his thumbs carefully along my jaw and leaned in to kiss me.

Our lips met in a tangle of heady lust, and I wrapped my legs around him. He supported me with one arm, the other tilting my head so he could devour me. When he broke away from my mouth to pepper kisses down the column of my throat, I was left gasping for air.

The first swipe of his fingers over my nipple made me whimper and grind against him. He groaned. "Fuck. You're going to be the death of me, Princess. Want to take a bite of you."

He hoisted me higher, until both of my breasts were bared to the cold, my nipples stiffening with the temperature against his lips, which wrapped around one taut bud and sucked. I arched my back, desperate for more as his free hand cupped my other breast and squeezed.

"Perfect," he whispered. He sounded so dazed, I wondered if he knew I could hear him.

"Søren," I moaned, reaching my hand down and between us to wrap around him. He stilled, his eyes meeting mine. I was caught in his gaze, wondering how my hand could be enough to render the most powerful man in the world helpless. Carefully, I ran my palm up and down him.

The sound he made sent a thrill down my spine. Because, yes, I wanted to come at his hands. But I also wanted to show him what I felt, to try and explain the depth of my emotion with this act.

In one swift motion, he turned me around so my back was pressed to his front, then guided my arms up and around his neck. "What were you dreaming about?" he asked, voice husky. "That night, when I put my cloak over you?"

His teeth grazed the edge of my ear and I had a brief flash of thought: Was he the kind to be gentle with a lover, or rough? Would he stretch out my pleasure, keeping me on the edge until I had no choice but to tip over? Or would he force me to come again and again until I was overspent?

My thoughts were cloudy with the possibilities, and I didn't comprehend his words. "Wh-what?"

His hands cupped my breasts, lifting and toying with them, and I rubbed my backside against him. "Think hard, Princess. When I laid my cloak over you that night? You were having a dream. At first I thought it was a nightmare—you whimpered, and I thought about waking you up. Until I realized you were rubbing your legs together beneath my blankets. In my bed."

"Oh, gods. I was?" Slightly mortified, my arms fell to grasp his wrists and still his hands.

When I looked over my shoulder, his pupils were so dilated, I could barely see the grays of his irises anymore. "Tell me I wasn't wrong, even back then. What were you dreaming about, Revna? Was it that boy you left behind, or . . ." I didn't miss the way he spat the word, as though referring to Arne as a boy were the gravest of insults. He traced the curves of my breast with one hand, fingertips landing just above where I wanted him most.

"It was you." The words spilled from me unbidden. "I was dreaming of this. Of your mouth on mine. Of your fingers inside me."

The noise he made then was feral, and it sent heat blooming between my thighs. "Good. *Good.* Even then I wanted you—wanted this. I've craved you from the moment you first pointed your sword at me."

He leaned in again, but I twisted fully in his arms to face him and pushed his shoulders back. "You were a complete ass back then!"

Søren dragged his hands up my sides beneath the water and pulled me to him. This time I submitted, every inch of me hyperaware of all the places we touched. "I had to be. The last thing I should have been doing was imagining my beautiful captive naked." His grin was sharp around the edges.

I traced the scar I'd noticed when I first saw him shirtless in the forge. It wrapped from his upper back over his right shoulder, ending just beneath his collarbone. "How did you get this?"

"My first battle," he said softly. "I was so nervous that day—only fourteen. The only people I'd killed before had been accidents. I didn't want to be there and I let someone get too close. This was before I knew how to use a sword."

His sorrow radiated, and I wanted to take the question back. I pressed a kiss to his chest, nestling into him with my head just below his chin. Søren wrapped his arms around me and for a long moment we embraced in the silence.

"Come back with me," I whispered. "Leave Kryllian behind. I'll protect you once I'm queen."

His next exhale was a sigh. "And leave my sister at my own queen's mercy? No. I can't." He tilted my chin up until our eyes met.

The fire was gone, replaced only by certainty. "You can't save everyone, Revna. And if I end up a casualty in this fight, so be it."

I wanted to protest, wanted to dig my heels in and hold on to my desperation. Because wanting Søren went far beyond a single night of pleasure, beyond a few weeks of forced proximity. Somehow, without me noticing, he'd carved himself into my soul. Forged a notch for himself that no one else could fill.

I knew intrinsically that I would feel the emptiness there for the rest of my days.

But I also had a war to end. Brothers to kill. A crown to seize. Priests to destroy. And as much as I wanted to reassure him that there would be no casualties, that everyone would emerge on the other side unscathed . . . I knew it wasn't the truth.

So instead I demanded, "Kiss me, then. Make me forget it all."

Determination set his jaw, and he obliged.

Gone were the soft, searching presses we'd exchanged earlier. Now lips were met with teeth scraping against tender flesh. Whimpers turned to groans, turned to "Oh fuck." Søren navigated us through the water to where a large rock rested, pressing me up against it and trailing the sharp edges of his teeth against the swells of my breasts.

"Are you wet for me?" he asked, his baritone voice hoarse. My legs were still wrapped around his waist, but his firm hand slid to the inside of my thigh, pushing it outward. "Open up for me, Princess. Let me feel."

I had no choice but to oblige, leaning back so that my head rested against the cool surface of the rock as he ran his fingers softly through my lower lips. I groaned at the sensation, the ghost of friction so close to where I needed it, but not enough to relieve any of the pressure building within. "Oh," he whispered reverently, like a worshiper at the altar of a god. "You're soaked. Even in the water, I can tell."

A thick finger breached my entrance and I gasped as he slid it in. My muscles clenched around him. "*Søren.*"

"You feel so perfect around my finger," he muttered, craning down to press sloppy wet kisses to my collarbones, my breasts. "Can't imagine how good this will feel when I get inside you."

An involuntary clench. "Please."

"Please what?"

"Touch me."

His thumb circled my clit. "I thought you'd never ask."

His movements were excruciatingly slow and gentle as he learned my body. Another finger slid in beside the first, the soft stretch making me keen. The world was awash in throbs of pleasure, my legs trembling as he whispered in my ear, comforting me through it all.

"You're so pretty when you let me touch you. So beautiful. After this, when we're back in bed, I'm going to splay you out so I can taste you. First you'll come on my hand, then my tongue, then my cock. Let me worship you until you can't remember any name but mine. Do you feel that stretch?" Here he slid a third finger inside of me, and a wordless sound escaped my mouth. "Perfect, pretty girl. Letting me finger fuck you. Let me make you moan."

Every word made me melt, and I was nothing more than a puddle in his hands, floating in the water. It could have been minutes or hours by the time my breaths began to shorten, my fingernails leaving crescent marks in the flesh of his shoulders as my hands tightened and the pleasure in my core began to spread through the rest of my body.

The pressure of his thumb, his filthy words, the steadily falling darkness—it all culminated in a release so overwhelming, I saw stars. My fingers scrabbled against his shoulders as I searched for purchase, and the sounds I made were ones I doubted I'd ever make again.

When I finally came down from the high, panting desperately, Søren was cradling me in his arms, murmuring, "Please, can I come inside you? Please, Princess, I need it—"

Gods above, I wanted to make him beg me for it every day until I died. I found myself thankful we'd had the necessary discussions about contraception on the hike over. I reached between us, lining him up with my entrance while I nipped at his jawline. "Hush, honey," I chided as he pleaded and I slowly came back to myself. "I'll take care of you."

He groaned, one palm slapping against the cool rock at my back as he slid in the first inch. Even that little bit stretched me despite the careful work of his fingers earlier, but my orgasm made me soft and pliable. With one fluid movement, he slid the rest of the way in, and we both panted as I adjusted and he tried not to move.

"I'm not hurting you?" He sounded concerned through his clenched jaw.

I shook my head, gripping his shoulders more tightly to support my weight. "No, I'm okay. I'm okay. Move, please? *Please*, Søren."

"Fuck. I love when you say my name." He thrust his hips, and the motion of him inside me sent a shiver up my spine. "Like I'm a person. Not a monster."

The words made me wish I could hold him so tightly, I never had to let go. Instead, I lost myself in the rhythm of his thrusting, caving to the carnal desire to run my tongue up the column of his throat. He groaned and cursed again, and my sated body was thrilled to know such a powerful man was shivering under my touch.

When he came, shuddering with every rush, head thrown back and eyes screwed shut, I pressed my mouth against his chest and held him through it. Spent, he inhaled deeply, then cradled my face in his hands and grinned before peppering me with a barrage of tiny kisses.

"Søren!" I couldn't stop laughing.

"You're incredible. That was . . ." He ran a hand through his hair while I settled my now sore legs back on the bottom of the hot spring. "It's never been like that before."

We couldn't keep our hands off each other. I didn't mind in the slightest, running my thumbs over his hip bones. He shivered. "Not for me either," I whispered, peering up at him shyly. "You liked it?"

"Liked it?" He looked so incredulous, I hid a smile behind my hand. "I more than liked it."

"Enough that you'd like to continue when we're back inside? If we're out here for too long, it will start snowing again."

Søren grinned, and for a moment everything was peaceful beneath the stars. "Race you back."

He bolted without a second thought, splashing hot water on me as if it would slow me down. I dressed faster than I ever had before, and as we sprinted back to the abandoned prison, I wondered if I might love a monster.

23

I STARTLED AWAKE WHEN SOMEONE DROPPED ME INTO A PATCH of freezing snow.

I gasped as the cold ripped through me. My only clothes were the Hellbringer's, a single layer of thin fabric. My armor crunched as it landed next to me.

The glare of the morning sun made it difficult to discern the person responsible for my plight, but when she bent to survey me, I recognized her. Mira.

Her face was uncovered, and I could see her mouth twisted into a scowl. A long, thick scar extended from her neck to her cheek, but I forced myself not to look at it.

"What the hell are you doing?" I demanded, pushing to my feet. The longer I stayed in the snow, the more likely I'd freeze to death.

She rolled her eyes, her blond hair glittering bright against the backdrop of white mountains. "He left you a note," she said without preamble. "'I've always hated goodbyes.' That's all it says." She crumpled the small piece of paper in her hand and tossed it into the snow.

I grabbed my cloak and threw it on, trying to piece together the information behind her words.

"Where is the Hellbringer?" I asked.

She sneered. "He told me to leave you outside of your camp. But his judgment is compromised. I'm doing what he should have done in the first place."

My eyes widened. "Which is what?"

Mira offered me a tight-lipped smile. "Leaving you in the snow to die."

She disappeared.

What had she seen? Had she realized the Hellbringer and I were together? Or was she making assumptions, since she wasn't aware of the real reason he'd been training me?

I tipped my head back to look at the sky. It didn't really matter what she was thinking. She was gone and I was alone in the frigid wastes. "What a great way to start my day."

◆ ◆ ◆ ◆ ◆

BEING ANGRY USUALLY HELPED ME FOCUS. TODAY IT DID THE OP-posite.

I'd been walking west for over an hour, hoping I was going in the right direction to run into someone—anyone, frankly. If I made it to a Kryllian camp and they didn't kill me on sight, maybe I could convince them to let me see the Hellbringer. And I knew my family's camp had to be out here somewhere.

Every step left behind a deep footprint. I wrapped my arms around myself and scowled. "Stupid Hellbringer," I muttered, teeth chattering. "Couldn't have brought me himself."

Last night, when we'd taken a moment to simply breathe in each other's arms, I found myself asking, "How do you sleep with that helmet on?" It had been over a week since he'd worn it in the prison with me. The last several nights had found him curled up next to me in bed without any armor on as we slept. It made me wonder about how he'd gotten any rest before he was willing to take the mask off in front of me.

"I don't do much sleeping," he said with a chuckle. "Now go to bed."

I rolled over in his arms and touched the mask, lying on the bed next to him. The hand-carved wood was rife with ridges invisible to the eye. I studied it instead of him, working up the confidence to ask my next question.

"Do you fuck your prisoners often?"

I tried to say it in a teasing voice so he didn't detect the uncertainty underneath. From the start, I'd known his power and political influence ensured that many wanted to woo him. Was he called for back in Kryllian?

And if he was, could I get over it?

"No," he answered, running his hand through my unbound hair. I'd tried to re-braid it on the way back to the prison, but he'd stopped me, admitting he liked it down. "I distance myself from most people. The life I live . . . well, it's not suitable for any kind of relationship. I'm sure you understand."

I thought about Arne. How we'd kept each other at arm's length to avoid the heartbreak we saw coming. I'd enjoyed my time with Arne, but he'd never been truly satisfied because of the emotional distance between us.

"I do," I said. "More than you know."

Eventually I'd fallen asleep.

Now, letting out a low growl of frustration, I watched my breath crystallize in front of me. Instead of bringing me to safety, the Hellbringer had tried to avoid a painful goodbye by letting his most trusted soldier take me herself.

Clearly an excellent decision.

As I approached the mountain looming in front of me, I sighed. Part of me was grateful we'd avoided an awkward farewell. What would I have said?

I could only hope Mira hadn't left me too far from my family.

Would Björn and my father be disappointed to find I was alive? Gods, I hoped so. Imagining the look on his face provided a surge of energy for me to continue.

Luckily, the skies were blue. No impending storm to kill me quicker.

After another hour of walking, the mountain in the distance was no closer. I stopped, letting my frustration build until I couldn't hold it in anymore. Then I took a deep breath and let out a scream.

A bird fluttered out of a pine tree as my voice echoed over the mountains. A low rumble came from the mountain as snow readjusted under the sound of my voice.

No one could hear me. No one was looking for me.

"Of all the places to die, this is probably the worst," I said aloud, kicking the nearest pine with all my might.

I kept walking.

◆　◆　◆　◆　◆

WHEN THE SUN BEGAN TO SET, MY WORRY SPIKED. NIGHT BROUGHT the killer cold, and this time I didn't have the Hellbringer to keep me warm.

Also, I was starving.

My stomach let out another gurgle and I swore. *Frode, if there's any way you can hear me, I could use your help right about now.*

That's when I heard it: the sound of galloping horses coming from the valley ahead of me.

My heart started pounding, and I ran for a patch of trees twenty feet away from me. There was a high chance the party riding toward me was made up of Kryllian soldiers, in which case I wanted to see them before they saw me. I needed some kind of advantage if I was going to convince them to take me alive.

Looking back at the path I'd taken, I noticed my footprints, clear as day in the fresh powder.

I swore under my breath. I would never be able to outrun horses, especially in the thick snow. Whoever was coming was about to find me.

Pulling Aloisa from its sheath, I crouched behind a tree, hoping it would provide me enough cover to remain unnoticed. The element of surprise might be enough to give me the upper hand.

The clatter of hooves slowed to a stop. I couldn't see them, but from what I heard, there were at least three or four riders, possibly more. The only sound was the horses snorting and shifting. Boots crunched in the snow as a rider dismounted.

I took a deep breath to steady my racing heart. This was it. The true test of what the Hellbringer taught me. I shifted my grip on the hilt of my blade. The footsteps came closer, until I knew the person was on the other side of the tree.

I lunged, aiming my blade for my unseen enemy, but they were ready for me, parrying my blow without a second thought.

"Maybe try being quieter next time you're hiding from an enemy," Frode said with a wry smile.

Relief flooded through me, and I couldn't stop the tears from pricking the corners of my eyes. I dropped my blade and without a second thought threw my arms around him.

"Frode," I gasped. "How did you find me?"

He hugged me back, squeezing tight. "You think loudly, little sister. Loud enough that I heard you from camp."

A laugh burst out of me, filled with emotion words couldn't convey. But then he leaned in. "Everyone came with me," he said in a low voice. "I'll talk to you later, but, for now, don't tell them anything of substance. Understand?"

You know I do. I pulled away from him and looked up to see my father and my other brothers watching us from several feet away. They'd remained on their horses while Frode came to retrieve me.

None of them spoke. Jac offered me a small grin. He, at least, was happy to see me alive. Björn sneered, the only expression he was capable of making nowadays, and my father and Erik remained stoic.

"Nice to see you all again," I remarked as I climbed behind Frode on his horse. No one answered, but Jac reached out and clapped me on the back. I smiled. From him, the gesture meant more than words ever could.

"Let's go," the king called, and they turned their mounts as one, moving back toward the valley.

I looked up to see the mountaintop far above us as we entered its shadow. Wherever we were headed, it wasn't the campsite I'd visited a few weeks ago. "Where is the camp, anyway?" I asked.

Frode glanced back at me. "Through this valley. We moved there two days ago. Didn't want to stay in one location for too long."

I sat back and sighed, wishing I believed in any gods so I could thank them. The Hellbringer's map must have been of the old campsite, so Mira had inadvertently dropped me closer to the new one.

"You're probably right," Frode mused. "I started hearing your thoughts about an hour ago. I wanted to come get you myself, but the rest of them insisted on joining me."

Not for sentimental reasons, I presume.

Frode chuckled. "You know them well. Father thought we might find the Hellbringer with you. I told him you were alone, but he wouldn't listen."

A sharp pain went through my chest. I already missed the Hellbringer. The memory of kissing him flooded my mind unbidden.

I felt Frode stiffen in front of me.

"Please tell me you aren't thinking about what I think you're thinking about," he seethed quietly.

Shame burned my cheeks. Not because it happened, but because the time that had been so special to me was no longer mine. Frode knew about it, too.

One of his hands held the reins firmly, but the other drummed fingers against his thigh. "Revna, please don't take this the wrong way, but you're an absolute idiot. Do not, under any circumstances, tell Father about this."

I'm not that *stupid.*

He slowed his horse enough that we fell behind the others and turned slightly to hiss, "Then next time you're a prisoner of war, *make better choices.*"

The comment stung like a slap and I fell into silence, seething internally. He didn't know anything about what I'd been through.

It took all of my willpower to keep my thoughts empty the rest of the ride. When we finally made our way to the largest tent over an hour later, Frode dismounted, clutching his head. As I walked alongside him, my legs almost collapsed under me. My ankles had supported my weight in the snow for too long. I let out a groan from the aches traveling up to my hips.

"Is your head okay?" I tried to sound normal, but my voice was stiff.

Frode pursed his lips. "I'm going to lie down. When you're done, come find me. We need to talk." He stalked away without another glance back at me.

I crossed my arms over my chest. A gust of wind toyed with my hair, still loose from yesterday. Frode and I rarely fought. I hated it when we did. But I was more than justified in my feelings for the Hellbringer. When I went to see Frode later, hopefully he would be more understanding.

"This way." My father grabbed me by the arm and pulled me toward the canvas tent. I stumbled with the force of it but managed to catch myself before I fell. I wrenched my arm out of his grasp.

"I'm capable of walking myself," I snapped. I pushed the flaps of the tent open.

Inside was warm. A fire blazed in a metal pit and the smoke escaped through a series of small holes in the top of the tent. To one side was a table with a map on it and three chairs. My father grabbed one and pulled it over to the fire. He gestured for me to sit.

I eyed him warily but obliged. The warmth of the fire seeped into my bones, thawing me from the inside out. I tried not to let my relief show.

"Now what?" I asked.

My father pulled one of the other chairs over to face me and sat.

"Now you tell us everything," he said. "Start talking. Spare no detail."

Oh, I was going to spare some details.

I took a deep breath. This was going to be complicated if I left things out. I couldn't tell him the *real* truth: the Kryllians wanted to put me on the throne and end the war.

But what would I tell him instead?

Might as well start with the truths I could share. "Well, the soldier who can teleport—she's the Hellbringer's number one. Only she can get to and from where he is staying. Where he kept me prisoner."

And where we kissed.

I turned to see Frode's expression before remembering he wasn't there. I swallowed the lump forming in my throat.

"And where was that?" Erik asked. He stood behind my father's chair, pausing his pacing to ask the question.

I shrugged. "We were in an abandoned prison." A glance between my brothers and my father showed various levels of interest in my words. Jac stood stoic in the corner. Björn sharpened his knife at the table, not looking up at me. "How long was I gone?"

Björn lifted his head and raised an eyebrow. "You don't know?"

"I hadn't seen the sun until they dropped me in the snow this morning. So, no, I don't know." I pursed my lips and raised an eyebrow in response, daring them to catch me in the lie.

"Five weeks," Jac supplied.

I let out a surprised laugh. "Well. That's a while. Did you all think I was dead, then?"

"It doesn't matter." My father's interruption caught me off guard, but I schooled my expression before he could see. He strode toward me, hands behind his back. His armor glinted in the firelight. "Do you know where the prison was? Could you identify any landmarks nearby? We have a teleporter in our ranks. The more we know, the closer we can get to taking out the Hellbringer."

Keeping my face neutral proved to be a challenge as fury swept through me. He held no concern for my safety, only the information I had to offer.

I gritted my teeth. "I wasn't able to see any significant landmarks from where I was. The mountains weren't in sight, so probably . . . east? Close to Faste. He confirmed we were still in Bhorglid, though."

"Why did they bother to take you?" Björn asked, continuing to sharpen his long knife. He paused to point it at me. I held my expression, and after a moment he sighed. "You're useless. Everyone knows that."

Heat flushed my cheeks. "Apparently not. They thought I was an easy target for information. Lucky for you, nobody tells me anything, including the locations of our camps. They had a mind reader come, and once they confirmed I didn't know anything, they kept me in a cell for a while and then dumped me in the snow to die."

My father leaned forward, placing his elbows on his knees. "What did they ask? What were they trying to find out?"

I shrugged. "They wanted locations of any hidden camps. Specifics on what attacks we were planning. What camps of theirs we were targeting. They wanted to know if we had any undercover godtouched. Anyone like the Hellbringer with a unique ability to turn the tide of the war."

"At the risk of being . . . insensitive," Erik said, "why didn't they kill you on the spot? Why would they risk anyone finding you?"

Hmm. I hadn't considered that.

Thankfully, with what they believed about the Hellbringer, the lie came to my lips easily. "The Hellbringer and his soldiers found it amusing that I would die in the wilderness without them needing to lift a finger." I looked at my feet, hoping they would think it a sign of shame. "They said it wasn't worth the effort of killing me."

"Yet you were worth the effort of taking to a remote location and dropping you off to die?" Björn scoffed. "I don't believe it."

I scowled. "I don't know what effort you mean. It took the soldier less than ten seconds to teleport me there, drop me, and teleport herself back. Besides, aren't you the ones who have been telling me Kryllian people are savages? They found sport in leaving me to die a slow, agonizing death in the freezing cold."

"Stop arguing." Father turned to me, his jaw working. "Was there anything else? Anything at all to lead us to the Hellbringer?"

I shook my head. "I've told you everything I know."

The fire had thawed me and was starting to make me sweat. It was too warm for comfort now. I wanted to go back outside. The cold would distract me from the hollow place inside my chest where my loss resided.

I missed Søren the same way I would miss a limb.

"Can I go now?" I didn't hide the emptiness in my voice. "I have nothing more to tell you."

"Maybe we find a truthteller," Björn suggested. "Are there any in this camp with that particular godtouch? Make sure she isn't lying."

My stomach twisted painfully, but Erik shook his head. "There are none at this campsite. And despite Revna's shortcomings, she knows better than to lie to us. Frode will be able to hear her thoughts, and if he notices anything amiss, he'll let us know."

My father sighed and stood, moving his chair back to the table. His expression of disgust and disappointment was familiar. "Go," he said. "You're as useless to me as before. I wish we'd found your frozen body in the snow."

Before my abduction, before the Hellbringer, I wouldn't have hesitated to fire back at my father. But now, instead of my blood boiling, defeat made my limbs heavy. I'd left Søren behind, only to return to this?

The sooner I won the Trials, the better. Then I wouldn't have to deal with constant condescension and insults.

Then I could order my father killed.

24

FRODE FOUND ME AN HOUR LATER, SITTING BY THE FIRE AT the center of camp. I'd re-braided my hair and taken to polishing my sword with enough fury that despite the frigid temperatures outside, I remained alone by the hearth.

The camp itself was bigger than I expected and the people who passed included not only soldiers but healers and the occasional priest as well. The tents were pitched in ever-expanding circles around the central fire. The snow around us was packed down by endless boot prints.

I wasn't blind. I saw how the eyes of soldiers who passed me widened and how they whispered behind their hands. As night had fallen, I'd become the main attraction in the camp. Many of the soldiers were from outer provinces, far from the capital, and had never seen the infamous Nilurae princess before now.

Frode touched me lightly on the shoulder to announce his presence. I turned to glare, but when I realized he wasn't a gawking soldier, I relaxed.

"You're out late," I said. The fire illuminated his face in the darkness as he sat beside me. Around us, the camp quieted. Most soldiers were in their tents, with a few posted as sentries.

"As are you," he replied. His green eyes glowed. "Are you okay?"

"I'm fine." I hated that he knew I was lying; he would always know.

"I suppose it's not as nice for you as it is for me." He smirked. "What did you tell them?"

I pulled the memory of the interrogation to my mind and walked through it, allowing Frode to see everything that had happened during the questioning. When I finished, he sighed and ran a hand through his hair.

"Father is determined to find the Hellbringer before the Trials. He says it's to help ease the transition of power, but we know it's so he can get the glory."

I leaned back, examining my sword. "He won't get far. I've never seen anyone protect a secret the way the Kryllians protect the Hellbringer's identity. I doubt anyone in the army knows who he really is."

Frode didn't say anything. I looked up to find him staring at me. "What?"

He shook his head. "There are things I shouldn't say here, so I'll keep them to myself for now. But I'll tell you exactly what I think of your time with the Hellbringer when we get home."

It felt like someone had closed their hand around my throat. "Why bother saying it when I can see it all on your face?"

He rubbed his forehead. "Revna, I don't think you understand the magnitude of what you've gotten yourself into."

My shoulders tensed as I stood and sheathed my sword. "Where do the foot soldiers sleep?" I knew better than to think my father had set aside a bunk for me in my brothers' tent.

Frode confirmed my assumption when he rose and pointed to a path leading out to the far edge of camp. "That way. I'll walk you there."

"No."

"Yes."

I wanted to punch him. I wanted to kick him in the groin. But, fine—let him join me. He wouldn't get a word out of me.

I started walking, chewing my lip as I realized he could read my thoughts, so it wouldn't matter if I didn't say anything.

Frode chuckled behind me.

"Leave me alone."

"What are you going to tell Arne, then?" he asked. "Or are we still not thinking about the consequences of our actions?"

"You know as well as I do Arne and I aren't together anymore."

For a few minutes the only sound was our steps through the snow. The silhouettes of trees towered over us, the fire in the center camp a mere glow in the distance now.

"Rev." He grabbed my shoulder but I shook him off.

"Let go of me," I hissed. "I won't listen to you berate me any longer."

"I'm not going to." He held his hands up in surrender. "I'm sorry."

I eyed him warily.

He sighed. "I've been under a lot of pressure. You don't deserve to have that taken out on you. I trust you. And if you decided to trust the Hellbringer . . . then, gods help us, I trust him, too."

I blinked. "Really?"

"Really."

I turned and shoved my hands in the pockets of my cloak, trying to warm them. A couple more minutes of walking and the foot soldiers' tents came into view. They were shabby, to say the least. Only a few torches were lit. Three sentries shivered in the cold.

"Not exactly war-ready, are they?" I muttered.

"The priests don't give a damn about the lesser godtouched either," Frode reminded me. "These soldiers are godtouched, so they were conscripted, but they can't do things like our family—or the Hellbringer. They can change the colors of their eyes or make someone else feel happier. Not much place for them on the war front."

I was surprised to realize I didn't feel sorry for them. But then again, they'd lived full, happy lives at home, never struggling for food like the Nilurae or wondering if their children would be born on the last day of the year and then sacrificed at the new year ritual. They were welcomed at the academies despite their minimal abilities. No one mistreated them simply for existing.

That's when I heard it floating through the trees. A familiar voice singing a tune I recognized. It was a Nilurae song.

My heart dropped to the bottom of my throat. In my naivete, I'd forgotten Arne might be stationed here. He still believed I was in love with him. Frode's comments about him made more sense now.

Shit.

I turned around. Frode was gone, on his way back to the royal family tent. Tentatively, I walked toward the fire, where a familiar silhouette sat on a fallen tree. "Arne?"

He turned and peered at me through the dim light. When he recognized me, his face paled. "Revna? What are you doing here?"

I didn't answer, too busy taking in his new appearance. The boy I'd cared about was gone, replaced by a hardened soldier. He wore an oversized uniform and armor. The side of his throat sported a crawling tattoo wrapping around the back of his neck like long fingers.

He ran over and pulled me into an embrace. "What the hell are you doing here?"

I disentangled myself from his arms like they were weapons. No one had told him. *I* hadn't told him. "I turned down the proposal. I'm competing in the Bloodshed Trials."

Utter silence.

Horror twisted Arne's mouth. "What?" he whispered. "No, no,

Revna. Why? I'd never want you to do that for me. Please marry the prince. You may not love him, but at least you will be alive and happy and"—he clutched my hand while I stared—"and don't be an idiot. Don't. Björn will laugh while he kills you in an instant. I can't stand to lose you—not like this. Please." His voice cracked.

An astonished laugh huffed out of me, my breath crystallizing in the air before falling away in the breeze. After all this time, after all we'd been through, after six years of friendship and two of something more, Arne still didn't know me. He thought he motivated my every action.

I gently pulled my hand from his. "I'm afraid there's been a misunderstanding. I did it for the godforsaken. For myself. Arne, I don't know when you fell in love with me, but"—I swallowed, steeling myself to deliver the blow—"it wasn't for you. I don't feel the same. You're one of my best friends. But I don't think of you that way."

He ran a hand through his hair, unease settling into his posture. The set of his jaw revealed his realization. "You're not here for me." He looked at our feet. "You didn't reject him for me."

I shook my head.

He grimaced. "I'm an idiot," he muttered. "I should have known."

I took a deep breath. "Arne, I'm sorry, but when you said you loved me . . . I couldn't say it back. I didn't mean to imply I loved you."

"So because you don't love me, you're going to get yourself killed?" he snapped. "Is it because you love Freja?"

I was trying so desperately to be patient as I explained it all to him, but my annoyance began to seep through every word. "I love her as a sister but nothing more. And if I did love her, wouldn't I be justified? She's been there for me through everything."

"*So have I!*" he bellowed, his face turning red.

I flinched and stepped backward, startled by his fury.

"Who was there when you broke your leg falling down the castle stairs when you were little?" Arne demanded. His voice was a harsh whisper now, like he'd realized yelling would wake the other soldiers. "Who came to you when you would cry yourself to sleep at night after your father beat you? Who encouraged you to marry the prince, to find the good in what you'd been given, only for you to reject it in favor of death? *Who?*"

"You," I said quietly. I couldn't meet his eyes.

"I *love* you, Revna," he said. "And you can't do me the decency of loving me back."

"The *decency*?" Gods, had he always been this frustrating? Or was it a symptom of being a soldier? "It isn't my job to give myself to you, Arne. You knew from the beginning this would never last. I've always been engaged to marry the prince. You chose to love me despite knowing it was impossible for us to be together."

"But it wasn't impossible," he retorted. "If it truly was never going to happen, you wouldn't be here. You wouldn't have refused the prince. Why did you change your mind?" He reached out, faster than I could have prepared for, and grabbed my chin, pulling my face close to his. "Is there someone else?"

I tried to pull out of his grasp, panic flooding me. Where was the gentle man I knew? Where was the boy I'd laughed with growing up, who lay in the grassy clearing with me and held me while I slept? "Let me go."

"I asked you a question."

"It doesn't matter whether there's someone else," I exclaimed, wrenching my face from his hand. "I'm here to save my fucking people—here to save *everyone*, including you, who's treated like trash by the godtouched. Is that not enough for you?"

He kicked at a dirty clump of snow, scowling. "No. It's not enough. When will you look around and realize you're not the only one trying to save the people they care about? I was saving you when I let you go. When I let them drag my ass out here and force a dull blade into my hands. When I killed my first godtouched. And you know what? Saving you made it all worth it." Arne shook his head. He wouldn't meet my eyes, which smarted with unshed tears. "Now I learn you took what I offered and threw it back in my face."

"Don't act like you're somehow the only victim here," I snarled, my own anger bubbling just below the surface, threatening to escape. "I'm under no obligation to accept your shitty *offering*."

"My love is worth so little to you?"

"Stop it, Arne. I tried to love you. But we kept each other at arm's length for too long and missed our chance. I'm sorry you're hurting. I'm here to save our people." At this, I took a step closer to him, forcing his eyes—hardened now, not soft and searching like they'd once been—to meet mine. "And anyone who gets in my way will see the sharp end of my sword. Including you."

Silence stretched out between us, taut as a bowstring ready to release. Finally, he cleared his throat. "Pick a tent and hope the occupants don't hate you. It's the best part of being godforsaken out here."

Arne turned and marched away, disappearing fast through the steadily falling snow.

I wrapped my arms around myself and shivered, mustering all my strength to keep from collapsing on my knees. My fury wasn't enough to ward off the cold, but it made me numb to everything else. I fought back the tears burning my eyes. In the space of barely more than a month, Arne had hardened into a shell of his former self.

Was it my fault? Did turning him away and falling for the Hellbringer make me responsible for his cruelty?

Dwelling on that was futile now. *I can't stay out here or I'll freeze.*

My survival instinct was louder than my anger. I turned and

walked ten steps into the nearest tent. As the flap closed behind me, I felt the subtle shift of bodies in the darkness. Gentle snores mixed with heavy breathing. I couldn't see, but I sensed the tent was packed with soldiers, each laid out in their sleeping bag.

I was furious with Arne, but one thing he said was correct: I didn't know how many of these soldiers were friendly. I couldn't risk waking anyone. My anger turned into hot tears, and when I tried to hold them back, a lump welled in the back of my throat.

I stepped backward and bumped into the pole holding up the front of the tent. It was cold, and I braced myself and slid down it. When I was sitting, I leaned my head back and took a deep breath.

There was an ache in my chest, and as I closed my eyes, I thought of Søren's arms wrapped around me. The memory of his lips on mine, his fingertips tracing over my collarbones . . . it soothed me.

More than that though, I recalled the way we'd pushed each other to fight harder. The way he had driven me to do better with my swordplay. The way he'd cradled me to his chest a few days ago, when I was having a particularly difficult moment. The careful attention he'd given my every word.

I dozed against the post, chin pressed to my chest, only starting awake when the Søren of my dreams reached out to brush my jawline.

25

SUNLIGHT STREAMED THROUGH THE TENT AND LIT MY FACE. I cracked my eyes open and ran my tongue across the roof of my mouth. It felt like sandpaper. I grimaced.

I did enjoy waking to the sun, though.

A quick glance told me I was the only one left in the tent. All the soldiers from the night before were gone.

Panic struck. Where were they? Why was I alone? I rose quickly, adrenaline rushing through my veins. The hair on my arms stood up straight. Outside was eerily quiet. And when I pushed through the tent flaps, an empty campground awaited me.

Trampled snow, empty tents, and the smoking ash of a campfire were all that remained. I turned in a full circle.

Had I slept through a mass exodus?

My eyes followed the trampled snow to the edge of the grove of pines. Those, at least, were familiar—I'd come that way last night. Beyond the trees, a trumpet blared.

I stiffened. Though it was my first time on the front lines, anyone in Bhorglid would recognize the sound. No good parent let their child grow up without knowing how to identify a battle call.

There was no time for hesitation. I sprinted down the path until I reached the center of camp.

I arrived gasping for air and clutching at a stitch in my side. The bitter wind tore like claws at my lungs. I'd strapped my sword on while I ran, fingers slipping over the buckle keeping the scabbard fastened to my waist.

It didn't take long to spot a flame of familiar curly hair.

Frode! Get the hell over here.

The last of the army trickled out of the camp, heading north. I had no doubt my father was at the head, Björn by his side.

Frode sauntered toward me, his two curved knives sheathed at either hip. "You sleep too deeply for your own good," he observed, reading my thoughts to learn the events of the morning. "Are you coming?"

Yes.

I was too out of breath to speak.

"Good. Your armor is in my tent. Bottom bunk on the left." He pointed to a tent at least five times larger than the one I'd slept in last night, but I didn't have time to dwell on his luxury accommodations. I rushed in, stripping out of my warm outer clothes to throw my armor on over my wool underlayer. My cloak went back on top. I ran my thumb over the hilt of my blade, and deep in my stomach I felt a rush of exhilaration.

I'd never truly fought in a war before. It was every godtouched child's dream to win honor for Bhorglid or die in search of it. I didn't pay much attention to godtouched socialites, but I knew those whose children didn't fight in the war were shunned. The social consequences piled on fast, but they were nothing compared to how the godforsaken lived.

I jogged out to where Frode waited for me, my horse saddled next to his. I clambered on, awkward with my armor. "Will this be like the battle in the canyon?" I asked him.

He shrugged. "Sure. It will be bloody."

I forgot my initial excitement. Of course he wouldn't want to talk about it. Battle destroyed him. He once described it as listening to the whole world scream directly in his ears.

We started riding, catching up with the marching army's rearguard. Why had I been excited in the first place? I may have been anxious to use my newfound fighting skills, but this wasn't the right place. Everything I'd learned from the Hellbringer was meant to bring my father down, not fight on his behalf.

I watched as Frode winked at me from his saddle and pulled a half-empty bottle of wine out of a saddlebag. My mouth dropped open. "Are you seriously about to get drunk before we go into battle?" I hissed. "I know you have a hard time, but that can't be a good idea. You're armed, for crying out loud."

He rolled his eyes and uncorked the bottle with a dagger, then raised it to his lips and took a long swig. "I'm offended you think I can't use my knives as well when I'm drunk. Besides, don't you know how to fight now? Just don't let me die." He shrugged. "And if I did die, it would only be a couple days early."

My mouth went dry. He was morbid, but . . . he might be right. This could be one of my last days with Frode. And Jac. One of my own last days alive. We had a plan, but there was so much room for everything to go wrong.

Frode reached over from his mount, nearly losing his balance, and shoved me playfully, laughing. "That's why I drink," he said, pointing to my head. "I can hear *allllll* of that. And it feels like shit."

No. No, I couldn't think about the Trials now. I needed to distract Frode or the whole bottle was going to disappear in an instant.

"Where are we going? For the battle."

He frowned and thought about it. "I dunno," he mumbled. Was he already tipsy? It hadn't even been two minutes since his first sip.

"Wait! I remember. A spy came and told us where to find some Kryllians."

I sighed. "You drank the other half of that bottle before we left, didn't you?"

"Yep!" He was far too cheerful for my liking.

With his focus entirely on keeping his balance, I was able to lean over and snatch the bottle from him. "Give me that." While he protested, I dumped the rest of its contents into the snow.

"Revna." Drunk Frode was usually out of it, but now he looked entirely too somber. "Gods, why are you being such a bitch?"

I would have taken the insult far too personally from anyone else. But this was Frode. "Because I love you."

We rode for over an hour, not stopping for any breaks. The foot soldiers eventually fell behind, muttering obscenities at us under their breaths as we passed. We had the luxury of riding, so surely that meant something substantial. I rolled my eyes. They had no idea what it meant to be nothing.

Eventually, my father held up his fist to halt us. Our procession slowed to a stop. If I stood in my stirrups, I could see down a hill in front of us to where ten small purple tents were arranged.

Was this it? We had brought our entire enemy to fight ten tents' worth of Kryllian soldiers?

"On my signal," the king said. And then we waited.

The couple of times I peered into the valley, I saw a few figures walking, going about their ordinary business. The pines around us sparkled with icicles in the morning sun. My horse adjusted her feet, snorting impatiently. It could have been minutes or hours for all I knew, but the sun didn't move far in the sky as we held our position.

And then, in a moment so ordinary I barely paid it any mind, my father raised his open hand, signaling our battalion to attack.

Battle cries roared out of every mouth and the horses galloped over the slope. Before Frode's mount could follow, I took the reins and led him over into the grove of trees, out of sight of the battle. "Stay here," I ordered. I wasn't sure if I was talking to my brother or the horse.

The foot soldiers charged, joining the fray. I felt bad for them—they'd had no rest before rushing right into the chaos. Though I wondered how it was possible the battle hadn't ended already, with so few Kryllians at the campsite.

Then I peered over the hill and understood.

We weren't the only ones lying in wait. The Kryllian army had known we were coming. Most of their soldiers had been waiting in the woods for us to charge. Now the colors of armor blurred together as a giant mass of soldiers collided.

Lurae were in action on both sides. I spotted Björn and my father at the head of our line of attack, breathing orange flames across the snow. Few soldiers came away with burns, though. They must have armor protecting them from fire. Smart.

Erik was on the other side of the front lines, his great axe effectively taking out masses upon masses of soldiers as he used his Lurae strength to annihilate them.

The Kryllian soldiers were as powerful if not more. I watched one summon lightning to his hands and use it to take out two Bhorglid soldiers on either side of him. Another pulled water from the patches of mud Björn and Father were creating and froze it over the hands of our soldiers. They'd cry out in pain and another soldier would step out from behind and decapitate them.

The snow brimmed with scarlet.

An explosion echoed across the valley and I whipped my head to the left to see smoke billowing like a cloud from a crater in the ground far too close for my liking. *Shit.* I couldn't go down there, not when it meant leaving Frode alone. He was in no shape to fight. Any Kryllian who stumbled upon him would kill him instantly.

I pulled my horse back by the reins, ignoring its unhappy snort and stomp. Apparently this mount had no qualms about going into combat. I cast one last glance down at the battlefield, wondering if Søren was there to turn the tide before moving back to where I'd stashed my brother.

My chest filled with panic when Frode's horse came into view without its rider. I glanced around and saw him instantly. He was curled up in the snow, hands over his ears, trembling like an autumn leaf about to fall. I stared at his green eyes, the whites so prominent, they matched the snow behind him.

"Come here, Frode," I said, bending to put an arm underneath his shoulders. I pulled until he sat up and used my other hand to pull my cloak off and drape it around him. The wet snow would soak through his clothes and freeze again, leaving him frostbitten if he wasn't careful.

I pulled him to his feet. "W-w-w-what the he-hell is hap-p-pening?" he gasped out.

"Down there? Ambush," I said, hauling him toward my horse. There was no way he could ride on his own. "We're going back to camp."

"W-w-we are?" I could hear the relief in his voice, and it was enough for me to hurry my efforts.

But before I could push him into the saddle, I saw a sudden movement out of the corner of my eye. I had to drop Frode in order to bring my sword up in time to parry a slash from a lone Kryllian soldier.

We were both breathing heavily as we stared at each other. I didn't know him; his dark hair and eyes were typical Kryllian features. But he raised a hand and a huge expanse of snow rose up behind me like a wave, blocking the bright glow of the sun and drenching me in shadow.

I barely managed to dodge the wave as it came down, grunting as I hurled all my force into a counterattack. The soldier's moves were practiced, every slice flawless—a deadly opponent. But he hadn't trained under the Hellbringer's strict tutelage.

Every strike was met by a swift parry of my own, keeping him too preoccupied to use his magic. Soon enough, I saw a gap in his dance, perfect for me to lunge forward, twist my sword, and shove it through the space between his ribs until I knew I'd struck his heart.

The soldier choked, gasping for air, and stared at his fatal wound. I pulled my blade out of him; there was no sense in leaving him to suffer longer for cruelty's sake.

He collapsed to his knees, the bright red stain in violent contrast with the pure white snow.

I didn't know what came next. Guilt? Relief?

Neither emotion rose to pull me from my numbness. Instead, I was met with a flutter of excitement. I had done it. I had fought a Lurae and won.

"Revna?" Frode's voice was hoarse. "I'm cold."

"Oh, shit." I left the lifeless body to rest in the snow and hauled Frode up, grateful the soldier hadn't managed to bury him during the attack. In a few moments my brother sat in the saddle and I managed to situate myself behind him, my arms around his waist.

I turned in the direction we came from and we started making our way back to camp.

26

OUR UNDERCOVER SOLDIERS, OFF ON MISSIONS TO GATHER intelligence behind enemy lines, returned at the same time as the rest of the army, dragging a snarling Kryllian in one of our uniforms with them. "Spy," I heard them inform my father. The king only grunted before disappearing into his tent with the newly captured prisoner and all my brothers except Frode. Agonized screams echoed through the camp for two hours before the man broke and revealed crucial information.

"Gather your weapons," my father announced when Frode and I joined the rest of our family at Jac's summons. "We are headed to their secret camp in the east. That's where the Hellbringer is hiding."

I heard him, but my mind was occupied with the gruesome sight of the spy, still tied to the chair they'd left him in. He was dead, head hanging limp and eyes sightless. He had been burned from the knees down; all that remained were charred bits of flesh on bone. A knife was buried in his back and blood dripped from his lifeless eyes and mouth.

"Jac will impersonate the spy," my father continued. "If we move fast enough, word of his capture will not have reached them yet. He will infiltrate the camp and learn where the Hellbringer will be at his most vulnerable. Frode will listen for his signal, and when it's given, we will move in."

Björn nodded, Erik's face serious. I turned away from the corpse to glance at Frode. Did they actually know the Hellbringer's location, or had the spy managed to give them false information?

Frode shrugged subtly at my thought. I knew the likelihood of us catching and killing Søren was slim to none, but it didn't stop my heart from beating faster in my chest, my stomach twisting at the thought of someone hurting him. Would I be able to stand back and watch without intervening while they tried?

Only time would tell.

A soldier came and hauled away the spy's body while my brothers strapped their armor on and grabbed their weapons. As soon as we were all prepared, we departed into the crisp afternoon.

◆ ◆ ◆ ◆ ◆

IT WAS DARK WHEN MY FATHER SIGNALED WE HAD ARRIVED.

The woods obscured the dim lantern Björn lit. Jac dismounted, and I watched with fascination as he turned into an identical copy of the Kryllian spy. The transformation was like watching a bucket being poured over my brother's head, but instead of water, a new identity washed over him. His hair turned light blond and grew out, his joints popped as he heightened several inches, and his eyes changed color.

Once he finished transforming, he dressed in the armor they had pulled off the spy before torturing him. Underneath, the too-big training garb I'd wondered about earlier was now a perfect fit.

We watched with bated breath as Jac's shadow disappeared into the darkness. The tiny glow of a campfire flickered in the distance, tents arranged in a half circle around it. Occasional figures from the camp passed by, silhouetted against the small fire.

Björn and Erik moved the horses into a concentrated area within the grove of trees, where they would be obscured from enemy sight. I followed suit, hitching my own horse to a tree and trying to draw as little attention from Björn and my father as possible. Honestly, I was surprised they'd let me come along in the first place. The only explanation I could fathom was they hoped the Hellbringer would kill me while we were here.

Frode cocked his head to the side, listening. He frowned. "I think the info we had was right. I'm pretty sure that's the Hellbringer I hear."

"What is he thinking?" Björn demanded.

Frode shook his head. "I can't make it out. His mind sounds like . . . a battlefield." Frode glanced at me questioningly. "It's as if there are hundreds of voices in his head. And they're all screaming at him."

I had no clue why it would sound like there was an army living in the Hellbringer's mind. *He seemed normal enough to me. Well, as normal as someone like the Hellbringer can be.*

Frode lowered his voice, and I was unsure whether his next words were addressed to me or to himself. "No wonder I've never been able to distinguish his individual thoughts in battle before."

We settled in to wait for our moment to strike.

Was Søren here of his own accord, or because the queen had ordered him here? It was impossible to know. The more important question was whether my brothers and father actually stood a chance at killing him.

I tried to imagine watching Björn slicing off the Hellbringer's head. Nausea rolled through my stomach. No. That couldn't happen.

A hand grabbed my wrist: Frode. "Stop worrying," he murmured. "You of all people know how capable he is."

I took a deep breath and tried to silence my mind.

Hours later, when the sun had begun to peer over the horizon, people began emerging from their tents.

"What's going on?" Erik muttered. "It's not dawn yet."

Frode frowned and inclined his head. "They're gathering for something. A . . . a speech, maybe? I think the Hellbringer is going to give a speech. And"—he squinted—"something else, but I can't make it out. There're too many voices; they're clouding my hearing."

"Should we get closer?" I asked.

No one was more surprised than I was when Björn agreed with me. "Yes. Use the snowdrift there for cover."

We crept toward the campground until we could hide behind the mound of snow Björn had pointed out. It rested just outside the border of the gathering crowd. Now, we faced the center hearth of the camp, the tents a backdrop against the speech Frode had learned was happening. If we listened carefully, we could hear voices over the wind.

My heart thudded an unsteady beat against my ribs. Søren was just through there, obscured by the soldiers. Anticipation swirled with anxiety in my stomach.

Father looked at Frode. "It's up to you now, son," he said.

Frode was pale. He fidgeted with the hilts of his knives. I knew the gesture—it most often appeared when he wandered the halls of the castle a day or two before leaving for the front.

I reached out and put a hand on his knee. He glanced at me, and I could see the anxiety in his eyes. *You can do this.*

He gave a curt nod.

The wind carried voices over the drifts. For a long while I didn't recognize any of them, but when a sudden snag of conversation caught my attention, I stiffened. Nothing could disguise the dissonance of the mask distorting the Hellbringer's tone.

"—a victory for Kryllian," he was saying. I tilted my head to try and hear better. "We are one step closer to destroying the heathens who dare lay claim to our land!"

Cheering echoed through the clearing. As it subsided, Frode turned to Father. "Something is wrong," he said, panicked. "They know it's Jac; they know he's a spy." He froze. "And they know we're—"

A hand reached over the snowdrift and grabbed me by the arm. Thanks to the Hellbringer's training, I moved on pure instinct, twisting in an attempt to remove myself from the attacker's clutches and lunging with my own blow.

My fist didn't connect, and I lost my balance, half falling. The hand adjusted its grip and pulled me up by the shoulder.

I looked into the familiar mask of my assailant.

"Hello, Revna," the Hellbringer said.

◆ ◆ ◆ ◆ ◆

I STARED AT HIM. MY THOUGHTS SWIRLED INTO SOMETHING UNIN-telligible in my brain, and a mixture of relief, adoration, and panic pounded through my veins. He pulled me over the snowdrift, and I cried out as my arm resisted being pulled from its socket.

Jac was the first person I saw as the crowd parted. He was tied to a chair next to their campfire, and soldiers swarmed, laughing and spitting on him. One of his arms shone red in the almost-dawn, shards of bone tearing through the skin. The transformation had worn off and his hair glowed in the firelight. His eyes were closed, his head lolling back. If he wasn't dead, he was at least unconscious.

"No," I whispered. The dull thud of my erratic heartbeat echoed through my skull. Everything Søren and I had done together meant nothing if he killed the brothers I was allied with. What the hell was he thinking?

Frode lunged over the drift, knives drawn, and slashed at the Hellbringer. The soldiers in the crowd drew their weapons, but stood back, allowing my brother to attack with no interference. My captor dodged, hauling me out of the way, then twisted me around, placing his familiar blade directly at my throat.

My heart plunged, but I didn't waver. Of course he'd use me as a hostage—if he'd done anything else, the eyes on us both would've turned hostile. Our deception, our partnership, would be known in an instant. I took a shaky breath, determined to play the game and play it well.

This was not Søren; this was the Hellbringer. And the Hellbringer was an enemy of Bhorglid.

Still, fury tore at my stomach when I thought of Jac's torture. I resisted the urge to wrench myself from his grasp. "Let Jac go," I demanded.

"None of you are in any position to bargain," the Hellbringer said. Father, Erik, and Björn were moving to the other side of the snowdrift, weapons ready. Frode shook—whether with anger or overwhelm at the voices he heard, I wasn't sure. "Would you look at that? The entire royal family of Bhorglid. What a treat."

My mind warred between panic and steadiness. The Hellbringer wouldn't kill me. This was a ruse, a way to prevent my father and brothers from discovering my plan to ally with Kryllian before the time was right.

You can trust him, I reminded myself.

But Frode's wide eyes met mine, his breath coming fast, and he shook his head.

I felt the blood drain from my face. Frode might be the one reading minds, but his message to me was clear as day, etched irrevocably in every terrified line of his face. Despite all the noise in the Hellbringer's head, Frode had ascertained the general's intentions.

You cannot trust the Hellbringer. Not anymore.

As I watched my breath shimmer in the rising sunlight, I realized we might not all make it to the Bloodshed Trials.

With a swift tug on the back of my collar, the Hellbringer marched me to where Jac was tied, pushing through his own soldiers as if they weren't there. They all backed away, eyes filled with something resembling respect—or fear.

The Hellbringer threw me in the snow at Jac's feet. I scrambled backward, trying to put distance between me and the black-clad figure.

I am not afraid of you.

When I had spoken those words to the Hellbringer, recovering from the injury he'd dealt me, I had meant them. Now, with him towering over me, sword reflecting the dawn, I wasn't sure if I could say them again.

The soldiers circled me and Jac, unconscious in his bonds. Then chaos erupted.

My father and Björn attacked, sending roaring flames into the crowd of soldiers, while Erik picked one up and hauled him over his head, tossing him ten feet like it was nothing. He proceeded to pull another soldier toward him by the arm. The soldier's scream echoed over the white landscape as his arm was pulled out of its socket.

The Hellbringer turned along with the rest of the soldiers in time to see Frode leap onto a soldier and slice his throat with his wickedly sharp knives. "Leave them alone!" he screamed, lunging for another.

As the army roared to life, drawing weapons to fight back, I took advantage of the general's distraction and pulled out one of my daggers, slicing through the ties holding Jac to the chair, grunting as I pulled him over my shoulder.

But the Hellbringer turned to reach for his blade and caught sight of us. "No you don't," he growled, advancing.

I turned to face him, using my free hand to draw my sword and flip it in the air until I could hold it steady. There was no way I could defeat him like this, not when I had barely managed to best him at full capacity. But honestly? I shouldn't have had to fight him.

"What the hell are you doing?" I growled, uncaring whether I was overheard. "Are you going to kill me *and* my family? What about the truce?"

He lowered his stance. "You would be hard pressed to remember the meaning of duty."

The battle raged on behind him. Flames burned away the snow, leaving only charred dirt in their wake, and a giant plume of fire exploded from within the crowd. Screams echoed along the mountains in the distance.

"You call this your duty?" I swung my sword, gesturing at the scene before us. Smoke billowed up in clouds. "Because it's going to shit."

His unoccupied hand clenched in a fist. "You know *nothing* about my duty," he hissed, and then he lunged.

I was able to block the swing with one hand on my sword. He was holding back despite his words. I shifted Jac's weight, ignoring the persistent ache building in my shoulder. "That's all you've got?"

He swung again, and by some miracle I stepped out of the way in time. But now he wasn't pulling punches. I barely had the time or ability to counter each strike. He took our duel to full speed, his strength overwhelming enough that I spent more energy than I wanted to simply not collapsing in the snow.

"Revna!" I could hear Frode calling my name, but looking was not an option. If I lost any degree of focus, the Hellbringer's blade would carve me to shreds. And Volkan wouldn't come to heal me this time.

"Was it all a lie?" I snarled, ducking to avoid another slice. My knees screamed as I pushed myself back up to full height, Jac's weight heavy and limp on my shoulders. My anger fueled me, and I forced it higher, leaving no room for the despair threatening to leave my limbs heavy and evaporating my will to fight. "Did you fake it all to get me on your side?"

His reply was a deep rumble. "I told you, Princess: I don't lie."

He lunged, but when I lifted my sword to parry, I stumbled, losing my balance. A flash of panic raced through my veins like lightning. *This is it.*

But there was a desperate cry and a blur of silver. The clang of metal on metal rang in my ears as I landed in powder, tumbling down a hill and away from the fight, Jac's deadweight tumbling right behind me. When gravity stopped pulling me, I looked up to see my savior.

Frode stood there, his two knives locked against the Hellbringer's blade, panting with the effort of holding his attacker back. His red hair shone in the light of the rising sun.

I made sure Jac was breathing, then scrambled to my feet, ready to strike at the Hellbringer again. Crawling up the drift proved harder than it looked. My feet slipped in the wet snow, stained with Jac's blood. Still, I kept an eye on the battle above me.

But the Hellbringer and Frode were motionless, their blades locked. My brother stared, brows furrowed, into the unseeing eyes of the mask. Why weren't they fighting?

Frode stepped back and dropped his knives. Even his opponent was shocked.

"Frode, what are you doing?" I screamed. I dug my feet in harder, trying to make it to the top.

"I understand," Frode called out. The Hellbringer lowered his guard for a moment. Frode glanced at me. His mouth moved, but the words were spoken too low to be heard. My brother held out his arms.

No. No, no, no . . . I hurled a dagger and it bounced off the Hellbringer's armor. The masked general stared at my brother for a moment, and then offered a single nod.

"No!" The scream echoed from me, shaking the mountains surrounding us.

But it wasn't enough to stop the Hellbringer from extending his hand, palm toward Frode, and then clenching it into a fist.

27

I T TOOK AN ETERNITY FOR FRODE TO FALL BACKWARD, LAND-
ing in the snow like it was a cloud. His eyes were lifeless from the
moment the Hellbringer closed his fist, staring straight ahead at
nothing.

The world fell silent, only a ringing in my ears.

I arrived at the top of the hill, but the Hellbringer was gone. The
smoke from the tents Father and Björn had set alight was a scar across
the morning's perfect sunrise, bleeding orange into the clearing.

Someone screamed in the distance. Feral screaming. Rage filled.

My hands shook as they turned Frode over. I pulled off my
gloves. My fingers immediately stiffened from the chill, but they
searched my brother's throat for any remnants of heartbeat.

Nothing.

A hand on my shoulder; muttering voices. My fingers were blue.
Was another Kryllian soldier coming to slide his blade softly
through my ribs and into my heart? I hoped so.

Where is your heartbeat? Where the hell are you hiding it? I
asked him, pressing my fingertips to his throat again.

I could hear his chuckle. *You aren't going to find it.* Frode's
voice was clear as day in my mind.

Hands lifted me—a support underneath my arms, pulling me to my feet. Other hands put my gloves back on.

"No," I whispered, tugging at the fabric. "No, I can't feel his heartbeat with them on."

A voice called my name but I ignored it, reaching for Frode again. A hand grabbed mine and pulled it back in.

Erik called my name again. "Revna."

Reality returned. Time moved normally once more. I could hear birds twittering in the trees, celebrating the morning. Celebrating death.

"I have Jac," Björn said. "He needs a healer as soon as possible; otherwise he might not make it."

I couldn't look to see if Jac's injuries were worse. I could only stare at Frode's face, devoid of color, devoid of laughter, devoid of life.

"Leave the body," my father snarled. "We'll ride back to camp." *The body.*

"What?" I whispered. "Why would we leave him?"

There was no reply. Maybe I spoke too quietly. I took a deep breath in to repeat myself. "Why would we leave his body?" My voice cracked midway through the words.

"I watched him die," Father said. I couldn't bring myself to look away. "He didn't fight. He held out his arms and *asked* the Hellbringer to kill him. He was so desperate not to compete in the Trials, he would rather die at the hand of an enemy."

"No." I shook my head and stars erupted at the edges of my vision. "That's not what happened."

"She's in shock." Erik's voice was smooth and sticky like honey. "Let's get her home." He placed one hand around my shoulders and the other under my knees, then lifted me into his arms.

I reached toward Frode. "You can't leave him."

I tore my eyes away to look at Erik's face. Was I imagining things, or did his eyes seem sorrowful? "We have to," he whispered. Behind him, I could see Björn and my father in the distance, trekking back to where the horses were hitched.

The words tumbled out of my mouth before I could think to stop them: "You're going to let them decide what is right when you already know? You're going to leave him here when I saw him sacrifice himself? You would dishonor your own brother that way?"

"Would you rather see his body burned to ash and swept into the gutters of the arena?" Erik snapped. I winced, turning away from his glare. "Of all the options, leaving him here is far more honorable than returning him to a place where he will be shunned for how he died. And I don't take orders from you, little sister."

He turned and started for the trees. Panic seized me and I arched my back, kicking and screaming. "You can't leave him! YOU CAN'T LEAVE HIM!"

Erik carried me the entire way back to where the horses were before placing me on his saddle and securing an arm around me. The entire time he said nothing, a figure of stone against the backdrop of my screams and sobs.

◆ ◆ ◆ ◆ ◆

THE HEALERS SPENT HOURS LABORING OVER JAC. I DOUBTED their abilities were as good as Volkan's, but they managed to put my one remaining ally back together. For that, I was grateful.

Jac kept his horse right behind mine for the journey home—back to the castle, back to Freja and Halvar.

At first, I pretended not to notice. He wasn't bothering me, and I was mostly grateful not to have Erik restraining me this time around. But eventually I felt the weight of Jac's stare on the back of my head with every step the horse took.

Finally, when I could tell my jitters were making my horse anxious, I twisted at the waist to face him, scowling at him through narrowed eyes. "Why are you following me?" I hissed.

He blinked, then shrugged. "Aren't we all going to the same place?" he asked. There was a strangeness in his voice I didn't recognize. His eyes weren't quite focused on anything.

I frowned. "What's wrong?"

Jac looked out over the snowy wasteland. The wind whipped my dark hair around my head and blew the light dust of freshly falling snowflakes onto my face. They stung.

"Do you think preparing for your own death makes it easier?" he asked the mountain path. "Or does it make everything harder in the end?"

I stared at him in silence for a moment, the only noise the wind and hooves breaking through the slightly frozen snow.

Jac tilted his head to the side. He wasn't looking at me. "I don't think I'm ready to die." He said it so softly I barely heard him.

There was a knot in my throat. I tried to swallow it, but it was stubborn.

"We aren't going to die," I said, feeling the lie of it in my very bones. I glanced forward, made sure Erik, Björn, and Father weren't listening in. "We're going to win. Together. You and me, remember?"

A sliver of fear made its way into the space between my ribs. Was our pact to work together no longer in play? Was he backing out?

"Jac?"

"I don't know if I can do this, Rev." He sounded utterly broken, and, gods, I didn't blame him. How could I when my own throat threatened to close every second I thought about Frode?

He should have been here. Should have been making snide comments about both of us losing our nerve, getting off our asses to fight another day. Instead, his body was frozen over somewhere in the wastes, unseeing eyes gazing up at the blue sky.

Did Jac feel as dead inside as he looked? A shiver ran through me, from my head through my toes. If he backed out, decided not to compete, they would kill him. But I wouldn't hold him to his deal. Not when everything was crumbling to pieces around us, an avalanche of loss sweeping away our determination like it had never been.

Am I ready to die?

Alone against Björn and Erik, death was my only possible fate.

I waited for a snappy response from Frode in response to my darkening thoughts, but none came. The wind whistled, filling the silence, but my heart felt like lead, sinking to the bottom of my stomach like an anchor.

"I suppose, whether I'm ready or not, Aloisa will come for me regardless," I murmured, running a hand over the pommel of my sword. "She comes to take us all eventually."

M Y HEART THUDDED AT THE THOUGHT OF SEEING FREJA again. After the way we had left things, I wasn't sure she would want my company, but knowing I might die without seeing her again left a ragged ache in my heart. Combined with the one Frode left, it was too much for me to stomach.

The hallways were dim and damp—the same as when I'd left for the front. They were lonelier without Frode or even Volkan keeping me company. I tossed my cloak over my shoulders, less for the warmth it provided than for something to dig my fingernails into and pull tight around my shoulders. Underneath, I'd concealed another cloak Halvar had given me. Though thinner, I had no doubt it would provide my friend some much-needed warmth.

Perhaps it would serve as a gift of reconciliation, too.

I heard Freja whistling as soon as I emerged from the stairwell. It might have put a smile on my face if a single thing about today were different. But instead I'd come to deliver the news my brother was dead, I'd been kidnapped by the Hellbringer, and Arne and I were no longer on speaking terms.

I wasn't looking forward to telling her all of that.

She heard my footsteps when I was several feet away. "Revna?" she called. "Is that you?"

She grinned at me when I peered into her cell. This time I couldn't keep the ghost of a smile from slipping across my face. Freja came over to the bars and reached out to brush her hand across my face.

"You look like death," she said.

She wasn't wrong—Halvar had said much the same when I stopped by before coming here. When I glanced in the mirror before leaving the Sharpened Axe, the circles under my eyes made me cringe.

I took in her appearance. The light was back in her eyes, and while her face was covered in dirt, she looked happier than when I had left for the front. There was a cloak around her shoulders already, but I noted goose bumps on her arms nonetheless. As much as I wanted to ask her how she was, I had to apologize first.

"Freja, I'm so sorry." I laid my forehead against the freezing metal bars. "The last time I saw you, I—"

"Stop." She squeezed my hand. "You don't need to apologize. If anyone does, it's me. What I said was cruel. I didn't mean it."

The wave of relief washed over me and made my knees weak. "I didn't mean any of it either," I said. "Oh, here. I brought you another cloak."

She squeaked with excitement, and when I handed it to her, she pulled it around her shoulders immediately, covering the thinner one she already wore. When she sighed with relief, I felt the cold leave my own veins. There was a blanket in the back corner of her cell, carefully hidden from prying eyes, but it surely wasn't enough on especially cold nights.

"You look better," I said.

She chuckled a bit. "I'm not as lonely anymore—I made friends with my neighbor." Freja gestured toward the cell to her left.

I leaned over enough to catch a glimpse of a wizened old person with pure white hair curled up in the corner. They didn't acknowledge me.

"How was the front?" Freja asked.

Dread sank like a rock in my stomach. I recounted the events of my time away, from my kidnapping to my confrontation with Arne to Frode's death. I left out significant amounts of my time with the Hellbringer, though, including how much I'd trusted him and cared for him, especially at the end. I already realized my own stupidity. I didn't need someone else to point it out. By the time I finished talking, the color had drained from Freja's face.

"You were kidnapped by the Hellbringer," she whispered, her hand moving to her mouth. I couldn't distinguish whether shock or amazement made her jaw drop. "What was he like? Is it all true? All of the legends?"

I shrugged. "He says they are, and I believe him. When I was with him in the prison, I started thinking there might be something more to him, something real hidden underneath the mask. But"—I shook my head—"he would have killed me. I don't know why he decided to kill Frode instead."

"That surprises me, especially since he offered you a truce from the queen." Freja frowned, chewing on her bottom lip.

I nodded. "I thought so, too." *I also thought he might have loved me.*

I ignored the disappointment welling in my stomach.

She pressed her face against the cell bars and lowered her voice to a whisper. "All the more reason for you to be queen, then. The godforsaken are ready to support you. Halvar says the rebellion is ready. All you have to do is win the Trials."

I smothered the words threatening to escape: that Frode was gone and I wasn't sure Jac was interested in our truce anymore. My odds of winning the Trials decreased with every passing minute.

"Good," I said, moving to sit on the dusty floor and hoping she couldn't read my hidden desperation. "It's been too long. Too many years. The godforsaken deserve a turn at the helm."

We lapsed into silence, and I rested my face in my hands. The space behind my eyelids throbbed. I couldn't get him out of my head. *Frode Frode Frode.* His name echoed like a song.

"I know you probably don't want to answer this, but . . ." Freja chewed on her lip. "Arne is okay, right? He wasn't dead last time you saw him?"

I chuckled at her tone. "Yes, I caught a glance of him after the battle I witnessed. He was fine. Maybe a bit scratched up, but nothing major."

"I can't believe you two actually ended things. And on such bad terms."

I shrugged. "He'd rather I marry the prince than fight for the godforsaken. In the end, it was a simple choice to make."

Simple for our relationship. But not for our friendship. I'd naively thought things could possibly stay light between us. But our argument in the war camp had proven otherwise.

I twisted my hands together, hoping the motion would distract me. I had to get Arne and Frode out of my head so I could concentrate.

"Are you okay?" Freja asked softly.

"I'm fine."

She reached through the bars to grasp my hand, and gratitude overwhelmed me.

I squeezed her hand in return. "I'm going to get you out of here," I said. "No matter what it takes. No matter who has to die. You deserve better than this."

A wiry voice floated over to us. "You'll be queen soon enough. No need for such dramatics."

Freja's eyebrows flew up and she let go of my hand, scrambling over to the front corner of her cell bordering her neighbor. "Say that again," she demanded. "Valen. You can't say that and then go quiet."

I peered over at the person in the next cell. They grumbled and pushed themselves to a sitting position, resting most of their weight on their elbows. There was no way they were younger than eighty.

"I *said* this one"—they pointed a finger at me—"is going to be queen. Listen harder next time."

Freja's eyes were wide. "Valen is a Seeing One," she whispered.

I glanced over at Valen's wizened features, twisted and gnarled like an oak tree. I had learned about the Seeing Ones growing up but I wasn't sure if I believed they were real. The books I read about the wandering clan of seers who rejected ideas of society for a truly blank slate fascinated me. They were neither men nor women, simply people, and used non-gendered pronouns.

I knew my father hated the Seeing Ones. He spoke of them only with disdain and disbelief, once going so far as to say they were Nilurae who pretended to have the gift of sight.

Valen's dark eyes bored into mine, an unspoken challenge. I knew how they expected me to treat them—with disgust and disdain, the only things my father had offered them.

I bowed my head in Valen's direction. "If I might ask, how did you end up imprisoned in Bhorglid? I thought your people were peaceful wanderers."

Valen cackled, an edge of derangement in their voice. "Are you also under the impression your father sentences people to this prison only when necessary?"

"No," I said. "I can assure you the opposite is true. Freja is only here because of what I've done."

"Not exactly true, but it doesn't surprise me you would say so," Valen said. When I opened my mouth to respond, the Seeing One held up a hand to stop me. "I know your destiny much more intimately than you do."

"And her destiny is to become queen?" Freja asked.

"Yes."

Freja's eyes lit up and she turned to me. "You *are* going to win," she breathed. "Revna, I knew it. You're going to be Queen of Bhorglid! Queen of the godforsaken! Can you believe it?"

I didn't have the heart to ask how long Valen had been locked in this prison; how long they'd had to sit with their thoughts and prophecies until the real world and dreams blended and became one.

"How?" I asked. I wanted to believe them, but without Frode, possibly without Jac . . . it seemed unwise to hope.

The Seeing One shrugged and turned to face the corner. "I cannot see the path, only the destination," they said. "But it will come to pass."

Freja was thrilled, and I managed to paste a smile on my face. "I hope it does," I said. "I hope it does."

◆ ◆ ◆ ◆ ◆

WHEN I FINALLY RETURNED TO THE CASTLE, I FOUND A HOT BATH waiting for me.

I didn't know who had left it—maybe one of the servants—but I didn't hesitate before pulling off my grimy clothes and sinking into the warm water. I sighed as the heat moved into my bones, defrosting my core. The war front had been traumatizing, yes, but more than that, it had been *cold*. I wasn't sure I remembered warmth.

The water looked dirty instantly. I pulled the tie out of my braid and unwove it, sinking my hair beneath the surface. I used the vial of soap that had been placed on a stool with a towel next to the tub to scrub at my scalp, working out all the sweat and filth.

The scent of death.

I shivered despite the heat. The last time I had bathed was . . .

No. I pushed the thought away. I didn't want to remember. Not right now—not when the Bloodshed Trials were tomorrow.

I toweled off and dressed in a comfy pair of clothes. Lying in bed, I surveyed my childhood bedroom. It looked the same as always, blankets draped everywhere and books in piles all over the floor. My dancing shoes from my youth were hung on the wall, from a time when Mother had actually praised my accomplishments and treated me like her daughter. That was before my lack of magic was confirmed.

I allowed reality to sink in. Tomorrow I would enter the arena and fight to kill my brothers. And if I couldn't, then one of them would kill me.

I wondered how they'd do it. Would Björn use his Lurae to burn me to a crisp? Would Erik smash his war hammer through my skull?

What was it like to die?

I reached my thoughts out to Frode, or whatever remained of him, lost somewhere in the freezing wasteland of the north. Did he sink into darkness like falling asleep? Or was there excruciating pain like nothing he'd ever experienced before?

What would my death be like?

The image of Frode laughing brushed across the backs of my eyelids.

I tossed and turned in my bed for hours, wishing a fitful sleep would overtake me. Being exhausted for the Bloodshed Trials was a sure way to get myself killed. Every time unconsciousness beckoned, however, the image of Frode's lifeless eyes appeared.

Was his body in the place we left it? The likelihood of a Kryllian battalion making camp there again was slim but not impossible. Kryllian bodies in their dark armor had been strewn across the bright snow, leaking blood from irreparable wounds. Had the Hellbringer been the only one to escape?

Would he return to bury the bodies of his fallen soldiers? Or would they be left there to freeze, like Frode?

If I hadn't fallen down the hill, would he be alive right now?

The thought tore me in two, and I curled in on myself, hoping to stay in one piece.

When sleep finally took me away, it was like being smothered.

◆   ◆   ◆   ◆   ◆

I CALLED FOR HIM.

Frode? Where are you? It's too dark; I can't see you.

My only answer was the haunting melody he'd been humming in recent weeks.

I sat straight up in my bed, covered in a cold sweat, tears streaming down my face. The cry caught in my chest and I covered my mouth as I let out a sob that wracked my whole body.

He was gone. He wasn't coming back. There was no one with the power to reverse the Hellbringer's deadly magic.

Nothing could stop the shaking echoing through me with every gasp. I shoved my fist into my mouth and bit down, trying to silence my own crying. Instead, blood seeped from my knuckles and into my mouth, coating my tongue with its bitter, metallic taste. The song from the dream played on a haunting loop in my mind.

This was my last chance to truly mourn him. I was alone now, but in the morning I'd stumble into the arena, a spectacle for the godtouched and a beacon of hope for the godforsaken.

For now, I would let the grief consume me. Let it eat me from the inside, let it crack my ribs and grow there. Tomorrow morning I would become the stoic competitor again.

When I forced myself to take a breath, the shaking faded, or at least lessened. I pushed aside the blankets covering me, except for one to wrap around my shoulders, and stumbled out of my room and into the hallway.

The torches were lit, reflecting off the stone floors. It was only a few steps to the door next to mine. I threw it open and stumbled into the room; it was identical to the one I'd left.

It looked the same as it always did: clothes strewn across the floor, the bed in the corner unmade, and the curtains drawn tight to block out the light. My tears continued to fall silently as I crept over to the bed and climbed in.

The pillow smelled like wine and childhood—like Frode. I curled up under the covers, knowing sleep was a fool's dream at this point but hoping to at least stave off the memories of his death for a moment longer.

"Revna?" There was a dark silhouette in the doorway.

"Jac? What are you doing here?" I asked with a sniff. Blood from the bites on my knuckles crept between my fingers and dripped onto the sheets.

He moved toward me. "Couldn't sleep." There was a strange tremor in his voice.

When he reached the bed, he crawled under the covers with me. Only when I touched his face did I realize he was crying.

"I'm not ready to die, Rev," he whispered. The anguish in his voice made me crack. "I'm only twenty-four. I wanted to get married. Have kids. Live a normal life. I didn't ask for any of this."

Not for the first time, the brutality of Bhorglid, of our own people, of the priests who claimed to speak for our gods, knocked the breath from my lungs. Jac, barely an adult, wanted to live. Wanted to disappear. He didn't want glory or bloodshed.

"You don't deserve any of it either," I said, staring into the pitch-blackness. But the thought of letting him go, doing it all alone, was almost unbearable. "You don't think we can win together? You have a powerful Lurae. The Hellbringer trained me while I was his captive—I'm not half bad with a sword or throwing knives. The two of us can take them on and still have a chance."

"I don't want to kill anymore." His voice was flat, lifeless. "I'm tired of being on a battlefield. Aloisa is the goddess of the soul, of death *and* life, and yet we're called to destroy in her name. What happened to creating? Bringing new life from the ashes?"

We lay together in Frode's bed in silence, darkness seeping through everything. I wondered when we'd become so close, my stoic, quiet brother and me. Perhaps Frode's last act had been to bring us together. I resisted my next words but forced myself to utter them. "What if you didn't have to compete?"

"That's impossible," he scoffed. But I could hear the flicker of hope in his voice. "And besides. I can't leave you. If you died in the arena, it would be my fault."

He sounded wistful, and that pushed me to continue. I sat up. "No one else is more equipped to escape this than you. Disguise yourself; flee to Faste. Volkan is here, in the castle for the Trials. Have him put together a map and a list of contacts for you and then go." Despite the prince's ties to the Hellbringer, I hoped he would be decent enough to do Jac this favor.

The last thing I needed was another heartbreaking betrayal.

I knew Volkan had arrived at the castle earlier that day to watch the Trials. But mustering the courage to go to him and ask whether he'd known of the Hellbringer's deception was impossible. Still, Volkan had proven himself to be good more often than not.

Jac hesitated. Then he shook his head, relaxing back into the bed again. "No. You need me to help as much as I can with Erik and Björn tomorrow. Without Frode, I'm the only thing standing between you and them."

His words stirred a gentle smile from me. "If I die tomorrow, it won't be because of you," I promised him. "It will be because of Father's cruelty. And the priests. And whichever brother strikes me down. You can make more of a difference if you survive. Go live a normal life somewhere, Jac. You've more than earned it."

I was surprised to see his eyes well with tears. "I can't leave you."

"And I can't watch you die." I squeezed his hand. "If I win the Trials, come back. If Björn wins, don't. It's simple. Now, pack a bag and get out of here."

He jumped up to leave but then doubled back.

"What are you—"

He pulled me into a bone-crushing hug. "Good luck," he whispered. "I'll miss you."

I wrapped my arms around him, trying not to let myself cry again. "I'll see you again, Jac. In this life or the next."

And then he was gone.

29

Dawn found me awake, dressed in my leathers and triple-checking the straps on my armor. My hair was pulled back into a single long braid I wrapped around itself and pinned at the nape of my neck.

The castle was eerily silent. I'd expected bustling halls, servants arranging everything for the coronation tomorrow morning, but it was so quiet, I wondered if the place was empty.

My thoughts turned to Jac. Had he made it out of the city without being caught? Considering his Lurae, I would have been surprised if he hadn't. The only one who might have turned on him was Volkan. I didn't want to entertain the idea of such a betrayal, but I had been blind to the Hellbringer's true motives. I wouldn't discount the possibility of Volkan's true loyalty lying elsewhere.

There was an hour or so until the Trials were to begin. I glanced at myself in the mirror, wishing I looked a little less plain—less Nilurae somehow. But I shook my head. No. I needed to look like my people as much as possible today. Even if today meant my death.

I turned to leave my room, hands twitching, when my eyes caught on something resting on a shelf. A jar of bright red paint, the same kind the priests used at their rituals. The only use I'd ever had for it was to highlight my lips. Today I had another idea.

I grabbed the jar and a brush, then turned back to the mirror, where I carefully painted a large X on my face, the lines intersecting across the bridge of my nose.

The symbol of Aloisa.

I raised my chin. She had dared to claim me once and I had escaped her grasp. Why not tempt fate another time?

Plus, my father and brothers would hate it.

There was a light rapping on the open door, and I turned to see Volkan dressed in his finery. "There you are," he said. "I worried when I didn't see you at all yesterday. Your father said you were out, but I wasn't sure whether to believe him."

"I was busy," I said, facing my reflection once more. "And I didn't want to talk to anyone."

Our gazes met in the corner of the mirror. He nodded and sighed, running a hand over his hair. "I heard what happened to Frode," he said. "I came to offer my condolences."

Condolences meant nothing. My pulse was erratic. Before I registered the motion, my shaking hand had pulled a knife from my belt and turned to him.

Volkan's eyes widened and he held up his hands. His throat bobbed as he swallowed nervously. "Let's be civil about this."

I stepped closer to him. "Did you know?" My voice trembled. "That he would turn on me?"

He shook his head. "I didn't."

"Swear it."

"I swear, Revna. I didn't know anything. The only time I saw either of you was when I came to heal you. That was it."

I relaxed my stance but didn't put the knife away. "He killed Frode. Instead of me. I don't know why."

Volkan shook his head, lips pursed in bitterness. "I don't know if his intention was ever to kill you. Maybe it was an intimidation tactic, a way to convince your father and brothers of your innocence. After all, the queen wants you to win, doesn't she?"

Yes, I wanted to scream, *she does, but it isn't enough to excuse him from murdering my brother.*

He must have seen something frightening in my expression because he took a half step back. "That was stupid of me to say. Please forgive me. I can't say I knew what he was thinking when he killed Frode. And you have every right to feel betrayed. And lied to. Because that's what he did." He sighed. "And if I had known, I would have stopped him. No matter what it took."

There was truth in his eyes. As he stood between the stone blocks making up my doorframe, my anger cooled for a moment. I slid my knife back into its sheath. "We were both fools," I said, grabbing my sword. I took one long last look at the bedroom. Would I ever be back?

As I walked to the stairwell, I heard Volkan murmur from behind me, "Yes. We were."

◆ ◆ ◆ ◆ ◆

LOCATED BEYOND THE EDGE OF THE CITY, THE ARENA'S GIANT steel walls were taller than the castle. The Bhorglid flag waved in the breeze from its post at the top of the structure. Dark clouds swirled overhead, and I grimaced as I viewed it from where I sat on my horse.

The arena's appearance was as cold and unforgiving as the occasions it hosted. Here, my father had competed to win the throne decades ago, slaughtering his two brothers without a second thought. It was where traitors were executed for their crimes. I swallowed hard as I rode nearer, staring over one of the rolling hills at the massive expanse of metal before me.

Realizing the freezing sandy floor of the arena might be where I took my last breath made me stiffen. My blood might stain the sand permanently.

There was no time to back out now. Though every part of me screamed to turn around, I clicked my heels gently on my horse's sides and rode to the arena.

By the time I made it to the bottom of the hill, it was swarming with people. Travelers from all over the country had arrived to watch the Trials and learn who would be their next ruler. They were wrapped in fur blankets to shield them against the harsh wind. Even the priests had come from cities far and wide to honor the sacred ritual sacrifice of heirs.

I realized suddenly all of this had started with a disrupted ritual sacrifice. Perhaps the gods had a twisted sense of humor; perhaps by saving one intended sacrifice, they balanced the scales by putting me in her place.

As I rode through the crowd, excited shouts turned to whispers at the sight of my face, covered in war paint.

I wondered what they thought. Were they as angry as my parents? Disgusted that a Nilurae would try for the throne?

Were there any who believed in me? Any who wanted me to win, like Jac and Frode did?

I resisted the urge to cower beneath their stares, holding my head high.

Let them see me. Let them whisper. Let them tell their stories and spread their rumors. What did it matter? By the end of the day, I would be queen or I would be dead. Either way, their opinions wouldn't matter.

I left my horse at the stables east of the arena and made my way toward the entrance. As I approached, I kept a steady grip on the hilt of my sword, my other hand hanging freely at my side. I didn't bother to meet anyone's stare.

The king and queen, both dressed in finery, waited at the edge of the arena, greeting people as they entered. Father's crown was perched on his head, a golden circlet with elegant twisting knots etched on every side. The peaks along the front of the metal were adorned with bloodred rubies. Next to my parents stood a priest. I made sure to glare at him as I passed.

This would all be over soon enough.

Father's lips curled into a snarl when he saw the paint on my face. Mother didn't spare me a glance. Her white gown and pale skin stood out against her black hair.

My father moved to the side so the entrance was blocked. I glowered at him. Murmurs flew through the crowd behind me.

"You dishonor our family by competing today," he said, his voice rough.

"Good," I said, meeting his gaze with my own. I hoped he could see the fire there, the hatred for his cowardice. "I compete for myself, not for this family." My smile was deadly as I leaned in to whisper, "No matter how today ends, I will never have to see you again."

I pushed past him, walking between him and my mother into the arena. The crowd parted for me, but I heard my name hissed over and over.

A few turns later, I arrived in a waiting area. My brothers and I would stay there until the Trials began. Erik and Björn were already there, sitting on benches haphazardly propped up in the dirt. At the sight of me, Björn sneered, and I shot him a glare that I hoped would silence him for the time being.

I stepped up to the wrought iron gate preventing us from entering the fighting pit before the competition was to begin. The bars were cold against my palms. While I looked at the arena before me, I kept half an eye on Björn. The last thing I needed was to be knifed before the Trials even began.

Above us, the sound of footsteps clanging against the metal stairs echoed along with the murmurings of the crowd. The seats ascending around the battleground filled steadily, mostly with citizens. Some visitors observed as well.

I shuddered, then turned my gaze to the more important part of the scene before me: the arena itself.

It had been changed for the Trials. What was usually an empty pit—a stone floor covered in a layer of sand to make blood from executions easier to clean up—was now a study in obstacles. There were large boulders scattered around to offer cover. There were also a few tall wooden poles erected in strategic places. They had no hand- or footholds, but were available for us to climb and perch on.

I'd gained a lot of muscle in my time with the Hellbringer, but I wasn't sure if I would be able to climb the poles. I pushed the thought from my head for now, deciding to come back to that option later.

Most concerning was the large trench carved into the ground around the arena. One good push and any of us could be sent tumbling ten feet down, unable to scramble back to level ground. I'd be a sitting duck if I fell, especially as I was the shortest of the three of us.

I moved away from the gate and sat across from my brothers, leaning back against the wall. The vibrations of footfalls through the metal echoed in my head. In a few hours this would all be over and we could move on with our lives. One of us, at least.

For the first time, the thought of dying didn't scare me. Maybe I would lose to Björn or Erik. But I wouldn't be shackled to someone else's will. Perhaps dying would prove to be peaceful in the end.

The footsteps continued to reverberate, pounding like a drum. How many Nilurae were here? Halvar and I had discussed our options the day before, locked in the cellar by candlelight before visiting Freja. He didn't know Jac had run, but the moment we entered the fighting ring, it would become clear. If I won—by some miracle—then our plan would move forward. Nilurae would rush for the priests, and we would do what we could to win control of our kingdom.

If I lost . . . well, they would try anyway. And probably be annihilated in the process.

I imagined my body lying on the ground, half of the crowd rushing to the king's seat, armed only with steel weapons and the element of surprise. No magic to be found.

It would be easier if I could win it all.

"Where is Jac?" Erik asked, peering out toward the arena's entrance, craning his neck to search for him. The flood of people entering had slowed, only a few stragglers still arriving. Two acolytes manned the entrance. It was the lowest of jobs; they wouldn't even get to watch us kill each other.

I shrugged, feigning ignorance. "I haven't seen him all morning. I thought he came down with you two."

Erik's frown was deep. "No, I haven't seen him either."

Björn huffed a laugh. "I didn't take Jac for a deserter. I suppose, now that Frode is gone, someone had to be the coward between us."

I clenched my hands and raised an eyebrow. It took all my fortitude to ignore the jab, but I managed. "Jac, a deserter? Not likely."

"I don't think so either," Erik said, shaking his head. The creases in his brow were pronounced. For the first time I noticed dark circles under his eyes. Had he been sleeping poorly despite the gods' reassurances that even his death would be holy? "I hope he's all right."

Part of me wanted to laugh at the absurdity of the statement. The hypocrisy was stark, like blood against snow—kindness until it required change, care for only those who were already gods-blessed.

From inside the arena a trumpet sounded, quieting the crowd. My heart raced, and I tugged on the loose edges of my armor, waiting for my father to start the competition.

Father's voice echoed through the chamber from outside. "Welcome to the thirteenth Bloodshed Trials," he announced. The crowd cheered and I shivered as a cold wind blew through the metal tunnel. "Here you will see my children compete for the throne. They will all enter the arena—but only one will leave. The gods have blessed this ritual sacrifice of heirs, and he who triumphs will be blessed."

Whispers of anticipation crawled through the crowd. I scowled at the use of *he* in reference to the winner. There was no acknowledgment that I was even competing. For the first time, though, I realized being here would have destroyed Frode. He would have tried to fight, but with so many people crowded around us, he would have gone out of his mind. Unable to make a difference. Erik and Björn would have killed him slowly and painfully.

Perhaps it was for the best that I was here alone.

The iron gate creaked open and Erik stood, straightening his shoulders, double-checking his armor and his weapons. He cracked his knuckles. There was no glance back as he strode into the arena, waving at the cheering crowd. Björn waited for the cries to die down before he walked out, too. The roars that greeted his entrance were significantly louder.

I swallowed, lightly touching the hilt of my sword and each throwing knife, one strapped to each bicep. A shaky breath wasn't enough to calm my racing heart, especially as Björn turned and offered me a smile with a tinge of bloodlust in the shine of his teeth.

I was going to die.

When I stepped into the arena, there was no cheering—only a chorus of boos, which I ignored. I scanned the crowd, catching the occasional glimpse of priestly white scattered among the citizens.

I took courage knowing Halvar was somewhere in the stands, the Nilurae organized and ready to fight when the time came. The fact that the priests were scattered would hopefully give the godforsaken a slight advantage.

When I brought my gaze back down to the bottom of the stands, a familiar visage stared back at me. My heart stopped in my chest.

Søren. He was here, his face lined with tension, eyes serious. The black cloak—the same one I'd slept under and admired—covered his shoulders. The rest of his clothing was all black, but it was strange to see him without his armor.

It was all too easy to imagine him standing next to me again, directing me to stand tall. His Hellbringer mask was nowhere to be seen, but still I wondered how Bhorglid's biggest enemy could sit with its citizens unnoticed. Couldn't they *feel* it emanating from him? The animosity, the calculated coldness of stolen lives? The sight of him made my heart stutter, and I resisted the urge to take a step back. We stared at each other, and I curbed my snarl.

He'd come to watch me die.

Disappointed you didn't get to do it yourself? I wished he could hear my thoughts, hoped he could see them clearly on my face. *Here to make sure I scream before I perish?*

When no one followed me into the pit, the crowd's cheers morphed into whispers. They started from the top of the audience and trickled down, much like the way Jac's shape-shifting took over his body. His disappearance had not gone unnoticed. My eyes flicked away from Søren and the distracting way his appearance made me dizzy.

I took a deep breath. Jac was gone now, far away, safe from the wrath of our father and brothers. Frode was dead, hopefully somewhere better than this. I didn't need to worry about either of them anymore.

And I could ignore the Hellbringer. Ignore Frode's murderer, here to see me make a spectacle of myself.

Björn crossed his arms over his chest, smirking. Erik strode to the west side of the arena, studying the obstacles around him with a keen eye. I looked up at the royal platform, where the king and queen sat with their retinue of priests. I spotted Volkan there too, looking uneasy.

Four priests made up the last of the royal designation. They stared into the pit, and Erik and Björn didn't so much as flinch at their veiled gazes. Standing in front of the crowd at assigned checkpoints were the few silencers my father employed. Their magic allowed them to keep the crowd from interfering with their Lurae, if any dared.

"It appears my third son has done the dishonor of running from his fate," my father drawled. The audience listened in hushed silence. "When we find him, he will be executed on sight."

The Lurae on all sides cheered at this declaration. My lip curled, and I made no attempt to hide my disgust.

"The audience may not interfere with the battle," the king continued. "There are no other rules except that only one of my children may leave alive. Let the Bloodshed Trials begin."

30

My BROTHERS AND I WERE POSITIONED FAR ENOUGH AWAY from each other that as chants and jeers began to fall from the crowd, none of us moved.

Erik was studying Björn, who studied me. I drew Aloisa, the satisfying sound of metal sliding from its sheath like a balm against my ears. I wasn't sure how to handle this, the very beginning of the battle. Did I hide and hope they killed each other first? Or did I plunge in and hope they didn't team up on me?

My heart pounded beneath my ribs, and against my will my eyes darted to the stands—to Søren, sitting right where I'd last seen him. Our eyes locked.

"This is your last chance, Revna." Erik's voice called out to me, bringing me back from my distraction. I narrowed my eyes at him as he twirled his greatsword, something akin to regret in his expression. "There is no possible way for you to win. I'll be merciful if you'd like. I can kill you quickly."

I was offended he would ask. But I was also sorely tempted.

Before I could reply, a lick of fire burst into being on the ground, tracing a path from Björn to Erik. My oldest brother leapt back, hissing as his shoes smoked.

But Björn wasn't out to kill—not yet, at least. "How kind of you to offer her an easy out," he spat. "But I want to play with my food."

Erik and Björn circled each other like predators, my presence forgotten for a moment. A cold gust of wind sent goose bumps up my arms, and I gripped Aloisa's hilt with all my strength. The crowd was divided—half cheering for Erik and the other half for Björn.

I scowled. This was nothing more than bloody sport to them. I took a step back from the impending battle, wondering what my best move was. Björn glanced my way for a half second, long enough to shoot me a feral grin. "Don't worry, little sister. I'll come for you once I'm done with him."

Erik moved first. He lunged forward, swinging his sword in a long arc, but Björn brought his own weapon up to parry. The sound of metal on metal echoed over the roaring crowd.

Erik's Lurae threw Björn back, but Björn twisted out of the way of a fatal blow and stretched out his hand to throw more flames at his attacker. Erik barely managed to drop to his knees and roll forward, swiping his weapon at Björn's feet.

I couldn't blink. If I did, I might miss the winning strike.

But my instincts screamed at me to hide, and I knew they were right.

I ran to the nearest boulder and began climbing as the fight continued behind me. The hiss of flame against the sand and Björn's war cries filled my ears, but I forced myself to focus on the rock, quickly finding handholds until I was at the top, a few feet higher now than either of my brothers.

I took a shaky breath at the realization they were both much, much faster than me. If I had to fight Björn, I'd be ashes in moments. I watched Erik expertly dodge Björn's blasts of fire, only possible because of his extensive years of military training.

As he leapt back and forth, trying to close the distance between himself and Björn, I gritted my teeth. If Erik didn't win this duel, I was most certainly going to die today. I found myself wishing I'd made the Hellbringer teach me how to use a bow and arrow. A ranged weapon could have performed miracles from my vantage point. But I wasn't willing to sacrifice one of my three daggers—not when I'd need them desperately when my remaining brother turned his attention to me.

Erik pulled out a knife he'd had hidden on his person and flung it at Björn. The fire wielder tried to dodge, but it had been an unexpected move, and the blade managed to slice his leg.

Björn hissed, his hand dropping to his wound, and Erik took his moment to dive. His greatsword came swinging toward Björn's free arm, but Björn whipped around before it connected and blasted fire so hot that the blade melted.

The crowd was in an uproar. Erik looked stunned, and I wondered if anyone had known that Björn was so powerful.

Despite his shock, Erik barely missed a beat. He was up close, fighting Björn as tightly as possible so his younger brother wouldn't have the chance to use his fire. Erik pulled his secondary weapon from its holster—a war hammer.

"Come on, Erik," I muttered, clutching Aloisa's hilt until my knuckles turned pale. "End him."

The clamor of clashing metal echoed throughout the arena. The crowd was enjoying this.

I watched Björn grit his teeth, arms shuddering against Erik's strength. Still, he managed to defend himself, though each clash of their weapons brought Björn's arms lower and lower.

Finally, Erik forced Björn to his knees. My youngest brother let out a cry of fury and tried to push Erik away, but to no avail. Then Björn looked over and made eye contact with me. His face contorted into a smile and my stomach sank.

In a flurry of motion so fast I nearly missed it, Björn twisted on his knees out of the locked weapon position in which Erik had him cornered. Before Erik had the chance to turn and strike again, Björn summoned his magic.

Flames pulsed from his fingers and met flesh.

The crowd screamed, not in victory but in horror, and I screamed with them as I watched Erik's body char under Björn's hands until flesh melted away to reveal bone and his ashes drifted away in the wind.

The crowd quieted. I swallowed the sour taste of bile.

And Björn tilted his head back and laughed and laughed and laughed.

◆ ◆ ◆ ◆ ◆

I DRY HEAVED ONTO THE BOULDER, BUT THE BATTLE DIDN'T STOP. There was no silence to honor Erik's short, misguided life. I hadn't even recovered before the first hint of flame flashed in my peripheral vision and I stumbled out of the way.

All around me people screamed.

Björn's hair shone bright fire red under the noon sun. Nausea roiled in my stomach, and I had to work to keep myself from vomiting right then and there.

He would kill me the same way he killed Erik. But with me, Björn would take his time. I tried to ignore my shaking hands, but as another pulse of fire forced me to dodge the other way, I turned, panic flaring in my chest.

There was no escape. There was no getting out of this.

I hefted Aloisa and the crowd exploded. If I had thought them loud before, this was a tsunami of sound barraging my ears.

I glanced toward the box where I knew Father sat, his face impassive. What must Mother think of me: a foolish twenty-one-year-old Nilurae, here to defeat her power-hungry brother? I couldn't do this. I *had* to do this.

An image flashed through my mind of Björn wearing Father's

crown and seated on the throne, ordering us to conquer more coun-tries until we dominated the world. Why wouldn't a war-hungry na-tion want that?

But I didn't. I wanted a choice. I wanted to see what it was like to live a different life than the one my father had organized so precisely for me and for this country.

I stepped toward the edge of the boulder, looked down at Björn's smug face, and imagined life as Queen of Bhorglid. Not married to Volkan. Not subjected to my father's prejudice. Not a slave to the priests' broken ideals.

Björn grinned, his armor flashing as he took his stance. "I won't lie to you, sister," he called out. "I truly am looking forward to this." His smile was blackened where the flame swallowing Erik whole had scorched it. I swallowed, pushing away the image of my oldest brother defenseless against Björn's fire.

"And yet, you aren't willing to fight me without your magic," I said. With a shake of my head and a click of my tongue, I radiated my disapproval. "That only confirms I'm the better fighter."

His eyes narrowed. "You want to duel without magic? Fine." He extended his arms wide. "Be my guest. No godtouch from me."

I narrowed my eyes. "You're lying."

He laughed. "What reason would I have to lie? I have every con-fidence I can beat you, and so does Father. Otherwise, you wouldn't be here. You'd be dead already, like our poor brothers." He ges-tured toward Erik's remains.

I clenched my teeth and slid carefully down to ground level. Then I got in position, sword at the ready. Maybe I would die.

But at least I would die fighting.

Björn drew his sword. People screamed their excitement. Couldn't wait to see me butchered, then fried, I supposed.

My eyes were on Björn, watching him carefully as he adjusted his hold and took a few steps toward me, raising his sword to slice through my throat.

Easy enough.

Blood pounding through my veins, I threw my sword up to meet his blade, parrying the way the Hellbringer had taught me.

The connection of our blades jarred me more than I expected—Björn was strong and it showed. When our swords collided, my very bones vibrated. My gritted teeth clattered and sent pain running through my jaw. There was no glimmer of sympathy in my brother's eyes as they bored into mine.

It sparked fresh anger in me. I escaped the hold and began to swing carefully, gaining a couple feet of ground.

Björn showed no sign of surprise. Did he know I would be such an equal match? His parries were swift and precise. No more movement than was absolutely necessary.

He watched carefully, deflecting every stroke before finally pushing back. Within a matter of seconds, I had given up twenty feet. The roar of the crowd's approval whipped around me as a breeze caught my hair.

I swore internally, arms burning from the force necessary to keep Björn from slicing my head off. Even if I could push back, his arms were far longer than mine and he had been practicing the art of fighting for years.

Panic filled my lungs and I struggled to breathe as we exchanged blows back and forth, over and over. I used my speed, size, and dancer's footwork to my advantage, jumping to dodge his blows where possible, moving quickly enough that he was forced to follow me.

I cannot die today.

The thought was desperate and nauseating. I forced myself to remain present, and the realization hit me:

I was going to lose. The competition and my life.

I could imagine Björn's wicked grin as he took his time slicing me open, carefully lighting me on fire. Watching me burn to death. He would take pleasure in my screams; I knew that much.

Forcing myself back to the present, I moved in time to block an attempt to stab me in the abdomen. Fear laced my every movement. I was growing tired. It was only a matter of time now before Björn overpowered me.

Then, before I could move to block the arc of his sword, a searing pain echoed in a flash across my upper arm. A small cry escaped me, and I resisted the urge to cover the wound with my other hand. His sword had sliced my bicep. How had he broken through my defenses?

Warm blood trickled down my arm as I hefted Aloisa again, our blades clashing together. "Why don't we turn up the heat?" Björn asked, his face wicked.

Flames erupted along his blade, reflecting in his dark eyes. I stumbled backward, losing my footing, hating myself for being Nilurae.

"You said no magic," I snapped through gritted teeth.

He smirked. "You should have known better. I've never kept my promises."

I couldn't resist glancing up at the audience to where my father watched. He smiled, waiting for Björn to gut me so he could move on with his life. Without a disobedient daughter in his way.

An idea flashed through my mind, and without a second thought I turned and bolted, running as fast as I could away from Björn, dodging obstacles along the way.

The crowd's noise overwhelmed my senses as I fled to the other side of the arena, breathing heavily. If I could get far enough away, maybe I could nail him with one of my daggers.

But I hadn't counted on the strength of his Lurae. I felt the flames lick at my ankles as a path of fire formed behind me. My throat closed up. I pulled one of my daggers from my belt and turned, blindly hurling it in Björn's direction. I missed, and the crowd laughed.

Exhaustion threatened to trip me, but I moved fast—until a wall of flame exploded in front of me, stopping me in my tracks. I turned to bolt the other way but was met by flames on all sides. Björn walked through the wall of fire, sword sheathed again. He held a single slim dagger, flipping it over and over in his hand. I threw one of my own in his direction. My aim was true, and it scraped across the side of his face, but he appeared not to notice it.

Blood dripped like tears down his cheek and he smiled. "Come, now, sister. Surely you never thought you could win this."

Shame flooded my cheeks.

I had thought I could win. I'd counted on Björn's arrogance being his downfall, but his Lurae overpowered me at every turn. There was no way out.

I drew my sword again, engaging him in battle once more. A step-ball-change kept the flesh of my leg safe from a more desperate strike of his. For a long moment it seemed I might be winning.

And then he disarmed me in a flash. His foot swept under my legs, and I couldn't think fast enough to recover my balance. I stumbled, my palms colliding with the dirt. Rolling over was a mistake—within seconds, Björn had grabbed my wrists in one hand, and planting a knee on my rib cage, pinned me to the ground. A hiss made its way through my lips and Björn put his hand over my mouth.

"Shh," he coaxed. "I have a gift for you."

He held his dagger over my face and I closed my eyes, waiting for death, waiting to be incinerated, but instead a sharp pain pierced my cheek. I cried out as I felt the dagger draw a thin, sharp line across my face, right where my war paint decorated my cheeks and forehead. The X-shaped marking, so delicately drawn there that morning, now streamed blood.

I screamed and writhed under the knife, but Björn murmured, "Be quiet, little Revna," as he carved my face like it was a piece of wood.

Eventually, he drew his arm back and admired his handiwork. He was kind enough to let me rub the blood from my eyes before he pinned my wrists in an iron grip once more. I sobbed, the incisions burning when my tears ran over the torn flesh.

Shame roiled in my stomach. Shame and fear. I was no warrior. No queen.

I hoped Søren had left. That the man who had ruined my life—the man I might have loved—wasn't watching my last moments.

"Please," I whispered to Björn as he lowered his knife to the base of my throat.

He clicked his tongue softly. "It's too late for that."

I took a deep breath—one of my last—and gathered my courage. I might die, but let them not forget the first Nilurae to fight in their Trials.

That thought sparked anger inside of me, replacing my fear, and without thinking I spat the blood and saliva in my mouth into Björn's face.

He reared back and I slipped my wrists from his hold, grabbed the last knife in my arm sheath, and shoved it upward with all my strength through the gap in Björn's armor, directly into his heart.

My brother's eyes went wide, and he gaped at the weapon lodged in his chest. Our eyes locked for a moment.

"You *bitch*," he whispered.

I pulled the knife from his body, and with a cough and a spurt of blood he fell forward on his face.

Dead.

31

SILENCE DESCENDED LIKE A BLANKET OVER THE ARENA—BUT only for a heartbeat.

Snow began to fall from the sky as a raging war cry echoed from the stands.

I looked up just in time to see Halvar slit the throat of the priest sitting nearest him. In slow motion the body tumbled, white cloth stained red, through the crowd. With a sickening thud, it flipped over the edge of the stands and landed in the trench carved along the sides of the arena floor.

I pushed Björn's deadweight off me and stood. Every muscle in my body trembled, and blood was still coursing freely down my face. But I raised Aloisa into the air, blade pointed high as cries began to echo through the crowd. "For the godforsaken!" I screamed, hoping someone—anyone—could hear me.

Chaos erupted and the arena became a stampede. Priests descended from their seats and clambered onto the sand, drawing scythes and rushing for me. The silencers were still in their positions, looking confused, and I was grateful. Their presence would significantly decrease the amount of damage the priests could do from a distance.

My traitorous eyes looked for the Hellbringer. He smiled smugly, sitting with one leg crossed over the other, leaning back as if the swarming crowd didn't bother him. For the briefest moment I considered ignoring the priests, clawing my way over the edge of the stands, and lunging for him, forcing my blade through his stomach. The idea thrilled me.

But before I could move, Mira emerged into existence beside him. She raised an eyebrow at me before grabbing his wrist. In less than a heartbeat, the two of them were gone.

Good. A distraction was the last thing I needed.

Only half looking, I swung Aloisa up to crack against the blade of a scythe, then swiftly sliced the wooden handle in half. The priest holding it stumbled and I kicked him in the stomach, sending him falling backward. One of the others rushing at me tripped over him.

They may have attended the military academy, but many of these religious figures hadn't used their weapons for battle in more than a decade. I had the clear advantage now. I whirled and parried, blinking blood from my eyes. Seriously, fuck Björn. He had to give me such an inconvenient injury before he died, making my vision blurry when it really mattered.

Adrenaline surged in my veins, the only thing keeping me upright through my exhaustion. The sounds of battle echoed from the stands, and I spared half a thought to hope Halvar was safe.

The next priest to lunge for me was not as lucky as the others before him. My training kicked in, muscle memory fresh from weeks in the abandoned prison, and the moment he faltered, I shoved my blade through his gut.

The sagging weight of him threatened to pull Aloisa from my hands, but I swiftly tugged my sword back, targeting the next priest with the blood-slick metal.

The rhythm of war was interrupted by scorching heat at my back. The priest in front of me retreated, and out of the corner of my eye I saw the others doing the same. The flames that followed their departure didn't touch me, and I straightened my shoulders, exhaling sharply before I turned to face him.

My father.

"I won," I called out. "Tell the priests to stop fighting and I'll call off the Nilurae."

He laughed, genuine mirth on his face. "You are not my successor. You're an impostor, a feeble excuse for a daughter. At least after today, we will be rid of you for good."

"This is only the beginning." My voice rose with every word. "We will never be content to be abused by you and your regime. You're already fighting one war; don't succumb to another."

"You think this will ever be a war? Look around you. The god-forsaken are already falling at the hands of the priests."

I didn't move my gaze from him, knowing that the instant I did, he would strike. But I did listen more closely to the cacophony around me. Beneath the clashing of swords and grunts of exertion, there were screams. And without looking I had no way of knowing whether they were coming from the Nilurae or our enemies.

"You will *die* for your insolence," Father spat. He raised a flaming hand high, aimed at my face. Dodging his death blow would be impossible.

At that moment, the world slowed, and I heard singing.

What is that?

The familiar tune wound around my father. My mother's old lullaby. I'd heard this song when first blood was shed on the snow of the canyon pass, when Frode's broken nose poured blood, in my unconscious dreams after the Hellbringer injured me. The humming was quiet and calm but excited. It moved with purpose, its pitch calling to my soul. And then I realized: the sound came from under Father's skin. His flesh sang to me. The tune lifted and carried to the beat of his heart. *Thud, thud, thud.*

I tilted my head to study him. Above me, I saw his mouth wide-open, screaming, preparing to kill me, but he was worlds away. A line connected my mind to the life housed under the skin covering him. An invisible string of sorts. I knew no one else saw it.

Curiosity and awe overwhelmed logic. I knew I should be panicking, fighting back, but why would I when this beautiful singing wound through every vein and artery beneath my father's skin?

Vaguely, I saw his hand move but I didn't care. Instead, I raised my palm and closed it around the mental string before giving it a sharp, experimental tug.

Without warning, my father flew across the arena, slamming into the wall closest to me. His flames disappeared in the same heartbeat.

Time snapped back into place and I blinked. The fighting continued around me, and no one except for a few priests seemed to notice the strange events that were unfolding. But none of those white-robed figures moved, even to help their king.

I pulled on the string again, hand curling into a fist with the movement, and Father's arm bent at an unnatural angle until it snapped. He screamed, the sound blurring with the others.

The singing grew louder, took over my ears until it told me what I needed to do to make him hurt. Force him to pay for all the faded burn scars strewn about my skin. I stretched my hands out in front of me and strode across the arena. With the dripping blood coating my face, I must have looked like something from the pits of hell.

I tugged the connection again and my father screamed. Whatever I pulled at, whatever listened to my commands, was breaking him—killing him.

And I liked it.

I watched him attempt to pull a flame from his fingers, but it sputtered and died.

He struggled against the force holding him back. He didn't

speak, only clenched his teeth from his place against the wall. My next pull was upward and I noticed blood flushed his face. He grabbed his head and screamed in pain.

His blood. I was controlling his blood. It sang to me.

It was as if I had done this a million times before. I crossed my arms so my wrists were in line and then pulled my elbows back with one sharp motion.

The crack of my father's neck breaking echoed through the arena.

Mother screamed. It echoed from the platform where she stood, safe from the battle, protected by the royal contingent of priests who stood guard around her. The sound seemed to break through the chaos somehow, and heads turned to see the king lying dead on the arena floor, his body one of many now.

In death, he was nothing more than a man.

The former queen pointed to the priests standing on either side of her. "Seize her!"

But they didn't move. Two in the front glanced at each other before slowly shaking their heads.

My hands shook. Why? Why weren't they moving?

Loyalty to their new queen?

Or were they afraid of me?

My eyes widened as it all hit me.

I was Lurae.

My mother sent a sharp spear of ice straight toward me. No part of my body felt like my own anymore; it was as if someone else controlled my every move as I stepped out of the way, then reached out until I felt my fingers connect with something no one could see.

The singing began again, low and beautiful.

I closed my hand, making a fist. Without warning, Mother's arm shattered, just like Father's had moments ago.

She screamed, bone breaking through the skin, blood flowing over her arm.

Waddell didn't move from his place with my father's guard. His face was pale, wan.

The hair on the back of my neck stood on end. When I looked around, Halvar was staring at me.

Battles continued around us, but they seemed to fall quiet. His face, often gruff but always filled with love, was twisted in an expression I'd never seen him turn on me before. But I recognized it from a lifetime of living with people who despised me.

Disgust.

There was another layer too, one I wasn't as familiar with: fear.

The emotions warred on his face, which was now pale. Blood was spattered across his visage, and I moved to take a step toward him.

He took a matching step back.

"Halvar?" I muttered, knowing he wouldn't be able to hear me over the distance.

"Retreat!" The cry shook me from my stupor and I turned to find who was yelling. My eyes lit on one of the priests in the royal retinue, voice magnified by what had to be magic. "Holy Order, retreat!"

As one, the priests began to flee, rushing for the exit.

I turned back, but Halvar was gone. I heard him over the stampede, yelling at the other Nilurae to pursue the escapees, to capture but not kill. The silencers had fled, but I knew they must still be close, otherwise the priests would be fighting back with a vengeance. I wasn't sure where they were going, but they'd more than likely find a place to regroup and return to wreak more havoc.

I grabbed the arm of a Nilurae woman jogging past me. "Tell Halvar to burn the temples," I instructed. "By order of the queen."

Emotions warred on her face: awe, trust, and fear. Only as she stepped away with a nod did I realize I'd left a bloody handprint on her sleeve.

My mother was screaming curses at me, so I stalked over to her. When I was close enough, I bent down where she had fallen and placed a finger over her lips. "Quiet," I commanded, tugging on her strings, softly this time—enough to keep her jaw closed. She couldn't open it even if she wanted to. "Your rule is over. A new era is beginning."

One of a few Nilurae who remained in the arena stepped up to me. "My queen. We can take her to the prison."

I glanced sideways at them. They were scrawny, underfed, and without magic. Even with a broken arm, I had no doubt my mother would overpower them. This was not a task for them.

A wave of exhaustion swept over me. It was all I could do to remain standing, to not fall on my knees and sob after the events of the day. This was all her fault. Hers and my father's. They could have been better than those who came before them; they could have nurtured us and not started the war, come to a truce while there was still time. Instead, they chose to be vindictive and warmongering. Instead, they forced me onto the arena sands with their every decision.

And now that same arena was littered with the dead and injured.

I took a deep breath and told the Nilurae, "There will be no need."

With a single movement of my hand, I stilled my mother's heart. She collapsed, lifeless in the sand.

I didn't look back.

Volkan was stepping carefully through the mess of bodies, occasionally kneeling down to heal someone. Checking pulses, offering comforting words while he did his work.

He hadn't been in league with the Hellbringer, I decided. Not when gentleness touched his every movement. Volkan was many things, but not a soldier. Not a killer.

I strode over to him, not caring about the eyes I felt following me. Not caring about the heaviness beginning to settle on my shoulders, in the space between my ribs, in my stomach. My knees shook slightly with every step. Hesitation radiated from the Nilurae I'd left behind me.

Why are they afraid? My thoughts felt like mud, so slowly did they slide through my mind. *Isn't this what they wanted?*

The Fastian Prince noticed my approach and frowned. He'd been closing the eyes of a Nilurae man, one I recognized from nights at the Sharpened Axe but whose name I didn't know. He stood now and asked, "Are you okay?"

"What do you think?" I hadn't meant the words to be harsh, but when they snapped out of me, I didn't take them back. The blood weeping from the wounds Björn had inflicted on me was now congealed, but with every facial expression I felt it crack and stretch. Did I look human anymore?

He spoke gently, the way people spoke to animals they were afraid of startling. "I think you're injured. I think you're losing a lot of blood. And I think you're probably in shock from what has happened." His eyes were full of concern, but I couldn't muster the energy to feel grateful for him.

The Hellbringer was gone, spirited away as soon as my win was confirmed. My brothers were all dead by various hands. My parents, killed by my own.

They deserved it, I told myself as heaviness bore down on me. I was drowning in exhaustion, drowning in the last hour, drowning in blood.

The pain in my head grew until I could barely get the words out, throbbing in time with my heartbeat. "I'm fine."

Volkan reached out to grab my arm, hoisting me upright. I blinked. I hadn't realized I was falling.

"We need to get you home." He threw my arm over his shoulder and wrapped his own around my waist.

My vision faded in and out. "Wait," I gasped. "I can't leave them." *Not like they left Frode.*

Volkan glanced at the myriad of corpses behind us. The arena was littered with them, but somehow he knew exactly who I was talking about. "I'll send someone back for Björn's body and Erik's ashes."

I relaxed, and the culmination of the morning landed on me like a heavy weight. I sank into darkness and stars and nothingness.

◆ ◆ ◆ ◆ ◆

I WOKE UP IN MY BED.

My headache was mostly gone. A full glass of water waited for me on my bedside table. I grabbed for it, pushing myself up halfway, and downed the whole thing as fast as I could.

Everything ached. I let out a small groan as I tested my range of movement. Nothing felt broken, but nothing felt completely right either.

There was something on my face. I reached up to touch it and recognized the softness of bandages, placed over the cuts Björn had carved on my face. I frowned and immediately regretted it. The movement sent pain lancing through the wounds.

"I'm not sure if you remember, but you asked me not to touch those," a wry voice said.

I looked up. Volkan sat in a chair at the foot of my bed, holding a book. He raised an eyebrow at me and grinned. "Glad to see you rejoin the land of the living."

My hand brushed the bandages again. "I don't remember."

He chuckled. "No, I imagine not. You were slightly delusional at best. Having your Lurae manifest so powerfully drained all your energy. You said something about remembering."

The vague memory came back to me. Volkan reaching for my forehead, and stopping him with my Lurae.

I'd meant, *I need them to remember.*

Never again would the Lurae look at me as the young, godforsaken princess who caused nothing but trouble. No. Now everyone who looked at me would be forced to remember exactly how I had earned my power.

"How long was I out?" I asked.

"Only a few hours," he said. "I haven't been here long. I wanted to make sure you were all right."

"Thank you," I whispered. I meant it. As flashes of memory flowed through my mind, I took a shuddering breath.

It was all over. Erik and Björn were dead. My parents were dead. And I was queen.

"Are people still fighting? What's going on out there?" I pushed up on my elbows, trying to peer out the window. On the clearest days, I could see out into the city from here.

"The temples are burning. A few more priests have been killed, but most of them have fled. I don't think Halvar has given any orders to pursue them."

I relaxed slightly. I'd worried there would be more of a fight ahead of us, but it was as we'd suspected. Once the seat of power was filled with a Nilurae, the priests saw no reason to do anything but save their own skins.

Though . . . perhaps the seat of power was no longer filled by a true Nilurae.

"How often has this happened before?" I said, stomach twisting. "How often does a person manifest a Lurae only as an adult?"

I watched Volkan's grin turn into a frown. "I don't know," he said with a shake of his head. "I can't think of a single instance I've heard of. Were you declared Nilurae by the priests when you turned nine?"

"Yes."

The prince shrugged. "Nine is supposed to be the age your

magic manifests," he said. "I've never heard of anyone else finding theirs afterward. Your case might be entirely unique. I don't know if anyone has studied Lurae magic in people under duress. Perhaps stress is what caused it."

"The Hellbringer wanted to know what my Lurae was when he held me captive," I recalled. "He kept asking me why I had been hiding it for so long. I didn't know what he was talking about. He was looking for me even before then." I shook my head. "He said the Queen of Kryllian had reliable sources that claimed I was Lurae. How could either of them have known? Especially before I did?"

Volkan rubbed his temples. "I don't know," he said. "Maybe they have a seer who foresaw you winning the Trials but didn't know you were declared Nilurae. That's the only thing I can think of."

"She only wanted me on the throne because she thought I was Lurae," I muttered, trying to work through it aloud.

"The Queen of Kryllian?" Volkan's confusion was plain on his face. "She wanted you on the throne?"

I hurriedly explained my deal with the Hellbringer. "At first I worried she was looking to put a Nilurae on the throne so she'd have an advantage if she tried to take over. But when the Hellbringer tried to make me admit I had a secret Lurae, then the whole arrangement made much more sense."

Before Volkan could respond, Freja, freshly bathed and clothed in finery I could only assume she'd stolen from my mother, burst through the door, launching herself into my arms.

"You won, you won," she whispered.

I clutched her as tightly as I could, squeezing my eyes shut to keep my tears from leaking out. I would do it all over again for her to be free.

Volkan smiled and excused himself. Freja sat back and traced a finger lightly over my bandages. "Why didn't he heal these?" she demanded. "Do I need to get him?"

I laughed. "No. I asked him not to. I want people to remember I earned my place on the throne."

"Speaking of your victory, I need to hear everything that happened," she said. "No one would tell me what was going on when they released me. Was it on your orders?"

"I think Volkan must have stepped in on my behalf."

She grinned. "Tell me everything."

My breath hitched in my throat. Freja didn't know. She didn't know I had a Lurae.

For a moment I considered lying. Could I bear to watch the light in her eyes turn to distrust? Betrayal?

Maybe not, but she would find out soon enough.

I took a deep breath, closed my eyes, and started talking. As I spoke, the scene flashed through my mind again: Erik's flesh melting away from bone, Björn's hushes while he carved my face, and the beautiful, ethereal singing that accompanied my new magic.

It swirled in my stomach, whispered in my ears, begged to be used. I ignored it.

"Bloodsinger." Freja's voice was breathless.

I opened my eyes. "What did you say?"

Her eyes were wide. "That's what Valen called you when I was released. 'Tell the Bloodsinger Queen I said congratulations.' I didn't understand. But Valen knew."

I opened my mouth, but nothing came out. Valen had known I was Lurae.

A knock sounded at the door and Volkan poked his head in. "Freja, Revna needs to rest. Why don't we let her sleep?"

Freja stood to go. The window she walked by showed a glimpse of the pink and purple skies scarred by smoke, the sun setting in the distance.

"Wait," I called. They both turned back to face me. "Before I sleep, there's something I need your help with."

◆ ◆ ◆ ◆ ◆

VALEN SAT ACROSS THE SMALL TABLE FROM ME IN WHAT USED TO be my father's office. I wasn't sure what to expect from this conversation, but an immediate comment on my face wasn't it.

"I always wondered where the scars came from," they said, gesturing to the bandages on my face.

Without consciously deciding to, I brushed a hand against the wrappings. They were starting to get annoying, blocking out enough of my vision to exacerbate my headache.

"When did you plan on explaining you've been having visions of me?" I asked, hands folded in my lap. The chair I sat in, intended for a person of my father's stature, was far too big, and I made an extra effort to keep my posture straight and regal. This was my first act as queen, after all.

Valen chuckled. "I planned to tell you from the moment I met you. Unfortunately, said meeting is occurring now and not twenty-one years ago."

"Why don't you start from the beginning?" I settled back and gestured for Valen to do the same. "I'd like to hear the whole story."

The Seeing One settled in, rubbing their wrists. "Considering your predecessor, I take it I'm the only Seeing One you've had the pleasure of knowing." When I nodded, they continued. "Seeing is unlike other gifts. Most Lurae are fairly standard, operating on a principle of magic wound into your deepest biology. It's an imprecise science—the worst kind. But when you have the Seeing Lurae, it can take a number of forms. Some Seeing Ones have no more knowledge than what will happen at a random location in the next two minutes. Others detail great prophecies of events to happen hundreds of years in the future. There are some who cannot function or lead normal lives because they are constantly stuck in the future while their physical forms remain here."

The Seeing One sighed, their wrinkled hands finding their place on the armrests of the chair. "And then you have me. My Lurae is focused on one person in particular: you."

My brows shot up. "Me? What exactly have you seen?"

"Only bits and pieces," they confessed. "When my Lurae presented my first true vision, it was of you winning the Bloodshed Trials. As Seeing Ones, we have a responsibility to share our visions with the appropriate parties, so I traveled here to see your father despite knowing of his hatred toward my kind. When I told him I came bearing a prophecy about the child his wife was carrying, he sent me to your prison without hearing anything I had to say. His prejudice overwhelmed his interest in knowing your fate."

I gaped. "That's horrible."

They laughed. "It was what I expected. I've been in that cell ever since—for over twenty-one years. But imagine my surprise when you showed up to see your friend and I realized you were Nilurae." Shaking their head, Valen said, "In my vision, you had clearly used your Lurae to kill your father. I thought perhaps I was wrong, but when I caught a glimpse of you, I knew it would happen. You would compete and somehow magic would flow through your veins like it never had before."

"Why?" I choked on the word. "Why do I suddenly have a Lurae?"

Valen sighed. "I'm not sure. I've seen other snippets of your future, but they are few and far between. I do know this, though: you will fulfill the prophecy of the first Seeing One. They were called Tam, a contemporary of Callum and Arraya who fought against their rule and formed our band of Seeing Ones."

"Fulfill the first prophecy?" I tried not to show how stunned I was. "What was the prophecy, then?"

Valen's eyes turned grave. "No one living knows the answer to your question, unfortunately. Tam was incredibly secretive about the prophecy, and the other Seeing Ones respected their decision.

But then they were taken captive by Arraya during the attempted revolution of the Fjordlands. Arraya forced Tam to be her personal Seeing One, torturing them when they wouldn't confess the prophecy."

I was surprised to see Valen's eyes brimming with tears. Tam had lived hundreds of years ago . . . Surely they hadn't known each other. Were all the Seeing Ones so emotionally close?

"What happened then?" I asked, afraid to know the answer.

Valen sighed. "Tam held on as long as they could. Eventually, they recited the prophecy to Arraya, and then she struck her killing blow. As far as the records show, Arraya never shared the prophecy with anyone else, including her husband, before she was killed."

"And yet you know I'm going to fulfill it?" I tried not to let panic overwhelm me. It stretched its maw wide, threatening to swallow me whole. "I don't understand."

"I wish I knew more, but my visions have been surprisingly limited." Valen's face slumped into exhaustion, a feeling I understood far too well. "Rest assured, if I see anything else regarding your future, you will be the first to know."

The Seeing One rose and moved to the door. "Where will you go?" I asked. "Now that you've been released, will you rejoin the other Seeing Ones?"

They smiled. "Yes. But first, I'm stopping by your kitchens for a proper meal. You should get some rest."

I stood and the world spun around me. "You're probably right."

"Oh," they said, hand on the door. "I failed to mention one part. You will not fulfill the original prophecy alone."

Breathing deeply, trying to clear the black spots from my vision, I asked, "Who else, then?"

"A young man whose true name I do not know." Valen shook their head. "I believe you call him the Hellbringer."

The world vanished into darkness.

• • ◆ • •

WHEN I WOKE, IN MY BED AGAIN, NIGHT HAD FALLEN. A FEW flickering lamps were lit, and I groaned, pressing a hand to my head. Would the ache there never retreat?

"Volkan?" I called out. My vision was blurry, but he was sitting in the same armchair as earlier, a book open on his lap. "I have a horrible headache. Can you heal it, or is it from the cuts on my face?"

There was a long sigh, and then a dark voice murmured, "Not Volkan, Princess."

I whipped my head around, ignoring the flash of pain. The Hell-bringer was sitting in my room, his wolf skull mask even more intimidating than usual in the flickering light. He wore his full suit of armor, the lantern's wavering flame reflected there.

There was no fear crawling beneath my sternum, not like I'd expected there to be. He could end me in a moment, sure. But he wouldn't—not when his queen had realized she was right and I did have power.

I, on the other hand, could kill him as slowly and painfully as I had killed my father.

I scowled, baring teeth I hoped were still bloodstained. "It's *queen* now."

He chuckled and closed the book before placing it on the armrest. He had one leg slung over the other, ankle balanced atop knee. "Don't I know it. Congratulations."

"You're here to gloat, then." I reached for the water on my nightstand, downing the glass. He didn't respond, so I asked, "Did Volkan let you in?"

"No. I let myself in."

"Did you consider knocking?" I demanded. "It's rude to watch someone sleep."

He hummed thoughtfully. "Would you say that's more or less rude than killing your lover's favorite brother?"

I inhaled sharply, eyes widening.

"This is probably the lesser of two evils," he mused, tapping his gloved fingers against the arm of the chair. "But I've done it all. So who knows?"

The fury building beneath my skin was red-hot. Had Björn and my father crawled into my body after they died? Had the god Hjalmar branded me for daring to kill them? Was I going to combust now, burst into flames from the anger?

The song from the arena began to play in my head again. It was louder this time. The notes, so soft and pleasant the first time around, jarred now. The tempo was faster and I could barely hear myself think.

The string that tied me to the Hellbringer, though . . . it was clearly visible. It trembled, far more taut than the one that had tied me to my father or my mother.

I didn't let myself think. I tugged it softly.

The Hellbringer hissed, arching his back and curling his hands into claws. Veins stood out in his neck, which was visible when he had his head tilted so far toward the ceiling. "The fuck are you doing, Revna?"

"If you're evil, don't you deserve to be punished?" I forced my voice to remain calm, even though the simmering anger hadn't faded. Instead of allowing it to explode out of me, I twisted his earlier words, tossing them back at him. "What's the greater sin: loving a monster or being one?"

He was silent, breathing through clenched teeth to mitigate the painful position I'd put him in. That was all it was; as much as I craved to tear him limb from limb, something stopped me. Instead, I held him frozen. Vulnerable. A state he likely knew little of.

With a sigh, I released him. He fell back into the armchair and I rolled over, facing away from him as I curled up under the blankets again. "Because I think I've done both now."

I heard a different pair of feet land on the floor, evidence of Mira's arrival. When they both left an instant later, the rage thrumming through my blood turned to gray melancholy.

32

REJA AND VOLKAN, BOTH WITH MY BEST INTERESTS AT HEART, pushed me to wait until I was further healed before holding the coronation. But I protested. With every minute we waited, the power vacuum would stretch ever wider, inviting those who took issue with my win to challenge me.

Best to cut potential rebellion off at the root.

The morning after the Bloodshed Trials was the first warm day of the year. Spring approached, and with it the subtle hints of growth. Green buds peered out of the ends of tree branches on the castle grounds. In other years, the sight would have filled me with excitement, but this morning there was no song in my step. The snow would be back to crush the coming spring without warning.

I looked at my hands as I sat in the dismal rose garden. No roses yet; only thorns.

When I had woken earlier, I'd performed what I suspected would become my new morning ritual: scrubbing my palms. They were already clean, had been since I woke after my time in the arena, but the sticky memory of blood in the creases remained.

A crown lay on the bench next to me. I didn't look at it. *Couldn't* look at it. It was the same one Father had been wearing when I killed him. It had been thoroughly cleaned, but I feared that if I looked too closely, I would find rust-red stains in the metal pattern.

Five graves lay before me. Volkan had been true to his word and retrieved Björn's and Erik's remains after dropping me off at the castle. Someone—maybe Halvar—had brought my father's and mother's bodies back to be buried as well. Frode's monument was only a headstone. The freshly turned earth marking the other graves was absent from his. His frozen body was buried in the snow, deep in the mountains to the north.

But now, on the bench, I pushed the thoughts of my brothers from my head. This wasn't the time to think about them.

Anxiety continued to gnaw at my gut, as it had all morning. It persisted like the itch of the freshly forming scabs across my face. All my discipline couldn't keep me from scratching at times. I'd removed the bandages against Volkan's wishes, knowing it was important for my new subjects to see my healing wounds during the coronation.

I was going to fulfill a prophecy with the Hellbringer.

Swallowing the bile rising in the back of my throat, I forced myself to breathe deeply. Perhaps the two of us had already fulfilled the prophecy. Valen hadn't mentioned any other details.

The image of the wolf skull mask flashed beneath my lids, and I shuddered. The Hellbringer was long gone, surely back in Kryllian by now. *And*—I set my jaw—*before any damn prophecy gets fulfilled, he's going to pay for what he's done.*

A single moment of mercy was all he'd receive from me. He shouldn't expect more, not from a monster.

The stillness became too much to bear. I stood and moved to the barn, saddling a horse, the crown hanging around my arm. All the while, I ignored the feeling of something heavy weighing on my stomach. Something new, impossible not to notice. The faint hum of magic.

I grimaced. Magic I wasn't supposed to have.

The ride down the mountain was quiet. I took the back roads to Halvar's, knowing most of the city streets would be full of townspeople walking to the burned-down temple for the coronation. I'd decided it was as good a place as any to hold the ceremony. After all, my rule would be built on the ashes of the priests who'd come before me—the ones who ran in fear the moment my power was truly revealed.

Stopping by the Sharpened Axe was going to make me late. But it didn't matter—I wouldn't survive this without a drink.

Wind tossed my hair behind me until I rode to a stop around the back of the run-down tavern. When my hand pushed the door open, it felt as if nothing had changed.

Halvar stood at the bar, wiping glasses with a cloth. He didn't look up when I closed the door behind me.

"Grab me a drink?" I asked. My shoes clacked with every step. The long, elegant gown I'd chosen was composed of light layers of red fabric draped into a long train. It was long sleeved and pulled back from my shoulders in a square neckline. The edges of each piece of fabric were lined with golden thread, and as much as I didn't love dressing up, I couldn't deny the thrill I felt when the dress shimmered in the light.

Halvar didn't answer. He continued his task silently, eyes refusing to meet mine.

I studied him. Dark circles hovered under his eyes. There was a mark on his lip from where it had been gnawed incessantly. He stared, unfocused, at a wall next to me.

"Are you okay?" I asked.

No answer.

"I came to get drunk before my own coronation," I said with a chuckle. Nerves began to claw through my stomach as he remained quiet. "But I was also thinking you should come to the castle after the ceremony. Help me start planning. Freja and Volkan will be there. We can pass the first legislation together, maybe ban the priests from returning. And then reach out to the Queen of Kryllian about ending the war . . ." I let my voice trail off.

Halvar closed his eyes and let out a sigh. When he spoke, his voice was hoarse. "Get out of my pub."

I stared. "Are you talking . . . to me?"

He threw the glass he was polishing, and it shattered on the hard floor. I started. He pounded his fist on the counter. "Who else would I be talking to?" His eyes were wild. "Yes, you. Get out. And don't come back. I don't want to see you again."

I threw my arms out. "What's your problem? We won the Trials! This is what you've been waiting for all this time."

"'We.'" He spat the word, as if it were bitter on his tongue. "There is no 'we.' You forfeited that right when you lied to me—lied to everyone. Pretending to be godforsaken so you could get in our heads."

I froze. "I wasn't lying. I have always been godforsaken. I have no idea what happened during the Trials to change that."

"Well, it doesn't matter," he seethed. "You're one of them now. You say you want equality. Maybe today that's true. But soon enough you'll be addicted to your magic, like they all are. And then what?" He shook his head. "Then nothing changes. And we're back at the beginning."

Frustration throbbed in the back of my throat, brought hot tears to my eyes. I held them in, desperate not to show weakness. "You don't know that. Give me a chance. I want to use my godtouch for good, to help the godforsaken become equal. That's what I've always wanted."

Halvar wouldn't look at me. "I don't believe you."

"We've been closer than family for *eleven years*," I protested. "You're practically my own father. Where is this coming from? Why would you abandon me?" Tears welled in my eyes, and I begged them to stay back.

"Everyone saw how much your blood father meant to you. Am I next? Are you going to snap my neck like you did his?"

I wanted to hit something, stab someone, take the anger out *anywhere* as it built to a crushing pressure beneath my skull. "That's different. You wanted him dead, too. You wanted me to be queen!"

He threw his rag down and slammed a fist on the counter, teeth bared in a scowl. "I wanted a *godforsaken* on the throne. Not one of *you*."

"After *years* of knowing me, teaching me, helping me, this is all it took to ruin our friendship? A *stupid*"—there was a roaring crescendo in my ears now—"*fucking*"—nothing would shut it out—"*godtouch*?"

It exploded.

My vision went red at the edges and nothing would stay in focus, but the thread in my stomach attached to my magic was taut with unrestrained power. Everything inside me demanded I pull it tighter and tighter.

The sound of blood pumping through a heart reverberated in my skull, and there was something else, something high-pitched and inhuman.

Screaming. Someone was screaming.

Pull harder, the magic whispered. *Harder.*

With another swift tug on the thread, the world splintered.

My vision went black as the magic in me disconnected altogether, disappearing in an instant. I stumbled backward, tripping over something I couldn't see. When I hit the ground, my vision began to clear.

Then I saw what I had done.

A thin trail of liquid seeped over the floorboards from behind the counter. I swallowed.

Blood.

My anger was replaced by fear. Overwhelming, all-encompassing fear.

"Halvar?" I called out, voice shaking. I pushed myself to my feet, brushing dust off my gown. I stepped toward the counter, wrapping my arms around myself. "Did I hurt you?"

My breath caught in my chest. The trickle of blood I had seen was a pool on the other side of the counter. And in the middle of the bloody mess, flat on his back, lifeless eyes staring at the ceiling, was Halvar.

I covered my mouth and dropped to my knees, crawling toward his body. Every part of me shook and my breath came in gasps. My trembling fingers fumbled at his neck, feeling for a pulse.

Nothing. His skin was already cold.

I screamed. The sound echoed through the silence around me.

Vomit rose in the back of my throat. I got to my feet and ran to the nearest trash can. The breakfast Freja had insisted I eat was gone in a matter of seconds.

I forced myself to look back at the corpse of my friend. His lifeless eyes. His blood soaked into his clothes, saturating them.

The sight would be burned into my dreams until I died.

I couldn't feel my fingers, but I saw them shaking. I raised them to eye level. Blood blurred with skin.

The bell above the door chimed and I whirled, panic lacing through every one of my limbs. I wasn't sure whether to be relieved or vomit again when Volkan's face stared back at me.

"What are you doing here?" he asked. "You're going to be . . ." His voice trailed off as his gaze drifted from my face to my hands, to my blood-soaked dress, to the trail of blood leading behind the counter. The pool of sticky red grew larger by the second.

"Shit."

I couldn't move. Volkan pushed past me and peered over the counter to see Halvar lying there. He swore and backed away.

A shuddering breath collected in my lungs, and I wondered distantly if I was about to start screaming again. Volkan paced back and forth in front of me.

"Okay. I'll deal with this, but you have to go. Now." He rubbed his palms over his eyes. "Don't tell anyone what happened here. We can fix this."

"My dress." I didn't feel myself utter the words, but it was my voice, so it had to have been me.

Volkan glanced at the hem, then pulled a dagger from his waistband. "Hold still." He knelt and sawed through the stained fabric until it was nothing but discarded scraps. "Wash your hands before you go."

He stood and I looked up at him. "Why are you helping me? I murdered him."

He raised an eyebrow. "I knew the Hellbringer before that was what they all called him. Back then, he was a scared little boy whose magic killed people by mistake." Volkan shook his head. "The two of you aren't so different, you know."

I forced myself to smother a sob threatening to emerge from my throat. *Is this who I am destined to be? Are we the same now? The Hellbringer—who murders soldiers, devastates armies, pretends to love, then betrays all trust—and the Bloodsinger Queen, who killed her brother and her father and her friend, whose magic tears the kingdom asunder?*

I picked up the crown on my way out the door and rode to the temple.

◆ ◆ ◆ ◆ ◆

NO CHEERS WELCOMED ME FROM THE CROWD WHEN I RODE UP TO the temple ruins and dismounted from my horse. The tall building was now reduced to ash and rubble, the remaining white marble scattered and coated in gray soot. Freja had told me this morning that the temple burned long into the night, a crowd of both Lurae and Nilurae standing silent vigil.

One of the tall statues remained standing, though. Aloisa stared ahead at a point far in the distance, her face stoic as ever, the rest of the pantheon crumbling on either side of her.

"She wouldn't fall when they took hammers to her," Freja had whispered to me over breakfast, despite the fact that we were the only ones in my room. "Some of the Lurae are saying it's a sign that you're a tyrant queen—that by banishing the priests, you've incurred Aloisa's wrath."

I'd merely scoffed over my bowl. Now I found myself strangely glad my blade's namesake was left here. She hadn't fallen in the face of fire. And neither had I.

Too bad she's a figment of the imagination and not a real goddess.

Whispers followed me like swooping vultures following the scent of death on the wind as I ascended the staircase. I ignored them, wishing I couldn't hear the fragments of their conversations on the wind.

Terrifying.

Murderer.

Tyrant.

Freja came over to me, her hair braided tightly against her head and wound into an intricate updo. She squeezed my hand as I moved toward the throne.

Would she have done the same if she had known whose blood had stained my dress mere minutes ago?

I sat on the throne, which had been brought down the day before. It was made of gold intricately twisted to form a seat. Compared to my father, who sat here last, I was tiny. Nothing.

How long would it take for someone to realize what had happened? For someone to learn I had murdered an innocent man? A Nilurae man. One of my own people.

The rest of the day played out in my mind. Freja, upon discovering Halvar and the evidence of my Lurae, would never speak to me again. If or when Arne returned from the front lines, Freja would tell him what I had done. And with reason enough to hate me already, I knew he would jump on the chance to further justify his animosity toward me.

I swallowed. Yesterday, walking into the arena to face Björn, I'd felt a tiny glimmer of hope amid my resignation. But now . . .

I had nothing.

I had no one.

I was alone.

For a moment, an ache tore through my chest, and I wished a stoic figure stood in the back of the crowd, arms crossed over his chest, dark mask expressionless. *We can be monsters together now,* he would muse, and I would hear the half smile in his voice even if I couldn't see it.

How could I love him after everything he'd done?

I bit back tears.

Voice steady, I spoke, hoping my words would carry over the crowd, wondering what they saw when they looked at me—their scarred princess, crowning herself on a throne of ashes.

"I don't know the words the priest would have used to declare me queen," I began. "But I don't need them. Because the priests no longer hold power here."

Freja let out a whoop, but it was the only sound. The crowd stared at me, expressionless.

"I am your queen. I am your ally. I will fight for your safety, for your rights. I will protect the vulnerable and raise up those who have earned it."

It was everything I'd come to say. I reached up and placed the crown on my own head.

Freja's cry was like a clap of thunder echoing in the silence. "All hail the Bloodsinger Queen."

ACKNOWLEDGMENTS

Taking this story from scattered words on a page to a real, published book on a shelf would have been impossible without having so many incredible people next to me every step of the way. I'm so grateful for every one of them!

Bethany Hendrix, my incredible agent—you saw the potential in this book from the very beginning, and I can never thank you enough for it. I am always most excited to send my work to you because of how well you see the vision of what I'm trying to create and help me get there. Thank you for your unwavering support through every obstacle we faced getting this book on shelves.

Gabrielle Pachon, editor extraordinaire and ultimate Hellbringer apologist—your enthusiasm and excitement for this book have quite literally changed my life. Thank you for every read-through, every note, every brainstorming call, every email answering my inane questions. Thank you for shaping this book into what it is now and for taking such good care of me as a debut author. I feel so lucky to work with you!

To the original Raging Feminist Riders—Megan Bates, Emily Pearson, McKenna Thomas, Celestina Flores, Emma Smith, and Mandy Darrington—your memes about the Hellbringer and Björn live rent-free in my head. Thank you for cheering me on as I wrote, revised, queried, and went on submission with this book. Your friendships mean the world to me, and I wouldn't be the writer or person I am today without all of you. And an extra huge thanks to Megan, who was the first to suggest that the Hellbringer should kidnap Revna!

To Maci Meriwether, who is still my very best friend after more than ten years—thank you for always believing in me. I remember talking about this moment when we were in high school together, and now it's real. I love our calls and I'm so glad we've managed to stay in each other's lives for so long.

To my internet friends, who have now become some of my best friends: Amber Ryberg, thank you for beta reading a (very) early version of this manuscript for me and cheering me on through it all! Sarah Marie Page, every time I hear "Mastermind" by Taylor Swift, I think of you. Thanks for being excited every time I text you with a crazy idea to do something I probably don't have time for . . . and then doing it with me. Annika, the way you've supported me through this entire endeavor cannot be overstated. I will forever be grateful for your advice and excitement. Your voice memos are my favorite podcast. Ria Parisi, my fellow Reylo March 2025 debut buddy—so grateful to talk fan fiction, *The Acolyte*, and life with you.

A huge thanks to Kathryn Purdie, who taught my class at Writing and Illustrating for Young Readers back in 2020. Your guidance helped me cross the last hurdle keeping my book from being query-ready. Your kind explanation that I had tried to shove two full-length novels into the space of one was the final push I needed to make this book what it is today.

To the Fairytale Trash group (otherwise known as my agent siblings)—we've been through it all together, and I can't wait to see where we all go from here. I love being on Team Bethany with you!

A huge thanks to everyone from Berkley/Ace who worked on

this book and helped promote it, including Jessica Plummer, Hillary Tacuri, Kristin Cipolla, Stephanie Felty, Lynsey Griswold, Emily Osborne, and Christine Legon. And thank you to Jason Raish, who illustrated the cover of my dreams!

I'm eternally grateful to all the authors who read and blurbed this book. Thank you for your time and support! And to all the artists who have brought my characters to life, including @balangawa, @winterofherdiscontent, Bronwyn, and Bri Bueno—your talents have carried me through any difficulties I had with writing and editing this book, because the art you created is so masterful.

A huge thank-you also goes out to the BookTokers and Bookstagrammers who helped with my cover reveal. To those who have shared excitement for this book on social media or even by word of mouth to friends, your enthusiasm means the world to me.

To my family members, who have shaped me into the person I am and offered their support, enthusiasm, and babysitting time—including my lovely parents, my siblings and their spouses (Noah, Claire, Sophia, Sam, and Lleyton), and my in-laws (Anna, Justin, Evan, Bronwyn, Chris, and Liam).

And, of course, to Owen. Our story is better than any rom-com. From the first moment I told you I wanted to be an author, you never doubted it would happen. You're an incredible spouse and parent, and there's no one I'd rather do life with.

To Reeve. Every time you sit next to me and declare you're writing a book, I know I'm headed in the right direction.

And, of course, to you, dear reader. A novel is nothing without someone to pull it from a shelf and bring it to life. Thank you for taking a chance on Revna, the Hellbringer, and especially me. Here's to many more.

Photo © 2024 Haili Jean Co

ALEXANDRA KENNINGTON has been writing fantasy stories since she was young. Now she's living her dream as an author of fantasy and science fiction novels. When she's not knee-deep in a world of her own creation, you'll find her reading a book with the enemies-to-lovers trope or obsessing over *Star Wars*. She lives in Utah with her spouse and child.

VISIT ALEXANDRA KENNINGTON ONLINE

AlexandraKennington.com

⬡ AlexKenningtonWrites

𝕏 Kennington_Alex

♪ AlexKenningtonWrites